Beneath a Silent Banner

A C Janes

First published in 2025 by Blossom Spring Publishing
Beneath A Silent Banner © 2025 A C Janes
ISBN 978-1-0684329-5-8
E: admin@blossomspringpublishing.com
W: www.blossomspringpublishing.com

Introduction

In the bleak pre-dawn light of an Afghan valley, Captain Maxwell 'Max' Fairchild surveyed the silent expanse with an intensity born from years spent in the shadows of war. A chilling breeze, carrying the arid scent of the desert, whipped across his face, a familiar caress in this unforgiving landscape. His eyes, trained to observe and calculate, betrayed his history — a history marked by secret operations and unspoken missions in the world's most dangerous corners.

The men under his command, a handpicked team embodying the essence of elite military prowess, waited for his signal. Among them was Sgt. Liam Connor, a trusted ally whose loyalty had been forged in the crucibles of countless covert operations. Their bond went beyond the typical camaraderie of soldiers; it was the bond of brothers-in-arms, shaped in the depths of adversity.

As the first rays of the sun pierced the horizon, painting the sky with a palette of fire and gold, Max gave the nod. The mission, meticulously planned and crucial in its execution, was to dismantle a cell of insurgents known for their lethal craft. Max led his team with a calm, calculated precision, every movement a testament to his years of specialised training, training that spoke of elite regiments and clandestine warfare.

The operation unfolded with a deadly grace, each step choreographed under Max's watchful eye. The insurgent cell, caught off-guard, was neutralised with swift efficiency. Yet in the aftermath, as Max surveyed the scene, the acrid smell of gunpowder and the sight of blood-stained earth stirred something within him — a reminder of the cost of war, a cost he knew all too well.

The return to base was marred by a sudden, violent ambush. In the ensuing chaos, Max's leadership was unflappable; his orders, precise and clear, cut through the haze of danger. But even the best plans are vulnerable to the caprices of war. As the dust settled, the lifeless body of Dan Jameson, a young soldier in his mid-twenties who had been on the team no more than six months, lay as a stark testament to the day's tragic turn.

The sombre journey back to the base was a procession of introspection and silent grief. Liam's presence beside Max was a wordless support, a shared understanding of the heavy burden they bore. Each life lost under Max's command was a weight upon his soul, a weight he carried with the stoicism of a seasoned soldier.

Weeks later, the news of his brother Michael's death came as a devastating blow. Delivered in the sterile confines of the base, the words echoed in Max's ears, a grim melody of loss and despair. Michael, who had followed his brother's footsteps into the military, had fallen to an IED blast — a fate all too common yet unbearably personal. The news shattered the last vestiges of Max's armoured facade, exposing a well of grief and guilt.

Returning home, Max found himself a stranger in his own life. His marriage to Emily, strained by years of absence and the unspoken horrors of his profession, had become a chasm of unshared pain and loss. His children, Lily and Alex, had grown in his absence, their faces a painful reminder of the time lost, the moments missed.

In search of solace, Max retreated to the Isle of Skye, a place where the rugged beauty and the relentless beat of the sea offered a respite from the ghosts of his past. But the solitude he sought proved elusive. The quiet of the island echoed with the whispers of his memories, the faces of those lost, the decisions made in the name of duty.

Before Skye, there was Iraq. Following his departure from the military, Max had entered the world of private security, offering his skills in the volatile environment of Baghdad. In the bustling streets and shadowed alleys of the city, he had navigated a different kind of conflict. Here, amidst political unrest and the ever-present threat of insurgency, Max had honed his instincts, adapting his military training to the unpredictable nature of civilian protection.

In this new arena, the rules were blurred, and survival often hinged on quick judgment and a deep understanding of human nature. Max's experiences in Iraq had further ingrained in him a vigilance that became second nature, a readiness that was as much a part of him as his own shadow.

Yet even in the stark isolation of Skye, the ghosts of his past life continued to haunt him. The small cottage he called home was filled with silent reminders of his military and private security days. Medals and certificates, once symbols of honour and duty, now seemed like relics of a life that felt increasingly distant. Max would spend hours staring into the horizon, the relentless Scottish waves crashing against the cliffs mirroring the turmoil inside him.

His days were filled with routine, each task a futile attempt to escape the relentless grip of his memories. The skills and instincts honed in the heat of Iraq's urban conflicts and the unforgiving Afghan terrain didn't fade in the tranquillity of Skye. They lingered beneath the surface, a constant reminder of the man he had been — a man defined by his ability to navigate through chaos and danger.

It was during one of these monotonous days that the call came, shattering the illusion of peace he had so carefully constructed. Lily's voice, strained and trembling with barely contained fear, pierced through the stillness. Alex, his son, had been attacked in London — an act of senseless violence that struck at the very heart of Max's world.

The news ignited a fire within Max, a burning mix of rage and helplessness that he had never felt before. The bureaucratic and indifferent response from the police only fuelled this blaze. The words 'no leads' and 'no suspects' echoed in his mind, a stark contrast to the decisive and immediate action he was accustomed to in his professional life.

The journey back to London was a blur, each mile intensifying the burning need for action that consumed him. He was returning not as the decorated Captain Fairchild, respected for his strategic mind and leadership, nor as the private security specialist who navigated the dangerous landscape of Baghdad with calculated precision. He was returning as a father, driven by a primal and unwavering determination to protect and seek justice for his son.

London's bustling chaos was a jarring contrast to Skye's quietude. The city's sounds, smells, and sights, once familiar, now seemed alien and overwhelming. Max moved through the crowded streets with a singular focus, his senses sharpened not just by his military training but also by the years spent in the unpredictable and perilous environment of private security.

His first stop was an old acquaintance from his days in the security sector – Frank 'The Armorer' Johnson. Their meeting was a terse, functional exchange of words, the kind shared by men who operated on the fringes of legality. Frank provided Max with the tools he needed for his new mission — a mission born not out of duty to country, but out of a deep-seated need for personal justice.

As Max stepped out into the dimly lit streets of London, the weight of the firearm against his side was a familiar yet foreign sensation. It was a weight he had carried in many forms across different continents, but this time it was imbued with a personal resolve that transcended his previous experiences in war zones and conflict-ridden streets.

His investigation into Alex's attack began with methodical precision. Max approached each clue, each lead with the meticulousness of a soldier and the streetwise acumen of a seasoned private security operative.

Yet as Max delved into the labyrinth of London's underbelly, he found himself confronting not just the city's dark corners but also the shadows within himself. The streets, once a backdrop to his former life, now became a chessboard where each move carried the weight of his son's trauma. The rules of engagement had changed; this was not the structured combat of military operations nor the defined objectives of close protection. This was personal, driven by a father's raw need for retribution.

The investigation took him through the city's heartbeat, from the pulsing neon-lit nightlife to the dimly lit alleys that breathed secrets. He moved with a ghost's subtlety, a skill fine-tuned in the bustling markets of Baghdad and the unforgiving terrains of Afghanistan. His every step was measured, every decision a product of years spent navigating the fine line between life and death.

Each day brought new revelations, each piece of information a fragment of the puzzle that was his son's attack. But with each revelation came new questions, new complexities that tangled the web he was unweaving. The simplicity of the battlefield, where friend and foe were clearly defined, was replaced by a murky moral ambiguity that clouded his mission.

The more Max uncovered, the more he felt the duality of his existence. The disciplined soldier and the seasoned private security operative were now overshadowed by the emerging figure of a vigilante, a role both unfamiliar and inevitable. The skills and instincts that had once served him in the name of national security and client protection were now repurposed for a cause that was deeply personal and fraught with moral complexities.

At night, as the city slept, Max found himself wrestling with the implications of his quest. The line between justice and vengeance blurred, challenging the principles that had once defined him. He was no longer just Captain Fairchild or the private security expert; he was a father driven to the brink, a man on stepping onto a path that offered no clear return.

As dawn broke over the city, Max stood by the window of his temporary lodgings, gazing out at the awakening streets. The man reflected in the glass was a far cry from the soldier who had once left for war with a sense of duty, or the private security operative who had navigated the complexities of Baghdad with calculated detachment. This man was fuelled by a deeper, more primal force — a force that propelled him into the day with a resolve forged in the depths of paternal love and a thirst for justice.

This descent into the unknown was more than a physical journey; it was a voyage into the depths of his soul. Max Fairchild, a man shaped by the rigours of military life and the shadows of private security, was embarking on a mission that transcended the rules and codes he had lived by. As the city awoke to another day, it remained oblivious to the storm that had arrived in its midst, a storm named Max, whose course was as unpredictable as it was determined.

Part One: The Descent

Chapter 1: A Soldier's Burden

In the shadowy embrace of the Afghan valley, the first hints of dawn were yet hours away. The landscape, a rugged tapestry of undulating hills and sparse vegetation, lay shrouded in the deep blues and greys of predawn light. The air was crisp, carrying the distinctive arid scent of the desert — a blend of dry earth and a faint, lingering smokiness from distant settlements. It was a scent Captain Max Fairchild had come to associate with the solemnity of his profession.

Max, standing motionless with a vigilance born from years of combat, surveyed the silent expanse before him. His figure, clad in tactical gear, melded into the darkness. The night-vision goggles perched on his head, integral to the high-tech nature of their operations, would soon be his window into a world unseen by the naked eye. His face, partly obscured by a scarf, bore the marks of a seasoned soldier — lines etched by stress and sleepless nights, eyes that held a story deeper than the visible scars on his skin.

Around him, his team, a handpicked group embodying military prowess, waited in silence. Each man was a shadow, their presence barely discernible in the dim light. They were equipped with the latest in combat technology: lightweight body armour that allowed agility, rifles outfitted with suppressors and thermal scopes, and packs that contained everything from medical supplies to demolition equipment. The faint hum of communication earpieces provided a subtle reminder of their connection to each other and the world beyond this desolate valley.

This operation, like many before, was meticulously planned. Intelligence reports had led them here, to this seemingly forsaken part of the world, where a cell of insurgents known for their brutal tactics had taken refuge. Max knew the importance of what lay ahead; the success of their mission could save countless lives, yet the weight of what might happen during the operation hung heavily on his conscience.

As he adjusted his gear, Max's thoughts drifted momentarily. He thought of the road that had led him here — the years of rigorous training, the covert operations in shadowed corners of the globe, and the many faces of those he had served with. Each operation left its mark on him, shaping him into the leader he was today, a man who could navigate the complexities of war with a calm, calculated precision.

Yet beneath the surface, there was a sense of foreboding, a feeling that this mission would be different. Max couldn't shake the feeling that what would unfold in the next few hours could change the course of his life in ways he could not yet comprehend.

The quiet rustle of gear brought Max back to the present. He glanced at his watch — it was time. With a subtle nod, he signalled his team. The operation was about to begin, and with it, a chapter in Max's life that would leave a lasting imprint on his soul.

*

Max's eyes swept over his team, each member bracing for the mission ahead. Among them stood Sgt. Liam Connor, his second-in-command. Liam's features were stark under the greenish glow of the night-vision goggles, his jaw set in a determined line. Where Max's leadership was like a silent current, guiding with an unseen force, Liam's was the pulse — the beating heart that kept the team alive and motivated.

Their camaraderie was born of shared trials, a bond forged through the fire of countless operations. It was Liam who would often echo Max's orders with a brotherly clout, ensuring every man knew the part they played. Yet there was a softness to Liam, a humanity that Max often relied on to temper the necessary hardness of command.

As the team conducted their final equipment checks, the atmosphere was thick with the electric charge of pre-mission tension. Each man was an embodiment of precision, from the way they secured their weapons to the silent communication that passed between them — a look, a gesture, a nod. The weight of their gear was a familiar comfort, the smell of oiled metal and worn leather a constant in the unpredictable landscape of war.

Max pulled Liam aside, their conversation low and measured. "This one's different," Max murmured, his voice almost lost beneath the whisper of the wind. "Intel suggests civilians in the mix. We keep collateral to a zero."

Liam's nod was almost imperceptible, his response a reflection of their shared understanding. "We'll bring them all home, Max. All of them," he promised, his words carrying the weight of a vow.

Max's gaze lingered on Liam's resolute expression, knowing well the unspoken truth that lay beneath — the possibility that not all would return. It was a silent acknowledgement that each mission might demand a price they had yet to pay.

The tension rose palpably as the time drew nearer. Max stepped forward, addressing his team with quiet authority. "Remember, we're the unseen. Swift, silent, and precise. Keep your focus. Watch your sectors. We do this clean — in and out."

Heads bowed in a collective nod as the men absorbed his words. Max's orders were more than directives; they were the thread that wove their actions into a singular purpose. As they moved into formation, the stark reality set in — they were about to step into the abyss, a place where the line between right and wrong blurred with every heartbeat.

And so, with the weight of the coming dawn on their shoulders, Max and his team set out. The valley, a silent witness to their passage, seemed to hold its breath, aware of the violence that was about to unfold.

*

The cloak of night was their ally as Max led his team through the rugged terrain, their movements a silent dance amidst the whispering sands. Each step was measured, each breath controlled — they were ghosts flitting through the darkness. The night-vision goggles turned the world into a monochromatic landscape, shapes and shadows sharply defined against the green-hued backdrop.

Max's hand signals cut through the darkness, orchestration without sound. The team fanned out, a fluid extension of his will. He could see the landscape before him through multiple lenses — not just the physical terrain, but the overlay of potential threats and tactical advantages. It was a mental map drawn from experience, honed by the knowledge that complacency meant death.

They approached the target location, a compound that sat like a scar on the barren landscape. Intelligence had been clear: high-value targets were inside, but so were non-combatants. Every decision now was a delicate balance on the edge of a knife.

The stillness of the night was a lie, a momentary peace that would soon be shattered. Max felt it in his bones, a tension that braced him for what was to come. As they neared the compound, the faintest hint of voices carried on the wind — a reminder of the humanity they were here to confront.

Then, without warning, the night erupted into chaos.

An improvised explosive device detonated, a violent bloom of light and sound that tore through the silence. The ground shook, and Max was moving, his training a guiding force in the sudden disarray. Orders were issued through clenched teeth, each word sharp with urgency. "Contact left! Push forward!"

The team responded with the precision of a well-oiled machine, returning fire, their shots muffled whispers in the tumult. The enemy was not the faceless shadow they had been briefed on; they were desperate men firing wildly, their shouts a cacophony of fear and aggression.

Max's world narrowed to the scope of his rifle, the clarity of his night vision turning the firefight into a series of stark, green-tinted images. His finger on the trigger was steady, his aim true. But amidst the adrenaline, a part of him stood apart, watching the unfolding violence with a sense of impending doom.

A structure on the edge of the compound caught his eye — too late, he realised it was not part of the insurgents' defences. It was a home, and the figures that stumbled out were civilians caught in the crossfire. His heart clenched, time seeming to slow as he shouted the order to cease fire. But the damage was done.

Max's decision had been strategic, the position advantageous — but in the chaos, innocent lives had been caught in the web of war. The weight of the moment sank into him, a heavy stone in his stomach. He had trained for many things, but the burden of collateral damage was a load that bore down on him with the gravity of a personal failure.

As the firefight waned, the stark reality of the operation's cost was laid bare before him. The compound was secured, the insurgents subdued or dispatched, but the air was thick with more than the smell of gunpowder. It was laden with the scent of loss, a pungent reminder of the price of war.

Max stood amid the aftermath, the sounds of his men securing the area a distant hum. His eyes, still behind the green glow of the goggles, were fixed on the broken figures of the civilians. This was the burden he carried, the soldier's burden, and it was a weight he would never truly release.

*

The gunfire had ceased, leaving a ringing silence in its wake. The compound, once an anonymous structure in the Afghan desert, was now a tableau of devastation. Max moved through the chaos with a stoic facade, but each step felt heavier than the last. The acrid stench of smoke mingled with the metallic tang of blood, an olfactory testament to the night's events.

Max's men were efficient in their grim tasks, checking bodies, securing the perimeter, and gathering intel. Their professionalism was a veneer over the raw shock of what had transpired. Among the insurgents' casualties were the civilians whose lives had ended as mere footnotes in a broader conflict.

Sgt. Liam Connor was at Max's side, his usual steady voice subdued. "We'll set up for exfil. Area's secure, but we should move out before they can regroup."

Max nodded, his response automatic. "Get the men ready. I want to be out within ten."

Yet his eyes remained fixed on the still forms of the civilian casualties. A woman, her features frozen in a silent scream, a child, too young to have known anything but war, and an old man, his hands still reaching out as if to hold back the tide of violence that had swept through his home.

This was the part of the operation that no debrief could sanitise, no report could adequately convey. The burden of command was never heavier than in the wake of such loss. Max had made countless decisions under fire, but the ghost of this night would haunt him, a spectre born of the clash between duty and humanity.

Liam's hand on his shoulder was a grounding force, a silent message of shared responsibility. "We did what we had to do, Max. You know that."

Max's gaze finally broke away from the casualties. "I know," he replied, his voice a low murmur. But the knowledge was a cold comfort, a distant beacon of rationale in the fog of his emotions.

The team began their withdrawal, retracing their steps through the valley. As they moved, Max's mind replayed the operation, each moment scrutinized with the brutal clarity of hindsight. The decision to engage, the placement of his men, the fatal crossfire — it was a cycle of thought he could not escape.

The journey back to their extraction point was a silent procession, each man lost in his own reflections. The weight they carried was not just the physical burden of their gear but the heavier load of experiences that would forever alter the landscape of their lives.

Max walked with the ghost of the night clinging to him, an unseen shroud that tightened with every step. The stars above were distant witnesses, their light untouched by the earthly events that had unfolded beneath them.

As they reached the extraction point, the first light of dawn was beginning to touch the horizon, a tentative caress that held no warmth for the men who waited there. The helicopter's approach was a distant thunder, a sound that promised an end to the night's ordeal.

Max looked back once, the valley now a part of his story. He knew that the dawn's light would reveal the scars of their operation, just as the night's events had etched new scars upon his soul.

The chapter of the soldier's burden was one that could never be closed, its pages forever turning in the restless wind of memory.

*

The roar of the helicopter blades cut through the early morning stillness, a jarring contrast to the silent expanse of the desert. Max and his team, now shadows against the burgeoning light, boarded the aircraft. Each man's entry was a heavy step, a silent testament to the night's burdens.

Inside the helicopter, the atmosphere was thick with unspoken thoughts. The familiar vibrations of the aircraft and the whir of machinery were a backdrop to Max's introspection. As the landscape retreated below them, Max's mind lingered on the ground, replaying the mission with a relentless scrutiny.

Liam sat opposite Max, his eyes meeting Max's with an understanding that transcended words. Their silent conversation was a shared debriefing, each man analysing the operation in the sanctuary of their camaraderie.

"You led us through hell and back," Liam finally said, his voice barely audible over the helicopter's din. "There's not a man here who would question your calls."

Max's nod was faint, the gesture more reflex than agreement. He appreciated Liam's unwavering support, the steadfast presence he had come to rely on. Yet it did little to assuage the churning thoughts that questioned every decision, every bullet's path.

The flight back to base was a limbo, a space between the raw immediacy of action and the reflective quiet of aftermath. As the adrenaline of the night ebbed, fatigue crept into Max's limbs, but rest was a distant prospect. He felt the strain not just in his body, but in his mind, the mental replay of the operation a loop that refused to pause.

Max's gaze shifted to the younger soldiers, their faces etched with the night's intensity. He saw in them the echoes of his earlier self, the initial resolve that had not yet met the test of such profound loss. Their silence spoke of processing the night's events, of trying to place them within the narrative of their service.

Upon landing, the team disembarked with mechanical efficiency. The base, a sprawl of temporary structures and permanent scars on the landscape, was a stark reminder of the ongoing conflict. They were back in the realm of harsh fluorescent lights and the ordered chaos of military operations.

Max's debrief with the commanding officers was a blur of tactical jargon and terse nods. He delivered his report with the clinical detachment expected of him, but the images of civilian casualties flickered behind his eyes, a stark contrast to the sanitised words he spoke.

Later, alone in the spartan confines of his quarters, Max allowed himself to feel the full weight of the night. He unpacked his gear methodically, each item a piece of the puzzle that was his service. The rifle, now silent, the body armour, no longer a shield against the chaos of war, and the night-vision goggles, their green lens void of the night's secrets.

Max sat on the edge of his cot, his hands clasped between his knees. The room was quiet, but the silence was an illusion. In his mind, the echoes of gunfire and the cries of the wounded were a cacophony that drowned out the stillness.

As the first rays of sunlight filtered through the narrow window, Max reflected on the operation's toll on his conscience. It was a ledger of lives saved against lives lost, a balance that seemed increasingly precarious with each mission.

The chapter of this night would close, filed away in a report, but its story would continue to unfold within Max. It would shape his decisions, haunt his dreams, and challenge his understanding of duty and honour.

And as he lay back on his cot, sleep a distant hope, Max knew that the true burden of command was not in the heat of battle, but in the quiet moments after, when the soul was left to wrestle with the cost of war.

*

As the base stirred to life with the routines of the morning, Max wrestled with a fatigue that sleep could not touch. His mind was a theatre where the night's operation replayed on a continuous loop, each decision, each moment of horror, each life lost a scene that refused to fade with the rising sun.

After a few hours of restless solitude, a knock at his door broke the silence. Max straightened, steeling himself for another round of debriefs or the mundane administrative tasks that would seem trivial after what had transpired. However, it was neither.

The figure who entered was not one of his immediate superiors but a liaison officer from the higher echelons of command, his presence unexpected and immediately concerning.

"Captain Fairchild?" the officer began, his tone formal yet tinged with an urgency that set Max on edge. "There's been a development. Command wants a debrief in the situation room, ASAP."

Max felt a twinge of alarm. It was unusual for such swift action after a mission, particularly one with such weighty consequences. Nodding in acknowledgement, he followed the officer through the base, his boots kicking up small clouds of dust with every step.

The situation room was abuzz with activity, the air charged with a tension that matched Max's internal state. Senior officers and intelligence analysts huddled around screens displaying satellite imagery and intercepted communications. Max's arrival quieted the room, all eyes briefly turning to him, some with respect, others with a hint of apprehension.

"Captain Fairchild," a senior officer greeted him, gesturing to a seat. "You've barely had time to breathe, but we need your insight. There's been chatter — the operation last night has stirred up more than we anticipated."

They briefed him on the aftermath: the insurgent network was reacting with a ferocity and speed uncharacteristic of their usual operations. It seemed Max's strike had hit more than just a tactical target; it had struck a nerve.

The room fell silent as the implications hung heavily in the air. The mission, which had already cost so much, was far from over. It had set off a chain reaction that promised to drag Max and his team back into the fray, into decisions even more complex and dangerous than those they had just faced.

Max listened, his expression unreadable, as the officer outlined the next steps. There would be no respite, no time to process or to grieve. The war waited for no man, and the weight of command was a mantle that granted no rest.

As the meeting concluded, Max's thoughts were not on the strategic implications but on the faces of his men, the lives that hung in the balance with every command he would give. The burden of leadership was a solitary path, and Max felt its isolation more acutely than ever.

He left the situation room with a new set of orders, a new mission that loomed on the horizon. It was a path that would lead him back into darkness, back into the crucible where right and wrong were not black and white but shades of grey stained with the blood of the innocent.

Max's decision at the ambush had indeed led to unexpected collateral damage, and now, the echoes of that choice were reverberating into the future, hinting at moral conflicts yet to come. The soldier's burden was not just the weight of the past but the shadow of the future, a darkness that stretched out before him, endless and unforgiving.

Max stood at the threshold of a new challenge, one that would test the very fibre of his being. The dawn that broke over the base was not a signal of hope, but a harbinger of the trials to come. However, he was unaware that the dawn's deceptive calm would soon be shattered by news that would test his resolve far beyond the battlefield — news that would irrevocably alter the course of his life.

Chapter 2: Tragic News

Shattered Normality

The relentless Afghan sun bore down on the dusty expanse of the forward operating base, mirroring the intensity of the day's operations. Captain Max Fairchild was in the midst of a routine debriefing, his mind wrapped around the tactical intricacies of their latest patrol. It was the mundanity of military life in a warzone, punctuated by moments of adrenaline-fuelled action and long stretches of strategic planning.

As Max wrapped up the meeting, his focus was on the next mission, the never-ending cycle of preparation and execution. But as he stepped out into the glare of the midday sun, a messenger approached with a solemnity in his steps that caught Max's attention immediately.

"Captain Fairchild?" The messenger, a young corporal whose name escaped Max at the moment, had an unreadable expression, a mask that military personnel learned to wear when bearing bad news.

"Yes?" Max responded, his senses already tightening, a soldier's instinct that something was amiss.

"You're needed in the CO's office, sir. It's urgent."

The urgency in the corporal's voice bypassed any further questions. Max followed swiftly, his heart rate picking up, not with the anticipation of combat, but with a dread that felt far more personal.

Colonel Edwards was waiting, his usual stoic demeanour softened somehow, his eyes holding a grave light. Max had seen that look before; it was the look of a man who bore the weight of lives in his hands.

"Max," Edwards began, his voice low, "it's about Michael."

Michael, Max's younger brother, the kid who followed his big brother into the army, the boy who grew up idolizing the uniform, the medals, the stories of heroism.

"What happened?" Max asked, his voice betraying none of the sudden tightness that gripped his chest.

"He was on patrol, an IED ..." Edwards trailed off, the details hanging suspended in the air between them.

Max felt the room spin, a sensation alien to the man who had faced down the barrel of enemy guns without flinching. Michael couldn't be gone. The base, the war, the very ground he stood on, all seemed to shift, a landscape altered in a way that he couldn't yet comprehend.

An IED — the impersonal, indiscriminate killer of this gruelling conflict had claimed his brother, his flesh and blood. Max's knees threatened to buckle, not from physical exertion, but from the sheer force of the news that hammered into him.

"Max, I'm sorry," Edwards said, and Max realised that the colonel had stood up, was standing beside him, a hand resting on his shoulder — a gesture of solidarity that bridged the gap between commanding officer and comrade-in-arms.

The room was suddenly suffocating, the walls closing in on him. Max needed air, needed space to breathe, to think, to feel. He nodded to Edwards, a mute expression of gratitude for his understanding, and stepped outside.

The brightness of the day was a mockery of the darkness that had descended upon him. Max walked, his gait unsteady, to a part of the base that overlooked the barren expanse of the desert. There, with no eyes upon him, he allowed the full weight of his grief to emerge.

Michael was gone, and with him, a piece of Max that he would never reclaim. The soldier in him was trained to move forward, to continue the mission, but the brother in him, the part that had known and loved Michael before he was a soldier, before he was a target for IEDs, that part crumbled beneath the burden of loss.

The desert, a place of extremes, of life and death, now reflected the turmoil within him. Max stood alone, a figure etched against the vastness, grappling with a pain that had no place in the order of his military life yet had irrevocably become the centre of it.

*

The news of Michael Fairchild's death spread through the base with a quiet ferocity, a wildfire of whispered condolences and shared sorrow. Max had always been a pillar among his men, a captain as respected for his compassion as for his tactical acumen. Now the brotherhood he had fostered was a source of solace, the men drawn together in a collective embrace of grief.

As the sun dipped toward the horizon, casting a golden glow that belied the sombre mood, the men of Max's unit gathered. They stood in the open space outside the barracks, a silent assembly united in their loss. Sgt. Liam Connor was at the forefront, his face a mask of stoic sadness.

"Men," Liam's voice broke the silence, strong yet tinged with emotion. "Today we mourn not just as soldiers, but as a family. Michael Fairchild was one of our own. His loss is a wound we all feel."

The men nodded, some reaching out to place a supportive hand on Max's shoulder as they passed. Words were unnecessary — their presence was their tribute, their silence a shared language of grief.

Max stood among them, the reality of his brother's death a relentless pressure against his chest. He watched as his men, toughened by conflict and hardened by loss, allowed their guards to drop. Eyes that had stared down the chaos of battle now glistened with unshed tears.

One by one, the soldiers shared their memories of Michael. They spoke of his laughter, of his unwavering courage, and of the small acts of kindness that had made him beloved by all.

Mark Owens remembered a night years back when Michael had taken extra guard duty so Owens could get some sleep before a letter from home arrived. Simon Bowdon recalled how Michael had fixed his radio during a tense operation, a small miracle that kept them connected and safe.

Each story added a layer to the tapestry of Michael's life, a life that had been inextricably woven into the fabric of their unit. The gathering was not just a moment to grieve but to honour, to ensure that Michael's spirit would endure in the memories they carried.

As the impromptu memorial drew to a close, Liam approached Max. "He was a good man, a good soldier," he said, his voice steady but his eyes betraying his pain. "He lived and died by the code we all swore to uphold. We'll make sure he's remembered, Max."

Max met Liam's gaze, a wordless communication that conveyed the depth of his gratitude. In this brotherhood, he found the strength to stand, to face the coming days with the resolve that Michael's memory deserved.

The grief was a shared burden now, each man carrying a piece of it within him as they returned to their duties.

The desert had claimed many lives, but it would not claim the legacy of Michael Fairchild. His memory, like their resolve, would endure beyond the setting sun.

*

The base returned to its nocturnal lull, a deceptive calm that settled over the cabins and makeshift barracks. Inside the command centre, however, the stillness was punctuated by the soft murmur of voices and the occasional crackle of radio communications. It was here, in the austere confines of a briefing room, that Max learned the details of his brother's final moments.

A field intelligence officer, a map spread out before him, pointed to a spot marked with the stark symbol of an explosion. "The IED was well-hidden, Captain," he said, his voice measured, professional. "Your brother's vehicle was the lead in the convoy. They didn't stand a chance."

The words were a clinical account of chaos, of a moment when life had turned to death with a brutality that was all too common in this unforgiving theatre of war. Max listened, his expression unreadable, but inside, a storm raged.

The reality of Michael's death was no longer an abstract concept delivered in hushed tones. It was raw and visceral, a narrative of violence that had snatched his brother away. Max's mind conjured the image of the blast, the searing heat, the deafening roar, and the silence that followed. It was a scenario he had seen before, but this time it was personal, a tragedy that bore his own blood.

After the briefing, Max found himself walking the perimeter of the base, a path he often took to clear his mind. The night sky was clear, the stars above indifferent to the sorrows of the world below. Max felt a bitter envy for their remote serenity.

He stopped, staring out into the darkness beyond the wire. The desert stretched out before him, an expanse of shadows and secrets. Somewhere out there, Michael had taken his last breath, had become another casualty in a conflict that seemed to have no end.

Max's fists clenched at his sides, the soldier within battling the torrent of emotions that threatened to overwhelm him. Grief, anger, guilt — they melded into a tight knot in his gut. He had always believed in the cause, had always been certain that their sacrifices were not in vain. But now, as he grappled with the loss of his brother, doubt crept in like a treacherous whisper.

Was it worth it? The question gnawed at him, a relentless itch that was offered no relief. He had been trained to fight, to lead, to protect — but he couldn't protect Michael. The helplessness was a foreign sensation, one that left him unmoored in a sea of uncertainty.

The harsh reality of Michael's death was a crucible, burning away the certainties that had once defined Max's world. What remained was a man who stood in the darkness, searching for the light of purpose that had always guided him.

As the night wore on, Max remained there, a solitary figure wrestling with the truths that soldiers seldom faced until the war followed them home. And when he finally returned to his quarters, the bed was an unwelcome reminder that rest would not come easy, and solace would be even harder to find.

*

Max sat alone in the dark of his quarters, the silence of the room amplifying his inner turmoil. The ghostly afterimage of the intelligence officer's map burned in his mind's eye, each detail etching a deeper furrow into his brow. The spot where the IED had claimed Michael's life was miles away, yet it felt as if it had detonated right there in Max's chest, leaving a crater of grief and unanswered questions.

The night was long, a stretch of hours that seemed to expand with each passing minute. Max replayed every conversation, every shared moment with Michael. Their last phone call echoed in his head, a casual exchange filled with the usual banter and promises to catch up when they both had leave. There was no hint of finality, no premonition that it would be their last.

Max's sense of duty had always been his compass, guiding him through the most challenging of times. Now, that same duty felt like a chain, one that bound him to the very cause that had put Michael in harm's way. The pride he once took in his uniform was now a weight, heavy with the burden of loss.

As dawn approached, the first faint light crept into Max's quarters, a daily rebirth that seemed at odds with the stagnation in his heart. He stood and dressed, his movements mechanical, each buckle and strap a reminder of the life he had chosen — a life that now demanded a toll he had never imagined paying.

The base was waking up, the hum of activity a stark contrast to the quiet vigil Max had kept through the night. He made his way to the mess hall, the smells and sounds of breakfast a mundane backdrop to his inner disquiet.

The men of his unit were there, their faces a mix of concern and respect. They made room for him, a small act of solidarity, but the usual camaraderie felt distant, as if Max were observing it through a thick pane of glass.

The conversations around him were muffled, the laughter a hollow echo. He pushed the food around his plate, each bite tasteless, an act of going through the motions.

After breakfast, Max sought out the base chaplain, a man who had counselled many through the valley of the shadow of war. The chaplain listened as Max spoke of Michael, of their childhood, of the shared dream that had led them both into the army's ranks.

The chaplain spoke of service and sacrifice, of the greater good, but the words felt like platitudes to Max. They were truths for another time, another place, not for this moment of piercing loss. Max nodded, the polite soldier still present, but the words did not reach the place within where doubt had taken root.

Throughout the day, Max moved through his duties as if through a fog. The familiar rhythms of military life, once so gratifying, were now a distant drum, a beat that he could no longer bring himself to step to.

He found himself at the training ground, watching the younger soldiers as they drilled. Their faces were determined, alive with the purpose and drive that he had once known. Max wondered if they could see the cost of their commitment, if they understood that the price of their service might one day be as steep as his own.

As the sun reached its zenith, the heat a blanket over the base, Max realised that the struggle within would not be easily quelled. The soldier in him would continue to serve, to lead, to do his duty. But the brother in him, the part that mourned Michael, would continue to question, to rage against the senselessness of a war that took so much and gave back so little in return.

The midday sun was relenting, casting long shadows over the base as Max made his way to the command office. The heat of the Afghan desert was in stark contrast to the chill that had settled in his bones since receiving the news of Michael's death. Each step felt like wading through a current, the resistance of a reality he still hadn't fully accepted.

Colonel Hammond was waiting for him. A career military man, Hammond's presence was always formidable, yet today, his usual sharp edges seemed tempered by the situation's gravity. He stood as Max entered, a gesture of respect that was not lost on the younger officer.

"Max," Hammond began, his voice resonating with a timbre that spoke of experience with loss. "I won't offer platitudes. I know there's nothing I can say that will make this easier."

Max simply nodded, the acknowledgement tight in his throat. He appreciated the absence of empty condolences. Hammond knew the cost of war, not just in strategic terms but in the human toll it exacted.

"But I want you to know that this command stands behind you. Your brother was one of us, and we share in this loss," Hammond continued, his gaze steady on Max.

Max felt a surge of gratitude for the colonel's directness. In the clarity of his words, there was a semblance of the order Max craved in the chaos of his grief.

"Thank you, sir," Max managed, his voice a little more than a whisper.

Hammond moved around the desk, coming to stand beside Max. "I've arranged for you to have some time away. Go home, be with your family, take the time you need."

Max hesitated. The thought of stepping away, of leaving his unit, even temporarily, was counterintuitive. The soldier in him wanted to bury the pain, to carry on with duty as a shield against the anguish.

"I'm not sure I can just ..." Max's words trailed off, the conflict evident in his expression.

"Max, you can, and you must," Hammond interjected with gentle firmness. "This is a time to mourn, to honour your brother's memory. The fight will still be here when you're ready to return."

It was the permission Max hadn't realised he needed. The acknowledgement from a superior officer that it was okay to step back, to feel the full measure of his loss without the constraints of his rank and responsibilities.

Hammond placed a hand on Max's shoulder, a solid, grounding pressure. "Your brother served with honour. Remember him not just as a soldier, but as the man he was. That's how you'll keep him alive."

Max met Hammond's gaze, finding a depth of understanding that bridged the gap between them. "I will, sir," he said, a newfound resolve in his voice.

As he left the office, Max felt a subtle shift within. The grief was still there, a constant companion, but now it was coupled with a sense of purpose. He would go home, face the family Michael had left behind, and find a way to begin the process of healing.

Colonel Hammond's words lingered, a reminder that leadership wasn't always about giving orders. Sometimes, it was about offering support and guiding those under your command through the trials they faced, both on and off the battlefield.

Max's journey back home would be a different kind of mission, one with challenges no less daunting than those he faced in combat. But it was a mission he would not face alone, bolstered by the support of his comrades and the strength of his brother's memory.

*

The transport to take Max home was arranged swiftly, the military efficiency in stark contrast to the turmoil of emotions that churned within him. As he waited on the dusty tarmac for the aircraft, his mind was invaded by memories of Michael — a cascade of moments that now bore the weight of finality.

Max recalled the last time they were together, on leave a year prior. The Fairchild brothers, both in civilian clothes, had raised glasses in a toast, a celebration of rare family time. Michael's laughter was a vivid sound in Max's memory, as was the light in his eyes as he spoke of his plans for the future.

The image of Michael, vibrant and full of life, clashed with the reality that he was gone, stolen by a war that Max had come to see as an endless cycle of sacrifice. As the aircraft's engines began to whir, the noise a growing crescendo, Max closed his eyes and allowed himself to sink into the memory.

He saw himself and Michael as children, playing in the fields behind their house, pretending to be soldiers in grand adventures. Those innocent games had been the prologue to their eventual paths, leading them both to the reality of military life.

Max's reminiscence was interrupted by the arrival of the aircraft. He boarded mechanically, his movements automatic. The interior of the plane was cold, the metal surfaces devoid of comfort. As it took off, the ground falling away, Max felt a disconnection not just from the land below but from the soldier he was.

In the quiet solitude of the flight, Max's thoughts turned to Emily, his wife. Emily, who had endured his absences, who had lived with the constant fear that one day she would receive the news that it was Max, not Michael, who had fallen. The strain on their relationship had been a slow-building storm, one they had both seen on the horizon but had hoped to navigate together.

Max remembered their last conversation, the strain in Emily's voice as she spoke of the latest news reports, of the mounting casualties. He had reassured her then, told her not to worry, but now those reassurances felt hollow. How could he comfort her in her fear when his own family had not been spared?

As the flight continued, Max knew that the homecoming would be a trial. The reunion with his family, the shared grief, the funeral — each step would be a march through personal sorrow. Yet as he thought of Emily, of the life they had built and the strains it had suffered, he knew this was also a chance. A chance to reconnect, to support each other, and to begin the healing process together.

The plane touched down in the soft light of early morning, the world waking up as Max's own seemed to pause. He stepped off the aircraft, a soldier returning not from war, but to the battle within, to the heartache that awaited him.

As he made his way through the quiet airport, Max carried not just the weight of his gear but the weight of memory, of loss, and the hope that in facing the days ahead, he could find a way to honour Michael, to mend the fractures in his marriage, and to reconcile the soldier with the man he needed to be for his family.

Chapter 3: Alex's Ordeal

The Retreat to Skye

Max stood alone on the craggy shores of Skye, the relentless wind of the Scottish Highlands tousling his hair and beard, both longer and more unkempt than during his years of military precision. Here, amidst the rugged beauty of isolation, he had found a stark refuge, a place where the ghosts of his past were mere whispers against the roar of the Atlantic.

Skye was an unforgiving canvas of brooding cliffs and moody skies, a reflection of Max's own internal landscape. He had arrived here a year ago, his soul weary from the deserts of Iraq, where he'd spent several tumultuous years providing close protection after his abrupt departure from the army.

Flashbacks came unbidden, as relentless as the Skye tides. He remembered the sterile military office where he had signed his discharge papers, the ink on his signature a full stop to the chapter that had defined his adult life. The grief for Michael had been a shadow that followed him out of the army and into the private military world, where the rules were different, but the danger was just as palpable.

Iraq had been a blur of VIPs and convoys, a high-stakes game of cat and mouse played out in the alleys of Baghdad and the endless stretches of desert road. The work was lucrative, the adrenaline a temporary balm for his loss, but it did little to silence the echoes of Michael's laughter or the growing distance in Emily's voice during their increasingly sporadic calls.

The memory of his last night in Baghdad was a visceral punch — the heat, the chaos, the sense that he was spiralling. And then, the final call with Emily, her voice breaking with a mixture of sorrow and resignation. "I can't do this anymore, Max," she had said, the end of their marriage not a question but a quiet surrender to the inevitable.

Now, in Skye, Max lived a life diametrically opposed to the one he had known. His days were marked by long walks along the cliffs, the solitude a balm and a curse. The house he rented was an old crofter's cottage, secluded from the small town by a winding, narrow road. It was here that he battled his demons, his only company the occasional visit from a neighbour bringing news or supplies.

Despite the isolation, the beauty of Skye was not lost on Max. There were moments when the sun broke through the omnipresent clouds, casting the sea in liquid gold and the hills in vibrant green, moments when he could almost breathe without the weight of loss on his chest.

*

The Skye landscape was a place of extremes, where the serene beauty of dawn could swiftly succumb to the brooding mists of dusk. This land mirrored Max's inner world, where moments of peace grappled with storms of turmoil. It was in this setting that Max often found himself adrift in the sea of memories that charted the course of his marriage to Emily.

Sitting by the fire that barely kept the damp at bay, Max let the memories wash over him. He remembered the early days filled with laughter and shared dreams, when the future seemed as bright and open as the sky above their heads. The military had been their shared cause, a noble path they walked hand in hand. But as the years passed, the path had grown rocky and their steps had faltered.

Flashbacks of their life together flickered like the flames before him — the excitement of each homecoming, the warmth of Emily's embrace, and the shared joy in each of their children's milestones. But as the deployments grew longer and the homecomings shorter, the space between them widened, filled with unspoken fears and unshared burdens.

The night Michael's death had been confirmed, Max had clung to Emily's words over the satellite phone, desperate for an anchor in the chaos of his grief. But in the wake of loss, even their shared sorrow could not bridge the growing divide. Emily's strength had been his rock, yet even rocks can crack under too much pressure.

The conversation that had marked the end of their marriage was not a quarrel but a quiet acknowledgement of the distance that could not be closed. Emily's tearful whisper over the line, "I miss the man you were," had echoed in Max's heart long after the call had ended.

The separation had been a slow peeling away, the formalities of legal proceedings an antiseptic balm to the raw wound of a life shared and then sundered. Max had thrown himself into his work in Iraq to avoid the emptiness, but the solitude of Skye offered no such distraction.

In the solitary confinement of his cottage, Max often found himself at the mercy of his own mind. Without the constant demands of protection details, his thoughts would inevitably turn to Emily. The memory of her smile, the sound of her laughter, the feel of her hand in his — they were ghosts that haunted the quiet corners of his life.

The fire sputtered, pulling Max back from his reverie. He placed another log onto the embers, watching as the sparks flew upwards, brief stars in the small cosmos of his hearth. He wondered if Emily ever thought of him, if she ever looked up at the same stars and remembered what they had once had.

The life he had built on Skye was one of isolation, the natural fortress of the island a reflection of the walls he had erected around his heart. Max's solitude in Skye was not peace, but a waiting, a holding of breath before the plunge back into the turbulent waters of the world he had left behind.

*

The stark landscape of Skye was both a sanctuary and a prison for Max. He had chosen this place for its seclusion, for the way the cliffs met the sea with uncompromising resolve, much like the way he intended to meet his days — with stoic endurance. The isolation of the island was both a salve for his wounds and a reminder of the distance he had placed between himself and the world he once knew.

Max's daily routine in Skye was one of simplicity and survival. He rose with the sun, the solitude of the dawn a time for quiet reflection. His mornings were spent tending to the small patch of land that came with the cottage, the physical labour a distraction from the turmoil of his thoughts. The earth under his fingernails, the sweat on his brow, were tangible evidence of his existence in a world that had become ethereal and disjointed.

His afternoons were spent wandering the rugged paths

that snaked along the coastline or across the moors. The walks were long and purposeful, a way to exhaust the body so that, come nightfall, sleep might grant him a brief respite from his memories. The vastness of the landscape, the unyielding nature of the terrain, it resonated with him. Here, nature was indifferent to a man's pain, and there was comfort in that indifference.

Max had few interactions with the outside world, his contact limited to the occasional trip to the nearest town for supplies. The townspeople had learned to respect his need for privacy, greeting him with nods and the occasional word but never prying. In their eyes, he saw their own hardships reflected, an understanding of grief and resilience that was as much a part of this land as the heather and stone.

The cottage itself was sparse, a reflection of his internal state. There were no decorations, no personal touches; it was functional, a place to rest, eat, and seek shelter from the relentless storms that would sweep in from the ocean. At night, the cottage creaked and groaned under the assault of the wind, a symphony of sounds that sometimes seemed like voices whispering across the threshold from another life.

Max's coping mechanisms were a blend of physical exertion and mental discipline. He read extensively, books on history, philosophy, and the occasional novel. They were company of a sort, voices that filled the silence without demanding anything in return. His evenings were often spent in front of the fire, a glass of whisky in hand, the golden liquid a slow burn that matched the smouldering in his heart.

Despite his self-imposed exile, Max kept up with current events, his satellite phone a lifeline to a world he had left but could not completely let go. The news was a constant stream of conflicts and calamities, a reminder that while he had stepped away from the chaos, it continued unabated.

The isolation of Skye, once a chosen balm, now felt like a shackle. He realised that the coping mechanisms he had developed were not shields against the world but mere illusions. The true test of his strength lay ahead, in facing the realities he had sought to escape.

*

The news came as the last light of day bled from the sky, painting the clouds in hues of fiery orange and deepening purple. Max had been about to stoke the fire for the evening when his satellite phone rang. The caller ID displayed Lily's number, and a surge of unease tightened his chest before he even answered.

"Dad." Lily's voice came through, a tremulous sound that gripped Max's heart with cold fingers. "It's Alex ... he's been hurt, Dad. It was an unprovoked attack. They just ... they wanted his phone, and when he resisted, they ..."

Her voice broke, the silence that followed filled with unspeakable fear. Max felt his world tilt, a sickening lurch as if the earth beneath him had given way.

"What happened, Lily? Tell me," Max urged, his voice firm despite the dread that was constricting his throat.

"He's in a coma, Dad. The doctors, they don't know if he'll wake up. You need to come home," Lily managed to say, her words punctuated by quiet sobs.

The details that followed were a blur. Lily told him of the knife, the senseless violence over something as trivial as a phone, and the blood — so much blood. Alex had been found unconscious, his life hanging by a thread, his fate now in the hands of surgeons who were desperately working to save him.

Max's mind raced, military training clashing with the raw instincts of a father. His son, his boy, was lying in a hospital bed, fighting for his life because of a random act of violence. It was a scenario Max had never allowed himself to consider; Alex had always been safe at home, far from the battlefields and the danger that Max had made his career.

"I'm coming, Lily. I'm coming right now," Max said, the words a vow, each one a step towards the door, towards the journey back to his children.

He ended the call, and for a moment, stood motionless, the phone still clutched in his hand. The isolation of Skye, once a haven, was now a cage, and every second he remained was a second lost, a distance that kept him from his son's bedside.

Max moved with a speed born of urgency, packing a bag with efficient haste, his movements a choreography of necessity. Within the hour, he was in his truck, driving down the narrow roads that led away from the cottage, away from the isolation he had sought, and back into the world he had left behind.

As he drove, the night closed in around him, the darkness a shroud that seemed to echo his despair. The single-lane winding roads to the nearest motorway, where he could really make up time, stretched out interminably. Each mile was a battle against the helplessness that threatened to engulf him.

Max's mind was a torrent of emotion, but overriding the fear and the pain was a burning sense of injustice. The attack on Alex was a manifestation of the world's cruelty, a senseless act that had stolen the innocence of his family's life. The disillusionment that he had felt with the military, with the system, now expanded to encompass a society where such violence could occur.

As the first hints of dawn began to touch the horizon, Max's drive became a metaphor for his state of mind — a relentless push through the night, seeking the light of hope, the promise of reaching his son in time.

*

The starkness of the pre-dawn hours matched Max's internal landscape as he navigated the empty roads. The news of Alex's attack had ignited a fury within him, the heat of which was unfamiliar in its intensity even to a man tempered by war. The system he had once upheld now seemed impotent in the face of random street violence that had left his son comatose.

His truck ate up the miles, but it was the phone call with David Rosenberg that consumed his thoughts. David, a voice from the past, had been an ally in the field and a confidant in darker times. The conversation they had had just days before Alex's attack now played in Max's head with prescient clarity.

"Max, it's all a farce," David had said, the cynicism in his voice a corrosive acid. "We prop up regimes, we fight the good fight, but back home, the real enemy is apathy and moral decay. Your son is more at risk walking down the street in the UK than he would be walking down the street in Baghdad."

At the time, Max had dismissed the sentiment as David's usual doom and gloom. Now the words were prophetic, a bitter truth laid bare by the attack on Alex. The disillusionment he had felt with the military's oft-misguided efforts had now spread, a creeping ivy, to the society he had believed was safe.

Max's hands tightened on the steering wheel, the leather creaking under his grip. The first light of dawn was breaking, a sliver of hope against the night. He stopped for fuel, the fluorescent lights of the service station harsh and unwelcoming. People moved around him, shadows in the periphery of his mission-driven focus.

Back on the road, Max's phone rang. It was David, responding to the urgent message Max had left hours earlier.

"Max, I heard about Alex. Jesus, I'm so sorry." David's voice was a mix of anger and sympathy.

"Sorry doesn't catch the bastards who did this," Max replied, his voice cold and hard.

There was a pause, a hesitation as David considered his words. "You know I'm here for you, whatever you need. Just say the word."

Max thought of the system, of the institutions that were supposed to protect and serve, the same institutions he had served. Now, when he needed them the most, they felt distant and impotent.

"I need to find out who did this," Max said, a steely resolve underlying his words.

David was quiet for a moment, understanding the implication. "I'll make some calls, see what I can find out. We're not without resources, you and I."

Max nodded to himself, a small gesture of gratitude. "Thanks, David."

The call ended, and Max was alone again with the

hum of the engine and the weight of his thoughts. The protector in him had been awakened, not the protector of diplomats and VIPs, but the primal guardian of his own blood.

As the landscape changed with the advancing daylight, so too did the landscape of Max's purpose. He was no longer a man fleeing the world; he was a father charging headlong into the fray.

The road ahead would lead him back to his family, to Alex's bedside. But it would also lead him down paths he had thought closed off forever — paths of investigation and retribution, of a father's rage against the violence inflicted upon his son.

*

The journey to the hospital where Alex lay was a long one, filled with silent pleas to every deity Max had ever heard of and some he hadn't. He clung to the hope that when he arrived, Alex would be awake, that this nightmare would be over, and they would all be able to put this behind them. But reality was rarely so accommodating.

When Max finally reached the hospital, the sterile smell of antiseptic and the sound of hushed voices in the corridors were stark reminders of the gravity of Alex's condition. His steps were heavy with dread as he approached his son's room, bracing himself for the sight of Alex, once so full of life, now lying still in a hospital bed.

After hours at Alex's bedside, whispering words of encouragement, of love, and unspoken fears, Max stepped outside to call Lily. His fingers were numb as he dialled, the cold of the hospital seeming to seep into his bones.

Lily answered on the first ring, her voice a balm to the raw edges of Max's spirit. "Dad? How is he? Have you seen him?"

"He's fighting, Lily." Max's voice was a low murmur, a controlled tremble as he pictured his son entangled in tubes and machines. "He's strong. But he hasn't woken up yet."

There was a sniffle from the other end, and Max could picture his daughter, trying to be strong, to be the rock that her father needed. "He has to wake up, Dad. He just has to."

"He will," Max said, more a statement of will than certainty. "He's a Fairchild."

There was a small, sad laugh from Lily. "Yeah. Stubborn as they come."

Max allowed himself a small smile. "Lily, I ..." He paused, the words catching. "I'm sorry. For being away for so long, for not being there."

"Dad, stop. We know why you had to leave. But you're here now, and that's what counts. We just need you to be here for Alex ... and for me."

Max felt the tightness in his chest ease just a fraction. Lily's forgiveness, her understanding, was a gift he hadn't known he needed. "I'm here, Lily. I'm not going anywhere."

There was a quiet understanding between them, the bond of family that had been stretched but not broken. "Come home, Dad. After this. Alex will need you. I'll need you. Come home."

Max's gaze drifted back to the hospital entrance, a gateway to the long vigil that awaited him. "I will, Lily.

It's time to come home."

Hanging up, Max felt the mantle of fatherhood settle around him with a new weight, a new meaning. It was a responsibility he had never abandoned, but one that had changed in the face of his children's needs. Lily's words were a clarion call to the protective instinct that had always been at the core of who he was, not just as a soldier but as a man.

With a newfound resolve, Max turned and re-entered the hospital. Each step took him closer to Alex, closer to the son who needed him, and closer to the realisation that his isolation in Skye was a chapter that was closing. Ahead lay a path defined by the needs of his children, a path that, despite its uncertainty, he would walk with the same determination with which he had faced every challenge in his life.

Chapter 4: Vengeance's Seed

The Echoes of War

In the quietude of the hospital's intensive care unit, Max sat motionless, his eyes unwavering from the rhythmic rise and fall of his son's chest. Each beep from the heart monitor sliced through the silence, cleaving the seconds into moments of raw, unyielding hope and despair. The stark white of the walls, the scent of disinfectant, and the soft shuffle of nurses' feet were a far cry from the windswept moors of Skye and the sun-scorched earth of Iraq. Yet to Max, this sanitised room felt like another battlefield, with stakes as high as any he had known.

Memories, unbidden and sharp as shards of glass, pierced the quiet. Max remembered the adrenaline of combat, the heat of a desert sun, the weight of a rifle in his hands, and the camaraderie of those who had fought beside him. These were the echoes of a past he could never fully leave behind, ghosts that had followed him to this sterile room, where the fight was for a single life, his boy's life, which hung in the balance.

Max's thoughts drifted to the days that followed his departure from the army — a time when the structure of military life gave way to the chaos of the civilian world. He had found a semblance of purpose in the private military sector, offering his expertise to those who could afford it. Baghdad had become his home, a city of ancient history now marked by the scars of ongoing conflict. He had navigated its streets with the same tactical precision required in the open desert, escorting dignitaries and businessmen with a watchful eye, always anticipating the unseen threat.

But Skye had called to him — a whisper of peace amid the cacophony of war. The remote island, with its rugged cliffs and sweeping vistas, was a stark contrast to the urban sprawl of Baghdad. It promised solace, a place to quiet the restless spirits that haunted him. And for a time, it had. He had walked the moors and climbed the crags, each step a meditation, each breath a respite from a life spent in the shadow of death.

Now, as Max watched over Alex, those days of solitude seemed like a lifetime ago. The hospital's constant artificial light was oppressive, bearing down on him with the weight of an interrogation lamp. He felt a kinship with the sterile room — it, too, was a place of stark contrasts and hidden battles. The fight here was silent, waged in the spaces between heartbeats, in the depths of unconsciousness where Alex now resided.

The steady beep of the heart monitor became a metronome to his spiralling thoughts. The world outside continued its ceaseless spin, but in this room, time was measured in breaths and the faintest movements beneath eyelids. Max's hand found Alex's, the touch a silent plea for his son to return to the waking world.

In the midst of the quiet, the call to action that had defined Max's life resurfaced with an intensity that was both familiar and terrifying. The soldier within him, the part that had faced down insurgents and navigated minefields, now faced an enemy that could not be seen or outflanked. The helplessness was a gnawing beast, its teeth sunk deep into the sinew of his being.

The idea of taking action, of reclaiming control, began to seep into his consciousness. It was a dangerous thought, one that skirted the edges of legality and morality. But as the days passed with no change in Alex's condition, that thought took on the weight of conviction. If the law could not find those responsible, then perhaps it was up to him.

Max's gaze never wavered from Alex's face, but his mind was now a battlefield of its own, a tumult of strategy and tactics not for a mission sanctioned by any government or agency but for a personal crusade born of a father's despair and rage.

*

Max's days and nights at the hospital melded into a continuous vigil. The sterile environment, the soft beeps and clicks, the hushed voices of medical staff, they all seemed to blur into a backdrop for his spiralling thoughts. As he sat there, a sentinel by his son's bedside, the line between the man he was and the man he was becoming began to blur.

The Max who had once stood firmly upon the foundations of order and discipline now found himself adrift in a sea of moral ambiguity. The soldier in him had been trained to respect the chain of command, to trust in the system. But as the father in him watched Alex lying still and silent, that trust began to fracture.

He wrestled with thoughts that were once unthinkable. The Max who had served with honour, who had upheld the rule of law, was now contemplating a path that lay in stark contrast to the ideals he had lived by. Vigilantism, a term that evoked images of masked avengers in the pages of comic books, was no longer a fantasy. It had become a potential reality, a course of action that, with each passing day, seemed more justifiable.

The police were doing their best, or so they said. But their best had yielded no arrests, no suspects, no leads. The faceless perpetrators remained free, their lives continuing as if they hadn't shattered his. The system that was supposed to protect and serve seemed impotent, leaving Max feeling like justice was slipping through his fingers like grains of sand.

In the dim light of the hospital room, as he watched the steady rise and fall of Alex's chest, the darkness in Max grew. It was a visceral thing, a shadow that spread through his veins and whispered in a language that spoke of retribution and wrath. The seed of vengeance that had been planted was germinating, fed by the helplessness and frustration that gnawed at him.

He began to imagine what it would feel like to confront those responsible. He envisioned himself not as a bereaved father but as an instrument of retribution. These thoughts, once foreign and repellent to him, now held a certain allure. They promised a sense of control in a situation where he had none, a way to channel the roiling emotions that threatened to consume him.

Each day that passed with no news, no progress, saw the unthinkable become a silent contemplation. The Max who had seen the horrors of war, who had faced down death in defence of his country, now considered a war of a different kind — a private war waged in the shadows of society.

As he sat there, his son's hand held within his own, Max felt the first stirrings of resolve. If the world would not deliver justice for Alex, then perhaps it was up to him to take it. This was not a decision made lightly, but with each tick of the clock, with each shuddering breath Alex took, it became increasingly clear.

The law had its place, but it was not here, not now. Not for Alex. Max's world had been one of black and white, but now he saw only grey. And in that grey, he began to see a path forward — a path that led away from the light of the law and into the shadows of vengeance.

*

In the washed-out hues of the hospital's cafeteria, Max sat across from Emily, their shared history hanging between them like a tapestry frayed by time and circumstance. They were two people bound by the profound love for their children yet separated by a chasm of past grievances and unhealed wounds. The fluorescent lights above did nothing to warm the scene, casting a clinical glow on faces marked by sleepless nights.

Emily's eyes, once the colour of summer skies in his memory, now reflected the stormy hues of worry and fatigue. They spoke, their conversation a navigation through a minefield of emotion, each word measured, each sentence laced with the subtext of their shared pain. It was Lily, the product of their union, who seemed to hold them together, her presence a bridge between the islands of their individual grief.

"Dad, we need to stay strong for Alex." Lily's voice was firm, with a touch of steel belied by her youth. "He's a fighter. He gets that from you."

Max looked into his daughter's eyes, seeing the reflection of his own determination. She was right; they needed to be strong, to forge a united front for Alex's sake. The familiar pull of duty that had once compelled him to leave for distant battlefields now anchored him to this spot, to the silent battleground where his son lay fighting for life.

The intimacy of the moment with Emily and Lily in the hospital cafeteria was a poignant echo of a time when they had been a family untouched by the ravages of war and loss. The connection that had once been unbreakable now showed the wear of strain, but it still held, tensile and resilient in the face of this new trial.

"We'll get through this together," Emily said, reaching out tentatively to touch Max's hand. It was a contact that bridged years of distance, a gesture that spoke of unity and shared strength.

Max felt the walls he had built around his heart since their separation begin to crumble under the gentle pressure of her touch. The need to be a pillar for his family, to be the man they could lean on, was a clarion call that drowned out the whispers of darkness that had begun to encircle him.

Yet even as he drew comfort from their togetherness, the seed of vengeance continued to sprout within the hidden chambers of his soul. It was a dark blossom fed by the undercurrents of rage and helplessness that the reunion could not quell. Max knew that the path he was contemplating was one he would have to walk alone, a shadowy trail that diverged from the unity they now presented.

*

The atmosphere in the hospital, once a sanctuary of strained hope, had become charged with an unspeakable dread. Max felt the shift before the news even reached his ears, a premonition that wrapped cold fingers around his heart. The call came at the darkest hour when the night held its breath before yielding to the dawn. Lily's voice, a delicate thread frayed by grief, carried the weight of the world.

"Dad, it's Alex ... he's gone."

The words were a blow, a physical force that drove the air from his lungs and buckled his knees. Max's vision blurred, the stark hospital corridors melting into a swirl of indistinct colours as he staggered to a wall, the phone slipping from his grasp. He barely registered the sound of it clattering to the floor, his entire being consumed by an abyssal void that opened within him.

Gone. The finality of that word echoed in his mind, a tolling bell that marked the end of a life too young, too full of promise. Alex, his boy, who had his mother's eyes and his father's stubborn chin, who laughed with his whole body and dreamed of a future that now would never be. The pain was a living thing, a beast that clawed at his insides, demanding release.

The sterile environment around him became a cage, trapping him with his anguish. Max's breaths came in ragged gasps, each one a struggle against the tide of sorrow that threatened to drown him. He had faced death before, had seen it steal away the bright flames of friends and comrades, but this ... this was a darkness so profound, so absolute, that it threatened to consume him.

And then, in the midst of the void, a spark. It was more than anger, more than rage — it was fury, pure and incandescent. It was the 'fuck it' moment, the point of no return where grief metamorphosed into something harder, something fiercer.

They would pay.

The thought was a lifeline pulling him from the depths of despair. It gave him direction, a purpose amidst the wreckage of his world. Max's mind, honed by years of military discipline, latched onto the thought with the tenacity of a drowning man clutching at a raft.

He retrieved the phone, his movements now driven by a cold, burning intent. Lily was still on the line, her soft sobs a distant sound as he brought the device back to his ear.

"Lily, listen to me." His voice was a low growl, barely recognizable even to himself. "Stay strong. I will take care of this. I promise you; they will not get away with it."

The promise was an oath, a sacred vow that etched itself into his very soul. Max had been many things in his life — a soldier, a protector, a father — but now he would become something else. An avenger. A bringer of retribution.

The seed of vengeance that had germinated in the shadows of his consciousness now blossomed into full, dark flower. The world had taken his son, and now he would take from the world. There would be no mercy, no quarter. For Alex, for Lily, for the life that should have been, Max would bring down the full fury of a father's wrath.

*

The transformation of Max Fairchild from grieving father to meticulous avenger began in the grim confines of his son's now-silent hospital room. The walls, which had borne witness to so many whispered prayers and fervent hopes, now enclosed a man whose purpose had shifted from preservation to destruction. As he sat in the cold, unforgiving light of morning, Max's mind worked with the precision of a well-oiled machine, a testament to his years of military and private security experience.

His first step was to disappear — a task at which he was adept. Max had always possessed an uncanny ability to blend into the background, to become the unseen observer. In Iraq, his survival had often depended on this skill, and now it became the cornerstone of his nascent plan.

He began to arrange his affairs from the confines of the hospital, using secure lines and coded language that he had not employed since his days in the Middle East. Contacts that had been dormant for years were subtly reawakened, cryptic messages sent that would draw no attention from the uninitiated but spoke volumes to those who knew how to listen.

Max knew the importance of surveillance and information gathering. He was clinical in his approach, methodical in his planning. From a safe distance, he began to watch, to wait, to track the ebb and flow of the city's underbelly. He used disposable phones, paid in cash, left no digital footprint that could be traced back to him. He was a spectre of vengeance that flitted on the edges of the tangible world.

As he pieced together the information he needed, Max maintained his facade. To the hospital staff, he was the stoic, heartbroken father. To the police, he was cooperative and appreciative of their efforts. But beneath the surface, his resolve hardened like steel tempered in fire.

He mapped out the movements of the gang members he suspected, learning their habits, their haunts, their weaknesses. Max had always been an excellent judge of character, a skill that now served him in a darker capacity. He identified the alpha, the weak link, the opportunist —

the key players who would lead him to his quarry.

And then there was Frank 'The Armourer' Johnson, a man whose name was whispered with a mixture of fear and respect in certain circles. Max had not forgotten the feel of a weapon in his hand, the weight of it, the promise of action it represented. Frank would be able to provide what he needed without asking why, a business transaction devoid of morality.

Max's planning was a slow, deliberate process. He anticipated every variable, considered every potential outcome. The act itself would need to be swift, a violence of action that was as decisive as it was lethal. There would be no room for error, no second chances. The strike, when it came, would be the culmination of all his preparation — a silent, deadly dance that would end multiple lives in exchange for the one that had been taken from him.

In his mind, Max rehearsed the scenario over and over, each step choreographed with brutal efficiency. The silencer on the pistol would be a whisper of death, the movements a shadow play of retribution. He would be judge, jury, and executioner, meting out the justice that the system had denied.

*

The world outside continued its routine, oblivious to the storm brewing within the confines of Max's mind. In the depth of his being, a chilling transformation was underway. The once honourable soldier, whose career had been defined by loyalty and service, now plotted in the shadows. The humanity that had bound him to the world seemed to unravel, thread by thread, replaced by an icy resolve.

Max spent the subsequent days in a state of cold detachment. His interactions were perfunctory, mechanical. He provided the necessary consolations to Lily, offered the expected gratitude to the sympathetic friends, but all the while, his true self receded further into the recesses of his calculated intent.

He moved through the city like a wraith, his presence barely registered by those he passed. Max's ability to render himself inconspicuous was a tool honed by necessity in foreign lands, where a soldier's survival often depended on the art of invisibility. Now that same skill served a darker purpose.

The brutality of his cause seemed to strip away the last vestiges of his empathy. Each step in his meticulous planning, each piece of intelligence gathered, was a step away from the man he had once been. The humanity of his targets was not a factor; they were objectives, nothing more. His son's attackers were faceless in his mind, dehumanized targets in a mission that had consumed him.

The emotional distance he cultivated was unsettling, even to himself. At times, a flicker of the man he used to be would surface — a father, a husband, a friend. But the flicker would quickly be extinguished, smothered by the overriding need for retribution.

Max understood the criminality of his intentions. He recognised the line he was about to cross and the abyss that awaited him on the other side. Yet the prospect didn't give him pause — it was the fuel that stoked the fires of his resolve.

In the quiet hours of the night, when the world seemed to hold its breath, Max made the final arrangements. His meeting with Frank Johnson was set, a clandestine encounter where he would acquire the tools necessary for his grim task. Frank's establishment, hidden in plain sight, was a place where questions were never asked — a sanctuary for those, like Max, who operated in the grey zones of morality.

As Max laid out the clothes he would wear — the dark fabrics that would blend into the night, the gloves that would leave no trace, the boots that would make no sound — he felt a detachment that was almost serene. The meticulous preparation was a ritual, the components laid out like sacred relics on the altar of his cause.

When he looked in the mirror, the man staring back at him was a stranger. The lines on his face were drawn by a hand that knew only the language of loss and vengeance. His eyes, once warm with life and laughter, were now cold and hard, like stones at the bottom of a deep and unforgiving sea.

Max's transformation was complete. He was no longer a soldier for hire, no longer a grieving father. He had become the embodiment of vengeance, a force of nature that would soon be unleashed upon those who had dared to tear his world asunder.

The brutality of his impending actions was a necessary end, a means to satiate the hunger for justice that gnawed at his soul. And yet, as he stood on the brink of this dark and violent act, there remained a whisper of doubt, a question that lingered in the air:

Was this the only way?

Chapter 5: Into the Shadows

The Armorer's Call

The city's breath was cool and heavy with mist as Max navigated the labyrinthine backstreets, moving towards an encounter that would cement his descent into the depths of vigilantism. Frank Johnson was a man who existed in the shadows, a merchant of death dealing in the currency of silence and steel. Max knew the risks of what he was about to do, but the hollow ache where his heart once beat demanded it.

He arrived outside an inconspicuous service entrance, the sort unnoticed by the casual observer. He waited, his body still but his senses hyperalert. After a moment that stretched taut with anticipation, a faint click sounded as the door unlatched from within.

The interior was stark, a void save for the narrow shafts of light that pierced the gloom, illuminating dust motes that danced like spectres. Frank's figure emerged from the darkness, his posture relaxed but his eyes sharp, missing nothing.

"Max," Frank greeted, his voice a low baritone that resonated in the confined space. "To what do I owe the pleasure?"

"Equipment," Max replied curtly. "I need to be a ghost and I need the same level of kit I'm used to operating."

Frank appraised Max with a look that took in every detail, weighing and analysing. "Follow me," he said after a moment, turning on his heel with the certainty of a man who knew his domain like the back of his hand.

They moved through a maze of corridors, the air

growing colder, the silence deeper. Eventually, they entered a room that served as a sanctum for the tools of Frank's grim trade. Here, the walls were lined with an arsenal that could outfit an entire battalion — each weapon meticulously maintained, each a promise of lethal efficiency.

Frank led Max to a bench where several items were laid out with precision — a tactical vest, an assortment of sidearms, and various implements of espionage. But it was the long-barrelled weapon that caught Max's attention — an HK416 rifle, its matte black finish absorbing the light.

"This is one of the best you can get," Frank said, following Max's gaze. "Custom build. Suppressor, enhanced optics, and a trigger action smoother than silk. It won't let you down."

Max picked up the rifle, feeling the familiar weight, the balance that spoke of deadly craftsmanship. It was an extension of his will, a tool that would deliver the justice denied to his son.

"I'll take it," Max stated, a tinge of the old fire in his voice — a fire that had been dampened by grief but now found new fuel.

Frank nodded, a flicker of something unreadable passing over his features. "There are other items you might consider," he suggested, gesturing towards gadgets and gear that were the trade's cutting edge.

Max looked at the vast stock in the room, his focus singular. "I'll also take the SIG 226, suppressors, extra magazines, flashbangs, some home wreckers, and the high-spec NODs, and the names of the best information brokers you know."

"You're diving deep, Max," Frank warned, his voice a

note of caution in the stillness. "Be sure you're ready for what you'll find."

Max met Frank's gaze, his eyes hard as flint. "I was born ready."

The transaction was completed with an exchange of cash, the bills as untraceable as the ghost Max was about to become. With the rifle securely packed in nondescript casing, he stepped back into the night, a shadow merging with shadows, the first step taken on a path from which there was no return.

The city would soon know a new spectre, one driven by vengeance and armed with the cold intent of a father who had nothing left to lose.

*

The room where Max met with the broker was shrouded in the kind of darkness that felt almost tangible, like a fabric woven from the night itself. The air was thick with the scent of old wood and faint traces of cologne, the kind used to mask other, less palatable odours. In the heart of this darkness sat a figure, ensconced in shadows as if she were part of them. Anastasia Sokolov — or the Black Widow, as the whispers in the underworld had named her — was a collector of secrets, a weaver of the invisible threads that connected the city's hidden sins.

Max had never been a man to dwell on the moral implications of his actions, and his current mission stripped away what little regard for such niceties he had once possessed. His communication with Anastasia had been arranged through a series of cryptic messages, each one a breadcrumb leading her to this clandestine meeting, and as he faced her now, he was an enigma, a man reduced to a single, burning objective.

"Mr Fairchild." Anastasia's voice was like silk, smooth and enveloping. "You've become quite the ghost. Rumour has it you're after some dangerous information."

Max's response was measured, each word deliberate. "Rumours are the currency you trade in, aren't they? I need names, locations, patterns. I need to know where the rats hide in their nests."

Anastasia regarded him with an intensity that might have unnerved another man, but Max was beyond such responses. His emotions, once a spectrum, had dulled to shades of grey, focused solely on the retribution that awaited.

"Such information comes at a price," she cautioned, a hint of steel underlying her words.

"I'm prepared to pay," Max replied, his tone leaving no room for negotiation.

The broker nodded once, curtly, her silhouette shifting as she reached for something beyond the pool of light. She slid a thin file across the table, its contents a Pandora's box of the city's darkest deeds.

"Everything you need is in here," she said, her gaze never leaving Max's face. "But be warned, Mr Fairchild, the path you're walking has no return. Vengeance is a chalice from which many have drunk deeply, only to find its dregs poison."

Max took the file, his hands betraying none of the turmoil that churned within him. "Some poisons are necessary," he stated flatly, his voice devoid of inflection.

As he stood to leave, Anastasia spoke once more. "Should you need further assistance, remember that the Black Widow's web is expansive. For a price, you can call upon my resources."

He acknowledged her offer with a nod, understanding the unspoken rules of their engagement. In this city, beneath the veneer of civilization, there existed a market for every commodity, including vengeance.

Max left as silently as he had arrived, the file tucked securely under his arm. He moved through the streets with purpose, a spectre on the hunt, his heart an ice-bound fortress where empathy had long since withered and died.

In the confines of his temporary hideout, Max pored over the file's contents. Each piece of information was a thread, and he was the loom, weaving together the tapestry that would reveal his prey. With a clinical detachment, he studied the gang's hierarchy, their territories, the ebb and flow of their illicit dealings.

The names of his son's attackers stood out like beacons in the night, and with each name, Max's resolve crystallized further. He would be the hand of retribution, the shadow that spelled their doom. And in this quest, there was no room for doubt, no space for the luxury of empathy.

Max Fairchild, once a man of honour, was now an instrument of vengeance. And in his new world, mercy had no meaning.

*

Max's preparation for the coming storm of retribution was meticulous. He had always been adept at the art of surveillance, a skill honed in the shadowed streets of Belfast and the treacherous terrain of Northern Ireland, where observing the IRA had been a game of life and death. Now he applied the same principles to his current quarry, the petty criminals whose fates were sealed by their own heinous act.

From a safe distance, Max observed the gang members through high-powered binoculars and long-range camera lenses. He followed their movements across the city, their routines becoming as familiar to him as his own. He noted their dealings in hushed alleyways, the hand-offs of drugs that were the lifeblood of their operation, and the violence that followed them like a shroud.

Through Anastasia's file, Max had been given the keys to their kingdom — the places they frequented, the times they were most vulnerable. And though finding such petty criminals was not typically her purview, she had understood the gravity of Max's request. Her usual clientele sought leverage over magnates and politicians, not street-level thugs. But the cold fire in Max's eyes had conveyed the necessity of his need, and Anastasia had delivered.

He operated alone, avoiding personal contact that could compromise his mission. His identity remained shrouded, his presence ghostlike. Max knew that the smallest slip could unravel everything. He could not afford to be seen, to be known. His interaction with the criminal world was a dance of shadows, each step calculated, each turn anticipated.

As he watched the gang members, Max couldn't help but notice the ripple effect of their actions — the way they influenced the community, the fear they instigated, the control they exerted. It was clear they were small cogs in a larger machine, a realisation that both simplified and complicated his objective.

The days passed, and Max's apartment became a war

room. Maps lined the walls, dotted with pins and strings that traced the gang's movements. Surveillance footage played on loops, revealing the patterns of the prey he stalked. He noted their interactions with other, more influential figures of the underworld, each encounter meticulously logged.

In one particular piece of footage, Max noticed a shift in the dynamic. A figure, cloaked in the garb of authority, met with the gang. This was no ordinary interaction; the deference shown by the gang was palpable. Max zoomed in, capturing the man's features, a face not found in Anastasia's file. This was someone new, someone of consequence.

He cross-referenced the image with public records, a process that took hours of painstaking research. Finally, a hit — an associate of Yuri Dubrovnik, a name that carried weight in the criminal hierarchy. This was the connection Max had been unconsciously seeking, the thread that, once pulled, would unravel a greater tapestry of corruption and power.

A cold smile touched Max's lips. The gang's end would be a message, a declaration of his intent. Their deaths would serve as a warning shot across the bow of a larger battle he was only just beginning to understand.

With each revelation, Max's mission evolved. What had started as a quest for personal vengeance was morphing into a crusade against the cancerous network of crime that had claimed his son. He was no longer merely a father seeking justice; he was becoming an executioner, a spectre haunting the periphery of a criminal world that would soon know fear.

*

Max spent the subsequent weeks in a state of near-constant surveillance, an invisible sentinel amidst the urban sprawl of London. The tools of his trade were extensions of his senses: monocular with night-vision capabilities for the late hours, directional microphones for eavesdropping from afar, and a collection of sophisticated, albeit not strictly legal, hacking tools that allowed him to follow the digital footprints of his targets.

His apartment, once a silent testament to his solitude, had become a nerve centre of operation. Screens flickered with feeds from hidden cameras, while scanners picked up the chatter of radio communications, some of which he knew belonged to the gang members. Max decrypted conversations with the methodical precision of a man who had nothing left but the mission.

The flat in a dilapidated estate that served as the gang's hub was under his watchful eye. It was in a derelict tower block, a monolith of the city's failures, its walls etched with the stories of neglect. The gang had turned one of the flats into their den, a nexus from which they sent out tendrils of influence, pushing their poison onto the streets, exploiting the vulnerable and the desperate.

Max had observed the comings and goings, noting the young faces, some barely in their teens, who were pulled into the orbit of the gang's activities. They were the foot soldiers of the 'county lines' drug operations, their innocence a currency spent in the service of their masters' greed.

He had watched the violence, too. It was casual, an everyday occurrence to the gang — a brutal lesson here, a display of power there. They wielded fear with the expertise of puppeteers, each act a string that pulled at the community, forcing it into a macabre dance of compliance.

With each observed atrocity, Max's resolve crystallized. These were not merely the killers of his son; they were a cancer that needed excising with a merciless hand. The people they hurt, the lives they destroyed — it was a litany of offences that justified what was to come. Deep down, Max wanted his family to understand this too, to feel the justness of his cause even as they would be shocked by the ferocity of his response. But he knew he must do all he could to protect them and his identity as long as possible.

He knew the flat's layout now, knew the shifts in guard patterns, the best angles of approach, the blind spots in their security. He had identified the sentries, the weak links, and the times when they were most relaxed, most vulnerable. It was in one of these lulls that he would strike, swift and lethal as the avenging angel he had become in his own mind.

The plan was set. Max had assembled a kit — a tactical harness, a suppressed long-barrelled weapon for the initial engagement, and his trusted sidearm for the close work. Flashbangs would disorientate any who were not immediately neutralised, and the night-vision goggles would give him the advantage in the ensuing chaos. The violence would be explosive, a choreographed sequence that left no room for mercy.

As he prepped his gear, Max felt a detachment from the man who would carry out the act. He was clinical, each item checked and rechecked with an emotionless efficiency. There was no pleasure in the preparation, no sadistic anticipation. There was only the cold calculus of vengeance.

Max understood the shock his actions would invoke,

the brutality that would stain his hands. But in his mind's eye, he saw only the faces of the young victims, the terrorized community, and the lifeless form of his son. They were the fuel for his impending storm, the justification for the hurricane of violence he was about to unleash.

This was the nature of his war — a solitary crusade against a blight that the law had failed to purge. Max Fairchild, once a protector of the innocent, was now the harbinger of death. And the gang that had thought themselves untouchable would soon learn the price of their transgressions.

*

Max's flat was silent, the only sound the soft clicking of his computer keyboard as he cross-referenced the faces of his son's killers with the latest surveillance data. The screen cast a pale glow, illuminating the stoic resolve etched into his features. It was in these quiet hours of analysis and planning that the memories of his past operations intruded upon the present, unbidden yet sharply clear.

The flashbacks came in disjointed fragments: the sombre Irish landscapes where he had tracked the IRA, his breath fogging in the chill air as he lay in wait, watching through the scope of his rifle. Each movement of the suspected militants was catalogued, each meeting documented with the meticulous attention to detail that was the hallmark of his profession. There had been violence then, controlled, and precise, a necessary response to the calculated moves of a dangerous adversary.

In Afghanistan, it had been the same — a different

enemy in the Taliban, but the same dance of surveillance and countermeasures. The dusty streets of Kandahar, the poppy fields that funded terror: they were the backdrop to his watchful eyes and steady hands. The crack of his rifle had been the punctuation to many a long vigil, the echo a testament to the deadly skills he possessed.

Now, as Max prepared to bring those skills to bear on the streets of London, he felt the weight of his past deeds coalesce into a singular purpose. The IRA, the Taliban, the gang that had taken his son from him — they were all threads in the tapestry of violence that he had been a part of for so long.

The gang's ruthlessness only fuelled Max's resolve. He had seen them in action, using teenagers as mules, pushing drugs with a casual disregard for the lives they ruined. The violence they perpetrated was without honour — beatings doled out with glee, stabbings in broad daylight, the laughter that followed the spray of blood. They were a scourge, their cruelty a stain upon the city that Max felt compelled to cleanse.

One particular memory stood out: a young man, no older than Alex, cornered in an alley by the gang members. Max had watched through his binoculars, the scene unfolding with sickening inevitability. He had memorized the faces of the attackers, their sneers of contempt, the way they had kicked the boy long after he had stopped moving. The police had found the victim later, another statistic in the growing epidemic of gang violence.

These recollections were a cold fire in Max's veins, each one a reaffirmation of the path he had chosen. The gang had no idea that retribution was coming, that their actions had sealed their fate. They continued their operations with arrogance, believing themselves untouchable by the law or by men like Max.

But Max was coming for them, an avenging spirit born from the union of his grief and the cruel history that he had been a part of. The skills he had honed in distant wars would now be used here, on the home front. The controlled violence of his past would pale in comparison to the storm he was about to unleash.

The night was drawing near, and with it, the moment of truth. Max's preparations were complete, his equipment ready. The flat, once a place of mourning, was now the calm before the storm. The storm of Max Fairchild, a man who had traversed the globe in the service of others, was now the instrument of his own dark justice.

*

Max stood in the dim light of his flat, a figure of meticulous preparation. On the table before him lay the tools of vengeance: a customized Heckler & Koch HK416 rifle with Aimpoint Micro T-2 sights, ideal for close-quarters combat, and a suppressor, its matte finish absorbing rather than reflecting the scant light, and a SIG Sauer P226 with a SilencerCo suppressor sidearm, equally muted. The weapons were the final pieces of a puzzle he had been assembling with cold precision, each part a critical component of the retribution he was about to inflict.

With methodical care, he began his transformation. Latex gloves sheathed his hands, each finger rolled down to ensure a skin-tight fit. Around his wrists, he secured tape, forming a seal against any stray fibres or skin cells that might seek to betray him. His beard, once a mark of his grief and isolation, fell away under the razor's edge, leaving behind the bare skin of a man reborn in the crucible of loss. His hair was covered with a cap, ensuring that not a single strand would be left in the wake of his passing.

Surgical boot covers encased his footwear, a barrier against the tell-tale prints that might speak too loudly in the silent aftermath. Every movement was deliberate, every action a step towards the inevitable. He was a ghost cloaked in the anonymity of his own careful design.

His equipment was laid out with the precision of a surgeon's instruments. He checked his ammunition, each round a harbinger of the justice he would deliver. The NVGs were tested and retested, their green hue a comfort in the pitch-black operation that awaited him. Flashbangs were secured in his tactical vest, their pins accessible, their purpose clear — to disorientate and disrupt, to shatter the complacency of those who believed the night belonged to them.

The old CCTV system of the flats was a relic, and Max had disabled it with ease days before. The feed had cut to static, a minor blip on the monitors that would draw no immediate concern, lost amid the white noise of the city's ceaseless surveillance.

The building's electricity was next, a simple matter of accessing a neglected maintenance panel and preparing to sever the lifeline that kept the gang's den illuminated. Darkness would be his ally, and he would command it with the flip of a switch.

Max slung the rifle across his body, feeling the familiar weight of it against his back. The sidearm rested in its holster, its presence a reassurance of the violence of action he was capable of. He was an instrument of death, honed to a fine edge by his singular purpose.

In the flat that served as the gang's stronghold, the nine lives that remained oblivious to their looming end continued their evening. They were the key players and their hangers-on — girls lured by the allure of danger, low-level dealers drawn by the promise of wealth. They laughed and revelled, a cacophony of the damned that echoed through the halls.

Among them was a girl, a witness to the carnage that was to come. She would be the one to survive, the voice that whispered of the ghost who had come calling, the shadow that had enacted a reckoning so swift, so brutal, that it would send ripples through the underworld.

Max stood at the precipice, the night stretching out before him, an abyss that called to the core of his being. He was ready, every fibre of his being attuned to the task at hand. The tension was a tangible thing, a serpent coiled within the confines of his chest, ready to strike.

And strike it would, with a ferocity that would shake the foundations of the criminal empire that had taken his son from him.

Chapter 6: The First Strike

Breach

Max's shadow loomed against the grim facade of the tower block, a dark wraith in a world of concrete and desolation. The flat that lay within was a cancerous cell, pulsating with the lifeblood of a gang that had long forsaken any claim to humanity. Tonight, that pulsation would cease; the hand of vengeance was at their door.

The air was thick with the anticipation of violence as Max surveyed the entrance. His preparations were complete, his kit meticulous — each item serving a purpose in the symphony of retribution he was about to conduct. With a final check of his gear, he slipped on his NVGs, the world transforming into varying shades of green — the hues of hunters and predators.

Silent as the night itself, Max approached the flat's main door. His tools were simple but effective; lock picks clicked into place with the softest whispers, betraying their deadly intent. With a deft twist, the lock yielded, and he was in.

The corridor stretched out before him, its silence soon to be shattered. He could hear the muffled sounds of laughter and music from within the flat, the revelry of the damned. They were oblivious to the fate that stalked them, a fact that would serve Max well.

He paused at the entrance to the flat, his heartbeat a measured drum against the cage of his ribs. This was it — the point of no return. He drew a flashbang from his vest, the pin between his fingers feeling like the trigger of destiny.

In one fluid motion, Max disabled the flat's power at the junction box, plunging the space into darkness. The music and laughter inside turned to confusion, then panic. It was in this disarray that Max made his move.

The flashbang sailed through the now-open door, a harbinger of chaos. It detonated with a blinding flash and a thunderous roar, the shockwave a physical force that swept through the room. Shouts of alarm and fear erupted as the gang members were engulfed in disorientation.

Max moved. There was no hesitation, no flicker of doubt — only the cold clarity of purpose. He entered the flat, the silenced HK416 rifle cradled in his arms, a lethal extension of his will. The gang members were shadows now, their figures outlined in the night-vision green that filled Max's sight.

The rifle's report was a whisper, the suppressor doing its grim work. Max was methodical, each shot a measured decision, each target selected with a calculated precision that was as ruthless as it was effective. The bullets found their marks with deadly accuracy, the gang members falling one by one, their lives extinguished before they could even comprehend their fate.

The room was chaos, the air filled with the sounds of screams and the desperate scuffling of those trying to flee or fight back. But Max was a maelstrom of destruction that left only stillness in its wake.

He advanced room by room, his movements a dark ballet danced to the music of death. Each space was cleared with the efficiency born from years of training — years spent in the shadow of war, where such actions were measured in survival rather than morality.

In the corner of a room, a figure huddled, a young girl clutching her arm where a bullet had grazed her. She was a silhouette of terror, frozen beneath a bed as the spectre of retribution passed her by. She saw only the green hue of Max's goggles, a pair of luminous orbs that would haunt her nightmares for years to come.

As the last of the gang members fell, Max stood amid the carnage. The silence returned, now laden with the weight of finality. He surveyed the room, his breath steady, his heart a stone within his chest.

The action had been clean, efficient — but as Max looked upon the aftermath, a thought crept into his mind, unbidden and insidious: it could have been cleaner.

*

The stillness that followed the storm of violence was not peaceful; it was charged with the lingering echoes of death. Max stood amongst the fallen, their bodies strewn across the squalid flat like grotesque marionettes with their strings cut. His breaths were controlled exhalations, a practised calm that belied the adrenaline coursing through his veins.

He surveyed the room with clinical detachment, his eyes scanning for any sign of movement, any hint of a threat that might still lurk in the corners. There was none. The silence was absolute, save for the faint, ragged breaths of the girl hiding under the bed, a lone survivor in a sea of death.

Max's mind was already cataloguing the event, dissecting each moment with the cold objectivity of a debrief. Eight targets down, the precision of the strikes undeniable. But one round had gone wide, grazing the girl. A mistake.

The pull to dispatch her too was a visceral tug, an

instinct honed by countless operations where loose ends could unravel entire missions. Yet something stayed his hand. She was not a combatant, not part of the threat matrix he had come to dismantle. She was a witness, yes, but her survival was a thread left hanging by choice.

As he stepped over a lifeless body, Max felt the hook sink deeper into his psyche. The operation's cleanliness was marred by that one errant shot, a blemish on an otherwise flawless execution. It was a deviation that would need to be rectified in future engagements. The need for perfection, for absolute efficiency, became a new mantra in his mind.

The ruthlessness of the gang had been mirrored in his actions, but there was a distinction in his mind. They had been parasites, feeding on the vulnerable, dealing in misery and death for profit and pleasure. Max's brutality was a calculated response, a necessary evil to purge the world of such parasites.

He glanced at the girl once more, her eyes wide with terror, a silent plea for mercy. Max's actions tonight had been the opening salvo in what he knew would become a broader campaign. The criminal world had many layers, and he had just peeled away the first.

The realisation that there would be more didn't unsettle him; it was an inevitability he had already accepted. There would be others who would fall to his silent wrath, others who would find themselves in the crosshairs of his scope. Max Fairchild the grieving father was fading, giving way to Max Fairchild the assassin.

As he prepared to exfiltrate, Max ensured his equipment was accounted for, his presence erased as much as possible. He wiped down surfaces, removed cartridges, and ensured that nothing could lead back to him.

The NVGs were switched off, the world returning to its natural palette of shadows and moonlight. He exited the way he had come, leaving behind the stench of cordite and blood, the flat now a tomb. The latex gloves and surgical boot covers were removed and placed in sealable zip bags ready to be incinerated with a quiet flame, the ashes scattered.

Outside, the night air was a cold caress against his skin, a reminder of the world that continued to turn, oblivious to the justice that had just been meted out within. Max's reflection on his actions was brief and pointed; it could have been cleaner, more efficient. It would be next time.

*

After the night's grim work, Max's return to his flat was not a retreat but a regrouping, a time to stoke the fires of a vendetta that had only just begun to burn. The route back was carefully planned to avoid CCTV, doorbell cameras, and potential areas for dashcams to pick up on his movement. The walls of his abode, once a place of solitude, now felt like a command centre for a war of attrition he had declared on the filth that had infested the streets.

He sat in the darkness, the only light emanating from the screen of his laptop as he began to compile a new list. This was no ordinary list; it was a ledger of death, each name a mark for the reaper he had become. These were the names whispered in fear in the underworld, the untouchables, the dealers of despair who believed themselves beyond the reach of justice.

The selection process was methodical, a distillation of information gathered from Anastasia's file, from street chatter, and from the digital shadows where the criminal elite liked to hide. Max's criteria were stringent; he targeted those who forced teenagers into servitude, who spread their poison across county lines, who revelled in the violence they sowed.

As he delved into the backgrounds of his new targets, Max felt the last vestiges of his former self slip away. The soldier who had once fought for queen and country was now a soldier of fortune, his cause personal, his war private. The darkness within him was a well that seemed to have no bottom, each new name on the list a stone cast into its depths.

The sound of the city at night, a symphony of the mundane and the chaotic, was a stark contrast to the silence of his flat. It was a reminder that the world remained ignorant of the cleansing fire he had become. Each name he etched into his list was a cancerous cell to be excised, a wrong to be righted.

As Max selected his marks, he considered the means by which they would meet their end. There would be no indiscriminate violence; each strike would be surgical, a precision that would become his signature. He was not a butcher; he was an artist, and death was his medium.

The girl who had survived would be the link, spreading the story of the ruthlessness of the unknown figure, the unwitting informant who would guide him through the labyrinth of the criminal network. Her survival had been no accident; she was the thread he needed to pull to unravel the tapestry of corruption he sought to destroy.

In the shadows, Max prepared for the next phase of his campaign. He gathered surveillance equipment, weapons, and tools with a ritualistic reverence. Each item was checked and double-checked, each plan meticulously plotted. The electricity that hummed through the veins of the city was at his command, and he would use it to plunge his enemies into darkness.

His apartment became a shrine to his mission, maps adorned with notes and photographs, strings connecting dots that only he could see. Max's world was now one of absolutes, black and white, life and death. The grey morality of his past was a distant memory, replaced by the clarity of his newfound purpose.

The descent into darkness was complete, and Max embraced it like a lover. The city's underbelly would learn to fear the shadow that moved with impunity through their ranks, the silent avenger who was the last thing they would never see.

*

Max's hands moved methodically as he cleaned his weapon, each part dismantled with mechanical precision, the smell of gun oil a tang in the air. The silence of the room was a canvas for his thoughts, and in the stillness, his mind wandered, unbidden, to the past.

Flashes of memory intruded: the oppressive heat of an Afghan village, the tension palpable in the air, and the weight of his rifle — a burden and a comfort all at once. There had been a mission, one of many, where the lines between right and wrong blurred in the face of necessity. An insurgent compound, intelligence of an imminent threat, and the order — clear and direct.

The operation had been clean, professional. But afterwards, amidst the rubble and the ruin, there had been survivors — civilians whose lives had been irrevocably altered by the choices Max and his team had made. The empathy he'd felt then, the questioning of the morality of his actions, had been a shackle he'd since cast off.

But now, as Max reflected on the gang members' deaths, the same questions began to resurface. He had been judge and executioner, delivering a final verdict with cold impartiality. In the moment, there had been no room for hesitation, no space for mercy. Yet in the quiet aftermath, the faces of the dead haunted him — not for their loss, but for what their abrupt silencing represented.

Max had embarked on a path that promised to be bloodier, one that would see him delve deeper into the criminal quagmire. Each name on his list was a death warrant waiting to be signed in lead. And as the list grew, so did the realisation that Max was becoming the very thing he hunted — a predator lurking in the shadows.

The violence he had unleashed had been righteous in his eyes, a purging flame. But as he prepared for the next strike, Max felt an unfamiliar pang — a whisper of the conscience he thought he had silenced.

He pushed the feeling aside, focusing on the tactile reality of his preparations. The NVGs, the flashbangs, the suppressed SG pistol — all were tools to facilitate his mission. Yet as he checked each item, the pang returned, more insistent now. It was a crack in the armour he had donned, a fissure through which the light of empathy began to seep.

Max's next targets were worse, he told himself. They were the orchestrators of violence on a grander scale, their hands stained with the blood of countless innocents. His actions, though extreme, were a counterbalance to the scale of their sins.

But the memory of the girl hiding beneath the bed, her

eyes wide with terror, was a haunting counterpoint to his justifications. She had been a bystander, an unintended casualty of his war. The realisation that there would be more like her was a stone in his stomach.

Max's journey was becoming a descent not into darkness but into a place where light and dark waged an incessant war. He had crossed a line, but where that line would ultimately lead, he could not say.

In his moments of solitude, Max was beginning to question the man he was becoming. The clarity of purpose that had driven him to this point was now muddied by the reality of his actions. The zero empathy he had prided himself on was proving to be an armour incomplete.

As he reassembled his rifle, the parts clicking into place with an almost musical rhythm, Max knew that the path ahead was one he would walk alone. The spectre of doubt, once banished, now walked alongside him — a constant reminder that the war he fought was as much within as it was without.

*

In the solitude of his flat, surrounded by the tools and weapons of his trade, Max sat in the stark glow of his computer screen, the list of names before him. Each one was a life he planned to extinguish, a debt he intended to collect. But as he reviewed his plans, the afterimage of the girl cowering beneath the bed flickered at the edge of his consciousness.

Max knew that to hesitate was to fail. He had embraced this path as the only means to exact justice for Alex, yet doubt was a persistent shadow that stretched longer in the cold light of retrospection. As a soldier, he had followed orders, believed in the cause for which he fought. But now, as a solitary agent of vengeance, the justifications were his alone to construct.

He replayed the events of the flat, the methodical precision with which he had executed the operation. It had been a manifestation of the skills he had honed over years of service — yet the purpose had been starkly different. There was no flag to rally behind, no camaraderie of fellow soldiers. There was only the silence of the dead and the whispers of his own conflicted soul.

The brutality of his actions was not lost on him. Each round fired from his rifle had been a deliberate choice, a balance of tactical necessity and personal retribution. The efficiency of the strike was cold comfort; it did not fill the hollow void left by his son's absence. Instead, it expanded it, a growing chasm fed by the blood of those he had deemed guilty.

Max's once unshakable conviction wavered as he considered the collateral damage of his crusade. The girl who had survived was a living testament to the chaos he had wrought. She would carry the trauma of that night forever, a scar not unlike the ones that marked his own psyche.

The reflections of his past missions intruded once more, uninvited yet insistent. He remembered the strict rules of engagement, the protocols that dictated when to take a life and when to spare it. In the shadowy realm in which he now operated; those rules were his to define. But with each life he took, the clarity of his moral compass dimmed, the needle wavering between justice and vengeance.

As the night deepened, Max turned off his computer, the names on the screen burning into his memory. He stood and approached the window, looking out over a city that slept in ignorance of the war being waged within its midst. The darkness outside mirrored the one within him, a once-clear path now muddied with the complexities of his actions.

He thought of Detective Inspector Sarah Bennett, a name that had surfaced in his enquiries — a woman who had made a name for herself by doggedly pursuing the shadows of the criminal world. Soon, he knew, he would become the subject of her hunt. The thought was neither a concern nor a challenge; it was simply another variable in the equation he was solving.

Max reflected on the moral line he had crossed. In the pursuit of retribution, he had become the very thing he hunted: a dealer of death, a shadow that moved with lethal intent. The righteousness of his cause was a flame that flickered in the gathering darkness, its light struggling to define the contours of his mission.

The dawn was a faint brushstroke on the horizon as Max prepared for rest, a brief respite in the unending campaign he had embarked upon. But sleep would not be easy; it was haunted by the faces of those he had killed and by the question that gnawed at him: In the quest to right the wrongs done to his son, what had he become?

*

The night relinquished its dominion to the creeping light of dawn, casting long shadows across Max's flat. In the aftermath of his actions, the space felt less like a refuge and more like a command post. Every item had its place, every piece of equipment served a purpose, and Max himself was the orchestrator of a symphony that played out in the silent cacophony of the city's underworld.

He moved with a purpose, gathering the tools of his trade. Each piece of surveillance equipment was wiped clean of fingerprints, each hard drive scrubbed of data. There was no digital footprint, no paper trail; Max had learned long ago that the most effective predator was one that left no trace.

His computer, once a fountain of intelligence, was now a blank slate. He had committed everything to memory, his mind a vault that required no keys, no codes. The names and faces of those he pursued were etched in the dark recesses of his thoughts, recalled with ease but hidden from any who might seek to follow his trail.

Max's training had instilled in him the necessity for operational security. He took no notes, kept no diaries. His plans were locked away behind the stoic façade that he presented to the world, a façade that betrayed nothing of the storm that raged within.

As the city awoke, unaware of the justice that had been meted out in its shadows, Max prepared for the day. He dressed in nondescript clothing, the uniform of the city's countless inhabitants. His gear was stowed away, innocuous in its containment, ready for when he would next need it.

He reflected on the path he had chosen, a path that had taken him deep into the heart of darkness. But unlike those he hunted, Max's darkness was a means to an end. He was not driven by greed or the lust for power; he was driven by a need for retribution and the unwavering resolve to prevent others from suffering as he had.

The professionalism with which he approached his

mission was his armour. It shielded him from the doubts that sought to creep in, the questions that society might ask of his methods. He was a professional in every sense of the word, his operations carried out with the same precision and attention to detail that had characterized his military career.

Yet as he looked out upon the city, Max knew that his actions had drawn attention. Detective Inspector Bennett's name had come to him during his research — a woman whose reputation for hunting down those who operated in the city's underbelly was well-founded. Sooner or later, their paths would cross, and Max wondered what that encounter would bring.

For now, Max was content to remain a ghost, a spectre of vengeance that haunted the nightmares of the criminal elite. He had crossed a line, yes, but it was a line that he had drawn in the sand, a demarcation of his own moral boundaries.

As Max stepped out into the light of a new day, he felt the weight of the path he had chosen. It was a burden he was willing to bear, a cross he would carry. He had become the arbiter of a justice that the law could not provide, a dark knight in a world that needed him.

The First Strike had been delivered, a message in blood and gunpowder. And though it could have been cleaner, more efficient, it was only the beginning. Max Fairchild was a man transformed, his purpose clear, his resolve unshakable.

The city would come to know his work, the signature of a professional who demanded retribution. A man who could kill efficiently. They would also understand the necessity of his existence in a world that was all too often cruel and unforgiving.

Chapter 7: Mentor's Concern

The Colonel's Intuition

The rain was a relentless torrent, drumming against the windows of the old service club where retired Colonel Hammond sat, nursing his scotch with a furrowed brow. The gloom of the London weather did little to dampen the concerns that clouded his mind. He was waiting for Max, his former protégé, a man he had once guided through the trials of military life and special operations.

Max entered the club like a phantom, his presence commanding yet subdued, in stark contrast to the warmth of the wood-panelled room reeking of history and tradition. Hammond noted the subtle changes in Max — a certain hardness in his eyes, a rigidity in his posture that spoke of a man reshaped by grief and fuelled by something darker.

"Max," Hammond greeted, his voice a deep rumble that mirrored the storm outside. "It's been too long."

"Colonel," Max replied, acknowledging the man who had been a mentor and a father figure.

They sat, the space between them charged with an unspoken tension. Hammond observed Max, the lines of his face etched with a tale of battles fought in shadows since they had last met.

"I've heard rumours, Max. Whispers of a vigilante striking at the heart of London's underbelly," Hammond began, his gaze locked onto Max's. "Tell me there's no truth to them."

Max's jaw tightened imperceptibly. He had been careful, meticulous in his efforts to remain unseen, untraceable. But he had underestimated the networks that men like Hammond had at their disposal — the old boys' club of intelligence and military connections that thrived on information.

"Rumours are dangerous things, Colonel," Max deflected, his tone even. "They can turn men into monsters or heroes, depending on the listener."

Hammond leaned forward, his concern evident. "You were a damn fine soldier, Max. But this path you're on …"

"It's one of justice," Max cut in, a steel edge to his words.

The colonel sighed, his fingers drumming a staccato rhythm on the leather armrest. "Justice? Or vengeance? There's a line, son. And once crossed …"

"I know all about lines, Colonel," Max interjected, his voice a low growl. "I crossed one the day I buried my son."

There was a moment of heavy silence, the air thick with the weight of unspoken words and shared histories. Hammond regarded Max, the man he had mentored, now a shadow of the soldier he had once known.

"George Blackwell," Hammond said abruptly, changing tact. "Do you remember him?"

Max nodded. George Blackwell, another name from his past, a man whose wisdom had often been a beacon in the chaos of war.

"He's been asking about you. Concerned about the stories he's hearing," Hammond continued. "He might be worth talking to. A different perspective, perhaps."

Max considered the suggestion. Blackwell had always had a way of cutting through the noise, of finding clarity in the confusion.

"Maybe," Max allowed, noncommittal.

Hammond leaned back, his eyes never leaving Max.

"Be careful, Max. There are unseen forces at play — powers that even we don't fully understand. This isn't just the criminal scum you're up against. There are players in this game that operate at a level even beyond our reach."

The indirect warning hung in the air, a veiled reference to entities that Hammond had always been wary of — shadow organisations that pulled strings on a global scale.

Max felt a chill that had nothing to do with the rain outside. His war, it seemed, was widening in scope, the battlefield extending into realms he had yet to fully comprehend.

"Thank you, Colonel," Max said, standing. "For the drink, and the advice."

As Max left the club, the rain seemed to intensify, as if mirroring the tumult within him. The meeting had been a reminder that his actions were not without consequences, that the ripples he created were being felt in circles he had once moved in.

He walked into the night, the darkness enveloping him, the words of his old mentor echoing in his mind. The descent into this life of shadows was not just a path of personal retribution — it was a journey that others were watching closely, a descent that might just draw the attention of powers that had so far remained in the shadows.

*

Max left the club feeling the weight of Hammond's words like a physical burden on his shoulders. The steady rhythm of the falling rain accompanied his footsteps as he walked the London streets that had become his new operational ground. He couldn't shake off the colonel's insinuations, the hint of larger forces at play, and the notion that his solitary campaign had not gone unnoticed.

The name George Blackwell surfaced in his thoughts, a beacon from his past that now cast a long shadow. Blackwell had been more than a source of wisdom; he had been a moral compass in times when the line between right and wrong had been blurred by the fog of war.

Max made his way to an old bookshop nestled between the more modern facades of a gentrifying neighbourhood. The bell above the door announced his entry with a jingle that seemed out of place in the world he now inhabited. The musty scent of old paper and leather bindings contrasted starkly with the sterile smell of gun oil and cordite that had become his new norm.

George Blackwell emerged from the rows of shelves, a slight figure whose age was betrayed only by the silver in his hair and the lines on his face.

"Max, I've been expecting you." Blackwell's voice was soft yet carried the same authority it always had.

They sat amidst the quiet fortress of knowledge, a world away from the chaos of Max's recent endeavours. Blackwell listened as Max spoke of his actions, of the night at the flat and the lives he had extinguished. There was no pride in Max's recounting, only the flat narration of facts.

Blackwell's gaze was steady, thoughtful. "You've started down a dangerous path, Max. What you see as justice is a knife-edge that cuts both ways. You've become the very thing you set out to destroy — a killer in the night."

Max bristled at the words, the defensive walls building

within him. "They were scum, George. They deserved to die."

"Perhaps," Blackwell conceded, "But it's not about what they deserve. It's about who you become in the process of delivering that justice. There's a cost to the soul, Max. And it's a price that's paid in more than blood."

The conversation turned to the unseen forces that Hammond had alluded to, the shadow players who operated in a world beyond the reach of conventional law. Blackwell's wisdom painted a picture of a chessboard, with Max as a pawn who had yet to realise the full scope of the game he was in.

"You've made an impact, that's certain," Blackwell continued. "But have you considered the attention you've drawn? Not just from the police, but from those who thrive in the shadows? You may find yourself caught in a crossfire from which there is no escape."

Max listened, the seed of doubt planted by Hammond now watered by Blackwell's words. The simplicity of his mission, once so clear, was now clouded by the complexity of a war with multiple fronts.

Before he left, Blackwell handed Max a small leather-bound book. "Read this," he said. "There are lessons within that even a warrior can learn from."

Max tucked the book away, the physical weight of it a testament to the gravity of their discussion. As he stepped back into the rain, the clarity of his mission was now obscured by a mist of uncertainty. The descent into darkness had seemed a straight path, but now it was a labyrinth, and Max was unsure if there was a way out.

*

As Max made his way through the maze of his mind, the rain-soaked streets seemed to mirror the turmoil within. Blackwell's words, laden with the wisdom of age, had struck deeper than expected. Max could not deny the undercurrent of truth: with every life he took, he was altering the fabric of his own being.

His footsteps led him to an isolated park, where the city's sounds faded into a muted backdrop. Here, beneath the cover of ancient oaks, Max allowed himself a moment of introspection. The faces of those he had dispatched flashed before him — not with regret, but as a stark reminder of the path he now walked alone.

The skills he possessed were honed for combat, for the defence of nation and creed, yet now they served a more personal code. Max contemplated the expanding arsenal of tactics at his disposal. The straightforward approach he had taken at the flat would not suffice for the larger war he faced. He needed to evolve, to become more than just a soldier. He needed to be a strategist, an unseen force that could strike with impunity and vanish into the ether.

Controlled explosives, the kind that could turn a car into a fiery tomb, were within his expertise. He knew the precise calculations of charge and placement, the art of timing that could make an assassination look like an unfortunate accident. Then there were the long-range sniper shots, a method that offered detachment, a way to deliver death from a distance that provided physical and emotional space.

Max envisioned the setups, the preparation, and execution with a detached efficiency. Each scenario was a puzzle to be solved, the pieces to be assembled in perfect order to achieve the desired outcome. This was more than tactics — it was a psychological chess match against adversaries who did not yet know they were playing.

The rain began to taper off, droplets falling from the leaves in a staccato rhythm that punctuated his thoughts. Max realised that his campaign would leave a trail of chaos in the criminal world, a disruption that would be felt by those who thrived in the darkness. There would be repercussions, a backlash from those who wielded power in the shadows. He was not naïve to the dangers, but the necessity of his mission eclipsed the risks.

As the skies cleared and the city's pulse returned to its regular cadence, Max felt the resurgence of his resolve. Blackwell's advice would not be discarded, but it would not deter him either. The mentor's concern was a reflection of a moral compass that Max had once shared, but his true north had shifted, recalibrated by loss and hardened by resolve.

Max left the park with the knowledge that his war had only just begun. The road ahead was fraught with peril, both known and unknown, but he would walk it with the same certainty with which he had walked into battle under foreign skies.

The city was his new battleground, and he would navigate it with the stealth of a wraith. The tools of war would be his allies, and he would wield them with a deftness born of necessity. The coming days would see a new chapter in his campaign — a shadow war fought with the precision of a scalpel and the impact of a hammer.

*

The city's cacophony returned as Max strode from the park, the early morning light casting long shadows that seemed to dance around his solitary figure. His mind was a whir of strategy and calculation, each step taking him deeper into his role as the unseen adjudicator of those who lurked in London's criminal underbelly.

Max's next move required precision, a delicate touch amidst the potential chaos. He retreated to his flat, a sanctum of solace that now served as the staging ground for his meticulous planning. Here, surrounded by the silent testimony of his military past, he began the intricate process of crafting his next operation.

He laid out maps of the city, marking key locations with precision. Potential targets were assessed not just for their complicity in the city's drug trade and violence, but for the message their demise would send. Max was becoming the invisible hand that would shake the foundations of the criminal hierarchy, leaving ripples that would turn into waves.

Controlled explosives were part of the plan, but they required a finesse that turned each setup into a calculated art form. Max procured the components with stealth, ensuring no trace led back to him. He crafted the devices with a deft hand, each one tailored for a specific purpose, for a specific moment.

The HK416 rifle was cleaned and prepared, its suppressor a silent promise of what was to come. Max loaded the magazines with a practised rhythm, the metallic click of each round a counterpoint to the beating of his heart. He considered the distances, the windage, the precise moment when his finger would caress the trigger and send a message that could not be ignored.

In the quiet of his flat, Max could almost hear the whispers of his former comrades, echoes of a time when he had fought alongside others. Now his war was a solitary affair, each victory and each sacrifice his alone to bear.

As the sun climbed higher in the sky, Max dressed for the day. His attire was nondescript, a facade that belied the lethal nature of his true intentions. Beneath the plain clothes, he wore a tactical harness, its presence a hidden truth against his skin.

Before leaving, Max wiped down every surface and removed every trace of his presence. He had become a master of the unseen, a spectre in a city full of spectres. The list of names that had once been etched into his computer was now locked away within his mind, a scroll of the damned that only he could read.

As he locked the door behind him, Max felt the weight of Colonel Hammond's and George Blackwell's words. They had seen something in him, a potential for darkness that Max had embraced as a necessary evil. But even as he stepped into the daylight, he could not shake the feeling that he was being watched, that the game he played had observers with keen eyes and unknown intentions.

The streets of London were a chessboard, and Max was a knight moving in silent arcs, poised to strike. Yet as he vanished into the crowd, he wondered who else was moving pieces across this grand board. Who else was watching the moves he made, and what moves would they make in return?

*

Max threaded through the bustling streets with the anonymity of a ghost. His days in the special forces had ingrained in him a skill set that he now employed with a ruthless efficiency. To the undiscerning eye, he was just another passerby, but beneath the surface, he was a maelstrom of calculated violence waiting to be unleashed.

He had selected his next mark — a mid-level enforcer known for his brutality and his role in the exploitation of the vulnerable. The man was a cog in the machine, but his removal would send a clear message: no one was beyond the reach of Max's justice.

The target frequented a pub in a less savoury part of London, a place where deals were made in hushed tones over pints of bitter ale. Max had observed the locale for days, his surveillance equipment capturing the patterns of life that swirled around the establishment. He noted exits, blind spots, and the time the enforcer would step out for a smoke — alone and vulnerable.

Max's plan was simple but lethal. The explosive device was small, no larger than a pack of cigarettes, and undetectable until it was too late. He planted it beneath the target's car in the early hours of the morning, his movements a whisper against the symphony of the city's slumber.

Later, as the enforcer's car ignited in a conflagration that consumed flesh and metal alike, Max was already miles away, his alibi airtight. He watched the news from a nondescript café, the headlines screaming about a tragic accident. There was no mention of foul play — the professionalism of Max's work left no room for such speculation.

The ruthlessness of the act was not lost on Max. Once, he had valued human life, had fought to protect it. Now he took it with an impassive demeanour, his emotions buried beneath layers of strategy and survival. The enforcer had been a parasite, and Max had become the cure — a poison that eradicated the disease of the criminal element with unrelenting resolve.

Max's lack of regard for life was not born of sadism; it was a product of necessity. In his mind, the world was a better place without men like the enforcer. If his soul was the price for such a world, then Max was willing to pay it.

He discarded the hacked digital scanner he had used to intercept digital communication systems he knew the police used, like the TETRA system, crushing it beneath his heel before tossing the fragments into the Thames. Every action was calculated to leave nothing behind, a trail that vanished into thin air.

That evening, Max stood on a bridge overlooking the city, the dark waters of the Thames flowing beneath him. The reflection of the city's lights danced upon the surface, a mirage of peace and normality that belied the violence that had just occurred.

Max considered the man he had been, the soldier who had once served with honour. That man was a spirit now, as ethereal as the fog that rolled in from the river. In his place stood a figure moulded by vengeance, a man whose hands were stained with the blood of those he deemed unworthy of life.

The city's underbelly would learn to fear the night, to whisper tales of the avenger who struck with precision and vanished without a trace. Max had become the embodiment of their nightmares, a myth in the making.

*

Max's return to his flat was under the veil of darkness, the cityscape a canvas of anonymity for his shadowed return. In the solitude of his concrete sanctuary, the echo of the explosion resonated within him — a symphony of destruction played out on the streets he had once walked with pride in his uniform.

He methodically dismantled and cleaned his equipment, each piece a witness to the night's work. The suppressor was unscrewed, its components laid out with the precision of a surgeon's instruments. He cleaned them with an almost ritualistic reverence, ensuring not a single trace of residue remained.

His rifle, a tool that had delivered death from afar, was stripped down. Max's hands worked with an artisan's touch, each part separated and cleaned, the muscle memory of countless disassemblies guiding his movements. The firearm that had been an extension of his intent was now just a collection of metal and polymers, devoid of its lethal purpose once more.

The tactical vest was stowed away, its pockets empty, its purpose served. The NVGs were returned to their case, the world they revealed — a world of sharp contrasts and clear targets — concealed within padded darkness.

Max's mind was a fortress, every thought, every memory of the operation locked away. There were no digital records, no notes scrawled in haste. His plans and actions lived and died in the moments they were conceived and executed, ephemeral as the smoke that had risen from the enforcer's car.

Yet even as he enacted his ritual of cleaning and storage, a sliver of doubt crept through the cracks of his armoured psyche. The reflection in the mirror showed a man hardened by resolve, but the eyes that stared back at him were not just the cold, calculating orbs of a hunter. They betrayed a depth, a flicker of something that was not as dead as he had believed.

The news had spread, the incident making national headlines — a tragic accident, they said, a freak occurrence. But Max knew the truth of it, and somewhere, buried beneath the layers of strategy and necessity, that truth clawed at him.

Max's thoughts drifted to DI Bennett, a haunting presence on the periphery of his consciousness. She would be piecing together her own narrative of the events, her mind sharp, her intuition honed by years within the Metropolitan Police. He knew it was only a matter of time before she began to see the pattern in the chaos he was orchestrating.

As the night waned into the early hours of the morning, Max sat in the darkness, the only sound the distant hum of the city. He pondered the invisible toll his actions had taken, the lives snuffed out by his hand. They were criminals, each one a blight upon the world, yet they were also human. The magnitude of his crusade was not lost on him — the shadow he cast was long, and it enveloped more than just those he targeted.

The first strike had been delivered, a message in fire and death. Max had crossed the Rubicon, and there was no turning back. The shadow's toll was etched into the fabric of the city, and Max Fairchild, once a soldier, now a vigilante, bore its weight.

As dawn approached, bringing light to dispel the darkness, Max prepared for the inevitable escalation. The war he waged was no longer just his own. It was a war that would draw in forces from both sides of the law, each seeking to uncover the identity of the phantom who had brought death to their doorstep.

Chapter 8: Yuri Dubrovnik

The Meeting

Max's steps were deliberate as he made his way through the early evening thrum of London's backstreets. He was headed to a meeting that could alter the very fabric of his campaign, a meeting with Yuri Dubrovnik, a name that whispered like a cold wind in the criminal underworld. Dubrovnik was known for pulling strings without getting his own hands dirty, a puppet master of vice and violence.

The rendezvous was set in an old warehouse district, where the walls held secrets and the shadows were long. Max had taken precautions — multiple routes to ensure he wasn't followed, checks for tails, a routine that was now second nature.

The warehouse was nondescript, a relic of industry past, but inside, it pulsed with life. It was a neutral ground of sorts, a place where the underworld could conduct its business away from prying eyes. Max entered, the dim light casting his face in sharp relief, the scars of battle hidden in the darkness.

Dubrovnik was there, waiting. He was a tall man with a presence that seemed to command the air itself. His eyes, cold and calculating, appraised Max as he approached.

"Mr Fairchild," Yuri greeted in a voice that was both smooth and menacing. "Your reputation precedes you."

Max didn't flinch. "You wanted to see me," he stated, a fact rather than a question.

Yuri smiled, the gesture more predatory than pleasant. "Indeed. I've heard about your ... exploits. You have a particular set of skills that could be useful to me."

Max weighed the man before him. Dubrovnik was offering an opportunity, but at what cost? The game was changing, the stakes getting higher. Max's foray into the underworld had started as a singular quest for vengeance, but now it was branching into something more complex, more dangerous.

Dubrovnik laid out his proposal — a series of operations that would require Max's expertise. They were not random acts of vengeance; they were calculated moves in a larger scheme that Yuri promised would bring about a significant shift in power within the city's dark economy.

Max listened, his mind racing. He thought of his family, the danger that each new operation could bring to their doorstep. His actions had already drawn the attention of the police, and now he was being offered a deeper role in the criminal sphere.

The risk was significant. Max's crusade had been a solitary one, his targets chosen for their direct connection to his son's death. But Dubrovnik was offering a path that led away from personal justice to become a mercenary in a broader conflict.

As Max sat across from Yuri, the warehouse around them felt like a stage set for a play that was both grand and macabre. The offer was tempting — a chance to strike at the heart of the beast that had taken so much from him.

But it was more than that. Max could feel the lure of the darkness, the seductive pull of becoming an agent of chaos. He had started down this path to honour his son's memory, to extract retribution. Now he was being tempted to become something else entirely — a shadow within the shadows, an assassin for hire.

Yuri awaited his response, the silence between them stretching.

Max knew that acceptance meant crossing yet another line, delving deeper into the criminal world than he had ever intended. But refusal would mean walking away from a chance to dismantle the network responsible for so much pain.

The internal conflict raged within him, a tempest that threatened to tear down the last remnants of the man he had once been. The soldier, the protector, the avenger — they were all at war within him.

As the warehouse's dim lights flickered, casting Yuri's face in a dance of light and shadow, Max made his decision.

"I'll do it," he said, his voice a low rumble of resignation and determination.

Yuri's smile widened, and Max could see the chessboard of the city's underworld reshaping with his words, the pieces moving into a new configuration of danger and possibility.

*

The meeting between Max and Yuri Dubrovnik was no chance encounter; it was the result of a carefully orchestrated series of events that began with the whispers circulating in the underworld. Max's actions, while ghostly in their execution, had not gone unnoticed. Yuri's extensive network, one that thrived in the exchange of favours and information, had picked up on the pattern of Max's vigilantism. To a man like Yuri, such talent was a resource to be tapped.

The arrangement of their meeting was through an intermediary known only to Max as 'The Broker', a figure as enigmatic as the shadows that clung to the fringes of the city's crime. The Broker had reached out to Max indirectly, through coded messages left in places only someone with Max's skill set would discern. It was a testament to Max's reputation that Yuri would reach out personally, an honour that bore its own set of risks.

As Max sat in the warehouse with Yuri, the weight of the decision pressed upon him. The assignment was clear: to eliminate a key family member of a prominent criminal dynasty, a strike that would send shockwaves through the underground hierarchy. It was a hit that would not only serve Yuri's ambitions but also sate the bloodlust that had taken root in Max's soul since his son's demise.

The target was no innocent; he was a man whose hands were stained with actions that merited retribution. Yet the act of killing him was not a simple execution of justice; it was an assassination that would bind Max to Yuri and the criminal world in ways he had never intended.

Max's mind flashed back to his days in the service, where the killing of an enemy combatant carried a certain clarity within the fog of war. Now, as he contemplated Yuri's proposal, that clarity was muddied by the murky waters of moral ambiguity. The family member was a criminal, yes, but he was also a son, perhaps a father. The ripple effect of his death would extend beyond the confines of the criminal world, touching lives innocent of his transgressions.

The potential risks to Max's family loomed large. He had been cautious, operating in the shadows, leaving no trace that could lead back to his doorstep. But an assassination of this magnitude would not go unanswered. The criminal family was known for its reach and its ruthlessness. Max's own kin could become targets in a vendetta that knew no bounds.

As Yuri outlined the details, Max felt the familiar tug of his special forces training. It was a call to action that had once defined his existence, a call that now beckoned him toward a precipice from which there was no turning back. He envisioned the operation with clinical detachment: the planning, the surveillance, the moment of truth when the target would fall.

The internal conflict raged within him, a battle between the soldier he had been and the avenger he had become. Max knew he was standing at a crossroads, one path leading deeper into the darkness, the other an uncertain route to redemption.

The silence that followed his acceptance of the assignment was a canvas for the storm of thoughts that churned in his mind. Max had agreed to a deed that would mark him in the annals of the criminal world, a deed that would etch his name into the ledger of those who operated in the darkest corners of humanity.

He left the meeting with a sense of foreboding, the cool night air doing little to ease the fire that burned within. The die was cast, and Max Fairchild, once a guardian of peace, stepped further into the abyss, his soul the currency with which he gambled.

*

Max had returned to the quiet confines of his flat, where the walls were lined with maps and the air heavy with the gravity of his decisions. He sat at his desk, a lone figure in the glow of a single lamp, the silence around him a stark contrast to the storm of activity in his mind. He was about to embark on an operation that would alter the very nature of his war, a meticulous execution that required all his skill and cold detachment.

He unfolded a map of the city, its streets a web of potential routes and chokepoints. Max's finger traced lines across the paper, marking the movements of his target, a dance of death that was yet to be choreographed. He plotted the assassination with the precision of a watchmaker, each element of the plan clicking into place with silent finality.

The logistics were complex. Max needed to factor in escape routes, police response times, the possibility of interference from the target's own security measures. He selected his equipment with care — the HK417 7.62 rifle, Schmidt & Bender PM II scope for its accuracy, and the explosives for their controlled destruction. Every item was a piece of a larger puzzle, and Max was the artisan fitting them together.

There was no room for emotion in the work he did. His features were set in an expression of grim determination as he checked and rechecked each detail. The preparation was exhaustive; the execution would need to be flawless.

As he immersed himself in the planning, his phone rang, slicing through the silence with an urgency that was jarring. It was Lily. For a moment, Max considered not answering, so focused was he on the task at hand. But the thought of her voice, the connection to the life he once had, was a siren's call he couldn't ignore.

"Dad?" Lily's voice was a tether to a world Max felt slipping away from him.

"Lily," he answered, his tone softening just for a moment. "How are you?"

"I'm okay. Have you seen the news?" There was a tremor in her voice, a mix of fear and disbelief. "The gang, the one ... They're saying it was gang violence, and some of the names thought to be involved in Alex's attack were mentioned on the news."

Max's gaze didn't waver from the map before him. "I saw," he replied evenly, giving nothing away.

Lily was silent for a moment, the digital connection crackling with unspoken words and shared grief. "I just ... I hope whoever did it feels justice was served."

Max felt the weight of her words, a heavy shroud that threatened to smother the flame of his resolve. "Justice comes in many forms," he said, a mantra for both her and himself.

"Just be careful, Dad," Lily added before they said their goodbyes, a plea that Max felt more acutely than any physical wound.

The call ended, and the room returned to silence. Lily's words echoed in his ears, a reminder of the stakes he was playing for. She was a beacon of innocence in the darkness that Max now inhabited, a reminder of the life he was fighting to protect, even as he spiraled deeper into the abyss.

Max turned his attention back to the task at hand. His daughter's voice was a lingering note in the symphony of his planning, a soft counterpoint to the hard edges of his lethal intentions.

He resumed his work, the professional soldier, the expert in death. Each piece of the plan was reviewed, each action rehearsed in his mind's eye. The target would be eliminated, and the message would be sent. But in the calculated coldness of his planning, a small flame of warmth remained — a connection to Lily, to the man he had once been, to the vestiges of humanity that still clung to his soul.

*

In the dead of night, Max stood atop a building that overlooked the city — a sentinel keeping a lonely vigil. The soft glow of his tablet illuminated the blueprints of the area surrounding the target's last known location, each alley and entry point marked and memorized.

His gear lay beside him, a testament to the coming storm. The HK417 rifle, its suppressor a promise of silence, the explosives, their power harnessed by science and shaped by intent: each item was checked and rechecked, a ritual that spoke of professionalism and the detachment required to utilize them.

Max's mind was a fortress of focus. Emotion had no place here. It was locked away, a beast in a cage, as he contemplated the cold calculus of his plan. The target, a scion of a criminal dynasty, was guarded, insulated by wealth and the loyalty bought by fear. But no fortress was impregnable. Max knew that. He had breached stronger defences in his time.

His finger traced the route on the tablet one final time before he steeled himself for the task at hand. It was not just about the elimination of one man; it was a surgical strike at the heart of a network that had bled the city for too long.

As he donned his tactical vest, each movement was measured, the heaviness of the fabric a familiar comfort. The night-vision goggles rested on his head, ready to cut through the darkness and guide his aim. His boots were silent on the rooftop, the sound swallowed by the vastness of the urban expanse below.

This was Max's element, the world where his skills could shine with deadly brilliance. The city below, a tapestry of light and shadow, was unaware of the judgment about to be delivered from on high. Max was the arbiter, the unseen hand that would tilt the scales.

The target's residence was a fortress in its own right, the security tight and alert. But Max had studied them, learned their patterns, and now knew them better than they knew themselves. He would strike when they least expected it, in the brief window when shifts changed and eyes were tired.

The anticipation of the act was not exhilarating; it was a sombre acknowledgement of what must be done. Max was not a murderer; he was a soldier in a war against a hidden enemy, and his heart beat with the rhythm of duty.

His phone vibrated softly against his leg — a message from an unknown number, a warning. *They're watching*, it read, the words stark against the screen. Max knew the risks, understood that eyes could be on him even now. But he also knew that fear was a tool to be used, not succumbed to.

Tonight, he would use that tool to his advantage. He would become the embodiment of fear for those who spread it like a disease. The city would sleep, unaware that its guardian angel was also its avenging demon.

The time was near, the moment of truth approaching with the inevitability of the rising sun. Max did not pray; he did not seek forgiveness for what he was about to do. Instead, he embraced the reality of his existence, the path he had chosen to walk.

*

Under the shroud of night, Max descended from his vantage point, each step calculated to avoid detection. The city around him was alive with the hum of the unaware, its inhabitants locked in their routines. Max, however, was moving against the current, a shadow amidst shadows on a collision course with fate.

He approached the target's stronghold, a modern fortress rising from the urban sprawl. His approach was methodical, the route practised countless times in his head now unfolding with silent precision. The explosives were in place, their presence unknown to all but him, the timer set to coincide with the changing of the guards.

Max found his position, a secluded spot with a clear view of the estate's entrance. The rifle felt natural in his hands, an extension of his will. He breathed slowly, his heartbeat a controlled drum in his chest as he peered through the scope. The night-vision goggles painted the world in a hue of green — details sharpened, movements highlighted.

Inside, the target was a man unaware of his looming demise, his life a series of actions that had led to this moment. He was a man who had chosen his path, just as Max had chosen his. There was a symmetry in that, a balance to the universe that Max appreciated.

The silence was palpable as Max waited, the city's pulse a distant thrum. Then the moment came — a flash of light, a muffled boom, and chaos erupted within the walls of the stronghold. Figures scrambled, silhouettes against the flames, confusion reigning as Max had planned.

He exhaled slowly, his finger caressing the trigger

with the familiarity of an old lover. The shot broke the night, a whisper of death that flew true to its mark. The target fell, a marionette with its strings cut, the finality of the act absolute.

Max did not linger on the sight; his escape was already in motion. The surrounding chaos was a cover, the panic a diversion that he used to slip away unseen. His path back was a mirror of his approach, a reversal of steps that left no trace, no sign of his passage.

The strike was not just an execution; it was a statement. Max had delivered his message with the subtlety of a sledgehammer, a declaration to all who would follow in the target's footsteps. There was a new player in the game, one who played by his own rules.

But as Max retreated into the night, his mind was not on his success. It was on the phone call with Lily, the innocence in her voice, the distance between his actions and her understanding. There was a gulf there, one that Max felt widening with every life he took.

He had become a dealer of death, a role he had assumed with the intention of justice. Yet with each pull of the trigger, with each fall of a body, Max felt the tendrils of the darkness he fought against entwining with his soul.

The internal conflict was a storm that raged within him, a tempest of doubt and certainty, of righteousness and sin. Max was aware of the fine line he trod, a tightrope suspended over an abyss. With each operation, with each kill, he danced along that line, a ballet of blood and shadows.

As he melded with the night, his actions complete, Max understood that the battle he fought was not just against the criminals of the city — it was against the darkness within himself. The soldier had become an assassin, the avenger a harbinger of death.

*

Max's retreat into the concealment of London's alleys was not just a physical withdrawal but a retreat into the recesses of his own psyche. The night had swallowed his violent act, just as the city swallowed the countless stories of those who walked its streets. But inside Max, there was no darkness large enough to engulf the reverberations of what he had done.

The rifle, now disassembled and stowed away in nondescript parts within his backpack, was devoid of its lethal purpose but heavy with the weight of consequence. Each component was a reminder of the life he had extinguished — a life that was part of a malignant web but a life, nonetheless.

Max's apartment welcomed him with silence, a contrast to the internal cacophony of his thoughts. He removed his gear methodically, each piece a symbol of the soldier he had once been and the man he had become. His reflection in the mirror was that of a stranger, the contours of his face unchanged but the gaze markedly different — a portal to a soul that danced with shadows.

The solitude of his room was a stage for the drama of his inner conflict. With Yuri's assignment completed, Max had solidified his place in the criminal hierarchy as a force to be reckoned with, a weapon for hire. But the cold professionalism that had marked his actions could not entirely mask the tremor of awareness that what he was doing was eroding the pillars of his former life.

He pondered the potential consequences of his

deepening involvement. His daughter, Lily, his connection to the remnants of a world where justice was more than a personal vendetta, was now at greater risk. The more entrenched he became in this war against the criminal syndicates, the greater the danger that those he loved would become collateral damage in a battle they had not chosen.

Max sat, the only movement the steady rise and fall of his chest as he breathed. The emotional armour he had donned — the lack of empathy, the ruthless efficiency — had been necessary for what he had set out to do. Yet now, in the aftermath, it felt less like armour and more like a shroud, one that threatened to suffocate the remnants of the man who had once cherished life.

The room's stillness was broken by the faint buzz of his secure phone — a message from Yuri, confirming the success of the operation and hinting at future assignments. Max regarded the device, a lifeline to a world that was as intoxicating as it was lethal. He understood that with each assignment he accepted, he would be drawn deeper into the abyss, his path marked by the blood of those he deemed guilty.

And yet there was no sense of triumph, no feeling of accomplishment. There was only the silent acknowledgement that he had crossed another line, had taken another step away from the light and into the enveloping dark.

As Max prepared for rest, sleep seemed like a distant prospect. The bed was no longer a place of respite but a tableau for the war that played out in his mind. He lay in the darkness, the sounds of the city a distant murmur, and allowed himself to feel — to mourn not just for his son, but for himself, for the man who had been consumed by the flames of vengeance.

Chapter 9: The Double Life Begins

The Illusion of Normality

The morning light filtered through the kitchen blinds, casting stripes across the breakfast table where Max sat with Lily. His hands cradled a mug of coffee, the steam rising like the mist on a battlefield, concealing the tumultuous thoughts behind his stoic facade.

"How's the project coming along?" Max enquired, his voice a controlled blend of interest and warmth, belying the strategic planner who had orchestrated a killing mere hours ago.

Lily, bright-eyed and unsuspecting, shared her enthusiasm about her university project on law and morality. "It's fascinating, Dad. We're discussing whether the ends ever justify the means," she explained, her innocent statement a piercing arrow to Max's conscience.

"That's quite a deep topic," Max replied, the irony hanging between them like a silent chime. He wondered if there would ever come a day when he would have to justify his means to her, to explain the actions that kept him away in the dead of night.

The duality of his life was never more apparent than in these quiet moments with Lily. Here, he was just her father, the man who had taught her right from wrong, not the vigilante who stalked the city under the veil of darkness, delivering his own brand of justice.

Across town, DI Sarah Bennett stood in her office, the wall before her a mosaic of crime scene photos and string connections. The latest addition — a charred vehicle and the remains of what had once been a high-ranking member of a notorious family — spoke of a calculated message, not an unfortunate mishap.

Bennett's intuition, honed over years of police work, sensed the undercurrent of a new player in the mix, noting on her pad *vigilante/ghost/who?* Her eyes scanned the evidence, seeking the thread that would unravel the identity of this ghost who executed justice outside the confines of the law.

Meanwhile, Lily's perception of her father had begun to shift, like a picture losing its focus. There were moments when Max seemed distant, his gaze lost in thoughts he wouldn't share. She had caught snippets of news, stories of gang violence curtailed by unknown means, and couldn't help but draw parallels to her father's sudden nocturnal absences.

Max, aware of the mounting suspicions, knew he had to reinforce the illusion of normality. He reached out to Anastasia Sokolov, the information broker, and Nadia Sokolov, a cyber-specialist, who provided him with insights into the underworld's machinations. They were conduits to the intelligence he required, yet they knew nothing of the true nature of his mission.

As evening approached, Max felt the strain of the mask he wore. Each role he played, each life he lived, demanded a piece of his soul, and he was unsure how much longer he could maintain the facade before it shattered completely.

In the confines of his home, with Lily talking about her day, Max's world was a delicate balance between light and dark. But as the night encroached, the darkness promised to tip the scales, and Max was all too aware that his next move could shatter the fragile peace of his double life.

*

Detective Inspector Bennett stood in her office as the sun dipped below the skyline, the city's silhouette a jagged line against the orange hue of dusk. Her eyes were fixed on the large pinboard that dominated the wall, a constellation of connected dots that mapped out the vigilante's actions. Each string, each photo, each report, was a breadcrumb, and she was convinced they led to a man who was systematically dismantling the city's criminal network.

It was her hunch, an instinct honed over years of detective work, that the latest incident — the spectacularly orchestrated demise of a known criminal — was no accident. It was a message. She had just begun to verbalize her theory to her partner when her phone rang, the shrill tone cutting through the room.

"Bennett," she answered crisply.

The voice on the other end was hesitant, an informant she had cultivated within the Kozlov organisation. "The one who died — he wasn't just some foot soldier. He was Marcus Kozlov's nephew. The family's in an uproar."

The pieces clicked into place, a chilling realisation dawning on her. This wasn't a one-off act of retribution; this was a hit with far-reaching implications. The nephew of Marcus Kozlov — a name that carried weight in whispers and fear in the criminal underworld — was the vigilante's latest victim. Whoever was behind this was not only skilled and lethal but was targeting the very pillars of the city's criminal hierarchy.

Back at his flat, Max sat in the dark, the only light emanating from the screen of his laptop. It was time to reach out to his sources again — Anastasia and Nadia. He needed information, the kind that could only be obtained through the clandestine channels of the criminal world.

As he encrypted his message, Max pondered the true identity of his last target. He knew the man was a key figure in the illicit operations plaguing the city, but the revelation that he was a Kozlov changed the calculus. The Kozlov family was not just a local problem; they were an international syndicate, their reach extending far beyond London's streets. His actions had undoubtedly sent shockwaves through their ranks, and there would be consequences.

At home, Lily watched her father with a growing sense of unease. He was there, but not present, his attention always split between the here and now and some unseen point in the distance. She wanted to believe in him, to trust in the man who had always been her protector, but doubt was a seed that, once planted, grew with relentless persistence.

"Dad," she ventured tentatively, "the news about the gang violence ... It's scary to think someone is taking justice into their own hands."

Max's gaze flickered to her, a silent war waging behind his eyes. "Sometimes the system fails us, Lil. Sometimes people have to take a stand."

His words hung heavy in the room, a veiled confession wrapped in the guise of a hypothetical discussion. Lily studied him, the man she called father, and wondered at the shadows that clung to him, shadows that seemed to grow longer with each passing day.

Max could feel the net of his double life drawing tighter, the strands of truth and fabrication woven so intricately that it became a challenge to navigate. He was aware that every encounter with Lily was tinged with the unspoken questions that danced in her eyes. Each look seemed to probe deeper, seeking the man behind the mask he wore so well.

Later that evening, as Lily retired to her room, Max took to his study, a space filled with the remnants of his military past and the tools of his new trade. He opened a secure line of communication, one that burrowed through the layers of the internet like a mole, reaching out to Anastasia Sokolov. She was an enigma, her loyalty tied to the currency of information, her allegiance as fluid as the data she traded in.

Sokolov, Max typed, his fingers a staccato beat on the keys, *I need everything on the Kozlov family.*

The reply was almost instantaneous, a testament to the broker's efficiency. *The Kozlovs are not pleased, Fairchild. You've stirred a hornet's nest.*

A frisson of danger threaded through Max's spine. He hadn't known the identity of his last target at the time, but now the implications were a heavy chain around his neck. The Kozlovs were a dynasty of crime, their vengeance legendary, their reach long. Max had underestimated the fallout, but he was too far in to retreat.

Across the city, DI Bennett was piecing together her own puzzle. The Kozlovs were a name she knew well; they were a file that never gathered dust on her desk. The connection between the vigilante's targets and the Kozlov family was becoming clearer, a picture emerging from the fog. She needed to find this vigilante, not just to stop him but to save him from the inevitable reprisal that was sure to come.

She pondered the nature of the vigilante — was he a hero or a villain? The line was blurred, the distinction muddied by the blood that had been spilled. Her duty was clear, yet she couldn't help but feel a grudging respect for the skill and precision with which he operated.

Max's next message was to Nadia Sokolov, the hacker who could find the skeletons in any digital closet. *Sokolov, I need a backdoor into the Kozlovs' operations. Financials, communications, I want it all.*

Her response was cautious. *Max, this isn't a game. The Kozlovs are dangerous.*

I know, Max replied, his decision set. *Just do it.*

He was playing a high-stakes game, and the chips were the lives of those caught in the crossfire. Max felt the weight of his choices, the burden of the lives he held in his hands. But there was no turning back. He had embarked on this path for justice, for retribution, and he would see it through to its bitter end.

The darkness outside mirrored the one within as Max continued his work, the lines between his two lives blurring further with each passing moment. He was a father, a soldier, an avenger, each facet battling for dominance. The web of lies he spun was intricate, but it was woven with the threads of noble intent.

*

The city was a different world under the cloak of night, and Lily found herself lying awake, staring at the ceiling.

The shadows seemed to play tricks, dancing with the possibilities her mind dared not entertain by day. Her father, her rock since childhood, now the source of her unrest, was a puzzle she could not solve.

Lily rose from her bed, compelled by a need for air, for clarity. She padded silently down the hallway, drawn by the faint glow emanating from beneath the study door. Max thought he had been discreet, but Lily had grown accustomed to the subtle changes in their home, the soft clicks of the keyboard at odd hours, the smell of burnt coffee that lingered in the mornings.

She pressed her ear to the door, her heart pounding. The muted sounds of her father's voice, the one-sided conversation with an unknown confidant, filtered through the wood. She couldn't make out the words, but the tone was one she had never heard before — it was commanding, urgent, a stark contrast to the warmth he reserved for her.

A shiver of fear ran down Lily's spine. The news reports, the whispers of vigilante justice, and now this — the pieces were coming together, forming a picture she was afraid to see in its entirety. She retreated to her room, the seed of suspicion now grown into a gnarled vine that wrapped around her heart.

DI Bennett's night was spent in the company of cold case files and crime scene photos. The flickering fluorescent light in her office cast a clinical glow over the documents that told tales of violence and retribution. She was building a profile of the vigilante, piecing together the fragments of a life she was certain held the key to understanding his motives.

Bennett was a woman of logic, but she couldn't deny

the undercurrent of empathy she felt for this shadowy figure. The precision of his actions, the choice of targets — it spoke of a personal vendetta, a crusade that had transcended the boundaries of law.

Her phone buzzed, a text message breaking her concentration. It was from her informant, a risky connection she maintained within the Kozlov organisation. *Be careful*, it read. *Kozlovs are on edge. They're looking for a ghost.*

Bennett knew the danger. The Kozlovs were a force unto themselves, their retribution swift and merciless. If the vigilante was indeed targeting them, he was in more danger than he realised.

Max concluded his communications. Each message sent was a thread in the web he wove. He shut down his computer, the screen's glow fading to black, reflecting his own darkening path. The room was silent, but the echo of his actions resounded in the space, a cacophony of consequences yet to come.

He stood, stretching the stiffness from his limbs. He thought of Lily, asleep down the hall, innocent and unaware of the war he waged. She was the reason for everything, the North Star in his night sky. The thought of her coming to harm was unbearable, a possibility that could not come to pass.

Max knew he was walking a tightrope, his double life a precarious balance that could topple with the slightest misstep. He had to be careful, for Lily's sake.

As he made his way to his own room, Max paused outside Lily's door, listening for the sound of her gentle breathing. It was a reassurance, a reminder of the stakes he played for. But as he finally lay in his bed, the comfort of her presence was in clear contrast to the turmoil that churned within him.

*

As dawn's light began to seep through the curtains, Max lay motionless, his mind a battlefield of strategy and consequence. Despite the exhaustion that clung to his bones, sleep had eluded him, chased away by the spectre of danger that now loomed over his family.

The day began as any other, with the routine of breakfast and the pretence of normality. Lily's eyes met his across the table, and Max could see the questions she wrestled with, her desire for the truth warring with the fear of what it might be. He offered her a reassuring smile, a silent promise that he would shield her from the darkness that encroached upon their lives.

DI Bennett was already at her desk as the city awoke, her eyes tracing the invisible lines that connected the vigilante's actions to the Kozlov family. She knew that the man she hunted was more than a mere criminal; he was a fulcrum upon which the balance of power in the underworld teetered.

Bennett's contemplation was interrupted by the arrival of her partner, bringing with him the latest reports. "Another one," he said, laying the file on her desk. "Someone's cleaning house, Sarah. And they're not stopping."

She nodded, her mind racing with the implications. Each act of vigilante justice brought with it a wave of instability. The city's criminal elements were on edge, and it was only a matter of time before they struck back in fear and anger.

The university day passed in a blur for Lily, her father's odd behaviours casting long shadows over her thoughts. She found herself jumping at shadows, the whispers in the hallways seeming to carry hidden meanings. She needed answers, but the thought of what those answers might reveal terrified her.

After university, she made a decision. It was time to confront her father, to demand the truth, no matter how it might shatter her world. But as she made her way home, resolve firm, she was unaware of the eyes that followed her, the unseen threats that her father's actions had drawn into their orbit.

Max's afternoon was spent in preparation. He had received word from Anastasia Sokolov that his next move needed to be calculated with even greater care. The Kozlovs were retaliating, their resources vast and their wrath fierce.

In the quiet of his study, Max pored over the intelligence provided by Nadia Sokolov, the data painting a grim picture of the network he sought to dismantle. As he planned his next strike, he was unaware of the net closing in on his own life, the danger that now stalked his daughter as she walked the streets of London.

The line between predator and prey was thinning, and Max was on both sides of it.

As the sun began to set, painting the sky with streaks of fire, Max received a chilling message from an anonymous source: *They know about Lily*.

His world stopped. The risk had always been there, lurking in the back of his mind, but he had believed he could keep it at bay. Now it was at his doorstep, and his daughter was in the crosshairs.

Max's decision was immediate. He would do what he must to protect her, to draw the danger away from the innocent life he had brought into this world. The double life he had been leading was collapsing, and he would have to move quickly to prevent it from crushing everything he held dear.

*

The London skyline was a jagged edge against the twilight as Max processed the dire message. His heart, encased in a shell of determination and ruthlessness, now felt a pang of pure, unadulterated fear for Lily. The boundaries he had drawn around her, the buffer zone of safety he thought impenetrable, had been breached.

Max's mind raced, crafting a plan with surgical precision. He would not — could not — allow his crusade to endanger his daughter. This was his fight, his burden to bear, and he would go to great lengths to ensure the shadows he operated in did not touch her life.

His phone call to Lily was a masterclass in emotional control. "Stay at a friend's tonight," he instructed, his voice a calm veneer over the storm of his emotions. "Do it for me, please."

Lily, sensing the urgency in her father's tone, acquiesced without understanding the gravity of the situation. She trusted him implicitly, not knowing that this trust was the shield he wielded against the dangers that hunted for her now.

DI Bennett was a woman who understood the dark undercurrents of the city. She saw patterns where others saw chaos, lines connecting the dots that others deemed unrelated. The vigilante's actions had escalated, becoming bolder, more strategic. There was a plan at work here, and it was her job to decipher it before the city was drawn into a maelstrom of retribution.

The pursuit had become her life's work, the vigilante a spectre that haunted her waking hours and her dreams. She pored over the evidence, each piece another step toward understanding the man behind the mask.

The night was now Max's domain, the darkness his cloak as he moved to secure his daughter's safety. Every resource at his disposal was activated, a network of favours called in, safe houses secured. His life had become a chess game, and he was the grandmaster, manoeuvring the pieces to ensure Lily remained out of reach of the encroaching danger.

Max's preparations were a testament to his special forces training — methodical, efficient, devoid of hesitation. Yet beneath the surface, there was a seething cauldron of fury. The underworld had dared to threaten his child, and for that, they would pay a steep price. His actions would no longer be just about vengeance; they would be about protection, a father's primal response to the threat against his progeny.

As he set the wheels in motion, Max was the embodiment of the dark avenger, the man who walked the fine line between hero and antihero. His love for his family was the fuel for his relentless drive, a drive that would see him through the abyss and back if need be.

Max had always known that his journey would be a solitary one, but now he faced the harsh truth that the battle could spill over, touching those who had never set foot on the battlefield. The double life he led was a shield and a sword which he wielded with the expertise of a seasoned warrior.

The night grew deeper, and Max's silhouette merged with the darkness, a part of the fabric of the city's secret war. The vigilante's crusade was no longer a silent undertaking; it was a clarion call to all who would listen that there was a new force at play, one that would stop at nothing to protect what was his.

Chapter 10: A Dangerous Reputation

The Shadow Emerges

In the undercurrents of London's criminal world, a name was beginning to circulate with a mix of fear and respect. It was not yet a name, per se, but a whisper of a figure — a shadow that struck swiftly and vanished into the night. Max's actions had created a ripple effect, and now those ripples were reaching the shores of faraway lands, carrying with them tales of a vigilante who could not be traced.

In Prague, Marcus Kozlov sat in his office, a room that spoke of power, with its dark wood and expansive views of the city. He was a man who controlled vast criminal operations with an iron fist, his influence extending across continents. The recent news from London had been a blow; the death of his nephew was not just a personal loss but a statement from an unknown enemy.

Kozlov's connections ran deep, even touching the untouchable — UK Members of Parliament and political elites who played their games of power and influence. Yet this vigilante was an anomaly, a wrench in the cogs of his well-oiled machine.

"Find out who is responsible," Kozlov commanded his lieutenant, his voice a calm that belied the storm of anger within. "I want a name, and I want it yesterday."

Back in London, Max was aware that the noose was tightening. His operations had been too effective, the silence of his approach too loud in its implications. He had become a spectre that haunted the criminal elite, and now that spectre had a target on its back.

Max's next operation was a calculated risk, a move against a mid-level trafficker who funnelled Kozlov's influence into the city's veins. It was a statement — Max was not done, not by a long shot.

As he prepared, the ghost of his daughter's suspicion and Bennett's determined pursuit lingered in his mind. He could not afford mistakes. Every step was planned with the meticulous care of a master craftsman, his tools laid out with reverence — the silent weapons, the disguises, the contingency plans.

The night of the operation, the city was a chessboard, and Max was a knight moving in silence, cloaked by the dark. The trafficker's abode was a fortress, but Max had learned its secrets and mapped its weaknesses. He moved through the shadows, a phantom enacting his retribution.

The operation was swift. The trafficker was no more, another message carved into the flesh of Kozlov's empire. But this time, something was different. As Max made his escape, the wail of sirens filled the air, a chorus that grew louder with each passing second.

Max's pulse quickened. He had been careful, but the police were on him faster than expected. The chase was on, the city's labyrinth a stage for a deadly game of hide and seek.

As he evaded his pursuers, Max knew that this escape was a turning point. His reputation was growing, a legend that whispered through the streets of London. But with that reputation came increased risk, a spotlight that sought to illuminate the darkness he operated within.

He ducked into an alley, his breaths measured, his mind racing. He had become the hunted, and though he was a master of evasion, he knew that every chase could end in capture.

The sound of footsteps echoed behind him, the police drawing closer. Max's training kicked in, his body moving with the instinct of survival. He was a ghost, but even ghosts could be ensnared by those who knew how to look.

As he slipped through a narrow passage, barely a sliver in the city's architecture, Max made his escape. It was narrow, too close for comfort, but he was out, back into the night that was his ally.

Unbeknownst to Max, his actions this night had interfered with a larger operation, one orchestrated by Kozlov himself. The trafficker had been a lynchpin in a more significant scheme, and Max had just pulled that pin.

Marcus Kozlov, receiving the news in Prague, felt the first stirrings of genuine concern. This vigilante was more than a nuisance; he was a threat that needed to be extinguished. Max's reputation had marked him, and Kozlov was not a man to forgive or forget.

*

Marcus Kozlov's stare was icy as he absorbed the news of the disruption in London. He stood by the window, gazing out at Prague's ancient skyline, a stark juxtaposition against the modernity of his criminal enterprise. The death of his nephew had been a calculated strike, a message he could not ignore. And now, the follow-up attack on his operations had revealed a persistent adversary.

"Expand our reach. I want eyes everywhere in

London. No stone unturned," he commanded, his voice the low rumble of distant thunder. Kozlov was not accustomed to being challenged, and the audacity of this vigilante was a bitter pill.

In London, Max's escape was a testament to his training and instincts. His movements were a blur, a dance with danger choreographed to the city's nocturnal rhythm. The sirens faded into the distance, a testament to his ability to vanish when all seemed lost.

Yet Max was no fool. He knew the stakes were rising, the waters he navigated now teeming with predators of a different ilk. The law was one thing, but the wrath of a man like Kozlov was an altogether different beast.

DI Bennett's frustration was palpable in the dim light of the incident room. They had been close, closer than ever to catching the phantom that haunted London's underbelly. She thumbed through the latest reports, the patterns there but just out of reach.

"Who are you?" she muttered to herself, a question directed at the empty chair across from her, as if the vigilante might materialize and provide an answer.

Her team was the best, but this man, this ghost, he was on another level. The pursuit was personal now, a challenge to her abilities, and Bennett did not like to lose.

For Max, the near-miss was a wake-up call. As he returned to his safe house, he felt the walls closing in, the city shrinking around him. His double life was a tightrope, and the wind was picking up. It was only a matter of time before he would have to confront the full force of the storm he'd unleashed.

He needed to be smarter, more cautious. The image of Lily's face, the sound of her voice, they were his anchors, the reason he could not falter. He would not allow his actions to reach her, to corrupt the life he'd so carefully shielded from the darkness of his own.

The night passed in a series of plans and contingencies, Max's mind a whirlwind of routes and strategies. He knew the Kozlovs would be searching for him, their resources vast and their network extensive. But Max had always been one step ahead, a shadow amongst shadows, and he intended to keep it that way.

As dawn approached, Max sat alone, the only company his thoughts and the looming presence of a dangerous reputation that was growing beyond his control. He was the eye of the storm, calm and still, while chaos raged around him. But Max was all too aware that the most dangerous part was yet to come.

*

The first light of dawn brought no solace to Max; it only emphasized the harsh reality of his situation. He knew that his operations had now placed him squarely in the sights of Marcus Kozlov, a man whose ruthlessness was legend. Max also understood that Lily's safety was paramount, and the time had come to take drastic measures.

As he deliberated his next move, Max knew that the only way to protect Lily was to remove her from the equation entirely. He needed to create a smokescreen, a diversion so convincing that it would draw Kozlov's gaze away from her. It was a gambit that required precision and the willingness to dive deeper into the fray.

He made a secure call, his voice altering with the use of technology, ensuring no emotional nuance could betray his intentions. "It's time," he said, speaking to a trusted ally from his military days. "I need the safe house ready. No traces."

His friend, a comrade bound by the unspoken oath of brotherhood, understood the gravity of the request. "Consider it done," came the terse reply.

Across the city, Lily's intuition was aflame. She could no longer ignore the signs that her father was entangled in something far greater than she had ever imagined. Her resolve hardened; she would confront him, demand answers, even if she was not prepared for the truths they might unveil.

In Prague, Marcus Kozlov received updates from his network, his influence casting a long shadow across Europe. He pondered the identity of this vigilante, this ghost who dared disrupt his dominion. "Bring me everyone he loves," Kozlov ordered, his words a death knell hanging in the air. "I want this shadow dragged into the light."

But Kozlov was not a man who waited idly by. He began to weave his own web: connections within the UK Parliament and political arenas that could be manipulated, levers of power he could pull to flush out the man who had become his nemesis.

Max's reputation as a lethal phantom was solidifying, and with it came the attention of law enforcement. DI Bennett had seen men like Max before — soldiers who found themselves lost when the war ended, unable to reintegrate into the society they had fought to protect. But this man was different; he was waging a war of his own making, and it was time to bring him to justice.

She coordinated with her team, their efforts now a manhunt that spread through the city's underbelly. "We're close," she assured them, sensing the breakthrough was imminent.

Max could feel the noose tightening, the forces of law and crime converging on him. But he would not be taken easily, nor would he allow harm to come to Lily. He had played the part of the hunted before, and he had always emerged victorious.

As he prepared to relocate Lily to the safe house, Max's mind was clear. His dual life was collapsing, but he would rebuild it, forge it stronger and more impenetrable than before. His love for Lily was the armour that no bullet could pierce, the drive that no threat could quell.

The day ended with Max executing his plan, the trafficker's demise just another move in the grand game he played. The streets were his to command, his escape routes as familiar as the lines on his palm. When the police arrived, sirens blaring and lights flashing, Max was already a ghost, slipping away into the night.

*

Max moved through the city's veins with the ease of a shadow flowing across the wall. His manoeuvres had become more than evasion; they were an art form, a testament to his resolve not to be caged by the consequences of his actions. But more than that, they were a testament to his unyielding determination to protect Lily at all costs.

The safe house was an unassuming structure nestled in the outskirts of London, veiled by the anonymity of suburban life. It was here that Max brought Lily under the pretence of a spontaneous getaway, a father-daughter retreat. She eyed him with a mix of suspicion and curiosity, her instincts telling her there was more to this sudden trip than met the eye.

"Dad, what's going on?" she asked, her voice steady despite the confusion that clouded her features.

Max met her gaze, the depths of his eyes swirling with secrets he longed to share but knew he must keep. "Just a precaution, Lil," he replied, the half-truth sitting heavily on his tongue. "We need to be careful."

Lily wanted to push, to demand the truth, but something in her father's demeanour halted her words. She nodded, a silent acceptance of the situation, trusting him despite the mysteries that wrapped around him like a thick fog.

Meanwhile, DI Bennett was orchestrating her network of informants and officers, a symphony of law enforcement that sought to capture the elusive figure haunting London's criminal element. The recent operation's fallout had brought them tantalizingly close to the vigilante's scent. It was only a matter of time before they cornered him, she was sure of it.

Marcus Kozlov, ever the strategist, began to see the pattern in the vigilante's strikes. They were calculated, a series of moves that were not random but pointedly disruptive to his organisation. Someone was waging a silent war against him, and Kozlov was not a man who took such challenges lightly.

He convened a meeting with his closest advisors, men

and women who operated in the shadows of the world's power structures. "Increase the pressure," he instructed, his voice the calm before the storm. "Our friend in London wants a war? Let's show him how we fight."

As the orders went out, the Kozlov organisation's machinery whirred to life, its gears oiled by the promise of retribution and the certainty of power.

Max was aware of the danger increasing with each passing moment. He had unleashed forces that would stop at nothing to bring him into the light, to expose him to the world he had so deftly navigated from the shadows.

But Max was not just a soldier or a vigilante; he was a harbinger of the storm he had summoned. As he laid out his weapons, his plans, he knew that his next move would be critical. It would be an operation that would define him, that would set the course for the war he waged.

That night, as Max set out from the safe house, leaving Lily under the watchful eye of his most trusted allies, he was more than a father or a shadow — he was the embodiment of the retribution he sought, a force of nature that would not be denied.

The operation was risky, a bold strike against a Kozlov asset that would draw the eyes of the world. But Max was not deterred by risk; he embraced it, for it was in the embrace of danger that he found his purpose.

The night air was crisp as Max slipped through the city, his every sense attuned to the task at hand. He was a predator in the urban jungle, and tonight he would claim his prey.

*

Max's movements were orchestrated with the precision of a maestro conducting a symphony. He traversed the cityscape, his path a series of shadows stitched together by the moon's silver thread. The Kozlov asset, a seemingly innocuous warehouse on the docks, was his destination — a node in a network that had spread like a cancer through the city's underbelly.

The warehouse was a fortress masquerading as a derelict relic, its true purpose hidden behind layers of legitimate facades. But Max had peeled back these layers, uncovering the pulsing vein of illicit activity that throbbed within. Tonight that pulse would stop.

He positioned himself, the cool metal of the HK417 sniper rifle familiar and reassuring in his grip. His breathing slowed, heartbeat a steady drumbeat syncing with the ebb and flow of the tides beyond the docks. The crosshairs found their mark, the silent confirmation of his impending action.

The shot broke the night's silence, a whisper of death that spoke volumes. It was the only sound Max allowed himself, the rest of his work silent as the grave. The warehouse erupted into chaos, but Max was already gone, his presence there as fleeting as a ghost's touch.

DI Bennett's phone rang with urgency, snapping her awake from the scant sleep she afforded herself. The voice on the other end was terse, conveying the news of an incident at the docks. "We believe it's him," the officer said, the 'him' hanging between them like a wraith.

Bennett was out of the door in minutes, her mind already racing. The vigilante had struck again, his actions bolder, more confrontational. She felt the undercurrents of change, the vigilante not just disrupting but declaring war.

As she arrived at the chaotic scene, Bennett's eyes took in the aftermath. The precision of the strike was undeniable; this was the work of a professional, a predator who had just made a significant move on the chessboard, one that would have repercussions they could not yet fathom.

Back in Prague, Marcus Kozlov received the news with a darkening scowl. The warehouse had been important, a critical link in his operations, and its loss was a blow to his network. The vigilante's message was clear, and it was written in blood and destruction.

"Enough," Kozlov muttered, the word a vow of impending violence. "This ends now."

He gave the order and his network activated, a dark tide rising to crash upon London's shores. Kozlov would not tolerate this affront to his empire; the vigilante would be found, and the price for his audacity would be steep.

Max returned to the safe house, his mind a whirlwind of what had transpired and what was yet to come. He knew he had marked himself, had drawn the ire of a man whose reach was long and unforgiving. But he also knew that he had struck a significant blow, had rattled the cage of a beast.

He checked in on Lily, watched her sleep for a moment, her innocence incongruous in the world he navigated. She was his light, his reason, and no matter the darkness that encroached, he would be her protector, her sentinel.

Max's escape from the docks had been narrow, the net of law enforcement closing in, but he was fluid, adaptable. He was the storm they chased, and storms were not easily caught.

*

The night was Max's domain, a realm where he reigned as both the hunter and the hunted. After the bold strike at the docks, he knew the rules of the game had changed. He was no longer an anonymous shadow; he had become a target, a name that carried weight in whispered conversations from London's dark corners to Prague's opulent halls.

Marcus Kozlov, with his vast resources, was now bent on retribution. The loss of the warehouse was more than a financial hit; it was a challenge to his authority, a blemish on the facade of invulnerability that he presented to the world. The orders had been clear — Max was to be found and made an example of.

But Max had always been adept at evasion, his senses honed to detect the faintest hint of danger. He operated within a network of safe houses and false identities, a maze designed to confuse and deter his pursuers.

DI Bennett, her mind a mosaic of case files and crime scenes, could feel the vigilante slipping through her fingers. The docks incident had all the hallmarks of his work, but it was more brazen, more aggressive. It was as if he was escalating, his actions a crescendo in a symphony of chaos.

As she stood amidst the aftermath, Bennett vowed to intensify her efforts. Her team was mobilized, their determination a mirror of her own. The vigilante had become a ghost story, but Bennett knew that every ghost leaves traces, and she was close to finding them.

Max's return to the safe house was a mixture of relief and restless anticipation. He had evaded capture once more, slipping away like smoke in the wind, but the night's events weighed heavily on him. Each move he made, each life he took, it was a step further into a darkness that threatened to consume him.

He checked on Lily, her peaceful slumber at odds with the violence that had unfolded just miles away. It was for her — for this moment of tranquillity — that he fought, that he risked everything. Max's facade as the untouchable spectre was cracking, the pressures from Kozlov and the law closing in.

But within Max burned a fire that the darkness could not extinguish. He was more than a vigilante; he was a father, a warrior, a guardian. And though the world sought to label him a criminal and a menace, he knew the truth of his cause.

As dawn approached, Max made a decision. He would not wait to be hunted; he would take the fight to them. He would dismantle Kozlov's empire piece by piece, a silent war fought not with guns and violence, but with intelligence and an indomitable will.

Max prepared to move once more, his next actions critical in the chess game he played with unseen opponents. The safe house had been a sanctuary, but now it was a cage, and he would not be caged.

As he stepped out into the breaking day, Max embraced his dual identity. He was the shadow that protected, the light that avenged. The hunter and the hunted, his reputation a dangerous weapon in its own right.

Part Two: The Veil of Darkness

Chapter 11: Echoes in Darkness

The New Doctrine

Max sat in the dimly lit room that had become his command centre, maps and photographs spread out before him like a mosaic of his new doctrine. He had welcomed his role as the arbiter of a justice that operated in the shadows, beyond the reach of the law. His creed was simple: strike hard, strike fast, and leave no trace.

The name Igor Savchenko was now at the forefront of his operations. A formidable figure in the criminal underworld, Savchenko's influence wove through the dark tapestry of corruption and violence that draped over the city. His connections were not just rooted in the seedy underbelly but extended into the echelons of power, implicating him in a potential political scandal that threatened to shake the foundations of the establishment.

Max knew the risks of targeting a man like Savchenko were immense. But the greater the risk, the greater the reward. Disrupting Savchenko's operations could deliver a critical blow to the network that had plagued the city for too long.

As he prepared for the mission, the silence of the room was a stark reminder of the path he walked alone. The few allies he had were shadows themselves, bound by the common goal of dismantling an empire of sin.

The operation was set for the morrow, targeting a high-profile event where Savchenko would be vulnerable. Max had all the details down, every second accounted for, every possible outcome considered. It was a dance with death, and he had been practising for this performance his entire life.

The night was still as Max sat alone, the weight of his creed a constant pressure. He allowed himself a moment to ponder the duality of his existence, the man who sought redemption through the crosshairs of his scope.

This was his life now, a life of purpose and solitude, a life where the only creed was the one he had written for himself. Max was ready, his resolve an unbreakable force that propelled him forward.

*

In the quietude that shrouded his planning space, Max's focus was laser sharp as he pored over the intelligence spread out in front of him. The room was silent, save for the occasional rustle of paper and the soft clicking of his keyboard as he cross-referenced data points. He was gathering the elements of a storm he was about to unleash upon Igor Savchenko.

Savchenko was no ordinary target; his name was whispered in reverence and fear in the circles Max now infiltrated with silent footsteps. With business ties that extended into the political stratosphere, Savchenko had insulated himself with layers of protection both human and systemic. But to Max, every layer was just another challenge, another puzzle piece in the grand strategy of his campaign.

The isolation Max felt was a double-edged sword; it shielded him from emotional compromise but also cut into the very fabric of his being, reminding him of the life he had once lived openly. He found an odd kinship with the solitary figures in history who had stood against tides of corruption, understanding now the toll such a battle took on the soul.

The plans for the mission against Savchenko were intricate and daring. Max had identified a high-profile event — a gala where the political and criminal elites would mingle under the guise of opulence and charity. It was there that Savchenko would be most exposed, a fact not lost on Max, nor, he assumed, on his target's security detail.

He had studied the blueprints of the venue and committed to memory the rotations of the guards, the placement of cameras, and the flow of service personnel. He would be a ghost amidst the revelry, his presence unnoticed until the moment he struck.

As Max readied his equipment, he allowed himself a rare moment of reflection. The mission was not just a strike against a single man; it was a declaration of war against a network that ensnared the innocent in its web of greed and power. His role as an assassin was clear, but the lines of morality were blurred in the shadows he now called home.

The evening of the gala arrived with a sense of foreboding. The sky seemed to echo Max's inner turmoil, heavy clouds promising a tempest. As he moved out, cloaked in the anonymity of the dark, Max felt the weight of his creed anchoring him.

He was the hunter in the night, moving with the certainty of a man who had nothing left to lose. The isolation of his double life was a small price to pay for the justice he sought to deliver. And as he neared the venue, the darkness around him seemed to pulse with the beating heart of the storm he was about to bring.

The gala was a bastion of wealth and corruption, its attendees a mix of the city's finest and the underworld's deadliest. Max, in the guise of a server, moved undetected through the throngs of glittering guests. His eyes, sharp and vigilant, scanned the room for Igor Savchenko. There he was, laughing heartily with a politician whose career was as tainted as the company he kept.

Max's heart was a drum of war in his chest, but his hands were steady as he adjusted the tray of champagne flutes. Each step was calculated, bringing him ever closer to his quarry. The weight of the hidden blade beneath his jacket was a reminder of the imminent strike, a burden he bore with silent resolve.

In the midst of opulence, Max was a shadow of vengeance. The chandeliers cast a golden glow, yet none reached the dark corners of his soul. He knew this was the point of no return, the moment where he fully embraced the creed he had written for himself.

Outside, the city was oblivious to the drama unfolding within the gala's walls. But for DI Bennett, the evening was anything but routine. The recent surge in vigilante activity had put the entire force on high alert, and a tip-off had led her to believe that tonight, something significant would unravel.

She surveyed the scene, her instincts on edge as she watched the guests with a keen eye. Among the faces of politicians, socialites, and tycoons, she searched for the one man who had become her enigma.

Savchenko, surrounded by his entourage of sycophants

and bodyguards, was a picture of confidence. But beneath the surface, his survival instincts were tingling. He had risen to the top through cunning and ruthlessness, and he was not oblivious to the threats that clawed at the edges of his empire.

Max edged closer, a silent predator among the flock. His mission was clear, his resolve unwavering. Yet as he manoeuvred into position, he felt the isolation of his double life more acutely than ever. Around him, life was a masquerade, and he was the only one unmasked — at least to himself.

The moment was upon him. With a fluid motion, he positioned himself behind Savchenko, the blade sliding silently from its concealment. But just as he prepared to strike, an unexpected commotion erupted at the entrance. Bennett and her team, acting on their lead, burst into the gala.

Max was forced to abort, retracting the weapon and slipping away as the crowd turned into a sea of chaos. Bennett's eyes scanned the room, searching for the phantom she knew was there. For a moment, their gazes almost met, but Max was a master of evasion.

The escape was a narrow one, but Max had lived his life on the razor's edge. As he disappeared into the night, the isolation of his existence was a cloak wrapped tightly around him. He had become the eye of the storm, and tonight the storm had raged without release.

*

Max's escape from the gala was a blend of serendipity and skill. The abrupt arrival of DI Bennett and her team had provided the perfect distraction, yet it also signified that his presence was anticipated, his actions monitored more closely than he'd considered. The walls seemed to close in around him with this realisation, and the weight of his isolation bore down with renewed gravity.

Retreating into the labyrinth of London's back alleys, Max moved with the urgency of a man who knows the breadth of his predicament. He had become the unseen adversary in a game that spanned from the grimy streets to the gilded halls of power. The failed strike at Savchenko was a setback, but it was not the end. Max knew the rules of engagement had shifted; his next move would need to be even more covert, even more decisive.

In the aftermath of the disrupted gala, Igor Savchenko was whisked away amidst a flurry of security. His eyes, cold and calculating, betrayed no emotion, but his mind was a whir of strategic countermeasures. The assassin had been within arm's reach, an unforgivable breach that would not go unanswered. Savchenko's connections were his armour, and he would leverage every contact, every favour owed, to fortify his position.

Back in his own dark corner of the city, Savchenko placed calls to his most trusted allies. His voice had a low, dangerous timbre as he issued commands that would set the underworld alight. The assassin would be found, he vowed, and the cost of his audacity would be steep.

DI Bennett stood amid the confusion of the gala's aftermath, her frustration a silent scream against the cacophony. She had been so close, yet the vigilante remained elusive, slipping through her fingers like smoke. The chase had become her obsession, the unnamed figure a question that gnawed at her ceaselessly.

Her team gathered around, their faces a mix of concern and determination. The operation had been a risk and it had not paid off. Yet Bennett was not one to dwell on failure. She was already piecing together the next step, her mind a razor honed on the edge of justice.

Max, now back in the sanctuary of his safe house, allowed himself a moment of introspection. The failed mission was a shadow on his record, a rare blip in an otherwise flawless campaign. The solitude of his double life clashed with the world he had just left behind, a world of lights and laughter that seemed as distant as a forgotten dream.

The silence of the room was a canvas upon which the echoes of his thoughts painted a sombre picture. The assassin's creed he had adopted was one of necessity, but it bore a cost that went beyond the physical. Max felt the isolation in his bones, a chill that the darkness around him seemed to amplify.

Yet within that isolation, within the very creed that dictated his actions, Max found a steely resolve. He would not falter, would not succumb to the doubts that clawed at him. His role was that of the unseen adversary, the deliverer of a justice that knew no accolades and sought no recognition.

As the city slept, unaware of the battles fought in its shadows, Max prepared for the next phase of his war. He was the unseen, the unnamed, the unrelenting force that would not be deterred.

*

The safe house was a cocoon, within which Max meticulously plotted his next move. The failed attempt on Savchenko had left a bitter taste, yet it also sharpened his focus. There was no room for error in the game he played; the stakes were life and death, not just for him but for anyone caught in the crossfire. He could not — he would not — let that be Lily.

In Prague, Savchenko's base of operations was abuzz with activity. Savchenko, a man who prided himself on control, found his anger simmering beneath a veneer of composure. The assassin had come for him and missed, but the message was clear. He was no longer untouchable. This realisation spurred him into action, and he dispatched his most trusted operatives with a new sense of urgency. Their orders were unambiguous: dismantle the assassin's network and bring him to light.

DI Bennett's pursuit of the vigilante had taken on a new edge. The gala incident had proven that they were dealing with someone highly skilled and incredibly bold. She spent hours reviewing security footage, looking for any sign, any clue that could lead her to the man who was now London's most wanted. Her intuition told her they were close, but the vigilante was a master of the unseen, his identity shrouded in mystery.

Her phone rang, breaking the silence of her concentration. The voice on the other end was urgent. "We've got a lead," it said. A tip had come in, a possible sighting of the man they sought.

The darkness was a cloak for Max as he set out once more. His target was not a person but information. He needed to unravel the threads that tied Savchenko to the world of politics, to expose the rot that lay at the heart of the city's elite.

Max moved through the back streets and alleyways with a predator's grace. His destination was an office building, nondescript but for the fact that it housed a server with information critical to his cause.

The infiltration was a silent ballet of shadow and light. Max bypassed security systems with devices born from his military expertise and the dark knowledge he had accrued in his new life. He reached the server room, the hum of machinery complementing the quiet focus that defined his movements.

His hands flew over the keyboard, commands entered with swift precision. Data scrolled across the screen, a litany of corruption and collusion that would shake the city to its core. Max downloaded what he needed, his heart pounding not with fear but with the thrill of the hunt.

But as he exfiltrated, a silent alarm he had missed was triggered. The sound of approaching sirens filled the air as Max made his escape. The lead had been accurate, and DI Bennett's team descended upon the building just as Max vanished into the night. They were always one step behind, but with each step, they gained ground. The web was tightening, and Max knew it. He had to move quickly.

Max melded with the shadows once again. The data he had secured was a weapon, one he intended to use, but at what cost? The veil of darkness was both his shield and his prison, and as he disappeared into the night, he felt its weight upon his soul.

*

Max, now back in the sanctuary of his chosen solitude, processed the information extracted from the depths of Savchenko's hidden servers. The glow of the computer screen cast ghostly shadows across the room, the digital evidence revealing a network of corruption that ensnared the city's elite in a net of power and vice. The data was explosive, the potential to shake the political landscape was enormous, and Max understood the gravity of possessing such information. It was a weapon of a different kind, but equally as lethal as any firearm in his arsenal.

He uploaded the data onto an encrypted drive, a modern-day sword waiting to be unsheathed at the right moment. Yet as he sat there in the dim light, the cost of his war weighed heavily upon him. The isolation of his double life was a chasm that seemed to grow wider with each passing day. He was a man standing alone against an empire, his only company the ghosts of his past actions.

In Prague, Igor Savchenko was made aware of the breach within moments of its occurrence. His expression remained unreadable, but there was a storm brewing in the depths of his eyes. He had underestimated this unseen adversary, a mistake he would not make again. Orders were issued in hushed tones, directives that set in motion a hunt that spanned continents. Savchenko would not rest until this vigilante was unmasked and destroyed.

DI Bennett stood outside the compromised building, her team combing the area for any trace of the phantom they chased. The frustration was etched deeply into her features. They had been so close, yet the vigilante remained a spectre, always just out of reach. But each encounter brought them closer, each brush with his shadow narrowing the field. She vowed to bring him to justice, her resolve hardened like steel.

As Max prepared to retreat once more into the night, a new sense of purpose solidified within him. The data he had acquired was not just a means to an end; it was a statement, a call to arms. He would use it to expose the rot at the core of the city's power structure, to tear down the facade that men like Savchenko hid behind.

He was ready to strike, to continue his crusade, but the revelation of his target's connection to elite politicians was a twist he had not anticipated. The network he fought against was more extensive, more entwined with the fabric of society, than he had known. Max now stood at the precipice edge of a revelation that threatened to change everything.

The night closed around him as he vanished once more into the darkness, a lone figure against the backdrop of a city that slumbered, unaware of the war waged in its shadows. Max, the assassin with a creed, felt the full weight of his isolation, a mantle that he bore as both his armour and his curse.

Chapter 12: Unseen Ties

The Web of Conspiracy

The threads of the conspiracy Max had uncovered were intricate and tangled, spreading out like a spider's web that ensnared not just the guilty but the unwitting as well. As he delved deeper, it became clear that his targets, once thought to be disparate elements of the city's criminal patchwork, were in fact bound together by unseen ties, a network of loyalty and betrayal that was as complex as it was hidden.

Max's latest lead had brought him to Dmitri Ivanov, a name that had surfaced repeatedly in his investigation. Ivanov was the lynchpin, a connector who bridged the gaps between the seemingly unrelated targets Max had previously taken down. As Max tracked Ivanov's movements, he began to see the pattern emerge from the shadows, a sinister picture that hinted at manipulation by forces within Marcus Kozlov's organisation.

Max's safe house was once again the scene of intense scrutiny as he pieced together the puzzle. His wall was a collage of information and photos connected with lines of string that wove a story of deceit. In the centre of it all was Kozlov, but as Max stared at the network he'd constructed, a creeping sense of paranoia began to take hold.

Was it possible that he had been manipulated from the start? Were his actions somehow serving the very beast he sought to slay? The thought was a splinter in his mind, impossible to ignore.

The feeling of being watched had grown stronger in

recent days. Max's once confident movements through the city were now tinged with the constant glance over the shoulder, the subtle check for a following shadow. It was during one such outing that he encountered Tariq Al-Fayed, a figure who was as enigmatic as he was dangerous.

Tariq was a ghost in the underworld, a man who moved with the silence of the grave. His allegiance was to the highest bidder, but his loyalty, Max discovered, was a currency as volatile as the markets. It was Tariq who revealed the extent of the network that Max had infiltrated, a revelation that made Max question the very nature of his crusade.

In the dimly lit backroom of a rundown building, Tariq laid out the reality of the situation. "You think you're the hunter," he said, a wry smile playing on his lips, "but even hunters can be hunted, Max."

The words struck a chord within Max, resonating with the paranoia that had begun to take root. He had always considered himself to be in control, the orchestrator of his fate, but Tariq's implications painted a different picture.

Max's eyes narrowed as he processed the implications. "Who's pulling the strings, Tariq?"

The other man leaned back, the shadows of the room embracing him like an old friend. "In this world, Max, there are layers upon layers. You may never see the hands that guide you."

As Max left the meeting with Tariq, the city around him seemed to pulse with unseen life, every passerby a potential observer, every car that lingered too long a possible tail. His mission was no longer just about delivering justice; it had become about uncovering the truth of his own involvement in the intricate dance of power that played out in the shadows.

His growing paranoia was a double-edged sword, sharpening his instincts while simultaneously eroding his trust. He had to stay focused, to remember the reason he had started down this path. Yet the question remained: was he a free agent, or just another pawn in Kozlov's grand design?

*

Max's safe house had become a crucible for his paranoia, every shadow a potential threat, every creak a whispered secret. He pored over the information Tariq had provided, cross-referencing it with the data he'd accumulated. What he saw was a morass of connections, with Dmitri Ivanov as a central node. It appeared Ivanov had been manipulating events from the shadows, orchestrating encounters and shaping the landscape in which Max operated. The illusion of choice in Max's crusade was beginning to crumble.

His introspection was broken by the buzz of his secure phone. It was a message from Anastasia Sokolov. *Watch your back*, it read. *Ivanov is more than he seems. Kozlov may not be the puppet master you think.*

The words were a cold splash of reality. Max had considered himself a player in this game, but the possibility that he might be a mere piece played by others was a twist he hadn't anticipated. It gnawed at him, a festering doubt that threatened to undermine his every action.

Max needed to see the full board, and for that, he had to seek out Tariq Al-Fayed once again. Tariq was a broker of information, but his allegiance was a slippery thing, as changeable as the wind. Max arranged a clandestine meeting, choosing a location that allowed him advantages should the encounter turn sour.

They met under the guise of night, two silhouettes against the backdrop of the city's ambient glow. "Ivanov is a ghost," Max began, his voice low and controlled. "What's his connection to Kozlov?"

Tariq's eyes were shrewd and calculating. "Ivanov is a kingmaker, a shadow that shapes the fates of men. His ties to Kozlov are ... complex. They are allies in some ventures, adversaries in others. Your actions have affected more than you know."

Max absorbed the information, his mind racing. The targets he had struck down, the operations he had executed – they were all part of a grander scheme, a war waged in a realm he was only beginning to understand.

The revelation that his targets may have been selected to serve Ivanov's shadowy agenda was a bitter pill to swallow. It suggested that Max's vendetta against the criminal underworld was perhaps not as righteous as he'd believed. The thought was a shackle on his soul, a chain that bound him to the realisation that his war might have been waged on false pretences.

Yet the mission remained clear. Igor Savchenko and the politics he was entwined in were pieces of a puzzle Max was determined to solve. He could not allow the possibility of manipulation to deter him from the path he had chosen. The data he had secured was a testament to the corruption he sought to eradicate. Max's creed was his own, regardless of the unseen forces that sought to use him as a weapon.

Max's departure from the meeting with Tariq was like a wraith fading into the mist. He moved with renewed purpose, his determination a burning flame in the growing dusk. The conspiracy he was unravelling was vast, but he was undeterred. He had faced insurmountable odds before; this was but another challenge.

The isolation of his double life had never been more palpable. Max was a solitary figure against a network of lies and loyalties that spanned beyond the city's skyline. His paranoia was a constant companion, whispering of betrayals and unseen eyes that watched his every move.

Yet in the heart of that solitude, Max found a steely resolve. He would not be a pawn in another's game. He would set the board ablaze if need be.

*

In the solitude of his hideout, Max laid out the pieces of the puzzle before him, the photos and strings forming a constellation of conspiracy. Each piece connected back to Dmitri Ivanov, the kingmaker, the shadowy figure whose influence seemed to touch every corner of the criminal underworld. The more Max uncovered, the more he realised the depth of Ivanov's control. It was like peeling back layers of an onion, each one revealing a new, more complex pattern beneath.

He knew now that Igor Savchenko was just one part of a larger mosaic, a cog in Ivanov's grand machine. But where did that leave him? Was he another cog, albeit unwitting, or was he the spanner in the works? Max's self-imposed solitude was both his sanctuary and his prison, providing safety and space for contemplation but also feeding the paranoia that was an ever-present shadow.

The name Igor Savchenko was a thread that led Max to an intricate web of financial transactions, political bribes, and backdoor dealings. It became evident that the political crime was more than mere corruption; it was an orchestrated symphony of power plays. As he delved deeper, the connections grew more ominous, hinting at a level of manipulation that extended beyond the city, beyond even the country.

Max's next move needed to be calculated with the utmost precision. He decided to confront Ivanov directly, to cut the head off the snake. But confronting a man like Ivanov was no small feat. He was a phantom in his own right, his appearances carefully choreographed, his locations always kept secret.

Utilizing his network of informants and leveraging the skills of Nadia Sokolov, Max narrowed down the possible whereabouts of Ivanov. It was a gamble, but every war required risks, and Max was playing for the highest stakes.

The confrontation with Ivanov took place not in the darkness to which Max had become accustomed but in the grey light of pre-dawn. They met on neutral ground, an abandoned warehouse that had once been part of Ivanov's empire but now stood as a relic of industries past.

Ivanov's silhouette was just as Max had pictured, tall and imposing, with an aura of untouchable confidence. "So, you are the one causing all this trouble." Ivanov's voice echoed in the vast emptiness, his tone almost amused.

Max stepped from the shadows, his posture relaxed but ready. "Your empire is built on exploitation and suffering. It ends now," he declared, his voice steady.

A dry chuckle escaped Ivanov's lips. "My empire?

You think too small. I am but a humble servant to the cause. You, however, have become quite the problem."

The exchange was brief, a dance of words and wits. Ivanov was a master manipulator, but Max was no ordinary adversary. The conversation veered between veiled threats and cryptic admissions, with Ivanov alluding to forces even greater than himself.

As they parted ways, Max felt a chill that had little to do with the morning air. Ivanov was not the endgame; he was a mere stepping stone to something much larger. The kingmaker had his own kings to answer to.

Max left the warehouse with more questions than answers. His target had ties that ran deep into a potential political scandal, one that threatened to shake the very foundations of the nation. The complexity and reach of the criminal network were daunting, but Max was resolute. His paranoia had not been unfounded; it had been a beacon, guiding him to the truth.

Max disappeared into the breaking day. He was a lone warrior in a battle that was far from over, his creed the only certainty in a world shrouded in deception and betrayal.

*

After the encounter with Ivanov, the city felt different to Max. The streets he walked were the same, the chill of the early morning as biting as ever, but the knowledge that his every action could be influenced by unseen forces cast a pall over everything. The echoes of truth that had reverberated in the warehouse with Ivanov lingered in Max's mind, a chorus of implications that hinted at a grander, more sinister orchestra at play.

Back in his safe house, Max's fingers danced across the keys of his computer, the encrypted drive containing the political data his conduit into a world he had only glimpsed the edges of. He had to tread carefully; the information he now possessed was a blade that cut both ways.

Ivanov had been a wealth of cryptic clues, but one name had stood out amongst the rest: Konstantin Belov. Ivanov had mentioned him in passing, a slip perhaps unintended, or perhaps a breadcrumb deliberately left behind. Max knew Belov was key to unravelling the web, a figure whose loyalties were as shadowed as the rest.

As he delved into the networks and transactions, a pattern began to emerge. Belov was everywhere and nowhere, a ghost in the system, his ties to Savchenko and Ivanov intricate and yet somehow obfuscated. It was as if he was a spider sitting at the centre of a web, pulling strings that moved the world in ways unseen.

Max's next mission was clear: he had to find Belov, to confront the network of loyalties and betrayals that he represented. It was a risk, but Max was beyond playing it safe. His paranoia had morphed into a tool, a sense that sharpened his focus and drove him deeper into the darkness in search of light.

His preparations were interrupted by a knock at the door, a sound that sent a jolt of adrenaline through him. Max approached cautiously, peering through the peephole to see a familiar face — Anastasia Sokolov. He opened the door, his expression questioning.

"You need to see this," Anastasia said, her voice urgent as she handed over a file. "It's Belov."

The file was thin, but the weight of it was heavy in Max's hands. Inside were photos, documents, evidence that Belov was not just a lynchpin but perhaps the architect of much of the chaos that had engulfed the city. And there, tucked between the sheets of information, was a single, stark revelation: Belov had been at the gala, a shadow amongst the crowd, his presence unnoticed but captured by a stray lens.

Max's mind reeled. Had Belov been the target all along? Was the attempt on Savchenko simply a means to draw him out? The possibilities multiplied, each more complex and disconcerting than the last.

Max set out into the city once more, the file burning a hole in his pocket. The network he had been dismantling piece by piece was revealing itself to be more intricate, more entrenched than he had ever imagined. The true nature of his assignments was now a question that demanded an answer.

The isolation he felt was now tinged with the sting of betrayal. The double life he led, once a choice, now felt like a trap. But Max was not one to be ensnared easily. He was the hunter, and it was time to draw out the spider.

*

Max moved through the city with a new sense of urgency. Belov's elusive nature made him a difficult target to pin down, but the information Anastasia had provided gave Max a place to start. He needed to find Belov, to pull on the thread he represented and unravel the web of conspiracy once and for all.

The clues led him to an affluent district, where the wealthy and powerful played at life far removed from the city's grime. It was here, in a high-rise that scraped the clouds, that Belov conducted his business. Max had always known that the city's elite were entwined with its criminal underbelly, but he had never seen it so blatantly displayed.

Max entered the building under the guise of a maintenance worker, his disguise as mundane as it was effective. The service elevator took him to the floor below Belov's penthouse suite. From there, it was a matter of bypassing a security system that was more a formality than a real barrier. He had done this dance many times, and his steps were sure and silent.

The door to the suite was ajar, which was the first sign that something was amiss. Max paused, his instincts on high alert. He pushed the door open slowly and stepped into the lavish space. It was quiet, too quiet. The opulence of the penthouse was a stark contrast to the violence that had visited it. Belov lay in the centre of the room, his lifeless eyes staring at the ceiling, a pool of blood expanding from beneath him.

Max stood over the body, processing the scene. Belov, the webmaster, the man who had pulled so many strings, now cut from his own web. Who had got to him first? Was this the work of Kozlov, a cleaning of house? Or something else entirely?

A noise from the other room snapped Max to attention. He moved swiftly, coming face to face with a woman who was as surprised to see him as he was to see her. She was poised, dangerous — a weapon in human form. Her hand hovered near her coat, where Max knew a gun likely waited.

"Who are you?" they asked simultaneously, a momentary connection formed in the crosshairs of suspicion and surprise.

Max didn't lower his guard, and neither did she. This was not a chance encounter. She was here for Belov, and now she was a loose end, a witness to Max's presence.

They circled each other, two predators uncertain if the other was prey or a fellow hunter. "Max," he finally said, offering only his first name.

"Isabella," she replied, her gaze never wavering from his. "Isabella Ivanova."

The standoff continued, a silent conversation of mutual assessment. Max needed information, and Isabella held the keys to many locked doors.

"Why are you here?" Max pressed, his voice calm despite the tension that crackled in the air like electricity.

Isabella's eyes flicked to Belov's body. "The same reason you are, I imagine. But it seems we're both too late."

Max knew he couldn't let Isabella leave, not until he had answers. But he also recognised the potential for an ally in her — someone who clearly shared his goals, if not his methods.

The air between them was charged, the beginning of an uneasy alliance forming out of necessity. They were both pieces on the board, but perhaps together, they could change the game.

*

In the shadow-draped luxury of Belov's penthouse, Max and Isabella remained in a standoff. The silent question hanging between them was who would blink first. Max's mind raced — Isabella was an unknown variable, but her presence suggested she was fighting a similar battle against the murky nexus of crime and corruption.

"You were after Belov," Max stated, more fact than question. "Why?"

Isabella's eyes held a glint of respect, acknowledging the shared pursuit. "Belov was a means to an end," she admitted. "I'm after the ones pulling the strings, same as you, I presume."

Max's suspicion mingled with the faintest relief. He wasn't alone in his fight, it seemed. "We might have a common enemy," he conceded. "But that doesn't make us friends."

Isabella's lips curved into a half-smile. "In this world, Max, friends are liabilities. Allies, however, are mutually beneficial."

Their conversation was cut short by the faint sound of sirens in the distance. The authorities would be here soon, drawn to the scene of the crime like moths to flame. Max knew they had to act quickly — both to escape and to leverage this unexpected partnership.

"Let's get out of here," Max suggested, his tone urgent. "We can cover more ground together. But I work alone."

Isabella nodded, understanding the sentiment. "Temporary allies, then," she said as they both moved towards the service exit. "Until our goals no longer align."

As they slipped through the building's underbelly and out into the dawn-streaked streets, Max and Isabella kept a cautious distance. They were like two feral cats who had temporarily set aside their territorial disputes in the face of a common threat.

Max felt the cold shroud of his isolation lifted slightly by Isabella's presence. The paranoia that had been his constant companion now had another voice, a sounding board that understood the stakes.

Once they were a safe distance from Belov's penthouse, Isabella turned to him. "I have resources, Max. Connections that could help you. This conspiracy is bigger than either of us realised."

Max weighed her offer. He had always been a lone wolf, but the complexity of the web he was untangling was daunting. Perhaps it was time to accept that going it alone was no longer the most effective strategy.

"Alright," Max agreed, his voice gruff with the unfamiliarity of compromise. "We pool our resources for now. But the moment I sense a double-cross, our alliance is over."

Isabella's nod was one of a warrior acknowledging the terms of a truce. "Understood," she said.

As they parted ways, each disappearing into the labyrinth of the awakening city, Max felt the burden of his mission's weight shared, if only slightly. The network of loyalties and betrayals that Belov had revealed was intricate, but now, with Isabella's help, Max hoped to trace the puppet strings back to the masters.

Chapter 13: The Rival's Introduction

The New Player

The city's undercurrent of crime and espionage was a chessboard, and Max had become one of its most unpredictable pieces. But now, a new player had entered the game — John Larkin, an enigma wrapped in the trappings of former American special forces. His emergence on the scene was as sudden as it was unsettling for Max.

Larkin's reputation preceded him: a ghost operative known for his ruthlessness and efficiency. Max had heard whispers of Larkin in hushed tones during his own operations — a rival whose methods and motivations seemed eerily reflective of his own. It was during an operation targeting a corrupt official with ties to the Kozlov empire that Max first crossed paths with Larkin.

Max had infiltrated the high-rise office under the veil of night, his every sense attuned to the environment around him. The intel was solid; the official was the key to unlocking another layer of the conspiracy. But as Max approached the target's office, he detected signs of another presence — subtle but unmistakable to a trained eye.

Inside, the official lay slumped over his desk, a clean shot through the heart. Max's gaze snapped to a figure retreating into the shadows — Larkin. Their eyes met briefly across the room, a silent acknowledgement of the rivalry that had just been born.

Max was quick to follow, but Larkin was a shadow, his exit as calculated and precise as Max's had always been. The realisation that he was not alone in his skill set was a jolt to Max. He had competition, and it was formidable.

The mission's outcome was a mixed blessing. The corrupt official was silenced, which served Max's purpose, but Larkin had beaten him to the punch. As Max retreated into the darkness, his mind raced. Who had sent Larkin? Was this a sign that his own network of contacts, including Yuri, could no longer be trusted?

Max needed to learn more about John Larkin. His operations were always meticulously planned, leaving no trace, no loose ends. But Larkin's presence was a variable he had not accounted for. Was Larkin working independently, or was he a pawn in a larger game, much like Max had feared he himself might be?

Back at his safe house, Max pulled up what little information he could find on Larkin. The man was a ghost in the system, his past a patchwork of redacted files and whispers of off-the-books operations. Larkin was a soldier who had traded the uniform for the shadows, much like Max. But his motivations remained a mystery.

As he delved into Larkin's background, Max found parallels to his own life. Larkin had been part of an elite unit, his service record impeccable until he had suddenly disappeared from the grid. What had driven Larkin to leave behind his life as a soldier? And what had brought him to the criminal underbelly of London?

This introduction of Larkin was a game-changer for Max. The city had become a battleground for two spectres, both highly skilled and both determined to achieve their objectives. But in this world of shadows, only one could emerge victorious.

Max settled into the chair, the glow of the computer

screen casting a sickly pallor over his features. His next move needed to be calculated with care. Larkin was a rival, yes, but also potentially a formidable ally — if he could be trusted.

*

Max's world had contracted to the illuminated glow of his laptop screen, data on Larkin pouring in through secure channels. He was piecing together the puzzle of Larkin's sudden appearance in London, each click drawing him deeper into the labyrinth of his rival's history. The more Max learned, the more he saw reflections of himself — a soldier forged in the crucible of war, now navigating the murky waters of a world without uniforms.

Larkin's trail led Max to the docks, where whispers in the criminal underworld spoke of an upcoming shipment that was of interest to both Kozlov's network and those who sought to dismantle it. Max felt the inevitability of a showdown, a confrontation that would pit him against Larkin in a race for the prize.

He arrived under the cover of darkness, the scent of salt and rust heavy in the air. The docks were a maze of containers and shadows, perfect for a man accustomed to moving unseen. But Max was acutely aware that he was no longer the only predator stalking these grounds.

The night was silent save for the distant cry of a lone seagull, its sound a harbinger of the impending clash. Max moved with care, his every sense strained for a sign of Larkin. It was a game of cat and mouse, but who was which was yet to be determined.

Their meeting was inevitable, two operatives

converging on the same target. Larkin emerged from the shadows, his presence a cold gust in the still night. Their eyes met, two soldiers recognizing the skill in the other, a mutual respect born of shared experience, albeit on opposing sides.

"We don't have to do this," Larkin's voice cut through the silence, his American accent stark against the backdrop of the Thames. "We're not enemies, Max."

Max's stance was wary, his hand near the weapon concealed beneath his coat. "We are if you're here to protect Kozlov's interests."

A tense laugh escaped Larkin. "Protect? No. I'm here to intercept the same as you. But I'm not your rival, Max. There's a bigger picture you're not seeing."

The conversation was a dance, each man probing for information, for weaknesses. But as the night wore on, it became clear that their goals were aligned, at least for the moment. Larkin had his reasons for being in London, reasons that dovetailed with Max's own mission to expose the corruption that lay like a blight upon the city.

In a temporary truce, they decided to join forces, to take down the shipment and retrieve whatever information it contained. The operation was swift, a testament to their shared expertise. The container, when opened, revealed not contraband, but documents — evidence of transactions that tied political figures to Kozlov's syndicate.

As they sifted through the papers, the alliance between Max and Larkin solidified, forged in the fire of their shared pursuit. But as dawn broke over the docks, casting light on the dark deeds of the night, Max's trust in his contacts, especially Yuri, frayed further. How much had they known about Larkin? About the true extent of the conspiracy?

Max left the docks with a new ally but also with new doubts. His life, once a solitary path, now included John Larkin — a rival turned comrade-in-arms. But in the world of espionage and shadow wars, how long could such an alliance last?

*

The first light of dawn cast a pale glow over the aftermath of their night's work. Max and Larkin stood side by side, a tableau of uneasy alliance as they surveyed the documents that sprawled before them. The papers whispered of deep-seated corruption, a network that entwined the city's political elite with the tendrils of Kozlov's empire.

"It's a mess, isn't it?" Larkin's voice broke the morning's silence, a hint of irony lacing his words.

Max could only nod, the extent of the conspiracy far surpassing what he had imagined. It wasn't just the criminal underworld; it was the very infrastructure of society that was rotten.

Max's distrust in Yuri, and by extension, all his contacts, had become a yawning chasm. The information that had guided his missions, the intel that had seemed so reliable — could it have been a ploy, part of a larger scheme orchestrated by the likes of Ivanov and Kozlov? The notion that he might have been an unwitting pawn was a bitter pill to swallow.

Larkin seemed to sense Max's introspection. "You're wondering if you've been played," he said, not a question but a statement. "I've been there. It's why I work alone."

Max glanced at Larkin, his expression hardening. "We

might be on the same side today, but that doesn't make us partners."

Larkin nodded, understanding the sentiment. "Fair enough. But you need to start questioning everything. Trust has to be earned, especially in our line of work."

The documents they had retrieved were a treasure trove of incriminating evidence, but they also posed a significant risk. If word got out that they had been compromised, the consequences would be swift and deadly. They needed to act, to use the information to their advantage before Kozlov and his associates could contain the fallout.

Max took the lead, his instincts as a tactician coming to the fore. "We leak it," he proposed, his mind already charting out the ripples such an act would cause. "We use the media, anonymous sources. We let the truth do the damage."

Larkin considered the plan, his eyes scanning the horizon as if visualizing the chaos that would ensue. "And become targets ourselves," he added, "if we aren't already."

Max's lips quirked into a grim smile. "We're ghosts, remember? Let them try to find us."

The uneasy quiet of the early morning seemed to portend the storm they were about to unleash. They parted ways, each to his own shadowed path, with a mutual understanding that their truce was temporary. Max felt the isolation of his crusade acutely in Larkin's retreating figure, a mirror to his own solitary fight.

As he made his way back through the city's waking streets, Max's thoughts were a whirlwind. The evidence they had uncovered would shake the foundations of the city's power structure, but the revelation of a rival in

Larkin was a complication he had not anticipated. He had to tread carefully, for in the world of shadows, allies were as dangerous as enemies.

The city was awakening, oblivious to the maelstrom that was about to descend upon it. Max, the orchestrator of the coming chaos, moved unseen, his presence an intangible whisper on the wind. The documents would be his weapons, the truth his ally, and the city's elite his unwitting pawns.

*

The streets of London began to stir as Max made his way back to his safe house, the weight of the documents in his bag a physical manifestation of the burden he carried. It was a risk, setting this information free into the world, but it was one he was willing to take. The truth had a way of finding its mark, and Max was counting on the chaos it would cause to cover his next moves.

At a secure location, Max sat down at a terminal, the keys clacking under his fingers as he composed the message that would serve as the fuse for the impending explosion. He had chosen a handful of reputable journalists known for their investigative tenacity and their lack of susceptibility to the city's elite's coercive influences. The message was encrypted, the trail cold, the identity of the whistleblower a mystery he intended to keep.

As he hit send, Max leaned back in his chair, the first rays of sunlight creeping through the blinds. The gamble had been made, and now it was time to see where the chips would fall.

The impact was immediate and far-reaching. The news

cycles were ablaze with the scandal, the documents painting a damning picture of collusion and corruption that reached the highest echelons of power. Politicians scrambled, denials were issued, and the machinery of damage control churned into overdrive.

Max watched the chaos unfold from a distance, a ghost observing the fallout. His actions had always been about justice, about righting the wrongs that the system had failed to address. Now he had struck at the heart of the beast, and the beast was writhing.

Amidst the tumult, Max's thoughts turned to John Larkin. The American had been a surprise, an operative with skills that matched his own, a shadow that was now cast alongside Max's in the narrative he had crafted. Max had to admit, albeit grudgingly, that Larkin's involvement had been instrumental in obtaining the documents. The question of trust, however, remained open.

Max had always been a lone wolf, but Larkin's emergence had forced him to reconsider the efficacy of standing alone. As the political scandal rocked the city, Max pondered his rival's motivations. Was Larkin truly an ally in this fight, or was there an ulterior motive behind his actions?

The day wore on, and Max remained cloistered in his safe house, his eyes glued to the screens that fed him information. The media frenzy was just the beginning. He knew the true players would be making their moves in secret, away from the prying eyes of the public. And Max needed to be ready to counter them.

As dusk approached, Max made a decision. He couldn't do this alone, not anymore. He needed to meet with Larkin, to lay down the groundwork for what was rapidly becoming a war on two fronts — against both

Kozlov's criminal empire and the political puppets it controlled.

He sent a message to Larkin: a location and a time. The safe house felt smaller, the walls closing in as he prepared to step out into the world he had shaken. The isolation of his double life was suffocating, but it was also his greatest defence. As Max set out to the meeting, he knew one thing for certain — the game had changed, and so had he.

*

Max navigated the city with a heightened awareness, the weight of his decision to reach out to Larkin pressing upon him. The streets, awash with the golden hues of the setting sun, seemed to hold their breath, awaiting the next act in the unfolding drama.

He arrived at the rendezvous point early, a greasy spoon café that offered a view of the street and multiple exits — a necessary precaution in his line of work. As he settled at a back table, his eyes scanned the other patrons, searching for any sign of surveillance. Paranoia was a survival trait in his world, and Max had honed it to an art form.

Larkin arrived with the punctuality of a man accustomed to military precision. His gait was relaxed, but his eyes were sharp, missing nothing. He nodded to Max as he approached, acknowledging the delicate nature of their meeting.

"You made quite the splash," Larkin commented as he sat down, his voice low but tinged with a note of respect.

"It needed to be done," Max replied, his eyes never straying far from the door. "The question is, where do we go from here?"

Larkin leaned back, considering the question. "We keep applying pressure. Your leak has them scrambling, which means they're vulnerable. We strike now, while the iron's hot."

Max mulled over Larkin's words. The man had a point. The political scandal had opened doors that were previously locked tight. It was an opportunity to delve deeper into the network they were both fighting against. But it also meant exposing themselves to greater danger.

"I have my reservations," Max admitted, his voice steady. "This alliance ... it's not something I'm used to."

Larkin's nod was one of understanding. "Neither am I," he conceded. "But sometimes, the mission requires adaptation. We don't have to trust each other completely, but we do need to trust that we're both after the same thing."

It was a sentiment Max could understand. Trust was a luxury in their world, one that was rarely afforded. Yet the circumstances had thrust them together, two soldiers fighting a hidden war.

Their conversation turned to strategy, plotting their next moves in the chess game that the city had become. They were pieces no longer acting in isolation but as part of a coordinated play that had the potential to bring down kings.

As the meeting drew to a close, Max felt a shift within him. The lone wolf was learning the value of running with a pack, however temporary. The documents had been his gambit, but it was clear that Larkin was a valuable piece in the game — one that Max could not afford to discard.

They parted ways with a nod, the silent understanding

between them speaking volumes. Max felt a new sense of purpose. The leak had been his, but the war ... the war was theirs. And as the sky darkened to the deep blue of twilight, Max felt the stirrings of an alliance that was as formidable as it was fragile.

*

As the café door swung shut behind him, sealing off the murmur of conversations and the clink of coffee cups, Max stepped into the cool embrace of the evening. The city hummed around him, a hive of the unsuspecting and the unaware, a world apart from the silent war he waged. The talk with Larkin had solidified something within him — a reluctant acceptance that alliances, however fragile, were necessary.

Max walked the streets, the city's pulse thrumming beneath his feet. His mind was a whirl of strategies and contingency plans, each step towards the safe house a calculation of the moves to come. Larkin's background and motivations remained opaque, but his skills were undeniable. Max had to admit, if only to himself, that Larkin's involvement brought an edge to his operations that he hadn't known he needed.

The political scandal, still unfolding across every news outlet and social media platform, served as a smokescreen for their movements. Max knew that the chaos of public attention would provide the perfect cover for their next strike. It was a narrow window of opportunity, but Max was accustomed to threading the needle.

Back in the safety of his hideout, Max's fingers flew across the keyboard, bringing up satellite imagery and encrypted communications. Trust in Yuri and others had eroded, but Max's reliance on technology remained steadfast. It was a bitter irony that in a world where trust in people faltered, trust in machines endured.

Larkin's words echoed in Max's head: "Keep applying pressure." The rival-turned-ally had a point. The entities they fought against were momentarily on the back foot, reeling from the revelations that continued to pour forth from the documents Max had leaked. It was time to capitalise on their disarray.

As he plotted the next mission, Max could feel the tendrils of suspicion that had wrapped around his heart since the beginning begin to loosen slightly. Larkin was an unknown, but he was also a variable that Max could influence. In a game as intricate and deadly as theirs, that was as much as he could hope for.

Night had fallen in full when Max finally stepped away from the screens, his mind heavy with plans and possibilities. The city outside his window was a network of lights, each one a life, a story, a potential ally or enemy. John Larkin's introduction into his life had changed the game, but Max was a quick study. He would adapt, evolve, and overcome.

As he prepared to catch a few hours of rest before the dawn broke, Max considered the web of unseen ties that had drawn him and Larkin together. They were soldiers on a battlefield devoid of flags, fighting an enemy that was as pervasive as the air they breathed. Tomorrow would bring its own challenges, but for tonight, Max had a plan, and that was enough.

He lay down, the city's nocturnal symphony a lullaby for the wary. In the world of shadows, he had found a kindred spirit, however temporary. And in the world of espionage and silent wars, that was as close to trust as one got.

Chapter 14: Collateral Damage

The Fallout

The operation had been meticulously planned, every variable accounted for, or so Max had thought. As he crouched behind the crumbled wall of the abandoned warehouse, the stench of smoke and burning rubber assaulting his nostrils, Max knew something had gone catastrophically wrong.

The mission's objective had been clear: to intercept a key exchange between two of Kozlov's lieutenants. Intelligence had suggested it would be a simple in-and-out job. But as Max and Larkin had moved into position, the night had erupted into chaos.

An explosion had torn through the east wing of the structure, a booby trap that none of his intel had hinted at. It was a setup, and they had walked right into it.

Through the ringing in his ears, Max heard the screams — the collateral damage of their botched mission. He pushed through the debris, his heart hammering against his ribs as he assessed the scene. There, amidst the rubble, lay casualties — workers who had been in the wrong place at the wrong time.

Larkin was beside him, his face grim. "We need to move," he urged, but Max was frozen, his gaze locked on the innocent lives lost. This was not the plan; they were not supposed to be here.

A name surfaced through the commotion, a whisper among the surviving workers — Carlos Ramirez. Was he a victim or a player in this twisted game? Max filed the name away for later; right now, he needed to contain the situation.

The aftermath was a blur. Max and Larkin retreated into the night, the weight of their failure a tangible presence between them. Max's mind raced — the operation had been compromised from the inside, the only explanation for the trap that had been so precisely laid out for them.

As they put distance between themselves and the warehouse, Max's thoughts turned to Colonel Hammond. He needed advice, guidance, something to anchor him in the roiling sea of chaos his life had become.

They parted ways with a curt nod, a silent agreement that there would be a reckoning for this night's events. Max made his way to the safe house, his steps heavy, his soul heavier.

Colonel Hammond was waiting, his figure silhouetted against the dim light of the safe house's interior. The Colonel's eyes were sombre, his usual stoic demeanour tinged with concern.

"Max," he began, his voice steady, "talk to me."

The conversation that followed was a confession, a debriefing, a search for solace. Max recounted the events, the explosion, the screams, the name — Carlos Ramirez. Hammond listened, his expression unreadable.

"You did everything you could," Hammond finally said, but his words were cold comfort to Max. The guilt was a vice squeezing his chest.

As dawn crept over the horizon, a new piece of the puzzle clicked into place. The failed mission was not just a setback — it was a message, a clear indication that there was a traitor within Max's circle. Trust, already a rare commodity, had just become even scarcer.

The realisation was a knife to Max's gut. The network

he had relied on, the contacts he had trusted, were now suspects in the worst kind of betrayal. Someone had set them up, and Max was going to find out who.

*

Max hadn't slept. The early morning light spilled into the safe house, casting long shadows that felt like accusations across the floor. His conversation with Colonel Hammond had ended with more questions than answers, and one name echoed in his mind: Carlos Ramirez. Who was he? A victim caught in the crossfire or a player in the deadly game that had just claimed innocent lives?

Max knew he couldn't let the weight of the night's disaster paralyze him. There was a traitor in their midst, and he had to be found.

The hunt for Ramirez led Max to a rundown tenement building in an area of the city that hope seemed to have forgotten. It was here that Ramirez was supposed to live, according to the scant information Max had been able to gather at short notice.

The building was a labyrinth of narrow hallways and cramped apartments, a place where secrets were currency. Max moved through the shadows, his presence as unobtrusive as a whisper. When he finally found Ramirez's door, he paused, listening. There was a tension in the air, the silent hum of danger that Max had come to recognise all too well.

He knocked. The man who answered was wary, his eyes flicking nervously to the hallway behind Max. "Carlos Ramirez?" Max asked, his tone leaving no room for evasion.

"Yes," the man replied, a tremor in his voice betraying

his calm facade. "Who are you?"

Max didn't answer. Instead, he pushed past Ramirez into the apartment, his eyes quickly scanning the room. It was sparsely furnished, the air heavy with the scent of fear.

"You were at the warehouse last night," Max stated, watching Ramirez closely.

"I ... I was just doing a job," Ramirez stammered. "I didn't know anything about ... about any exchange."

Max's eyes narrowed. "And yet you survived the explosion that killed your co-workers."

Ramirez's face went pale, his guilt as clear as daylight. "I was warned," he whispered. "Someone told me not to go to that section of the warehouse."

The revelation hit Max like a physical blow. Someone inside the operation had warned Ramirez, had known about the setup. It confirmed Max's worst fears — the traitor was one of their own.

Max pressed Ramirez for more information, but the man knew little else. He had been a pawn, a disposable asset in someone else's play for power.

As Max left Ramirez's flat, his mind was racing. He had to confront Yuri, to ascertain his involvement. But as he navigated the streets back to his safe house, a sinking feeling took hold. What if Yuri was the traitor? The possibility had been unthinkable before, but now doubt cast long shadows over every alliance Max had formed.

Yuri's workshop was as Max remembered it, cluttered with the tools of his trade. The man himself was hunched over a workbench, his focus on the piece in front of him. He looked up as Max entered, a flicker of surprise crossing his features.

"Max, what's wrong?" Yuri asked, but Max's expression

was grim.

"We need to talk," Max said, his voice heavy with the burden of betrayal.

The conversation that followed was tense, fraught with the gravity of the situation. Max laid out the events, the setup, the death of innocent workers, and the warning Ramirez had received.

Yuri's denial was vehement, his shock genuine — or a masterful performance. Max couldn't tell, and that uncertainty was a poison, corroding the trust that had once been unshakable.

As Max left Yuri's workshop, the early morning's clarity had been replaced by the fog of suspicion. The failed mission was a setup, and now Max had to consider the possibility that every move he made was being watched, manipulated by a traitor who had marked him for a fall.

*

Max had always operated in the shadows, but now those shadows seemed darker, more treacherous. His meeting with Yuri had left him with a seed of doubt that refused to be dismissed. If Yuri was innocent, then who within his trusted circle was the traitor? Each step he took now was tainted with the fear of unseen eyes tracking his movements.

The city was waking up, the usual cacophony of traffic and voices in sharp contrast to the silence of his safe house. Max needed to clear his head, to find a space where he could piece together the fragments of truth he had.

He found himself at an old haunt, a secluded park bench that offered a view of the Thames. The river's constant flow was a reminder that life moved on, despite the undercurrents that threatened to drag one down.

As he sat, his mind replayed the operation, the explosion, the screams. The collateral damage of their actions had been real, innocent lives extinguished. The weight of it pressed on Max's conscience, a heavy cloak of remorse that he couldn't shake off.

It was in this moment of vulnerability that Colonel Hammond found him. The older man approached with measured steps, his demeanour calm but his eyes reflecting a deep concern.

"Max," Hammond began, his voice steady. "This isn't on you. We both know the risks that come with the territory."

Max looked up, the lines of his face etched with fatigue. "That doesn't make it any easier to accept," he replied, his voice rough with emotion.

Hammond sat beside him, the two soldiers sharing the silence. "War has a way of extending its reach beyond the battlefield," Hammond finally said. "The enemy you fight is not bound by honour or rules of engagement."

Their conversation turned to the mission, to the potential leak within their network. Hammond listened intently, his years of experience evident as he dissected the possibilities.

"The setup was professional, calculated," Max said. "It could only have been orchestrated by someone with intimate knowledge of our operations."

Hammond nodded, his expression grave. "Then you proceed with caution. Trust has to be earned, now more than ever."

Max felt the truth of those words. Trust was a currency that had been devalued, it's worth diminished by the shadow of treachery.

As the day wore on, Max knew he had to make a decision. He could no longer operate as he had before; the rules had changed. The traitor's mark was on him, a target he couldn't see but felt, nonetheless.

The failed mission was a message, one that read loud and clear — you are not as untouchable as you believe. Max's response would have to be equally clear. He would find the traitor, and he would end this game of cat and mouse on his terms.

As he parted ways with Hammond, the Colonel's parting words were a warning: "Be careful, Max. You're in uncharted waters now."

Max walked away, his resolve hardening. The web of lies that had been spun around him would be untangled, and he would be the one to cut the threads. The city, with its ever-moving tides of people and traffic, was a chessboard, and Max was a king moving to checkmate.

*

Max's departure from the park was like the retreat from a battlefield, leaving behind the dead and the wounded, carrying only the scars and the lessons learned. The walk back to his urban stronghold was a march through the enemy territory of his own making, every face a potential spy, every car that lingered too long a possible threat.

In the solitude of his safe house, Max's mind was a tempest, thoughts crashing into one another with the force of a gale. The mission's failure was not just a misstep; it was an unravelling of everything he had believed to be true about his role in this shadow war.

Max booted up his secure computer systems, a network of his own creation, untouched by any other hands. He began to retrace every mission, every contact, every piece of intel that had passed through his network. If there was a mole, a traitor who had set them up, there would be a trail, no matter how well covered.

Hours passed, and Max's eyes grew heavy with the strain of analysis. Lines of code, encrypted messages, financial transactions — they all told a story, but it was like reading a book where half the pages were ripped out.

A breakthrough came in the form of an anomaly, a small discrepancy in a financial ledger that didn't match the rest. It was a clue, a thread hanging loose from the fabric of their operations. Max pulled at it, unravelling the trail of digital breadcrumbs that led him to a name: Carlos Ramirez.

Ramirez was the key. His name had surfaced as a survivor of the warehouse explosion, but as Max dug deeper, he found that Ramirez was more than just a lucky soul who had escaped death. He was a ghost in the system, his financial records a maze of shell companies and dead ends.

Max needed to find Ramirez again, knowing he would have scattered following their first encounter, to confront him, to understand his role in the setup. But as he prepared to leave, a knock at the door froze him in place. He approached cautiously, weapon at the ready.

The figure that greeted him was unexpected — Colonel Hammond, his face etched with urgency. "Max, we've got a problem," he said without preamble. "Ramirez is dead."

The words hit Max like a physical blow. Another casualty in a game that was growing deadlier by the day.

Hammond stepped inside, his eyes scanning the room, taking in the maps, the photos, the web of conspiracy that

Max had been tracing. "I've just come from the scene," Hammond continued. "It was made to look like a suicide, but we both know better."

Max's fists clenched the anger and frustration a fire in his belly. "Set up to take a fall," he growled. "Someone's tying up loose ends."

"Which means you're getting close to something they want buried," Hammond said. "You've rattled someone's cage, Max. And they're rattling back."

The revelation that the failed mission was a setup, now with a dead man as evidence, was the spark that lit the fuse. Max's mission had just become a vendetta. Whoever was orchestrating this betrayal had just signed their own death warrant.

As Hammond left, Max returned to his screens, his every movement deliberate and purposeful. The hunt for truth was now a hunt for vengeance. The traitor had revealed their hand, and Max was ready to play his.

The city outside was unaware of the storm that was brewing within the walls of Max's safe house. The hunt was on, the prey was known, and Max was a hunter without equal. The collateral damage of their war had just become personal, and Max was a weapon aimed squarely at the heart of the conspiracy.

*

Max sat alone, the digital glow of his screens painting him in shades of blue and grey. The death of Carlos Ramirez had transformed the mission. It was no longer just about uncovering a traitor; it was about justice for the fallen, a vow of retribution for the collateral damage caused by a war they never asked to join.

He pored over the data once more, seeking the connection that would lead him to the mole. The anomaly in the financial ledger that led to Ramirez was a clue, but it was not the end of the trail. There had to be more — a mistake, a slip — something the traitor had overlooked.

As he combed through the digital records, cross-referencing and analysing, a pattern began to emerge. Transactions that didn't fit the narrative, communications that ended abruptly. They were breadcrumbs, and they led to a startling revelation — the traitor was someone with high-level access to operational data.

Max's mind raced as he considered the implications. This wasn't just a mole; this was someone with intimate knowledge of their strategies, their tactics, their movements. Someone who had been with them since the beginning.

The pieces of the puzzle clicked into place, forming a picture Max had refused to see until now. It was a betrayal of the highest order, a violation of the brotherhood of arms he had held sacred.

He knew what had to be done. The traitor had to be confronted, exposed, dealt with. But he would proceed with caution; the enemy was cunning, and Max would not underestimate them again.

Night had fallen when Max set out, the city a play of light and shadow. He moved through the streets with a single purpose, his destination clear. The confrontation would be on his terms in a place of his choosing.

The place was an old warehouse, abandoned and forgotten by the city's relentless march forward. It was here that Max would face the traitor, here that the truth would be laid bare.

He waited in the shadows, the silence his companion.

Then a figure emerged from the darkness — Yuri. The man's steps were hesitant, his posture that of a condemned man walking to his execution.

"Yuri." Max's voice was ice, his form stepping out into the dim light. "Why?"

The conversation that followed was a symphony of lies and truths. Yuri's justifications, his reasons — they fell on deaf ears. Max listened, his expression unreadable, the betrayal a wound that ran deep.

The failed mission, the setup, it had all been orchestrated. Yuri had played them from the start, a double agent in a game where lives were the currency.

"I had no choice," Yuri pleaded, but Max's response was a cold echo in the empty space.

"There's always a choice."

The silence that followed was a chasm between them, a gulf of trust that could never be bridged again.

As Max left the warehouse, leaving Yuri to the darkness, he knew that the war had just begun. The traitor had been unmasked, but the network they served remained, a hydra with many heads.

Max's vow of retribution was a promise to the innocent lives lost, a pledge written in the ashes of betrayal. He would dismantle the network, piece by piece, until justice was served.

Chapter 15: Questioning Morality

The Echoes of Doubt

Max's every step was shadowed by the ghost of what had transpired; the echoes of the explosion and the screams of the innocent were a cacophony that only he could hear. He'd set out to dismantle a corrupt system, to punish those who operated above the law. But now, he found himself questioning the very fabric of his mission. Was his brand of vigilante justice just another form of chaos in an already fractured world?

As Max wandered the city, lost in his turbulent thoughts, he stumbled upon a small, tucked-away memorial garden. It was here he met Mrs Agnes Sullivan, an elderly woman with gentle eyes and a presence that seemed to calm the disquiet in his soul.

Agnes was tending to a rose bush, her hands skilled and sure as they pruned and cared for the living thing before her. She looked up at Max, and in her gaze, he found an unexpected reservoir of understanding.

"You look like you're carrying the world on your shoulders, young man," she said, her voice carrying the lilt of a life lived long and fully.

Max hesitated, then took a seat on a nearby bench. "It feels that way," he admitted.

Agnes set down her gardening tools and joined him. "I grew up in a generation that lived through a war. Seen the best and worst of humanity," she shared, her eyes reflecting memories of a past era. "I've learned that violence only begets violence. It takes a stronger person to break that cycle."

Her words struck a chord in Max, resonating with the part of him that longed for a different path.

As the conversation flowed, Max found himself opening up about the collateral damage of his past, the lives lost, and his role in it all. Agnes listened, her expression one of compassion rather than judgment.

"You've been given a chance to make a difference, but the direction you take is up to you," she advised, her hand resting lightly on his arm. "Sometimes, the hardest battles we fight are with ourselves."

The sun began to dip below the horizon, casting a warm glow that seemed to wrap around them. In Agnes's simple wisdom, Max found a solace he hadn't known he'd been seeking.

The day waned, and Max knew he had to leave, to return to the shadows from which he'd emerged. But Agnes's words lingered, a counterpoint to the cacophony that had been haunting him.

As he walked away from the memorial garden, Max felt the weight of his internal conflict reaching a boiling point. The path he had chosen was fraught with darkness and doubt. Could he continue down this road, knowing the potential cost?

Night had fallen by the time Max sought the counsel of George Blackwell, a former mentor whose own moral compass had always pointed true north. Blackwell had seen the darkness of the world and had come out the other side with his integrity intact.

Max laid bare his soul, confessing his fears and his uncertainty. Blackwell listened, his seasoned eyes reflecting the moonlight that filtered through the window.

"You've reached a crossroads," Blackwell finally said.

"The decisions you make now will define you. But remember, redemption is not beyond reach, nor is change beyond possibility."

Max absorbed the words, feeling the tumult within him subside into a semblance of clarity. It was time to make a decision, one that would alter his course irrevocably.

As the night wore on, Max sat in the quiet of his safe house, a decision forming in the depths of his conscience. He could no longer blindly follow a path of retribution that risked the innocent. There had to be another way, a means to achieve justice without becoming the very thing he fought against.

The next morning, Max would begin anew, his actions influenced by the wisdom of a woman who had seen the cost of war and a mentor who believed in the power of change. His vigilante justice would take a different form, one not mired in the same violence he sought to eradicate.

*

Max spent the night in a restless sea of contemplation, the words of Agnes Sullivan and George Blackwell echoing in his head. The first rays of dawn brought clarity, a resolution hardening within him. He could no longer be the judge, jury, and executioner. There had to be a line, and he had to draw it before he lost himself completely in the darkness.

With the new day came a new resolve. Max decided to reach out to contacts he had been wary of, to seek a different path for his crusade. The network he had been fighting could be dismantled with precision, without the need for more bloodshed. It was a risk, a deviation from the lone-wolf approach he had always taken, but the stakes had changed.

The city was waking up, and with it, the machinery of daily life began to churn. Max found himself outside the small café where he had met with Larkin, the memory of their conversation fresh in his mind. It was time to set a new plan in motion, one that would require allies.

He sent a message to Larkin, proposing a meeting. If they were to proceed, it would be with a shared understanding of the new rules — no more collateral damage.

The meeting with Larkin was brief, the air between them charged with unspoken tension. Larkin listened as Max laid out his new approach, his face unreadable.

"You're changing the rules of engagement," Larkin finally said, his voice neutral.

"We never set out to hurt the innocent," Max replied firmly. "It's time we remember who we're fighting for."

Larkin nodded slowly, the implications of Max's decision weighing heavily on him. "Alright," he agreed. "But we need to be smarter, more strategic."

The rest of the day was a whirlwind of activity. Max reached out to old contacts, re-establishing lines of communication he had let go cold. Each conversation was a step towards building a new coalition, one that would operate within the bounds of a morality that Max was redefining for himself.

He knew that some would see this as weakness, but Max saw it as strength. To change course required courage, especially when it would have been easier to continue down the path of vengeance.

As the sun set, Max felt the weight of the past few

days begin to lift. He was still a warrior, but now he fought with a clearer sense of purpose, one that didn't compromise the values he held dear.

That night, as Max prepared for the days ahead, he felt a sense of peace that had eluded him for so long. The road ahead would be fraught with danger, but it was a road he chose with a clear conscience.

The city's nocturnal symphony played on while silent battles were fought in its shadows. But Max knew that each quiet victory was a note in a larger harmony, a song of justice that he was slowly composing.

*

Max had always known that the night was full of eyes, but now he felt them more than ever, watching as he walked a tightrope between the man he was and the man he aspired to be. The silent city seemed to hold its breath, reflecting Max's internal struggle. The decision to change tactics wasn't just a shift in strategy; it was a transformation of self.

The early evening found Max at a small, quiet bar, an unlikely place for a man whose life was steeped in shadows. The dim light and hum of soft conversations were a backdrop to the pivotal meeting unfolding in a secluded corner.

George Blackwell sat across from him, a figure from a life that seemed both a lifetime ago and just yesterday. Blackwell's eyes held a depth of understanding that came from years of navigating the grey areas of morality in service to a greater good.

"You've made the right choice, Max," Blackwell said, his voice carrying the weight of conviction. "The line between right and wrong is often blurred, but you must draw it somewhere."

Max listened, his mentor's words reinforcing the new direction he had chosen. "The cost was becoming too high," Max admitted, the words tasting like truth.

They discussed tactics and alliances, the conversation ebbing and flowing around the rocks of ethical dilemmas and the hard decisions that came with them. Blackwell had contacts, people who could help — not with guns or brute force, but with information, with access, with the power to influence from the inside.

The new path would be dangerous, fraught with the risk of exposure and the ever-present shadow of betrayal. But it was a path walked with the light of conviction, and Max found strength in that.

As the night deepened, Max left the bar with a network of new contacts and a burgeoning plan. He would dismantle the corruption that plagued the city, not with bullets, but with truth. It was a more complex, more challenging battle, but it was one worth fighting.

Max lay in his bed that night, the events of the past few days swirling in his mind. The sound of Agnes Sullivan's voice, the steady gaze of Colonel Hammond, the strategic mind of George Blackwell — they had all played a part in bringing him to this juncture.

He thought of the innocent lives lost, the collateral damage of a war they never knew existed. Their memory would be the bedrock of his renewed crusade, a silent vow that their deaths would not be in vain.

The quiet of the safe house was a balm to the turmoil within Max. He was at the centre of a maelstrom he himself had conjured. But he was no longer the tempest; he was the calm, the resolve, the promise of a new dawn.

As the first light of morning filtered through the curtains, Max rose. There was work to be done, contacts to meet, information to be gathered. He was a man on a mission, a mission that had evolved, as he had.

The city would awaken to a new day, unaware of the man who moved through its streets with a quiet determination. Max was a warrior reborn, his every step a testament to the power of change.

*

The city was stirring to life as Max stepped out of his safe house, the crisp morning air soothing to his wearied spirit. With each breath, he felt the weight of the previous night's decisions solidifying into a suit of armour, tempered with the wisdom of Agnes Sullivan and forged in the strategic fires of George Blackwell's counsel.

Max had a series of meetings lined up, each one a careful step on the newly-charted path he was carving out for himself. He met with informants, not in dark alleys or secluded warehouses, but in bustling cafés and crowded parks, places where the everyday joy and pain of life flowed freely. His questions were no longer just about targets and timings; they probed deeper, seeking the root of the rot he aimed to excise.

With each piece of intelligence gathered, Max built a clearer picture of the network he was up against. It was a tapestry of greed and power, each thread interwoven with the next in a complex pattern of exploitation. But where once he would have pulled on those threads with force, now he sought to untie them, to unravel the tapestry without tearing it.

The change in Max did not go unnoticed. His contacts

whispered of a new approach, one that didn't end in the usual bloodshed. It was a ripple of change in the underworld, a shift in the winds of the city's hidden wars.

As the day progressed, Max's resolve only grew stronger. He felt as if he was waking from a long sleep, his senses sharpened, his mind clear. The path of violence he had walked seemed like a distant memory, a chapter of his life that was closing, giving way to a story yet to be written.

The sun was dipping below the skyline, painting the city in hues of orange and pink, when Max's phone vibrated with a message. It was from Larkin, a simple statement that read, *I'm in*. The alliance, it seemed, was holding, the foundation of their concerted efforts against a common enemy growing stronger.

That night, Max met with Colonel Hammond once more. They stood on a rooftop overlooking the city, the sprawling metropolis a map of the lives they sought to protect.

"War is not just fought with weapons, Max," Hammond said, his gaze on the horizon. "It's fought with hearts and minds. You're proving that."

Max's reply was a nod, his eyes reflecting the last light of day. "I'm tired of the darkness," he confessed. "It's time to bring some light to this fight."

The decision Max had made was like a declaration, a promise to those who had fallen and those who still stood. He was a warrior, yes, but a warrior of a different kind now — a conscious one, whose every action would be measured not just by its efficacy, but by its righteousness.

As Max looked out over the city, he knew the road ahead would be fraught with challenges. But for the first time in a long while, he felt hope. Hope that the war he was waging could be won without losing himself in the process.

Chapter 16: The Journalist's Lead

Unravelling Secrets

Rebecca Turner sat in the cluttered cubicle that served as her office at the London Chronicle, surrounded by stacks of papers and a collage of sticky notes. Her eyes were fixed on the computer screen, where articles, photos, and notes formed a web of intrigue. She was on the verge of a breakthrough, her journalistic instincts telling her that the scattered pieces before her were connected by a common thread — the vigilante actions that had been a thorn in the side of London's criminal underworld.

Meanwhile, Max was threading his way through the city's veins, the network of back alleys and shadowed streets that he knew like the back of his hand. He was aware of the new threat, a determined journalist who had taken too keen an interest in his missions. Rebecca Turner was becoming a name that elicited caution rather than curiosity.

The game was delicate, a balancing act between continuing his operations and ensuring that the keen eyes of the press didn't pry too deeply. Rebecca's tenacity was admirable, but it was a wildcard that Max couldn't afford to overlook.

A tip had brought Max close to a warehouse by the docks, a place that promised more secrets to uncover. But as he positioned himself atop a nearby building, surveying the scene with his night-vision binoculars, a figure in the distance caught his attention. It was DI Sarah Bennett, her silhouette unmistakable even from afar. The close call was a stark reminder of the fine line Max walked — one misstep and he could fall into the hands of the law he sought to serve from the shadows.

The night passed with Max remaining just out of Bennett's reach, a ghost in the urban landscape. But the encounter was a sobering one, emphasizing the risks that came with every move he made.

The following day, Rebecca's investigation took a dramatic turn. Her sources had been reliable, a mixture of whispers from the streets and leaks from within the Met. But nothing had prepared her for the discovery that linked a string of vigilante actions to a high-profile crime that had rocked the city months ago.

Her heart raced as she connected the dots, the implications staggering. Could the enigmatic figure behind these actions be tied to something much bigger, much more dangerous than anyone had realised?

She leaned back in her chair, the weight of the potential story pressing upon her. This was more than just a scoop; it was a revelation that could change everything.

Max, unaware of Rebecca's discovery, continued his work. He had cultivated a network that operated on trust and discretion, but Rebecca's digging threatened to expose him to daylight.

As he planned his next move, he considered the journalist. Rebecca Turner was not an enemy, but her pursuit of the truth could inadvertently become one. Max knew he had to be cautious, to stay one step ahead not only of the criminals he pursued but also of those who pursued him.

The city was a chessboard, and Max was a knight

moving in silence. But the game was changing, new players emerging, each with their own agenda. Max's fight for justice was evolving into a fight to remain an enigma, the faceless crusader in a city full of prying eyes.

*

Rebecca's fingers paused over her keyboard, her mind racing with the implications of her latest findings. The link she'd uncovered between the vigilante's actions and the high-profile crime was more than just a story; it was a potential crisis. The pieces of the puzzle were coming together, but with each piece, the picture grew increasingly dangerous. Journalism was about exposing the truth, but Rebecca knew that some truths came with a heavy cost.

Max moved through the night, a shadow among shadows, always watching, always aware. He had operations to conduct, a mission to continue, but now he had to account for the watchful eyes of a determined journalist. Rebecca Turner had become a thread in the tapestry of his crusade — one that could unravel everything if pulled too hard.

His work led him to the underbelly of the city, to the places where light seldom reached and voices were seldom heard. It was here that Max gathered the intelligence he needed, always careful to remain unseen, a whisper in the dark.

The close call with DI Sarah Bennett the night before had left him wary. Their paths had almost crossed, a near encounter that would have brought an unwanted end to his mission. Bennett was a formidable adversary, dedicated and relentless in her pursuit of justice — qualities Max respected even as he sought to evade her grasp.

The day brought a sense of urgency. Max's contacts had become more cautious, their meetings more coded. The landscape was shifting, and Max with it. He had to be more than the vigilante; he had to be a phantom, untouchable and ever elusive.

A meeting with one of his most trusted allies revealed the extent of Rebecca's investigation. She was drawing connections that were too close to the truth, her questions too pointed, her gaze too keen. Max knew he had to address this new complication.

As the sun began to set, painting the city in shades of gold and amber, Max found himself outside the London Chronicle building. It was a calculated risk, but necessary. He slipped inside, a face in the crowd, and made his way to Rebecca's cubicle.

She looked up in surprise as Max approached, her expression one of shock that quickly shifted to recognition. "You," she said, the word a breath in the quiet hum of the newsroom.

Max nodded, his presence an answer to the unspoken questions in her eyes. "We need to talk," he said, his voice low and urgent.

Rebecca glanced around, then gestured to a small meeting room. They entered, the door closing with a soft click that seemed to seal their fates.

The conversation that followed was a dance of revelation and concealment. Rebecca had questions, and Max offered truths, but only those he could afford to share. He acknowledged her drive, her passion for the truth, but he also painted the picture of a city on a knife-edge, a balance that could too easily tip into chaos.

"You're playing a dangerous game," Rebecca said, her journalistic instinct for the story warring with the very real danger Max represented.

Max met her gaze, his eyes a mirror of the city he fought for. "It's the only way to bring about change," he replied, his voice carrying the weight of every action he had taken, every line he had drawn in the invisible sand.

*

The clandestine meeting room was a world away from the dark corners where Max usually operated. Here, facing Rebecca across a stark table, the usual anonymity of the night was stripped away, replaced by the stark fluorescent reality of her journalistic determination.

Rebecca's mind was a whirlwind, her journalistic instincts at war with the human element before her. She had questions, so many questions, but the gravity of Max's presence grounded her. "You're saying there's more at stake here?" she asked, the pen in her hand forgotten.

Max nodded, his expression sombre. "There's a network, a web of corruption that's not just criminal; it's systemic. If you pull on one thread without understanding the entire tapestry, it could all unravel, harming those it should protect."

Rebecca considered his words, the potential story of her career weighed against the potential cost of lives and stability. "And you're what, the city's silent guardian?" she asked, a touch of scepticism in her voice.

Max leaned forward, his gaze never wavering. "I'm someone who saw an opportunity to make a difference, albeit from the shadows."

As they parted, Rebecca with a promise to consider

her next steps carefully, Max returned to the night, his path ever winding, ever hidden. The journalist's lead had brought a new dimension to his mission, but Max was determined to stay the course.

As they spoke, DI Bennett was only blocks away, her own investigation leading her down parallel paths that dangerously flirted with Max's world. The vigilante was a question mark in her case files, but she was drawing ever closer to an answer.

The close call Max had experienced the night before was not lost on him. Bennett's dedication was commendable, her skills formidable. He respected her, perhaps more than any other adversary he had faced. But respect was a luxury that could not slow his mission.

After leaving Rebecca, Max felt the gravity of the situation pressing down upon him. The journalist's lead, the close encounters with law enforcement — they were tightening the noose around the operation he had fought so hard to keep covert.

The night was young as Max slipped through the city, the echo of his meeting with Rebecca a constant murmur in his mind. He had to move quickly now, to act before the story Rebecca was piecing together could threaten the delicate ecosystem of his campaign against corruption.

The following days were a blur of motion, Max's operations escalating in both intensity and risk. His network was tightening, information flowing like a lifeline as he worked to stay one step ahead of both Rebecca's exposé and Bennett's pursuit.

The close call with Bennett had left Max's heart hammering, a reminder that the line he walked was razor-thin. They were in a dance of shadows, Bennett, and he, always just a beat out of sync. It was a dance that could not last forever.

Rebecca's investigative prowess had unearthed a connection between Max's vigilante actions and a high-profile crime that had gone unsolved for months. It was a link that could not be ignored, a piece of the puzzle that suddenly fit all too well.

As Max absorbed the implications, the world around him seemed to pause, the city holding its breath. The story Rebecca had uncovered was explosive, a truth that could shatter the fragile balance Max had fought so hard to maintain.

Now, faced with the consequences of his actions, Max had to decide how to proceed. The truth was a powerful weapon, but in whose hands would it do the most good?

*

Max's mind raced as he processed the information that Rebecca had uncovered. The linkage of his covert activities and a major unsolved crime could not have come at a worse time. The narrative he had carefully constructed to stay below the radar was unravelling, and the consequences were sure to follow.

Sitting alone in the dim light of his safe house, Max weighed his options. Every move up until now had been calculated to avoid this exact scenario. Yet there it was, a glaring connection that put both his mission and his life at risk. It was time for damage control.

Rebecca sat at her desk, the glow of her computer screen casting a pallor over her determined face. The story she had pieced together was more than a career-defining scoop; it had the potential to ripple through the city's power structure, causing untold fallout. She held her breath as she readied the article for publication, aware of the lives it could change, including her own.

Meanwhile, DI Bennett was closing in. The recent developments in her case had provided new leads, and her intuition told her she was on the verge of a breakthrough. The vigilante who had been a ghost in her investigation was now leaving traces, faint but discernible. She reviewed the evidence laid out before her, a mosaic of clues that were beginning to form a coherent picture.

The close call with Max had been a moment of pure instinct. She had felt his presence, sensed the vigilante's shadow before it slipped away. It was only a matter of time before their paths crossed again, and she intended to be ready.

The hours ticked by as Max enacted his contingency plans. He reached out to his network, warning them of the potential storm on the horizon. Every ally, every contact was on high alert. The foundations they had built together were shaking, and Max could only hope they were strong enough to withstand the pressure.

A critical decision lay before him, influenced by the guidance of George Blackwell. Max had always operated in the shadows, but perhaps it was time to step into the light, to confront the narrative head-on. It was a gamble, one that went against every instinct he had, but the rules had changed.

As the city slept, Max made his move. He met with Rebecca, providing her with a new angle and new information that would steer her investigation away from the dangerous precipice it was headed towards. It was a calculated risk, divulging just enough to keep her from the truth he couldn't afford to have revealed.

Rebecca listened, her reporter's scepticism battling with the understanding she saw in Max's eyes. They were two sides of the same coin, seeking justice in their own ways, and in that moment, a silent agreement was forged. Her article would go forward, but with Max's amendments.

Morning broke over the city, the first light of day heralding a time of change. Max's face was not among the crowds that moved through the streets, his presence erased from the world he had influenced from the shadows.

Rebecca's article hit the newsstands, sending shockwaves through the city. It was explosive, yet it protected the invisible line Max had drawn. And somewhere in the shadows, DI Bennett read the lines, knowing there was more to the story, a deeper truth that was still to be uncovered.

Chapter 17: Crossfire

In the Line of Fire

Max's latest operation was supposed to be straightforward: infiltrate a warehouse where a key exchange in Kozlov's network was taking place. But as he positioned himself in the dark rafters, the warehouse doors burst open and Larkin's team stormed in. Almost simultaneously, the sound of sirens wailed in the distance — law enforcement was on their tail.

The situation deteriorated rapidly. Max watched as Larkin's men took positions, unaware of the police closing in. Max had a choice: intervene and risk exposure or slip away and let the chaos unfold. His decision was made when he saw a figure he recognised.

Alexei Morozov was an old contact from Max's military days, a man who had once saved his life during a covert operation gone wrong. Alexei, former Polish Special Forces and now a freelance operator, had clearly been drawn into Kozlov's web. Their eyes met, and a silent understanding passed between them. They were not enemies here, not today.

Max descended from the shadows, moving with purpose through the confusion. "Alexei," he called out softly, ducking a stray bullet.

"Max? I thought you were a ghost," Alexei replied, surprise etched on his weathered face.

"In many ways, I am," Max answered. "But right now, we need to get out of this alive."

As they communicated with hand signals above the roar of gunfire, a plan took shape. They needed to create a diversion, something to give both Larkin's team and the police the slip. Working together amidst the flying bullets, they rigged a forklift with a makeshift incendiary device.

The explosion was deafening, a shockwave that rippled through the warehouse and provided the necessary distraction. Max and Alexei moved quickly, now not just avoiding Larkin's men but also dodging the law enforcement officers who had breached the building.

In the aftermath, as sirens and smoke filled the air, Max and Alexei found a moment's respite in the chaos. "I didn't expect to find you in the middle of this mess," Max said, catching his breath.

Alexei grimaced, wiping soot from his face. "Kozlov's money is good, but I didn't sign up for a war with the police."

A revelation dawned on Max — Alexei's position within Kozlov's organisation could be exploited. He was the unexpected asset Max needed.

"Help me take Kozlov down," Max proposed, his gaze intense.

Alexei considered the offer, the sound of approaching footsteps lending urgency to his decision. "Alright," he agreed, "but we do this my way."

As they slipped away into the night, Max could feel the game changing. The operation had been salvaged, and with Alexei's insider knowledge, a new avenue to dismantle Kozlov's network had opened. The night had been a crossfire, but Max had emerged with something more valuable than he had anticipated — an ally with access to the enemy's lair.

*

Under the cloak of chaos, Max and Alexei made their retreat through the labyrinth of shipping containers. The disarray at the warehouse was their smokescreen, granting them precious minutes before the clash between Larkin's team and law enforcement would turn into an all-out manhunt for anyone involved.

"Got a place we can lay low?" Max asked, vaulting over an obstruction with an agility born of necessity.

Alexei nodded, leading the way to an unassuming panel van parked a discreet distance from the warehouse. "I keep a few tricks up my sleeve," he said, his voice rough with the adrenaline still coursing through him.

Inside the van, equipped with an array of surveillance monitors, Max and Alexei surveyed the aftermath of their escape. Through static-laden feeds, they watched as DI Bennett directed her team with a commanding presence that Max both respected and evaded.

"Who's she?" Alexei enquired, noting Max's fixed stare.

"DI Sarah Bennett. She's sharp," Max replied. "Too sharp."

A tense silence fell over the pair as they considered their next move. Alexei had made his choice, but the reality of standing against Kozlov was a heavy one.

The next hours were a dance of strategy and survival. Max and Alexei plotted their moves; each step forward was carefully weighed against the risks. Their newfound partnership was a fragile thing, yet it held the promise of turning the tide in their silent war.

Max's phone buzzed with a message from an encrypted sender. It was Larkin, his message concise: *Situation contained. Meet at Rally Point Echo.*

Alexei raised an eyebrow, a silent question. Then he asked, "So, you're rolling with ex-SEALs now? You know

Americans only ever serve Americans, right? Someone higher is always pulling the strings."

"A temporary truce," Max explained. "Larkin and I, we have an understanding."

Their meeting with Larkin was terse. The dockside clash had left everyone on edge, and the presence of law enforcement had escalated the stakes.

"We can't afford a screw-up like this again," Larkin stated, his eyes cold as steel. "Next time, we might not walk away."

Max agreed, the sentiment echoing his own thoughts. "We need to hit Kozlov where it hurts, dismantle his operation piece by piece."

"And how do you propose we do that?" Larkin challenged.

Max turned to Alexei. "He's going to get us inside."

Alexei's introduction to Larkin was a study in cautious diplomacy. Two men from different worlds with a common enemy found themselves in an uneasy alignment of goals.

"We hit the financials, the logistics," Alexei suggested. "I have access to both."

The plan was daring, a surgical strike that required precision and a deep trust in each other's capabilities. Max could see the questions in Larkin's eyes, the same he had asked himself.

Could they trust Alexei? Was the enemy of their enemy truly their ally?

As night fell once again over the city, the trio dispersed, each to prepare for the operation that would either break Kozlov's grip on the city or break them. Max's mind was awhirl with the possibilities and the dangers. The crossfire at the docks had been a warning shot, a reminder of the fine line they trod.

Max now found himself caught between the indomitable force of Larkin and the immovable object of DI Bennett's law enforcement. It was a precarious position, one he had to navigate with care.

*

In the quiet before the storm, Max found himself at a crossroads of trust and necessity. Larkin's cooperation was crucial, but the introduction of Alexei, a ghost from Max's past now resurrected, added a new layer of complexity to the operation. They needed to strike Kozlov's operation, disrupt the financial flow, destabilize the logistics — actions that required a mole on the inside. Alexei was that mole, but the question of his loyalty lingered like a shadow.

They reconvened in a nondescript safe house, a place off the grid where Max felt the walls didn't have ears. Larkin arrived first, his presence like a tightly coiled spring. Alexei was last, carrying with him the air of a man who had seen too much and yet had more to see.

"The plan," Max began, laying out a map of the city with various points marked, "is to dismantle Kozlov's operations piece by piece. We hit him in the resources, the money. We freeze his assets, flag his shipments, choke the life out of his network."

Larkin leaned over the map, his finger tracing the routes of Kozlov's known operations. "And how do you propose we do that without drawing attention?"

Alexei stepped forward, pulling out a slim laptop, the screen alive with lines of code and cascading numbers. "I have access to Kozlov's financials. With a few keystrokes, we can set off a series of transactions that will red-flag his accounts to every major financial institution."

The operation was set in motion under the cover of darkness. Max and Larkin provided the distraction, a well-timed heist on one of Kozlov's lesser caches of contraband, drawing the attention of both Kozlov's men and the watchful eyes of the law. Meanwhile, Alexei worked his digital magic, his fingers a blur as he navigated the labyrinth of the criminal financial network.

But as Max slipped through the night, a sense of unease settled over him. The operation had gone too smoothly, the responses too predictable. It wasn't until he heard the distant sound of sirens converging on their location that he realised they had walked into a trap.

Crossfire. The word rang in his ears as bullets began to fly, the air thick with the sound of chaos. They were caught in the middle, a literal crossfire between Kozlov's angered forces and the law enforcement drawn to the scene by their diversion.

Max and Larkin fought back to back, their years of training taking over as they fought their way out of the trap. But it was a voice on the Icom radio that gave them their chance, a voice that was both unexpected and familiar — Sgt. Liam Connor, Max's old comrade, now a Met detective and part of DI Bennett's team.

"Max, it's a setup," Liam's voice crackled through the static. "Get out now."

Despite Max's disbelief, the warning was all they needed. Using the chaos as cover, they retreated, disappearing into the night as quickly as they had come.

In the aftermath, as they licked their wounds and counted the cost, Alexei's true colours were revealed. "I didn't know about the trap," he insisted, his eyes haunted. "But I did what I came to do." He slid a USB drive across the table to Max. "Everything is there — names, dates, accounts. It's your move now."

The twist was a bitter pill to swallow. The operation had been a double-edged sword, yielding crucial information but exposing the fractures in their makeshift alliance. Max took the drive, his mind already racing with the possibilities it opened.

"We're just getting started," he promised, a steely resolve setting in. Kozlov had made his move, and now it was Max's turn to make his. The game was far from over.

Chapter 18: The Mercenary's Code

An Unlikely Meeting

Max's breath formed misty plumes in the cool night air as he navigated the derelict streets of London's East End. His contact had chosen an out-of-the-way pub, the kind that thrived on anonymity and the kind of discretion that money can't buy. The Bear had said he would be there — Dimitri 'The Bear' Petrenko, a man whose name was spoken in hushed tones, the kind of man who could either be a valuable ally or a formidable enemy.

The pub was dimly lit, with walls that could tell a thousand stories. As Max entered, the low murmur of conversations paused, a dozen pairs of eyes sizing him up before returning to their drinks. He spotted The Bear at a secluded table in the back, a hulking figure who seemed to command the space around him.

"Petrenko," Max said, nodding as he approached.

"Mr Max," Dimitri responded, his Russian accent thick and his handshake like a vice. "I was beginning to think you wouldn't show."

Max took a seat, the wooden chair groaning under his weight. "I'm interested in what you have to say about Kozlov's influence."

The Bear poured two glasses of vodka, pushing one towards Max. "To understanding," he toasted, and Max touched his glass to Dimitri's before taking a sip.

Dimitri leaned in, his voice a low rumble. "Kozlov is not just a thug; he's a visionary in his own twisted way. He's building an empire, and he's not afraid to topple anyone who stands in his way."

Max listened intently as The Bear outlined the extent of Kozlov's reach. It wasn't just the underworld that he had his fingers in; it was politics, high finance, and international logistics. Kozlov was a spider at the centre of a vast web.

"The man has his hands in too many pies," Dimitri continued. "He's ambitious, but ambition can make a man reckless."

Max pondered Dimitri's words, the gravity of the situation settling upon him like a leaden cloak. He needed more than just muscle and guns to bring Kozlov down; he needed information and leverage.

The Bear seemed to read Max's thoughts. "You need something concrete, yes? Evidence of his dealings, something that can't be washed away in the tides of corruption?"

Max nodded. "Exactly."

Dimitri smiled a grin that didn't quite reach his eyes. "I may have something for you. But it comes at a price."

The price turned out to be a job, a task that would benefit them both. Dimitri needed a shipment intercepted, one that was vital to Kozlov's operations. It was risky, a venture that would put Max directly in the crosshairs of Kozlov's wrath, but it was a necessary evil.

Max agreed to the terms. The operation would be a two-pronged approach; while Dimitri's men created a diversion elsewhere, Max would strike at the heart of the shipment, securing the evidence they needed to expose Kozlov's dealings.

As they shook hands, sealing their agreement, Max felt the weight of the mercenary's code binding him. It was a code of honour amongst those who operated in the shadows — a code that Dimitri lived by and now Max was a part of.

Max left the pub with a new sense of purpose. The night was silent, but the echoes of his meeting with The Bear rang loud in his ears. Kozlov had made many enemies, and now those enemies were aligning against him.

But as he made his way back to his safe house, a warning from Yuri Dubrovnik reached him, a text message that was as foreboding as it was cryptic: *Be careful how deep you swim, Max. The ocean is vast, and there are monsters lurking in the depths that even you can't fathom.*

Max stopped in his tracks, considering Yuri's words. The dangers of going too deep were real; he had seen what happened to those who got in over their heads. But he also knew that to take down a man like Kozlov, he would have to dive into those very depths.

*

The plan was simple in concept yet complex in execution. Max's role was to be the infiltrator, while Dimitri's men executed a diversionary raid on one of Kozlov's known drug dens across the city. Timing was critical; even a minor slip could spell disaster for both operations.

Max spent the days leading up to the operation in meticulous preparation. He scouted the warehouse where the shipment was due, a plain lifeless building that sat in the shadow of the city's industrial heart. Security was tight, with patrols at regular intervals and surveillance cameras sweeping the cold concrete expanse.

The night of the operation, the air was thick with the tension of impending action. Dimitri's men struck with the precision of a well-oiled machine, their assault on the drug den a calculated chaos that lit up the night. Police scanners erupted with the news, drawing the attention of the city's law enforcement as planned.

Max used the commotion to slip unseen into the warehouse district. The Bear's intel had been good; the guards were fewer, their attention split between their duties and the distant sirens. Max disabled the cameras with a localized EMP device, plunging the perimeter into electronic darkness.

He picked the lock of a service entrance and slipped inside, the smell of oil and metal greeting him. The warehouse was a maze of crates and containers, but Max moved with purpose, guided by the map he'd memorized.

He found the shipment hidden beneath a tarp in the back, a nondescript container that belied the value of its contents. As Max worked to open it, his ears pricked at the sound of footsteps. He stilled, his hand inching towards the gun holstered at his side.

It was then that Yuri's warning replayed in his mind, a stark reminder that he was swimming in dangerous waters. Max knew he wasn't alone, and the realisation was a cold splash of reality. He was in the lion's den, and the lions were prowling.

The container clicked open, revealing a stack of hard drives, each marked with a cryptic set of numbers. Max quickly began transferring them to his bag, aware that each second was precious.

Suddenly, the lights came on, flooding the warehouse with a harsh glow. Max was exposed, caught in the act. He dived behind a crate just as bullets began to ricochet off the metal walls.

Caught in the literal crossfire, Max had to think fast. He couldn't go back the way he'd come; it would be suicide. Instead, he spotted a high window, an escape route that would require a climb, but it was a chance.

He returned fire, providing cover for his ascent, and began to scale the shelving units. Bullets whizzed past, some so close he could feel their heat. He reached the window, smashing it with the butt of his gun and hoisting himself through the jagged opening.

Max tumbled into the outside, the cool night air a welcome relief. Alarms were blaring now, the warehouse a cacophony of noise and confusion. He didn't stop to catch his breath; he ran, clutching the bag of hard drives against his chest.

As he made his escape, he realised the full weight of what he'd done. He'd secured a small piece of Kozlov's empire, but at what cost? The warehouse operation would have repercussions, and Max knew that Kozlov would be on the warpath.

He disappeared into the night, a ghost once more, with the knowledge that the real battle was just beginning.

*

Max's escape from the warehouse was a blur of adrenaline and close calls. His heart thundered in his chest as he weaved through the labyrinth of alleyways, the stolen hard drives a weighty testament to his success — and to the new level of danger he had invited. The warehouse's alarms faded into the night, replaced by the pulsing of his own blood in his ears.

Once he was a safe distance away, Max allowed himself a moment to lean against the damp brick of a building, his breath visible in the chill of the night air. The mission had been a success, but the taste of victory was bittersweet. He had the information he needed to strike at the heart of Kozlov's empire, but the risks were mounting. Yuri's warnings rang in his ears, and he knew he couldn't ignore them.

Later, in the dim light of a safe house, Max examined the hard drives. Each one was a piece of a larger puzzle, and as he began to fit them together, the scope of Kozlov's influence became horrifyingly clear. It wasn't just the criminal underworld Kozlov had in his grasp; it was legitimate businesses, political figures, even elements within law enforcement.

Max realised he was dealing with an adversary whose reach extended far beyond anything he had anticipated. Kozlov wasn't just a kingpin; he was a spider at the centre of a global web.

It was then that Max received another warning from Yuri Dubrovnik, a message that arrived like an omen: *Max, you've gone too deep. There are things about Kozlov's operation even you can't understand. Pull back before it's too late.*

Yuri had at times been the voice of reason, a beacon of caution in Max's often reckless pursuit of justice. The message was clear: Max was in over his head, playing a game with stakes higher than he'd realised. He pondered his next move, the hard drives before him a Pandora's box of information that could either cleanse the city of its festering wounds or plunge it into further darkness.

Max needed guidance, and there was only one person who could provide it — The Bear. He was a man who knew the operator's code, who lived by a creed that balanced on the knife-edge between honour and survival. Their meeting was tense, the air thick with unspoken fears and the weight of decisions yet to be made. The

Bear's gym was quiet in the early morning hours, the two men alone amidst the echoes of past fights.

"I've seen what's on the drives," Max began, his voice steady despite the turmoil inside him. "Kozlov is more than a crime lord; he's a power broker."

Petrenko nodded, his expression grim. "I warned you, Max. Kozlov plays a game most don't even know exists."

Max leaned forward, his hands clasped tightly. "What would you do, Dimitri? You know the operator's code better than anyone."

The Bear's reply was measured, his eyes reflecting the harsh fluorescent lights. "The code says to fight, to stand against tyranny in all its forms. But it also says to survive, to live and fight another day."

Max considered The Bear's words. Survival meant pulling back, reassessing the situation. But fighting meant continuing on, using the hard drives to unravel Kozlov's empire piece by piece.

The choice was Max's to make, and it would define his path forward. The operator's code had brought him this far, and now it would guide him through the storm he had helped conjure.

*

The silence in the gym was palpable as Max weighed Petrenko's words. The code was clear, yet how it applied in this labyrinth of espionage and crime was anything but. Max knew that to survive, he had to be as ruthless in strategy as he was in combat.

"The code also speaks of justice," Max finally said, breaking the stillness. "If I have the means to bring down a man like Kozlov, don't I have the obligation to pursue it?"

Petrenko nodded, the corners of his eyes crinkling. "Justice is the endgame, Max. But remember, the path to justice is not a sprint, it's a marathon. Sometimes you have to circle back to move forward."

Max understood. A direct assault on Kozlov would be foolhardy. He needed a layered approach, one that dismantled Kozlov's network piece by piece without exposing himself to unnecessary danger.

Together, they outlined a strategy. Petrenko would use his contacts to spread disinformation, sowing discord within Kozlov's ranks. Max would continue to gather evidence, staying in the shadows, hitting Kozlov where it hurt most — his finances and his reputation.

"I have someone who can help," Max disclosed, thinking of John Larkin and the resources he commanded. "We'll need to coordinate our efforts, maintain a united front."

Petrenko grunted in agreement, his mind already turning over the logistics. "A three-pronged attack, then. We'll need to be precise, leave no trace."

They shook hands, the grip firm and resolute. It was more than a partnership; it was a brotherhood forged in the pursuit of a common cause.

As Max left the gym, the early light of dawn crept across the sky, painting the city gold and pink. He felt the weight of the hard drives in his bag, each gigabyte a piece of the puzzle that would dismantle Kozlov's empire.

He met with Larkin in an abandoned office building, the city sprawling out beneath them like a kingdom awaiting its king. Larkin listened to the plan, his eyes calculating the risks and the rewards.

"We'll need airtight alibis, ironclad ops. No room for error," Larkin stated, his gaze never leaving the cityscape.

Max nodded. "And if we pull this off?"

"Then Kozlov falls," Larkin replied, the ghost of a smile on his lips. "And we rise."

The plan was set. Max would play the role of the unseen hand, guiding the pieces into place for the final takedown. The Bear would be the shield, deflecting attention and creating turmoil within Kozlov's ranks. Larkin would be the sword, striking swiftly and without mercy when the time came.

As Max walked the streets, the city coming to life around him, he felt the burden of his mission. But it was a burden he chose to bear, a weight he carried with honour. The operator's code dictated his path, and he would follow it to the end — whatever that end might be.

Chapter 19: Deeper in the Web

The Web Tightens

The information from the hard drives Max had secured was a beacon in the murky waters of Kozlov's criminal operations. He had known that Kozlov was influential, but the depths of his reach were proving to be abyssal. Max now found himself in his safe house, surrounded by screens aglow with data, the lines between legality and crime blurred into a complex network of transactions, names, and illicit deals.

As Max delved deeper into the encrypted files, the links began forming a chilling picture. Kozlov wasn't just involved in the criminal underbelly; he was a puppet master, with tendrils extending into the highest echelons of global politics.

It was Dmitri Ivanov who provided the next piece of the puzzle. Ivanov was a hacker of unparalleled skill, a man whose conscience had driven him to turn against Kozlov. He arrived at Max's safe house under the veil of darkness, a messenger bearing the digital equivalent of Pandora's box.

"Dmitri," Max greeted, acknowledging the risk the hacker had taken to come here.

"Max," Ivanov replied, his voice weary, his eyes haunted by the things he'd seen in the digital shadows. "I have something for you. But it's dangerous information — the kind that makes you a target."

Max accepted the flash drive Dmitri offered, feeling the weight of consequence heavy in his hand.

The data was a revelation. Kozlov had been manipulating

political strings, orchestrating events to serve his interests. But it was the connection to a specific political figure that turned Max's blood cold. A high-ranking official, a name whispered in the corridors of power, was in Kozlov's pocket. This wasn't just corruption; it was a coup in slow motion.

Max was faced with a decision that would determine his next move. He could use this information to strike a critical blow to Kozlov, but in doing so, he would expose himself to the world. Alternatively, he could remain in the shadows, but that meant allowing Kozlov's machinations to go unchallenged.

The choice tormented Max as he sat alone, the ghostly glow of the computer screens the only light in the room. Ivanov's warning echoed in his mind, a grim reminder of the stakes. Max realised that his next actions could very well determine his fate in the criminal world.

He pondered the politician at the heart of the web, a person whose influence could sway policies, start wars, or end them. Kozlov had chosen his puppet well, and now Max held the scissors that could cut the strings.

Max decided to meet with Larkin and Petrenko to share the critical information and to formulate a plan. They convened at an abandoned warehouse, a place where their conversation would not be overheard.

"The political figure in question," Max began, revealing the name that had been shielded by layers of encryption and deniability.

Larkin's reaction was immediate, a frown creasing his brow. "This changes everything," he said, the implications clear to all of them.

Petrenko leaned against a rusted girder, his arms crossed. "If we move against him, we're not just fighting

Kozlov anymore. We're fighting an idea, a belief system that's rooted in the foundation of society."

The news lay heavy in the air between them. The politician was not just any official; he was a candidate for prime minister in the upcoming general election. Kozlov's plot was to place a leader at the head of the government who would dance to his tune.

Max's resolve hardened. "We can't allow this to happen. This is beyond criminal — it's an attack on the very democracy we stand for."

Larkin nodded, a grim set to his jaw. "We'll need to be strategic, swift, and silent. The public cannot know of this — not yet."

They parted ways, each man burdened with the knowledge of the task ahead. Max's place in the criminal world was now set on a collision course with the halls of power. He would either emerge victorious or not at all.

*

Max sat in the oppressive silence of his safe house, the gravity of his discovery anchoring him to the spot. The political figure, a well-respected leader poised for the prime ministerial seat, was nothing more than a marionette with Kozlov pulling the strings. The implications were staggering; this was no longer about street-level crime or even international syndicates. It was about the sovereignty of a nation.

He pondered his next steps. Public exposure would be met with denial and possibly a lethal silencing. To dismantle this plot, he would need incontrovertible proof delivered in a manner that left no room for doubt, no chance for Kozlov to wriggle free.

Max reached out to Ivanov, whose digital prowess had unearthed the conspiracy. *Dmitri, we need to meet.* Max's message was urgent. *It's about the politician. We need a way to expose him without exposing ourselves.*

Ivanov's reply was swift, a string of coordinates and a time. Max prepared, deleting the message instantly, leaving no trace of their communication.

In a small, quiet café, they sat across from each other, two men burdened with knowledge that could alter the course of history.

"We need something undeniable," Max stated, his voice low. "Something that ties Kozlov and the official together beyond a shadow of a doubt."

Ivanov nodded, his fingers tapping on the table. "There is one thing. A recorded conversation, encrypted and hidden within the drive. It's a confession in their own words."

The recording was a bombshell. It revealed a candid discussion between Kozlov and the official, outlining plans for the future, deals made in the shadows, and favours that would be owed from the highest office.

Max knew this was the key, but releasing it was akin to lighting a fuse that would ignite a political firestorm. The timing had to be perfect; the method of release had to be untraceable.

"Can you do it?" Max asked, his eyes locking with Ivanov's.

"Yes," Ivanov replied, a resolute steel in his voice. "But once it's done, there's no turning back."

As Max left the café, the streets of London seemed different, as if the city itself was holding its breath. He walked with purpose, knowing that the next steps would redefine his war against Kozlov.

Max's mind was a whirlwind of scenarios, each potential outcome more daunting than the last. He needed allies, and there were none better than Larkin and Petrenko. Together, they would have to act with precision, ensuring that the blow they struck was decisive and final.

The meeting with Larkin and Petrenko was a confluence of determined wills. They gathered under the guise of night, a triad of resolve against a common enemy.

"We release the recording, and we release it soon," Max asserted, laying out the plan. "Once the public hears it, Kozlov's grip on the political figure will crumble."

Larkin's response was a nod, his mind already calculating the fallout. "We'll need to prepare for the aftermath. Kozlov won't go down without a fight."

Petrenko added, "And the politician will fall with him. We're changing the course of the river, not just diverting the flow."

As they parted ways, the night seemed to close in around Max. The decision had been made, the path set. He would release the recording, expose the corruption, and watch as the dominoes fell. It was a path that could lead to redemption or ruin, but for Max, there was no choice. The truth was his weapon, and he would wield it without hesitation.

*

The plan was in place, a digital dagger poised to strike at the heart of Kozlov's manipulation. Max, Larkin, and Petrenko understood the gravity of their endeavour; it was a move that could redefine the nation's future. The evidence they held was volatile, and its release needed to be as anonymous as it was absolute.

Ivanov had orchestrated a network of proxies, servers bouncing across the globe to mask the true origin of the recording. The file itself was encrypted within layers of seemingly innocuous data, set to be released to major news networks and social media platforms simultaneously.

"This goes beyond any hacktivism I've done before," Ivanov admitted, his usual stoic demeanour betrayed by a flicker of apprehension. "This ... this is revolutionary."

Max placed a hand on Ivanov's shoulder, a silent show of solidarity. "It's necessary," he said firmly. "Kozlov's reach must be severed."

The countdown began, each second ticking away with the weight of consequence. Max watched from the safe house, the city sprawling before him unaware of the imminent upheaval. The tension was palpable, shared looks between the men speaking volumes of the unspoken risks they were all taking.

The moment arrived, and Ivanov initiated the release. There was no fanfare, no dramatic surge of electricity — just a single keystroke that sent ripples through the digital world, and soon, the real one.

The effect was immediate and explosive. The recording, clear and undeniable, hit the airwaves and the internet, sending shockwaves throughout the political landscape. Kozlov's puppet, the would-be prime minister, was exposed, his credibility shattered by the revelation of his collusion with the criminal mastermind.

The public outcry was instantaneous, a roar of collective betrayal that echoed through the halls of power. Kozlov's name became synonymous with corruption, his years of careful manipulation unravelling in a matter of hours.

Max and his allies watched the chaos unfold, a chaos they had orchestrated for the greater good. Larkin's connections within the intelligence community ensured that the fallout was contained, while Petrenko's influence kept the criminal elements from capitalizing on the disorder.

But the victory was not without its shadows. As the political figure's career disintegrated, the man himself became desperate, a loose end that posed a new threat. His downfall could lead him to divulge information, to point fingers in an attempt to save himself. Max knew they had to be prepared for any retaliation.

The day bled into night, and the city felt different, as if a storm had passed, leaving the air clearer but charged with the potential for new tempests. Max felt the fatigue of the long hours weigh on him, but there was no time for rest. They had struck a significant blow, yet Kozlov was still out there, wounded but dangerous.

Max realised that their actions had not just cut the strings of one puppet; they had begun the unravelling of Kozlov's entire network. Now they had to watch as it all came undone, ready to act on whatever came loose in the fray.

Max had taken a step deeper into the web, and now he had to navigate its sticky strands, wary of what lurked in its darker corners, ready to pounce.

*

As the city's heartbeat returned to a semblance of normality, the reverberations of Max's actions continued to echo through the streets, the homes, and the highest offices. The exposed MP became the focal point of a scandal that gripped the nation. Journalists, politicians, and the public alike were all trying to make sense of the implications of such a betrayal.

Max watched from the shadows as the dominos continued to fall. Kozlov's empire, once an indomitable fortress, now showed cracks in its foundation. The release of the recording had done more than clear the smog of deception; it had illuminated the dark corners where Kozlov and his ilk operated.

The political figure, now stripped of veneer and title, scrambled to disassociate himself from Kozlov, but the evidence was irrefutable. His career was in tatters, his ambitions dashed upon the rocks of his own greed.

The choice Max had made haunted him in the quiet moments. He had stepped into the role of judge and executioner, wielding the sword of truth against the Goliath of corruption. It was a role he had never sought, yet it was thrust upon him by the circumstances of his own creation.

In the midst of the turmoil, an unexpected piece of the puzzle fell into place. Dmitri Ivanov unearthed a connection that tied the politician to a high-stakes plot far more insidious than they had anticipated. Kozlov had been planning a coup not just of power but of ideology, seeking to install a regime that would serve his interests and his alone.

Max received the new information with a heavy heart. Each revelation seemed to pull him deeper into a web he was unsure he could ever escape. Yet with each thread uncovered, his resolve hardened. Kozlov had to be stopped, no matter the personal cost.

In a meeting with Larkin and Petrenko, the gravity of their situation became clear. They were no longer facing a criminal — they were up against a potential dictator in the making.

"We need to continue," Max asserted, his voice firm despite the fatigue that pulled at his edges. "Kozlov's ambitions are a threat to the fabric of our society."

Larkin nodded, his usual stoicism giving way to a rare flicker of concern. "We've started this. Now we have to finish it. We need to ensure Kozlov's influence is eradicated."

Petrenko's agreement was silent but no less determined. They all knew the stakes had never been higher.

As Max left the company of his unlikely comrades, the city around him seemed to be holding its breath, waiting for the next act in this drama to unfold. Max knew that their clandestine war was far from over; it had simply evolved into a new battle, one that would require all the cunning, strength, and fortitude they possessed.

In the days that followed, Max and his allies worked tirelessly, combing through the hard drives for any shred of evidence that could further dismantle Kozlov's schemes. They operated in the shadows, unseen warriors fighting for a future free from the corruption that sought to strangle their city and Max's country.

The web had been shaken, but the spider at its centre was still weaving, still plotting. Max understood that the true test of their mettle was just beginning.

Chapter 20: Shadows of Doubt

Reflections in the Dark

Max found himself at his favourite vantage point atop a city building, where the London skyline stretched before him, lights glittering against the encroaching darkness. Here, amid the hum of the metropolis, he allowed himself a moment of introspection. The recent victories, the unravelling of Kozlov's network: it all felt hollow when weighed against the internal turmoil he felt. His creed, the unspoken oath he had taken to fight corruption, now seemed like a double-edged sword. Every move against Kozlov had consequences, ripples that disturbed the waters of his conscience.

He was so deep in thought that he barely registered the faint click of the rooftop door. Footsteps approached, and Max didn't need to look to know who it was.

"Emily," he said, as he turned to face her.

"Max," she replied, her voice a mixture of warmth and concern. "I've been watching the news. Lily has had nothing else on. I see your handiwork."

Max's gaze returned to the horizon. "It had to be done. They had to pay."

Emily moved closer, her presence a reminder of a life once lived, of a time before the shadows. "But at what cost, Max?" she asked softly. "The Max I knew wouldn't recognise himself now."

Her words stung because they were true. The reflection Max saw in the mirror each morning was that of a stranger, a man driven by revenge and justice, yes, but at what point did one consume the other?

"You don't know what I've seen, Em," Max replied, his voice tight with emotion. "The depth of all this is madness, and their influence, the rot they spread through the city — it's pervasive."

Emily reached out, her hand tentative on his arm. "But where does it end, Max? When will you decide you've done enough?"

Max pulled away, a restlessness within him. "It ends when Kozlov is stopped, when the city is free from his grip."

Their conversation lingered with Max long after Emily had left. He was at a crossroads, one where the path he walked seemed to stretch into an unending night. The more he fought, the more elusive peace became. He wondered if he was becoming the very darkness he sought to vanquish.

The city lights flickered below, a mimicry of the stars hidden by their glow. Max felt the weight of his actions like a shroud, doubts creeping in like the first cool whispers of autumn. Had he been so focused on the fight that he'd lost sight of what he was fighting for?

In the solitude of the rooftop, the shadows of doubt grew long and deep. Max wrestled with the creeping sense that his campaign against Kozlov was transforming him into something unrecognizable. Each victory, each revelation of corruption brought satisfaction, yes, but also a gnawing sense of unease.

What if his quest for justice was leaving a trail of collateral damage in its wake? What if, in his pursuit to expose the darkness, he had allowed it to seep into his soul?

The night offered no answers, only the echo of his turmoil and the distant sound of a city that never truly slept.

The nights grew longer, and so did the list of Max's concerns. The crusade against Kozlov had taken its toll, and the echo of Emily's words haunted him. Max began to see the toll of his creed not just in the mirror but in the eyes of those he interacted with — acquaintances who once greeted him with nods now looked away, their gazes loaded with questions they dared not ask.

Max's next move was to seek solace in the place where his journey had begun. The army barracks stood as stoic as they had years ago, the walls reverberating with the echoes of a past life. Here, among memories of camaraderie and simpler times, Max sought clarity.

He walked the grounds, his presence unnoticed by the new crop of soldiers training under the watchful eyes of their instructors. It was here, in this cradle of discipline and order, that Max had been moulded into the soldier he had once been — the soldier he sometimes missed.

Max's phone broke his reverie, pulling him back to the present. "Max," called out a familiar voice. It was Liam Connor, his old friend, now bearing the rank of detective in the Met.

"Liam," Max responded, pleased to hear his friend's voice. "It's great to hear your voice, and thanks for the heads up in the warehouse." The contact had spoken volumes of the bond forged in service and battle.

"I heard about the operations, Max" Liam said, his tone careful. "You're making waves, Max. Dangerous ones." Again, Liam's tone was cautious and respectful. "After the incident with those scum-bag gangbangers, the cameras, the power, the brutal efficiency, I knew it could only have been you. Don't worry, no one here knows, but

Bennet is sharp and getting closer."

Max's jaw tightened. "It's necessary," he insisted. "You know as well as I do — the rot runs deep."

Liam sighed in unspoken acknowledgement. "But at what cost, mate? You've always been the one to charge ahead, but you're no longer in a warzone, Max. The rules are different here."

The conversation with Liam was a mirror of the one he'd had with Emily. It seemed everyone could see the path he was on except for Max himself.

He left the barracks with a sense of unease, the kind that settles in the stomach and clouds the mind. His resolve, once as solid as the concrete beneath his feet, now felt like shifting sand.

Max's next step took him to an old haunt, a quiet café where he and his military friends used to decompress after tours. The clink of coffee cups and the murmur of conversation were a balm to his frayed nerves.

It was there that Max experienced a moment of profound realisation. A veteran at a nearby table was speaking to a young girl, his granddaughter. The stories he told were not of battles and bloodshed but of hope, of the people he'd helped and the lives he'd seen changed for the better.

Max listened, the narrative striking a chord within him. His own story had been one of relentless pursuit, of a shadow war that seemed to have no end. Had he become so focused on tearing down Kozlov's empire that he'd forgotten the very people he was fighting to protect?

His return to the safe house was a walk through a fog of contemplation. Max knew he stood at the edge of a precipice, his next actions critical not just to his mission but to his very soul. The shadows of doubt were lengthening, and as he sat down to review the latest intelligence from Ivanov, he knew he faced a choice.

He could continue down the path of vengeance and retribution, or he could look for a way to heal the wounds his war had caused. The battle against Kozlov was far from over, but perhaps it was time for a new strategy — one that didn't just destroy but also rebuilt.

*

The clatter of the safe house door closing behind him echoed like a gavel in a courtroom, marking the commencement of his self-trial. Inside, the dim glow of the computer screens illuminated Max's furrowed brow as he sank into the chair that had become his command post. The data on the screens flickered, each byte a piece of the battle, each file a fragment of the war he waged.

Max replayed the veteran's words in his mind, their essence in opposition to the cacophony of conflict that had become his life's soundtrack. The old soldier had spoken of building, of helping, of leaving places better than he found them. Max's reflection on these sentiments was a stark realisation that his current trajectory promised no such legacy.

In the stillness, Max reached for the phone, dialling a number he had almost forgotten. It was a number that connected him to a life before the shadows, to a time when his motives were clear and his spirit less burdened.

The call connected, and Emily's voice came through, tinged with surprise. "Max? I didn't expect —"

"I just wanted to hear your voice," Max interrupted, his usual stoicism giving way to vulnerability. "To remind me of who I am ... or at least who I was."

There was a pause, a silence that spoke volumes before Emily replied, "You're someone who cares, Max. Someone who's always fought for what's right. Just ... don't lose yourself in the fight."

Her words were a balm to the raw edges of his resolve. Max ended the call with a promise to be careful, a promise he intended to keep. It was a pivotal moment, one that marked a shift in the tides of his soul. He was at a crossroads, and the direction he chose now would define not just the outcome of his war against Kozlov but also the essence of his being.

The choice before him was clear: continue down the path of relentless retribution or pivot towards a course that might offer not just victory but also healing.

As dawn crept through the blinds, casting slatted shadows across the room, Max stood and stretched, his body aching from the tension it housed. He approached the window, peering out at the city that was slowly waking up. London was a landscape of contradictions, of beauty and blight, of tradition and transformation.

Max knew that he could be an agent of change, not just a harbinger of justice. His actions could foster hope as much as they punished wrongdoing. The realisation was a seedling of purpose, one that began to take root in the fertile soil of contemplation.

He made his decision. Max would not abandon his mission — Kozlov's malignant influence had to be curtailed — but he would adjust his tactics. He would ensure that his actions didn't just dismantle but also paved the way for rebuilding. For every blow struck against the dark web of Kozlov's empire, Max would strive to support a foundation of restoration and growth.

This was the new creed he would live by — a balance between the warrior's code and the healer's compassion. It was a delicate equilibrium, fraught with challenges, but Max felt a renewed sense of purpose as he embraced this broader vision.

Part Three: Redemption or Ruin

Chapter 21: The Fateful Assignment

The Assignment's Burden

Max Fairchild sat in the half-light of dawn, the only illumination coming from the glow of his computer screen in the otherwise darkened safe house. The starkness of the room reflected the starkness of the choice laid before him. On the screen was a document, clinical in its brevity, outlining his new assignment. Yet it was the name at the centre of the document that ensnared his focus and tightened his chest: Eleanor Petrova.

Surveillance photos of Eleanor, vivid and numerous, were scattered across the desktop. Images captured in shadow and sunlight, through rain-streaked windows and across crowded rooms. She was always poised, a figure of elegance and control, whether she was stepping out of a London law firm or navigating the social labyrinths of high society. And always, that undercurrent of something more, something that the camera's indifferent eye could never quite capture.

Flashbacks flitted through Max's mind unbidden, his memories painting a very different picture to the woman depicted in the photos. There was a time when his missions were clearer, the objectives set and the enemy lines drawn with certainty. But Eleanor's case was different — it blurred the lines between past and present, between enemy and ... something else.

He remembered the first time her name had come up

in a briefing, almost two years back when Max had started to piece together the full extent of Kozlov's organisation and its firm hold on London's underworld. Mikhail Patrov, Kozlov's right hand, had mentioned his niece with a hint of pride in his gruff voice, a note that had stuck with Max through the years.

Now, as Max sifted through the details of Eleanor's life — her routines, her associations, her habits — he saw the meticulous patterns of a life lived in plain sight yet shrouded in secrets. Her role as a lawyer within Kozlov's empire and her connection to Patrov made her an adversary, yet there were moments, fragments of compassion and humanity, that seemed to pierce through the veil of her public persona.

Max leaned back, the creak of his chair breaking the silence. He grappled with the conflicting images of Eleanor — the professional, the niece, the enigma. She was a part of the world he had sworn to dismantle, but as he watched her moving through her life with a grace that seemed at odds with the coldness of her uncle's empire, doubt crept in.

He wrestled with the implications of his task. To eliminate Eleanor was to remove a key player in Kozlov's organisation, yet something about her — the way she paused to drop change into a homeless man's cup, the genuine smile as she spoke with an earnest young intern — made him question the righteousness of his mission.

As the sky outside lightened, signalling the start of a new day, Max closed his eyes, seeking clarity. The warrior in him knew the path he was expected to take. But the healer, the part of him that still believed in the chance for atonement and redemption, hesitated.

With a heavy heart, Max made his decision. He would not act from the shadows this time. He needed to meet

Eleanor Petrova, to look into her eyes and find the truth hidden behind the façade. Only then would he know the course to take — not as an executioner, but as a judge imposing justice in a world mired in shades of grey.

He powered down the computer, the finality of the decision settling in his bones. The assignment was clear, but the path he chose to follow was his own. Max Fairchild was no stranger to the darkness, but with Eleanor Petrova, he sought a light that might yet change everything.

*

The morning air was crisp as it seeped through the cracked window, yet the chill it brought was no match for the cold knot of apprehension in Max's stomach. He had seen the faces of many targets before, but Eleanor Petrova's visage haunted him, stirring a turmoil that felt both foreign and familiar.

Max pulled up the surveillance logs, the keystrokes echoing in the quiet room. As the detailed reports of Eleanor's daily life populated his screen, her pattern of life unfolded before him — a pattern that spoke of routine and yet whispered of covert intricacies. She navigated the corridors of power with a lawyer's acumen, defending the indefensible within the Kozlov organisation. But between the lines of recorded meetings and shadowed exchanges, there were anomalies that intrigued Max, points where Eleanor's professional facade seemed to slip, revealing glimpses of the woman beneath.

There was an intensity to her that the dossier couldn't convey, a passion that seemed to be at odds with her uncle's cold empire. Her connection to Mikhail Patrov was a bond of blood, but Max questioned how deep that loyalty ran. Was she bound by familial ties, or was there a fissure in her allegiance waiting to be exposed?

Max delved deeper into the files, watching video footage that showed Eleanor in the courtroom, commanding and articulate, battling with words as he did with weapons. And yet, in other, more candid moments, she displayed a gentleness that belied her connection to one of London's most ruthless men. It was in the way her hand rested on the small of a child's back, guiding them gently through a crowd, or the way her laughter rang clear and bright at a charity event, unburdened by the shadows of her lineage.

The warrior in Max wanted to dismiss these contradictions as irrelevant — after all, wasn't it the mark of the best in his business to be a chameleon? But the healer, the part that had been awakened by the tragedies he'd seen and caused, urged him to look closer, to question the easy answers.

His mind wrestled with the complexity before him. He had been trained to see the world in absolutes, in targets to be eliminated and missions to be accomplished. But Eleanor was challenging that worldview, her very existence blurring the lines he had once believed to be indelible.

A particular piece of surveillance caught his eye — a candid shot of Eleanor walking alone in a park, her expression pensive. It was a rare unguarded moment where her beauty was not a polished armour but something more vulnerable, more real.

The image stirred something in Max, a pull towards her humanity that went beyond his mission. He found himself admiring her — not just her poise and intelligence but the compassion that seemed to radiate from her when she thought no one was watching.

Max closed his eyes, taking a steadying breath. He was trained to observe and act, but now, observation had led to an unexpected empathy. He was questioning not only her role within Kozlov's empire but also the righteousness of his own task. Was it justice he sought, or was it vengeance? And could Eleanor, with her intricate ties to his enemy, be an unexpected ally in his quest?

The first light of day had given way to the full brightness of morning. Max stood up, the decision still firm in his mind. He would not make his next move from behind the lens of a scope or the safety of a screen. He would meet Eleanor Petrova face-to-face. He needed to know the person behind the name, the soul behind the role she played.

His course was set, a course that diverged from the orders given but aligned with the moral compass that had begun to steer him. Max Fairchild was not just a soldier; he was a man, and it was as a man that he would confront the enigma of Eleanor Petrova.

With the finality of his decision weighing upon him, Max stepped out of the safe house and into the light. Ahead lay the complexities of a mission that was no longer just about the cessation of a life but about understanding its value. It was a mission that could redeem or ruin, and Max walked towards it with his eyes and heart open.

*

Max stepped through the throng of London's morning rush, the cacophony of the waking city contrasting with the stillness within him. He was headed to a place that didn't exist on any map, known only to a few — a small, secluded bookstore nestled between the ever-changing facades of the high street. It was a front for the kind of intelligence gathering that couldn't be officially sanctioned, run by an old contact, Mikhail Aslanov.

Mikhail was a relic of the cold war, a spymaster who had navigated the fall of empires with the same ease as he navigated the shifting allegiances of the modern age. He owed Max a debt, one incurred under the cover of darkness in a world that bore no witness.

The bell above the door chimed as Max entered the bookstore. Rows of books, from dusty tomes to recent bestsellers, lined the walls, but they were merely a façade for the real business conducted in the shadows. Mikhail emerged from the back room, his presence commanding yet subtle, a trick learned from years of moving unseen.

"Max, it's been too long," Mikhail greeted, his voice a low rumble of Russian-accented English. "To what do I owe the pleasure?"

"Eleanor Petrova," Max stated without preamble, his gaze steady. "I need to know everything. The files I have don't tell the whole story."

Mikhail's eyes held a flicker of understanding. "Ah, the lawyer with the blood of Kozlov flowing through her veins. A dangerous subject, my friend."

Max nodded, the weight of his task a tangible thing between them. "There's more to her than the role she plays in Kozlov's game. I need to see the unseen threads."

Mikhail motioned for Max to follow him into the back room, where the air was thick with the smell of old paper and secrets. He booted up a computer hidden beneath a desk, the screen coming to life with the tap of a key.

"The Petrova you see is but a mask," Mikhail began, his fingers dancing across the keys as he brought up files, surveillance images, and intercepted messages. "Eleanor plays a long game — one of vengeance and justice. She's a sleeper within the organisation, waiting for the right moment to strike."

Max leaned in, absorbing the flood of information. "Vengeance for what?"

"Her father," Mikhail answered, pulling up a grainy photo of a younger Eleanor, grief etched into her features. "Mikhail Patrov was not just her uncle by blood but the man she held responsible for her father's death. He was collateral in a power play within Kozlov's ranks."

A silence hung in the air as Max processed the revelation. Eleanor's motives suddenly shifted in his perception, her actions painting the picture of a woman driven not by loyalty to Kozlov but by a deep-seated need to right a past wrong.

"Thank you, Mikhail," Max said finally, his voice firm. "This changes everything."

As he stepped out of the bookstore, the city around him seemed to shift into a new light. Eleanor Petrova was not just a target; she was a potential ally with her own score to settle. And for the first time, Max felt a flicker of hope that together, they might just take down Kozlov once and for all.

Max knew what he had to do next. It was time to meet the woman behind the mask.

*

Max merged back into the city's lifeblood, his mind racing with the new revelations about Eleanor. She was not just an appendage of Kozlov's empire, but potentially its undoing. The weight of the mission, which had always pressed heavily upon him, now felt different — it had dimension, texture, and a new shade of urgency.

The truth about Eleanor's father had cast her in a new light, one that softened the edges of her image in his mind. She was no longer the faceless part of a criminal machine but a woman marked by loss and fuelled by retribution. This knowledge didn't absolve her of her actions, but it did complicate the simplistic narrative he'd been sold.

Max found himself outside a café that Eleanor was known to frequent. It was a place that boasted an air of exclusivity, with patrons who whispered over gourmet coffees about the latest political dramas and stock market tremors. Here, he would observe her in her element, unguarded and authentic.

He took a seat outside, a vantage point that offered a clear view of the entrance. The waiter approached, and Max ordered a coffee, his eyes never straying from his task. As he waited, his thoughts drifted to Alex, his son, whose own death had redefined Max's world and understanding of loss, rage, and strength. It was Alex's death that had sharpened his resolve to end Kozlov's reign, to ensure that no more lives were shattered by the man's ambition.

A sleek car pulled up, and Eleanor stepped out. She moved with an understated grace, her posture perfect, yet there was a tension in her shoulders that spoke volumes to Max's trained eye. She was carrying the weight of her own mission, a mission driven by a personal vendetta that Max now understood.

As she passed by his table, their eyes met briefly. In that fleeting exchange, Max saw the depth of her resolve, and he recognised the reflection of his own. Here was a woman who had mastered the art of wearing masks, just as he had. But beneath those masks, they were both warriors, fighting a war that had become personal.

Eleanor's laugh reached him then, a melodic sound that seemed incongruous with the image of a woman on a vendetta. She was an enigma, one that Max was more determined than ever to understand.

He sipped his coffee, the bitter taste grounding him in the moment. His next steps needed to be calculated with precision. The path he was about to take with Eleanor was fraught with danger, but it was a path that could lead them to a shared goal.

Max left the café, the echo of Eleanor's laugh lingering in his ears. He would approach her, but not as an enemy. He would come to her as an ally in a war that had claimed too much from both of them.

The next move was clear. Max would seek out Eleanor, not with a sniper's scope but with an offer of alliance. Together, they might just have the power to dismantle the empire that had caused them both such irrevocable pain.

As the day gave way to the cool embrace of evening, Max felt a resolve settle over him. He was ready to meet the woman behind the mask, ready to join forces in a battle that was long overdue.

The game had changed, and Max Fairchild was ready to play.

*

Max chose the hour and the place with deliberate intent — the hour, when the cloak of dusk would grant them both the anonymity they needed; the place, a quiet corner of St. James's Park, where the natural chorus of rustling leaves and distant chatter would mask their conversation.

He arrived early, the soft light of the setting sun

filtering through the autumn leaves, casting a golden glow over the serene landscape. This was where he would lay the foundation for an alliance with Eleanor Petrova, an alliance that felt as dangerous as it was necessary.

Max positioned himself on a secluded bench, away from prying eyes, his gaze fixed on the winding path where Eleanor would soon appear. His mind was a whirlwind of strategy and anticipation. In the complex chess game he played, Eleanor had become a queen — a piece with the power to move freely, to make or break the game.

As the minutes ticked by, Max felt the familiar itch of adrenaline beneath his skin, a silent echo of the many times he had waited like this, for targets, for threats. But this time was different; he was not waiting for an enemy but for a potential ally with shared enmity for Kozlov.

The sound of measured footsteps approached, and Max straightened. Eleanor emerged from the shadowed path, her figure a silhouette against the fading light. She moved with confident strides, her eyes scanning her surroundings until they locked with his.

She took a seat beside him, her posture relaxed but her eyes sharp. "Mr Fairchild," she greeted, her voice betraying none of the surprise she must have felt. "To what do I owe the pleasure?"

Max turned to her, the last rays of sunlight illuminating her features, highlighting her cautious curiosity. "Ms Petrova," he replied, his tone even. "We have a common enemy, and perhaps, a common cause."

Eleanor's gaze didn't waver, though Max saw the slightest flicker of interest in her eyes. "Go on," she urged, a challenge woven into the words.

He leaned forward, his voice low. "Marcus Kozlov has

taken much from both of us. I believe you want to see his empire crumble as much as I do."

A pause hung in the air, heavy with the weight of unspoken truths. Then Eleanor nodded, a subtle concession. "And why should I trust you?"

Max's answer was immediate, decisive. "Because I know about your father, about the real reason you've stayed so close to Kozlov and Patrov. You seek justice, as do I."

The revelation might have shaken another, but Eleanor simply regarded him with a newfound appraisal. "It seems we may be more alike than I thought, Mr Fairchild."

They spoke then, of plans and possibilities, of the risks they would face. The conversation was a delicate dance around details too dangerous to voice outright, but understanding passed between them with each measured word.

By the time they parted ways, the park was shrouded in the velvet blue of twilight. A pact had been formed, not with handshakes or signatures, but with the unspoken agreement of warriors on a battlefield.

Max watched Eleanor disappear back into the maze of paths, her figure swallowed by the night. He felt a strange sense of camaraderie, a bond forged not by friendship but by the shared resolve to fight back against the darkness they both knew too well.

The alliance was formed, and with it, the course of the war had shifted. Max Fairchild and Eleanor Petrova would take on Kozlov's empire together, and only time would tell if they would emerge victorious or if their union would be their undoing.

*

Max remained seated, alone now in the quietude of the park, the conversation with Eleanor replaying in his mind. Their alliance was a fragile thing, born of mutual need and a shared history with a man who cast a long shadow. He pondered her last question, the one she had posed just before slipping away into the night's embrace: "Did Kozlov send you to kill me?"

He had answered truthfully. "He did, or at least I believe he has engineered this entire sequence of events from afar. But some orders are meant to be questioned, not followed."

Now, as the night deepened around him, Max considered the implications of that truth. Eleanor knew the lengths to which Kozlov would go to maintain his power. She knew, too, the depths of the darkness they faced. Yet in her eyes, he had seen not fear, but a fire that matched his own.

Eleanor Petrova was no damsel to be saved; she was a fighter, a survivor in a war that had taken from her as it had from him. She would be a formidable ally, but Max knew that their path would be fraught with peril. Trust was a commodity in short supply in their world, and while their goals aligned, the spectre of betrayal would always linger close.

As Max stood and made his way out of the park, he felt the weight of the path he had chosen. There was no turning back now. Eleanor was a part of this — part of the fight against Kozlov, part of the tangled web of his own redemption. Together, they would have to navigate the treacherous terrain that lay ahead.

The city around him was a labyrinth of light and shadow, and Max was a creature of both. He moved through the streets with a newfound purpose, aware that the game had changed, that new players had entered the fray.

In the days to come, they would need to plan carefully. Each step would have to be measured, each decision weighed against the possible cost. Max had allies — John Larkin, Liam Connor, and now Eleanor Petrova. Each brought their own strength to the table; each carried their own scars from battles past.

But it was Eleanor who stood at the centre of the storm now brewing, Eleanor who held the key to dismantling Kozlov's empire from within. And it was Eleanor who knew the true face of the man who had come not as her executioner, but as her ally in a fight for justice.

Max's next move would be to solidify their plan, to ensure that all pieces were in place before they struck. Kozlov was a man who dealt in absolutes, but Max and Eleanor would fight him with guile, with cunning, and with a resolve born of shared loss.

The night air was cool as Max disappeared into the darkness, a silent figure moving with certainty in a world where certainty was the rarest of things. The alliance was forged, and the battle lines were drawn. The war against Marcus Kozlov was about to enter a new chapter, and Max Fairchild was ready to play his part.

Chapter 22: Eleanor's Secret

Hidden Depths

In the confines of his dimly lit safe house, Max delved into the encrypted files he'd obtained from Mikhail. The glow of the screen cast an artificial pallor on his face as lines of code cascaded before his eyes, a digital waterfall hiding secrets within its depths. He was looking for the unseen, the unspoken truth behind Eleanor's façade, the keys to her past that had shaped her present.

The decryption software completed its sequence, and a new dossier opened on the screen. This was not the cold collection of surveillance and conjecture he had been fed before; this was personal, a file that smelled of betrayal and hidden vendettas. It detailed Eleanor's earliest involvement with Kozlov's empire, a history painted in shades of grey and red.

Max's eyes narrowed as he read. Eleanor Petrova, it seemed, was the cousin of the first Kozlov family member he had killed almost eighteen months ago. That death had been a statement, a declaration of war against the empire, and it had been Eleanor who Kozlov had tasked with unmasking the ghost who had struck from the shadows.

As he absorbed the information, Max felt the picture shift. Eleanor had been hunting him just as he had been hunting her uncle's associates. Their lives had been intertwined long before they knew each other's faces, playing roles in a tragedy neither had written.

The revelation was a jolt, a paradigm shift that sent a ripple through the fabric of Max's understanding.

Eleanor's pursuit had not been born of loyalty to Kozlov but of a desperate need for answers about her parent's death, a death she believed Kozlov had orchestrated. Her life within the organisation was not servitude; it was a long, calculated infiltration born of a need for vengeance.

Max leaned back, the chair groaning under his weight. The drive to uncover the truth about Eleanor had become personal, transcending the parameters of his mission. She was not just a target; she was a kindred spirit, another soul scarred by Kozlov's ruthless machinations.

The soldier in him understood duty, but the man in him, the one who had felt loss and the sting of betrayal, understood Eleanor's pain. His perception of her shifted, like a lens coming into focus, revealing the intricate details of a person who was much more ally than enemy.

He had to speak to her, to hear her story from her own lips. The dossier was a map, but Eleanor was the territory, and the territory was always richer, always more complex.

*

With the newfound knowledge of Eleanor's past, Max set out into the brisk London evening, the city's historic facades a silent testament to his own internal resolve. He needed to confront Eleanor, to bridge the gap between what was written in files and the reality that breathed life into her actions.

He found her where he expected, in the quiet solace of a small, private garden tucked away behind the library she frequented for legal research. It was a place that whispered of contemplation and refuge from the tumultuous world they both navigated.

Eleanor was seated on a wrought-iron bench, her

profile etched against the dusky sky. Her eyes, when she looked up at Max's approach, held a wariness tempered by a cautious interest.

"Max," she greeted, her voice betraying a hint of surprise at his appearance. "I didn't expect to see you so soon."

Max took a seat beside her, the iron cold and unforgiving beneath him. "I've learned more about you, about your past with Kozlov and your family," he began, watching her closely.

Eleanor's gaze didn't waver, though a shadow passed over her features. "And what have you found in your quest for truth?" she asked, a challenge underlying her words.

Max told her then of the dossier he had uncovered, of her hunt for the man who had struck down her cousin, and how that path had led her to him. He spoke of her father's death and the suspicion that Kozlov had engineered it.

Eleanor listened, her face a mask of composure. When he had finished, she looked away, her eyes lost to the twilight for a moment. "My father's death was the catalyst," she admitted, her voice a mere whisper carried on the evening breeze. "I knew Kozlov was involved, but I had no proof. My position in his organisation was the means to an end — a way to find the truth and to make them pay."

Max understood then the magnitude of her resolve. Eleanor was not an accomplice to Kozlov's schemes; she was a spectre within them, seeking justice from the inside.

"And now?" Max asked, the question hanging between them.

Eleanor turned to face him, her determination clear.

"Now I fight alongside you. We both seek the same thing — to see Marcus Kozlov's empire fall."

The decision that had weighed heavily upon Max lifted in that moment, replaced by a sense of clarity. Their experiences with Kozlov had set them on a collision course, but now their paths had converged into one.

"You were sent to kill me," Eleanor stated, not a question but a fact. "Why didn't you?"

Max's reply was simple and honest. "Because I saw in you the same drive that fuels me. Your fight is my fight. And together, we stand a chance against Kozlov."

The air around them held a charge, the kind that precedes a storm. They were two forces united by a common goal, their alliance sealed not by trust but by the mutual desire for retribution and change.

As they stood to leave the garden, their steps in sync, Max felt the first true sense of partnership. They were no longer solitary warriors in the dark; they were allies, each a beacon for the other in the fight against a shared darkness.

The night around them was no longer an abyss to be navigated alone. It was a battlefield, and they were ready to face it together.

*

Max and Eleanor left the seclusion of the garden, their steps leading them through the labyrinth of London's heart. The city around them was a living entity, pulsing with life, yet for Max, it had transformed. No longer was it just the backdrop of his solitary crusade; it had become the staging ground for a joint operation that held the promise of ending Kozlov's reign.

As they walked, the conversation turned to strategy. Eleanor's insight into Kozlov's legal fortifications was invaluable, her knowledge of the organisation's inner workings unparalleled. She described the layers of protection Kozlov had built around himself — legal loopholes, political connections, a network of influence that spanned across continents.

"But he's not untouchable," Eleanor said, her voice carrying the steel of someone who had seen the monster behind the mask. "There are cracks in his armour, weaknesses only someone on the inside could know."

Max listened intently, his mind already weaving her information into his existing plans. Every detail she provided was a piece of ammunition, a potential key to unlocking Kozlov's downfall.

They reached a quiet café, its windows fogged from the warmth within, a stark contrast to the chill of the evening. Here, they could continue their discussion with a semblance of normality, two figures lost in the crowd.

Over cups of steaming coffee, they outlined their approach. Eleanor sketched a rough structure of Kozlov's empire on a napkin, circles and lines that represented the hierarchy of power. Max, in turn, laid out his network of contacts and resources — John Larkin's investigative prowess, Sgt. Liam Connor's tactical expertise, and the backing of other shadowy figures who, like Max, had scores to settle.

"The first Kozlov you killed, my cousin — he was the beginning," Eleanor confessed, tracing the outline of a circle with her finger. "But it's Marcus who needs to pay for my father. For everything."

Max saw then not just the lawyer or the avenger, but the daughter who had lost a parent, the human being behind the façade. "We'll bring him to justice, Eleanor. For your father, for my son, and for all the lives he's destroyed."

Their planning stretched into hours, the café's patrons ebbing and flowing around them. They discussed timelines and contingencies, the need for subtlety and precision. When they parted that evening, it was with a shared sense of purpose, a joint mission that was larger than either of them alone.

Max walked the streets, the night now an old friend, its shadows comforting rather than oppressive. Eleanor's presence in his life had become the catalyst for change, her secret — her vendetta — now a shared cause that bound them together.

Their alliance was forged in the fires of their respective losses, tempered by the desire for a justice that had long been denied. As Max disappeared into the night, he knew that the road ahead would be perilous, fraught with danger from both Kozlov and the law.

But he was no longer alone, and the fight ahead was no longer just his own. Together, he and Eleanor would face the darkness, and together, they would seek the light of a dawn that was yet to break over London's storied skyline.

*

The following days were a blur of activity. Max and Eleanor met in clandestine locations, each encounter building upon the last as they pooled their knowledge and resources. They were like two architects drafting the blueprint for the fall of a dynasty, each line drawn, each plan set, bringing the endgame ever closer.

Max reached out to John with the care that such a communication required. They convened under the guise of darkness in an abandoned warehouse on the outskirts of the city, a place where secrets echoed off the walls and vanished into the void.

John arrived with the silent tread of a man accustomed to the shadows, his eyes revealing nothing of the thoughts behind them. "Fairchild," he greeted, with a nod that served as the extent of pleasantries.

"Larkin," Max acknowledged. "I need your eyes on this," he said, passing a flash drive across the space between them. "It's everything we have on Kozlov's operations — schedules, routes, financials. And more."

John pocketed the drive, his expression unreadable. "And what's the 'more'?"

"Eleanor Petrova," Max revealed, watching as John's eyebrow arched slightly. "She's inside Kozlov's circle. And she's on our side."

The news seemed to pique John's interest, a spark igniting in his gaze. "That is more," he conceded. "Alright. I'll see what threads I can pull, what shadows I can chase. We'll bring this empire down, Max. From the top down to its very roots."

As John melted back into the night, Max felt the first stirrings of what could be victory, or perhaps the calm before the storm. He knew that the information he'd given John could unravel the network that supported Kozlov's empire, exposing the underbelly of the beast they sought to slay.

Meanwhile, Eleanor worked her own channels, setting quiet fires within Kozlov's organisation that would soon blaze into infernos of confusion and dissent. With her knowledge of the legalities and illegalities that bound

Kozlov's operations together, she was the perfect saboteur, her actions as precise as they were devastating.

But as they set their plans in motion, the danger grew. DI Sarah Bennett was closing in, her investigation drawing tighter around the acts of vigilantism that had shaken the city. Max knew it was only a matter of time before she connected the dots leading to him and Eleanor.

Max met with Liam next, in a pub known for its discretion and its clientele who asked no questions. Liam was solid, a rock in the ever-churning sea of chaos that Max navigated.

"Max, you look like you're about to start a war," Liam observed, clapping him on the shoulder as he slid into the booth.

"In a way, I am," Max admitted, his voice low. "But this is one we've been fighting for a long time. We just didn't know it."

He briefed Liam on the situation, on Eleanor's role and the impending strike against Kozlov. Liam listened, his face a mask of concentration, only nodding when Max finished.

"We've been through hell and back, haven't we?" Liam said, a wry smile touching his lips. "What's one more battle?"

It was the confirmation Max needed. With Liam on board, they had the tactical edge, the experience, and the loyalty that would be crucial in the coming days.

As Max left the pub, the weight of the world on his shoulders, he knew that the path they had chosen was fraught with peril. But it was a path they walked together, a united front against the darkness.

The storm was gathering on the horizon, and Max

Fairchild was ready to face it head-on.

*

In the grey light of pre-dawn, Max met Eleanor in a deserted warehouse, one that bore the scars of industry long since decayed. Here, they would weave the final threads of their intricate web, a trap set for a kingpin who had long believed himself untouchable.

Eleanor arrived, her face set in determination. She carried with her a series of documents, each one a silent testament to the years she had spent under Kozlov's thumb, each one a piece of the puzzle they were about to complete.

"I've secured the last of the evidence we needed," Eleanor said, her voice echoing in the vast emptiness of the warehouse. She spread the documents out before Max, a mosaic of corruption and crime meticulously documented. "This is the leverage we need to turn Kozlov's closest allies against him."

Max examined the papers, seeing in them the culmination of Eleanor's life's work, a dedication to justice that mirrored his own. "And the risks?" he asked, his eyes not leaving the sheets.

"High," Eleanor conceded. "But necessary. Kozlov's empire is a fortress, but even fortresses have their weak points."

They spent the next hours poring over the documents, discussing each move, anticipating Kozlov's counterstrikes, and devising contingencies. Max could feel the momentum building, a current that was now flowing inexorably toward their final confrontation with Kozlov.

Yet even as they planned, Max was aware of the

delicate balance they maintained. DI Bennett's investigation was closing in, her own web of inquiry beginning to intersect with the one they wove. Max knew that any misstep now would not only jeopardize their operation but could also land them both in Bennett's net.

Eleanor's next words broke into his thoughts. "We need to act soon. Kozlov is planning a gathering — a display of power and unity for his closest associates. It will be the perfect opportunity to strike."

Max nodded, the idea slotting into place like the final piece of a puzzle. "We'll need to be careful. Ensure that our tracks are covered. Bennett is thorough; she'll use anything she finds."

Eleanor's lips quirked in a grim smile. "Then we'll give her nothing to find."

As the sky began to lighten, signalling the start of a new day, Max and Eleanor finalized their plans. They were two parts of a whole, a team forged from the fires of vengeance and the ashes of their pasts.

Max left the warehouse with the knowledge that the next time he and Eleanor met, it would be with the fate of Kozlov's empire hanging in the balance. The day of reckoning was upon them, and the storm they had been chasing was about to break.

Their paths had led them here, to this moment where the past and present were poised to collide. And Max Fairchild, once a lone soldier in the darkness, now stood shoulder to shoulder with Eleanor Petrova, ready to face the dawn.

*

As Max stepped out into the chill of the early morning, the city was just beginning to stir from its slumber. The day ahead was one of profound significance; it was the eve of the confrontation they had meticulously orchestrated. The plan they had set in motion was like a finely tuned instrument, and every move from now on had to be executed with precision.

The air was crisp with the bite of approaching winter as Max made his way through the desolate streets. His mind was alight with the final details of their strategy, the contingency plans, and the myriad of ways things could unfold. He had been in situations of high tension before, but the stakes had never been quite like this.

He had one last stop before the day's end — a meeting with Isabella, a contact whose loyalty had been bought at a price, but whose information had always proven reliable. They met in the shadow of an old church, its spire a silent witness to their clandestine rendezvous.

Isabella was already there, her breath forming small clouds in the cold air. "Max," she greeted him with a nod, her face partially obscured by the scarf wrapped tightly around her neck.

"Isabella," Max acknowledged. "Do you have it?"

She produced a small envelope from her coat pocket and handed it to him. "It's all there. Routes, times, passwords. Everything you need to get inside the gathering without raising alarms."

Max tucked the envelope away securely. "And the payment?" he asked, reaching into his own coat.

Isabella held up a hand, stopping him. "Consider it settled. I'm not doing this for Kozlov or his blood money. I'm doing this for the same reason you are. I want to see him fall."

Max searched her eyes, finding an echo of his and Eleanor's resolve within them. "Thank you," he said sincerely.

With a final glance, Isabella turned and disappeared into the morning fog, leaving Max alone with the weight of the coming day.

Returning to the safe house, Max found Eleanor waiting for him, her expression one of focused anticipation. Together, they reviewed the information Isabella had provided, integrating it into their plan.

"The gathering is our best chance," Eleanor reiterated, her finger tracing the perimeter of the estate on the map before them. "Kozlov will be vulnerable, surrounded by his own sense of security."

Max nodded, feeling the familiar surge of adrenaline that came with the promise of action. "We'll only get one shot at this. We need to be ready for anything."

Eleanor met his gaze, her eyes steady. "I am ready. Ready to end this, one way or another."

Their preparations continued late into the night, and when they finally rested, it was with the understanding that the next day would change everything. They had set out on this path separately, each driven by their own demons and desires for vengeance, but they would walk into the lion's den as allies, united by a shared purpose.

The morning would soon arrive, bringing with it the culmination of their efforts. Max and Eleanor would step into the fray together, facing down the darkness with the light of their unwavering determination. Kozlov's empire would be challenged, and the power he had wielded so ruthlessly would be put to the test.

As Max lay in the quiet before dawn, the pieces were

in place. The stage was set for a reckoning, and the echoes of the coming storm whispered promises of retribution and the hope of a new beginning.

Chapter 23: A Protector's Vow

Vigilance

The night wrapped around the safe house like a shroud, the quiet hum of the city a stark contrast to the storm of activity that had taken place within its walls over the past few hours. Max surveyed the perimeter one last time, his eyes scanning for any anomalies in the shadows. Eleanor's safety was his top priority, and he'd be damned if he'd let anything slip past his watch.

The room was secure, a temporary stronghold against the threats that lurked just beyond the reach of the light. Eleanor sat at the central table, her focus on the array of documents and digital screens before her. She had traded the sharp lines of her lawyer's suits for the functional ease of dark, form-fitting attire more suited to their clandestine operations.

Max approached, his footsteps silent on the concrete floor. "The security measures are in place," he announced. "I'll take first watch."

Eleanor lifted her gaze, meeting his with an intensity that matched his own. "Thank you," she said, though the words seemed inadequate for the depth of her gratitude. Max had become more than just an ally; he was her shield in the tangible darkness that had descended upon her life.

As Eleanor returned her attention to the work at hand, Max took his position by the window, his eyes a constant sentinel. The night was young, and the true test of their alliance had yet to come. But as each hour passed with the quiet assurance of safety, the foundation of their trust grew stronger.

The silence of the space between them was a comfortable one, filled with the unspoken language of shared purpose and the mutual recognition of the stakes at hand. Max was more than a guardian; he was a partner in the truest sense, and as the night deepened, so too did the bond that had formed between them in the face of their common enemy.

*

The digital clock on the wall marked the passing of midnight. Eleanor, still engrossed in the labyrinth of legal documents and encrypted data, paused as a particular file caught her eye. It was a hidden ledger detailing transactions that even Marcus Kozlov didn't know she had access to.

"Max," she called softly, beckoning him over.

He moved to her side, his presence a comforting solidity. "What have you found?"

She pointed to the figures on the screen, lines and numbers that would seem innocuous to the untrained eye. "Proof," she stated. "Transactions that link Kozlov directly to several high-profile politicians. If we can expose this ..."

Max understood the gravity of her discovery. It was the kind of ammunition they needed — not bullets or blades, but the undeniable truth that could unravel Kozlov's web of influence.

"It's risky," he cautioned, his mind already assessing the dangers of leveraging such information. "But it could be the tipping point."

Eleanor met his concern with a resolute nod. "Risks

we knew would be part of this. I'm ready if you are."

Max's response was a nod, the silent affirmation of their shared commitment. He watched as Eleanor encrypted the file, securing it within layers of cyber protection before dispatching it to a trusted contact who could make the necessary arrangements for its release.

As the file was sent off into the digital ether, Max felt the axis of their battle shift. They were no longer merely reacting to Kozlov's moves; they were actively setting the stage for his downfall.

With the ledger sent, Eleanor leaned back in her chair, the fatigue of long hours etching shadows beneath her eyes. Max's protective instincts surged. "Get some rest," he insisted gently. "I'll keep watch."

Eleanor hesitated, the weight of the mission and the gravity of their situation pressing upon her. But eventually, she conceded, her body acquiescing to the need for rest even as her mind continued to race.

Max watched over her as she settled into a makeshift bed, her breathing eventually evening out into the steady rhythm of sleep. In her rest, she seemed more vulnerable, a stark reminder to Max of the solemn vow he had made.

He returned to his post by the window, his gaze steadfast into the night. The protector's role was one he had taken up without hesitation, but it was more than duty that tethered him to her side. It was the unyielding desire to see justice served, to right the wrongs that had brought them both to this point.

And as the city slept around them, Max Fairchild stood watch, a silent vow renewed with every passing hour — to safeguard Eleanor Petrova, to shield her from the storm they were destined to face together.

*

The city's nocturnal heartbeat throbbed distantly, a muted reminder of the world beyond their sequestered reality. Max remained vigilant, his eyes periodically scanning the monitors, each showing a different angle of the surrounding streets. The sanctity of their haven had to be preserved; Eleanor's trust in him was not something he took lightly.

In the quiet hours of the night, Max's thoughts drifted. He considered the journey that had brought him here, to this room, to this moment of calm before the inevitable storm. His mind replayed the missions, the faces of those he had served with, the ones he had saved and the ones he had not. Each memory was a thread woven into the fabric of who he had become.

Eleanor stirred, her sleep uneasy, troubled by dreams or perhaps the weight of their shared burden. Max moved to her side, his hand hesitating just above her shoulder, wanting to offer comfort but reluctant to cross the unseen line their professional relationship dictated.

"Eleanor," he whispered, and at the sound of her name, she awoke, her eyes fluttering open to lock with his.

"It's still night," she murmured, a question in her gaze as she took in his proximity.

"Just checking in," Max reassured, his voice low. "You should rest. We have a long day ahead."

Eleanor sat up, pushing back the strands of hair that had fallen across her face. "I can't stop thinking about it," she confessed, the shadows of the room playing across her features. "About all that could go wrong."

Max understood her fears all too well. "We've planned for every contingency," he reminded her, his voice steady.

"Kozlov won't see us coming."

She nodded, though the crease of worry remained etched between her brows. Max's resolve hardened. "I made you a vow, Eleanor," he said, the words more than mere comfort. "I intend to keep it. You're not alone in this."

Their eyes held, and in that prolonged gaze, something shifted. A connection, deeper than strategy and shared objectives, formed between them. It was the bond of two souls who had recognised the echo of their own pain in each other, the understanding that they were united in more than just their fight against Kozlov.

Eleanor reached out, her hand finding Max's. Her grip was firm, grounding. "Thank you," she said, her voice stronger now. "For everything."

Max returned the pressure of her hand, a silent pact between them. "Together," he affirmed.

With a nod, Eleanor lay back down, her eyes closing once more, this time finding a more peaceful slumber. Max watched over her, a silent guardian whose vow was etched in the very marrow of his bones.

As the darkness of the night deepened, so too did the bond they shared, forged in the quiet hours before the dawn, before the world would demand they step back into the fray. For now, they were simply two allies, two kindred spirits finding solace in the presence of one another.

*

The first light of dawn crept through the cracks in the blinds, casting a pale glow that signalled the end of night's dominion. Max watched the subtle change in the room's ambience, the shift from shadow to light reflecting the transition in their own circumstances. Today was the day they would put their plans into action, and the weight of it rested heavily on Max's shoulders.

Eleanor roused herself, her movements deliberate as she prepared for the day. She caught Max's eye and nodded, a silent acknowledgement of the risks they were about to take. There was a steely determination in her posture, an echo of the vow they had shared in the quiet hours of the night.

They gathered their gear, each item a testament to their readiness. Max checked every weapon, every piece of equipment, ensuring their functionality. Eleanor, meanwhile, organised the documents and data they had amassed — evidence that would expose Kozlov's corruption and dismantle his empire piece by piece.

Max approached her, his hand resting on one of the packs. "Once we step out of this door, there's no turning back," he said, his voice low and steady.

Eleanor's hands paused, and she looked up at him. "I haven't looked back since the day I learned the truth about my father," she replied. "I'm ready to see this through, Max. Ready to end Kozlov's tyranny."

Max nodded, the bond between them a source of strength as they stood on the brink of action. "Then let's begin," he said. "We have a vow to fulfil."

Together, they left the safe house, stepping into the cool morning air that carried the promise of the confrontation to come. The city was waking up, its citizens oblivious to the battle about to be waged in the shadows.

As they made their way to the rendezvous point where they would meet John and Liam, Max felt the protector's vow surge within him. It was more than a promise to keep Eleanor safe; it was a commitment to stand by her side, to fight for justice, and to strive for a future free from the corruption that had tainted their lives.

The streets of London unfolded before them, a chessboard of infinite possibilities and perilous gambits. But Max and Eleanor were no longer mere pieces in the game controlled by Kozlov's hand. They were players in their own right, masters of their fate, moving with purpose and the unshakable resolve of those who have nothing left to lose.

The day was upon them, and with it, the culmination of all they had worked for. Their steps were measured, their spirits unyielding as they moved forward, not just as allies, but as avatars of retribution and guardians of the vow that bound them.

*

Max and Eleanor arrived at a derelict building on the outskirts of the city, a place that had long been forgotten by those who walked the well-trodden paths of London's bustling streets. This was to be their rallying point, where they would unite with John and Liam, completing the circle of their compact resistance.

The building loomed like a spectre, its walls etched with the passage of time, yet within its desolate halls, there was a pulse of life. John was already there, his form emerging from the shadows as they entered. The special operator turned assassin had traded his solitary existence for the more familiar team life and action he had honed as a SEAL, his role as silent partner set aside for the more immediate call to arms.

"Max, Eleanor," John greeted them, his voice a low rasp that spoke of nights spent in vigilance. "The pieces are set; the board is ready."

Liam followed, his military bearing unmistakable even in civilian clothes. He nodded to Eleanor with the respect of a soldier to a comrade, recognizing the steel in her that had been forged in the fires of loss and vengeance.

"The team's ready," Liam confirmed, his gaze sweeping over them. "We've got one shot at this. Let's make it count."

Max looked between his allies, feeling the gravity of their shared purpose. They were an unlikely fellowship, each driven here by different roads, yet their intentions were the same — to bring down the tyrant who had cast such long shadows over their lives.

Eleanor stepped forward, her presence commanding attention. "We have truth on our side," she stated, her voice resonant with the power of her conviction. "Kozlov's reign ends today."

Max watched the resolve on the faces around him and felt it in his own bones. He stepped into the centre of the gathering, his eyes meeting those of his allies. "We've all made sacrifices to get here. Today those sacrifices pay off. Today we reclaim our lives and our futures."

John and Liam nodded, the unspoken language of warriors in their glances. They understood the stakes, the price of failure, and the reward of success.

Max turned to Eleanor, her gaze steady and unwavering. "You ready?" he asked, though he knew the answer before she even spoke.

Eleanor's reply was a mirror of his determination. "Let's finish this."

The alliance was solidified, the plan set in motion. They were no longer solitary agents in the dark; they were a united force, standing together on the threshold of retribution.

With the early morning light creeping through the

broken windows, casting a mosaic of shadows and illumination across the group, they set out. Each step was a march towards an uncertain destiny, but they walked it together, bound by the vows they had made, by the trust they had forged in the silent hours of the night.

The city awaited them, and so did their adversary. The day of reckoning had arrived, and Max, along with Eleanor and their band of steadfast allies, stepped out to meet it head-on.

*

The first rays of dawn gilded the edges of the horizon as Max, Eleanor, John, and Liam made their way through the deserted streets, moving towards the epicentre where Kozlov would be holding his gathering. The air was thick with anticipation, each of them aware that the actions of the next few hours would irrevocably change the course of their lives.

The city was quiet, holding its breath as if it too sensed the impending upheaval. Max led the group with a calm assertiveness, his every sense attuned to the environment around them. He had walked into danger many times before, but never with so much at stake, never with a burden shared so deeply with those at his side.

Eleanor moved with a grace that belied her tension, her mind undoubtedly replaying the plan they had meticulously put together. She carried with her the evidence that would not only incriminate Kozlov but also sever his ties with the powerful allies who had protected him for so long.

John's eyes were watchful, darting to every shadow,

269

every alleyway they passed. His usual role of uncovering the truth for the world to see had shifted, for today he would be part of the truth being laid bare.

Liam's presence was reassuring, the soldier in him ready for whatever might come. His experience in the field was invaluable, and his loyalty to Max was unwavering. He was the backbone of their operation, steady and unshakable.

As they neared the venue, the reality of their mission settled around them like armour. They were ready to pierce the heart of Kozlov's empire, to dismantle it from within and watch it crumble.

Max paused, turning to face his companions. "Once we go in, keep to the plan. Watch each other's backs," he instructed, his voice low and firm. "We'll communicate through the earpieces. Stay sharp, stay focused. We'll come out of this together."

Eleanor nodded, her eyes meeting Max's with a steely determination. "Together," she echoed, her voice resolute.

With a final check of their equipment and a deep collective breath, they moved forward. The venue loomed ahead, a facade of grandeur that masked the corruption within. Today that facade would crack, and the truth would pour out like light into the darkness.

The group split as planned, each heading to their designated positions. Max felt the familiar adrenaline surge as he took his place. The protector, the avenger, the ally: today he was all these things and more. Today he was the hand of justice, and he would not falter.

The city began to awaken around them, the usual rhythms of life resuming as the sun climbed higher in the sky. But for Max and his allies, life had paused at a crossroads, one path leading back to the world they had known, the other foraying into uncharted territory.

As Max awaited the signal to move in, he allowed himself a moment to reflect on the vow he had made. He was here to protect, to fight, to serve. He was here for Eleanor, for the city, for the very concept of justice. And as the signal finally came, Max stepped into the fray with a clarity of purpose that felt like the first true breath of his new life.

Chapter 24: Converging Paths

The Assassin's Watch

John Larkin stood in the shadows, his eyes fixed on the opulent building where the gala would take place. A former operative of the U.S. Special Forces turned assassin, he had always been a solitary figure, but his alliance with Max had brought him back into the fold of a team, a concept he had long distanced himself from.

His current position offered a clear view of the venue's entrances and exits. From this vantage point, he could observe the comings and goings of the guests — each one a potential puppet of Kozlov's grand design. Larkin's role tonight was crucial. He was the overwatch, the safeguard against unexpected threats, and the first line of defence should things go awry.

A light flickered from a nearby building, a signal from one of his placed informants. Larkin's gaze didn't waver as he acknowledged it with a subtle nod. Information was key, and tonight, it would be the currency that could buy them victory or spell their doom.

As he waited, his thoughts briefly turned to Max and Eleanor. They were inside, weaving through a maze of deception and power. Larkin knew the weight of the task they shouldered, the tightrope they walked upon, and he felt the old, familiar surge of adrenaline that came with the proximity to danger.

The net was closing in on Kozlov, but Larkin was aware that they were not the only players in this game. DI Sarah Bennett and her team from the Met were drawing their own circle around the same target. It was a delicate dance of timing and intent, and Larkin was prepared to ensure that Max and Eleanor would not be caught in the crossfire.

As guests began to arrive, their finery the antithesis of the darkness of Larkin's attire, he remained vigilant. The gala was a stage, and tonight, the performance would be one for the history books.

*

Detective Inspector Bennett of the Metropolitan Police had been piecing together the puzzle for months, her team's investigation leading them through a labyrinth of leads, false starts, and breakthroughs. Now it all culminated in this gala, where the upper echelons of society mingled with those who wielded a darker form of power.

Bennett stood across the street from the venue, her eyes hidden behind the lenses of her binoculars. She wasn't here for the canapés and champagne. Her presence was the culmination of sleepless nights and relentless pursuit, the hunt for the truth behind the vigilante actions that had shaken the city's criminal underbelly.

Next to her, Detective Constable James Fletcher monitored the live feed from their surveillance van, a hub of technology that was their window into the gala's heart. "DI Bennett, we have eyes on several known associates of Kozlov," Fletcher reported, his voice a low whisper.

"Keep tracking their movements," Bennett instructed, her gaze not leaving the scene before her. "Any sign of them?"

"Not yet," Fletcher replied, his fingers flying over the keyboard as he cycled through camera feeds.

Bennett knew the vigilante's reputation: a ghost

operative with a code of honour that had led him down this path.

He was the key to this entire operation, the one who could unravel Kozlov's grip on the city. Bennett felt a grudging respect for him; his motives might align with the law's intentions, but his methods stood firmly outside it.

As the guests continued to flow into the gala, Bennett's focus remained unwavering. She was aware that there were others like her, hidden in the night, watching and waiting. The game was complex, the players numerous, and Bennett was determined to stay one step ahead.

Tonight, the paths of law, order, and vigilantism would intersect, and Sarah Bennett would be there to ensure that justice, her brand of justice, would prevail.

*

Elsewhere in the city, Rebecca Turner, the journalist who had been tracking the vigilante's trail, sat in the back of a cab, her laptop open to a sea of notes and articles. She had connected the dots leading to the Kozlov empire and the shadows that moved against it, her articles painting a target on the organisation that the public eye could not ignore.

Rebecca had always had a nose for the stories that mattered, the ones that lurked beneath the surface, and this was her biggest yet. She knew that tonight's gala was more than a social event; it was a nexus where many threads in her investigation would come together. Max and Eleanor, who had until now remained phantoms behind the curtain, might finally emerge, and Rebecca intended to be there when they did.

Her phone buzzed with a message from an anonymous

source, one who had proven reliable in the past. It was brief: *The storm is coming. Be ready.* Rebecca's pulse quickened. This was it, confirmation that tonight's events would be pivotal.

She arrived at the venue and slipped into the crowd, her eyes scanning the opulent hall for the key players in her narrative. Rebecca moved with a practised ease, her recorder discreetly tucked away, ready to capture any slip, any revelation that might unfold.

As the evening progressed, her anticipation grew. The air was electric with the tension of unspoken intrigues, and Rebecca could almost taste the story that was about to break. She positioned herself with a clear view of the grand staircase, where the evening's honourees would make their entrance.

The click of her camera went unnoticed amidst the murmur of conversations and the clinking of glasses. She was a ghost, a watcher, her pen poised to write the first draft of history.

Above all, Rebecca Turner was ready. Ready to document the fall of an empire, ready to shine light on the truth, and ready to reveal the names and faces of those who would bring about Kozlov's undoing.

*

The grandeur of the gala was a facade, a veil that masked the undercurrents of power and manipulation beneath. As the guests donned their masks and indulged in the opulence of the night, the true spectacle was not the one performed on stage but the one that was silently orchestrated in the wings.

Max and Eleanor had entered separately, their

appearances calculated to avoid drawing attention. Max blended into the background, his eyes sharp and alert, watching the crowd for the signs he had come to recognise — the subtle exchange of glances, the brief handshakes that were more than mere greetings. He moved through the throng with purpose, every step bringing him closer to their target.

Eleanor, for her part, navigated the social landscape with the grace of one accustomed to such events. Her attire was elegant, her demeanour poised, but her mind was focused on the mission. She carried with her the weight of the evidence that would dismantle Kozlov's empire, her every interaction laced with the intent to expose the corruption that festered at the heart of this gathering.

In the midst of the revelry, DI Bennett and her team maintained their vigil. Their presence was discreet, their observations keen as they monitored the crowd for any sign of the individuals they were tracking. Bennett's eyes were constantly moving, her instincts telling her that the night would not pass without incident.

And then there was Rebecca Turner, the journalist whose pen was as mighty as any sword. She watched from the periphery, her camera at the ready, her senses attuned to the story that was about to unfold. She knew that beneath the surface of this grand event lay a network of deceit, and she was determined to drag it into the light.

As the evening wore on, the tension grew palpable. The guests were unaware of the play within the play, of the actors among them who performed not for applause but for the highest stakes imaginable.

The clock ticked closer to midnight, and with it, the moment of revelation approached. The gala's veil was about to be lifted, and the true drama was set to begin. Max and Eleanor were in place, Bennett's team was on alert, and Rebecca's camera was focused on capturing the imminent climax of this intricate dance.

The stage was set, the players were ready, and the paths of many were about to converge in an event that would shake the very foundations of the city's power structure. The gala ball was only the beginning, and as the hands of the clock moved inexorably towards the hour, the fate of those gathered hung in the balance.

*

As the gala swirled with the gaiety of the unsuspecting elite, a different kind of dance was underway — a dance of fates intertwined by the looming confrontation. Max, a silent predator among the prey, had positioned himself on the periphery of the main hall. He was the unseen sentinel, watching as Kozlov's main man, a key link in the chain, conversed with a high-ranking Member of Parliament.

Eleanor, with the poise of someone who belonged to this world of glitter and guile, kept a careful eye on the interactions, her mind cataloguing every detail that would later be used to unravel the net of corruption. The evidence she carried was more than mere paper and data; it was the power to ignite the downfall of an empire.

DI Bennett, vigilant and unyielding, watched the crowd through a different lens. Her focus was twofold: to ensure the law was upheld and to prevent the vigilantes from stepping over the line. Her team, scattered strategically throughout the venue, was a silent force ready to act on her command.

Rebecca Turner, with her journalist's instinct honed to a razor's edge, observed the crowd, her camera discreetly documenting the night's faces. Among the laughter and the clinking of glasses, she waited for the moment that would reveal the rot beneath the veneer.

As the clock neared ever closer to the stroke of midnight, the atmosphere shifted subtly. A disturbance at the edge of the crowd caught Max's attention — the arrival of a new player, an informant whose allegiance had been one of the night's uncertain variables. This was the wildcard, the thread that, once pulled, could hasten the unravelling of Kozlov's meticulously woven tapestry.

Max gave a subtle signal to Eleanor, who excused herself from a conversation with a grace that belied the urgency of the situation. They converged near a secluded alcove, their voices a whisper.

"The informant is here," Max informed her, his words clipped with tension.

Eleanor's eyes flashed with a mixture of surprise and anticipation. "Then it's time," she said. "We move on your lead."

Across the room, Bennett's sharp gaze caught the exchange. Her hand moved to her earpiece, a quiet order issued. The team tensed, ready to close in.

Rebecca, ever the observer, sensed the shift in the tide. Her camera lens found Max and Eleanor, capturing the moment of silent communication that spoke volumes to her trained eye.

The gala, for all its opulence and celebration, was the stage for a far more dangerous game — a game of justice and retribution, of law and order, of truth and deception. And as the chimes signalled the arrival of midnight, the game reached its crescendo.

The informant made his move, approaching Kozlov's right-hand man with a demeanour that spoke of urgent news. Max and Eleanor prepared to intercept, to leverage the new information that could tilt the balance in their favour.

And just as the pieces were set to fall into place, an unexpected figure approached Max and Eleanor, one that hadn't been accounted for in their plan — a figure that would leave them questioning the fate of all involved.

*

The figure navigating through the sea of opulence and carefree laughter was not dressed in the evening's required finery, nor did they carry themselves with the affected grace of the gala's attendees. Instead, their approach was purposeful, their demeanour incongruous with the surrounding revelry. It was clear they were not another guest but an interloper with intentions unknown.

Max's hand instinctively moved closer to the concealed sidearm beneath his jacket. Eleanor's posture tensed, ready for whatever threat or opportunity this new variable presented. They had planned for many scenarios, but the appearance of this unexpected player added a wildcard to the already high-stakes game.

As the figure drew closer, the light caught their features, and a murmur of recognition passed between Max and Eleanor. It was a face from the past, one intertwined with the origins of their mission, a ghost from the chapters of their lives they thought had been firmly closed.

The figure stopped before them, their eyes locking onto Max's with a piercing intensity. The surrounding sounds of the gala seemed to dull into a distant echo as the three stood in a silent standoff, the weight of history pressing down upon them.

"You shouldn't have come here," Max uttered, his voice barely above a whisper but edged with a sharp warning.

"I had to," the figure responded, their voice a mixture of resolve and something that sounded like desperation. "There's something you don't know, something that changes everything."

Eleanor's gaze narrowed, her mind racing to piece together the puzzle this new piece presented. "What information?" she demanded.

Before the figure could reply, a sudden commotion erupted at the edge of the room. Shouts rang out, piercing the orchestral music, and the guests turned in alarm as uniformed officers led by DI Bennett made their presence known. They moved through the crowd with authoritative strides, their purpose clear and their targets identified.

Max's eyes met Eleanor's, a silent communication that spoke of contingency plans and immediate action. They had prepared for the possibility of law enforcement intervention, but the timing was far from ideal.

The figure seized the moment of distraction, pressing a small, hard object into Max's hand. "It's all here," they hissed, urgency lacing their words. "Use it."

Max pocketed the object without breaking eye contact with the figure. "Stay out of sight," he instructed before turning to Eleanor. "We need to move, now."

Eleanor nodded, and together they began to navigate the chaos, their exit strategy unfolding just as the gala began to crumble around them. The masquerade had fractured, the illusion of the night shattered by the sharp reality of the pursuit.

Rebecca Turner's camera flashed, capturing the pandemonium that ensued — the startled faces of the elite, the determined approach of the police, and the enigmatic figure standing amidst it all.

The fate of Max and Eleanor hung in the balance, and their next moves were critical. The information pressed into Max's hand by the ghost from his past promised to be the key to a new chapter, one that could shift the balance of power and lead to Kozlov's undoing or their own downfall.

The gala's veil had been torn away, exposing the intricate dance of predators and prey beneath. And as the clock struck midnight, the true face of the night was revealed — a face marked by the impending storm that was about to break.

Chapter 25: Betrayal Unveiled

The Broker's Deception

The glittering remnants of the gala lay behind them, the opulence of the night shattered by the chaos that had erupted. Max and Eleanor, having slipped through the fingers of the Met thanks to the diversion, found themselves in the dim backstreets, where the city's façade of grandeur gave way to the stark reality of steel and concrete.

Isabella, the broker who had once been a lynchpin in Max's network, emerged from the darkness of an alley, her face a canvas of tension and fear. "Max," she hissed, her eyes darting around nervously. "I need to talk to you. It's urgent."

Max regarded her with a steely gaze, his hand subtly reaching for the weapon concealed beneath his jacket. "Talk," he commanded, his body language protective of Eleanor, who stood slightly behind him.

Isabella's eyes flicked to Eleanor, a flash of something unreadable passing across her features. "It's a trap," she confessed, her voice barely above a whisper. "The Kozlovs ... they know about your plans. They've been one step ahead the whole time."

The revelation struck Max like a physical blow, the implications of her words like the tightening of a noose. He had always known that the Kozlovs were formidable adversaries, but the depth of their infiltration was more extensive than he had anticipated.

Before Max could probe further, Isabella's hand whipped out, a small revolver suddenly aimed at Eleanor.

It was a movement born of desperation, the act of a cornered animal.

Max reacted on instinct, his own gun drawn and fired in one fluid, practised motion. The shot rang out, a stark declaration in the silent street, and Isabella crumpled to the ground, her weapon skittering away into the darkness.

Eleanor stood frozen, the brush with death leaving a pale shadow on her elegant features. Max moved to her, his eyes scanning the area for any further threats, his mind racing to understand how Isabella, the broker he had trusted, had turned against them.

In the wake of the gunfire, Max knew they needed to move — and quickly. He took Eleanor's arm, guiding her away from the scene, his mind working through the implications of Isabella's betrayal.

They needed a new place to regroup, to realign their fractured plans in the face of this new threat. The betrayal had been a sharp lesson; trust was a luxury they could ill afford. Max's vow to protect Eleanor had never been more critical, and as they vanished into the labyrinth of the city, the weight of his promise bore down upon him with the force of a solemn oath.

*

Max and Eleanor moved swiftly, putting distance between themselves and the scene of Isabella's betrayal. The echoing sound of their hurried footsteps on the wet pavement was a stark counterpoint to the cacophony that had engulfed the gala just moments ago.

"Max, why would Isabella turn on us like that?" Eleanor's voice was steady, but there was a tremor of disbelief beneath her words.

Max kept his eyes forward, scanning the path ahead while his mind raced. "Isabella was a broker; her loyalty was to the highest bidder. It seems the Kozlovs made her an offer she couldn't refuse," he said, his voice edged with bitterness.

"But to kill me?" Eleanor's question hung in the air, a chilling reminder of the night's grim turn.

"The Kozlovs are desperate," Max replied. "Desperate enough to use any means necessary to maintain their grip on power."

They found sanctuary in another safe house, an unassuming apartment nestled within a maze of buildings. Once inside, Max secured the door, and they both allowed themselves a moment to process the night's events.

Eleanor's mind was a whirlwind of emotion and analysis. The realisation that Isabella had been coerced into becoming an assassin for the Kozlovs was a testament to their ruthlessness. It also meant that there might be others, once allies or neutral parties, who could have been similarly compromised.

Max saw the dawning understanding in Eleanor's eyes and knew it mirrored his own. "We have to assume that the Kozlovs have more than one card up their sleeve," he said, his tone grave. "We can't trust anyone outside of this room."

The stark reality of their situation settled upon them with oppressive weight. Their list of allies had been dwindling, and now they had to consider the possibility that anyone could be a potential enemy. The lines had been drawn, and it was clear that the Kozlovs were not the only ones capable of manipulation and deceit.

Eleanor approached Max, her resolve solidifying. "Then it's just us," she declared. "We need to reassess our strategy, use what we have to expose the Kozlovs before they can strike at us again."

Max nodded, the gears in his mind already turning. "We'll need to be unpredictable, stay mobile, and make our moves count."

Their eyes met, and in that gaze, they found a renewed sense of purpose. The betrayal had not weakened their resolve; if anything, it had strengthened their determination to see their mission through to the end.

With fresh urgency, they set to work, poring over the evidence they had collected, the leads they had yet to follow, and the assets they still had at their disposal. The path forward would be fraught with danger, but they were committed to walking it together.

As the night gave way to day, Max and Eleanor realigned their loyalties to each other, their shared mission the only beacon in the encroaching darkness. They were a united front against an enemy that had shown they would stop at nothing to retain their power.

*

With the first light of dawn creeping into the safe house, Max and Eleanor sat amidst a sprawl of papers and open laptops, a silent tableau of urgency and focus. The betrayal had not only narrowed their circle of trust but also forced them to re-evaluate their strategy under the harsh light of new realities.

Eleanor broke the silence, her voice a mix of fatigue and determination. "We've been reacting to Kozlov's moves. We need to take the initiative, turn the tables on him."

Max, his mind a battleground of tactical scenarios,

nodded in agreement. "We have enough evidence to start a fire under Kozlov, but we need to make sure it burns hot and fast before he can snuff it out."

Eleanor leaned back, rubbing her temples. "We've been playing chess, but Kozlov's been playing poker. He's been bluffing and forcing our hand."

"It's time we change the game, then," Max said, his eyes meeting hers. "We use the evidence we have as leverage, not just to expose him, but to dismantle his support. If we take out his pillars, the roof will cave in."

A plan began to take shape, born of their combined experience and the harsh lessons learned. They would need to stay under the radar, use secure lines of communication, and perhaps most importantly, they would need to be swift and decisive.

Eleanor sifted through the documents, her finger pausing on a photo of a key Member of Parliament — someone with enough influence to make or break Kozlov's hold on power. "We start here," she declared, tapping the photo. "We expose this connection and watch the dominoes fall."

Max considered the implications, the potential for backlash, the escalation it would undoubtedly provoke. It was a bold move, but boldness was a currency they were not short on.

As the city awoke, oblivious to the undercurrents that ran beneath its streets, Max and Eleanor prepared to resurface from the depths of their clandestine world. Their next moves would be critical, each action rippling through the network of power and crime they sought to destroy.

Max and Eleanor emerged from the safe house, their evidence concealed on encrypted drives, their steps measured but certain. The quiet dawn was behind them, and ahead lay the storm they would conjure — a storm that would sweep through the city and leave Marcus Kozlov exposed and vulnerable.

*

The city was stirring to life, the early morning bustle beginning to swell into the arteries of London's streets. Max and Eleanor found themselves blending into the crowd, their presence as unremarkable as any other commuter. Yet beneath their ordinary façade, a plan of extraordinary consequence was taking shape.

Their first move was to contact Dmitri Ivanov, an associate of Yuri Dubrovnik, whose loyalty to Max had been proven in past operations. Dmitri's expertise in cyber-espionage would be invaluable in disseminating the evidence they had against the Kozlov empire. A secure message was sent to Dmitri, a digital baton passed in their relay against corruption.

Meanwhile, a new figure had entered the fray, one whose name had been whispered in the dark corners of the city's underworld — Igor Savchenko. Igor, a significant figure in the criminal hierarchy, had his own reasons for wanting Kozlov's downfall. The enemy of my enemy is my friend, as the adage goes, and while Max did not trust him implicitly, Igor's resources could not be ignored.

Eleanor, her legal mind always strategizing, suggested they leverage Igor's desire to ascend in the pecking order. "If Kozlov falls, it creates a vacuum. One that Savchenko would be keen to fill," she said.

Max knew the risks of engaging with someone like

Igor but also recognised the tactical advantage. "We'll need to keep Savchenko on a tight leash," he cautioned.

As they navigated their next steps, they remained acutely aware of the delicate balance they had to maintain. Their alliance with John had already shown the strength that former adversaries could bring to a common cause. It was time to expand that strength, to draw in new allies from the shadows.

Their day was spent in constant motion, their plans adaptive and fluid. They met with John in a nondescript café to update him on their strategy. John, his experience in covert operations a valuable asset, listened intently, his mind already calculating the myriad of ways he could contribute to their offensive.

"Kozlov won't know what hit him," John assured, the ghost of a smile on his lips.

This resulted in an impromptu war council, held in an abandoned warehouse that had once been a Kozlov storage site. Max, Eleanor, John, Dmitri, and now Igor Savchenko each stood like chess pieces on a board that spanned the entire city. Their moves were plotted with care, each player aware of their role in the greater strategy.

As night began to fall, their plans were set, the pieces in motion. Max looked at each of his unlikely allies, knowing that the coming days would test them all. Yet there was strength in this makeshift fellowship, a determination that bound them together in their pursuit of a common goal.

The cityscape was silhouetted against the twilight sky, the lights beginning to twinkle like stars fallen to earth. In the heart of that urban constellation, a silent battle raged — a battle that would determine the fate of those who dared to defy the darkness.

*

The warehouse, once a silent keeper of illicit goods, now resonated with the hushed tones of conspiracy and resolve. Max, Eleanor, John, Dmitri, and Igor stood around a makeshift table littered with blueprints, digital tablets, and a network of interlaced strings connecting photographs and documents — a tangible representation of Kozlov's sprawling empire.

Igor, whose motivations were as murky as the Thames at twilight, presented his own intelligence — locations of Kozlov's safe houses and the names of officials on his payroll. His information was a goldmine, but Max received it with the caution it warranted, knowing that in the shadows of their war, every piece of information could be a double-edged sword.

John, his demeanour as unreadable as ever, suggested a series of coordinated strikes — disinformation campaigns, strategic leaks to the press, and tactical disruptions of Kozlov's operations. Each suggestion was met with nods of approval; they were actions that would sow chaos in the ranks of their enemy.

Eleanor's legal acumen shone as she outlined the prosecution of their case in the court of public opinion. "The evidence we release must be irrefutable," she insisted. "We'll need to make Kozlov's allies distance themselves out of fear and self-preservation."

Dmitri, his fingers skating over a tablet screen, nodded in agreement. "I can ensure that the evidence is seen far and wide," he offered. "By morning, Kozlov's name will be synonymous with corruption."

As the evening waned, the collective spirit of the group solidified. They were an ensemble cast in the theatre of justice, each playing their part to bring down the curtain on Kozlov's reign.

Max, who had once borne the burden alone, found strength in this unlikely fellowship. He looked at each face, from Eleanor's determined gaze to Igor's inscrutable expression, and felt the tide turning.

The meeting adjourned with a silent vow, each member disappearing into the night, a phantom force against the backdrop of a sleeping city. They had laid their plans, set their traps, and now, as London slumbered, the unseen web of war stretched across its breadth, ready to ensnare the unsuspecting Kozlov in its strands.

Max and Eleanor were once again in the shadows, watching the city from their vantage point. The night was still, but the energy of impending action charged the air. They shared a quiet moment, a breath in the eye of the storm, before the battle would truly begin.

Max, Eleanor, and their allies have set their plans in motion. The city becomes the grand stage for their machinations against Kozlov. As dawn approaches, the consequences of their actions will soon unfold, and the next part will follow the dramatic fallout of their intricate war dance.

*

With the city ensconced in the vulnerability of pre-dawn stillness, Max and Eleanor remained in the shadows, their watchful eyes tracing the skyline they were about to challenge. The air was thick with anticipation, the sort that heralded storms on the horizon. London, in its unsuspecting slumber, was the stage for the day's silent symphony, one composed of clandestine whispers and the soundless steps of operatives in the dark.

Eleanor, her mind a whirlwind of statutes and legal precedents, considered their next legal manoeuvre. "When this is over," she murmured, "we'll have to ensure the evidence can stand up in court."

Max nodded, his focus on the tactical aspects of their operation. "Evidence will be worthless if we don't survive to present it. Our first move is to ensure Kozlov's immediate circle begins to doubt him. Once suspicion sparks, it spreads like wildfire."

They were interrupted by the vibration of Max's secure phone — a message from Dmitri confirming the dissemination of the evidence. In the digital realm, the first salvo had been fired. Kozlov's financial records, his network of bribery and coercion, were now laid bare for the world to see.

Simultaneously, John, from his vantage point, executed a series of diversions designed to spread Kozlov's forces thin, creating vulnerabilities. These feints and forays were subtle, yet their impact would be significant.

Igor, in his role, manipulated the undercurrents of the criminal world, sowing discord and fear among those who once served Kozlov with blind loyalty. The dissonance was a quiet knife, one that began to cut the ties that held Kozlov's empire together.

As the first light of dawn touched the horizon, Max and Eleanor prepared to move. They had orchestrated a symphony of subterfuge, and the overture had just begun. Their steps were measured and their minds sharp as they initiated the day's gambit.

The city began to wake, the early morning light casting long shadows that seemed to play out the drama unfolding in its heart. Max and Eleanor were shadows among them, moving with purpose, driven by a cause that was righteous and true.

And somewhere, in the burgeoning daylight, Rebecca Turner prepared her pen to write the history they were making. Her role as a journalist was not just to observe but to document the fall or the rise of those daring to stand against the darkness.

London stirred, and with it, the operation against Kozlov began to unfold in earnest. The stage was set, the actors in place, and the first act of the day's play was underway. The outcome was uncertain, the risks high, but the determination of Max, Eleanor, and their allies was unyielding.

They stepped forward into the burgeoning dawn, the harbinger of reckoning for Marcus Kozlov. The day would be long, and the fight would be hard, but they were ready — ready to face what was to come, ready to change the city forever.

Chapter 26: The Enemy Within

Unravelling Deceit

The fallout from the gala left a tangled web of chaos and uncertainty in its wake. Max and Eleanor, having narrowly escaped the fray, found themselves holed up in a dimly lit basement room that had once served as a safe meeting place for those who operated in the city's underbelly. Now it was their impromptu command centre, the walls lined with monitors displaying various feeds and documents that held the clues to their next move.

The question that gnawed at Max was not just who had turned Isabella against them, but why. It was a thread that, when pulled, would unravel the deeper machinations within Kozlov's organisation. "We need to figure out who flipped Isabella," Max stated, his voice low but firm.

Eleanor was already sifting through the data, her eyes scanning lines of communication, financial transactions, and personal profiles. "There has to be a trace," she murmured, "some sign that we missed."

As they delved into the digital evidence, patterns began to emerge — subtle anomalies in the communication networks, strange financial transfers, and most telling, a series of coded messages that had all the hallmarks of Kozlov's handiwork. But within those messages lay the contradiction, the duality of an enemy who might once have been a friend.

Max leaned over the computer screen as Eleanor pointed out the discrepancies. "This ... this is language I've seen before. It's not Kozlov's usual style," he said, the realisation dawning on him. "It's someone mimicking him."

The betrayal cut deeper than Max had anticipated, the possibility that someone within his trusted circle had been turned against them, a mole who had been hiding in plain sight.

As they traced the digital breadcrumbs, the trail led them to an unexpected name, one that had been allied with them since the beginning — Dmitri Ivanov. Max refused to believe it. Dmitri had been a loyal ally, a crucial element in their fight against Kozlov. But the evidence was irrefutable, painting a picture of a friend turned foe, of a trusted ally who had been compromised.

Max was faced with the duality of the enemy within, the painful acknowledgement that the war they fought was fraught with deception, that those they counted as friends could be turned against them, their loyalty bought or coerced.

The realisation forced Max into a corner, demanding a decision that would alter the course of their mission. He could confront Dmitri, seek an explanation, perhaps even attempt to turn him back to their side. Or he could cut him out, sever the connection and lose a valuable asset.

Eleanor watched Max closely, her expression one of concern. "Max, we need to be sure. If we confront Dmitri without proof ..."

"We have proof," Max interrupted, his jaw set. "The only question now is what we do with it."

The gravity of the situation settled around them like dust after an explosion. Max knew that the choice he made would send ripples through their operation and would impact the lives of everyone involved.

He stood up, his decision made. "We bring Dmitri in. We need answers, and we need to know exactly where he stands."

Eleanor nodded, her hand reaching out to squeeze his arm in a gesture of support. "Then we do this together," she said. "We face the enemy within, and we find out the truth."

Max's next steps were critical. The future of their mission hinged on the loyalty of their allies and the veracity of the evidence they held. The enemy within had been unmasked, and now it was time to confront the truth, no matter how painful it might be.

*

The atmosphere was thick with tension as Max and Eleanor prepared to confront Dmitri Ivanov. They had relocated to a small derelict warehouse on the outskirts of the city, a place where privacy was guaranteed and the potential for unwanted ears was null. Dmitri, upon receiving Max's terse message, had agreed to meet, his response time adding another layer of suspicion to his already questionable loyalties.

As they awaited his arrival, Max went over their approach. "We need to be direct but cautious. If Dmitri is under Kozlov's influence, he could be dangerous," he cautioned, checking his sidearm.

Eleanor nodded, her legal mind formulating the questions that needed to be asked. "We'll start with the evidence, make him explain the discrepancies. If he's innocent, he'll have answers."

The sound of a vehicle pulling up outside broke their strategizing. Through the small, grimy window, the headlights of Dmitri's car cut through the darkness, signalling his arrival. The moment of truth was upon them.

Dmitri entered the warehouse, his expression one of

confusion and concern. "Max, what's this about?" he asked, looking between Max and Eleanor.

Max didn't waste time on pleasantries. "Dmitri, we've found evidence that suggests you've been leaking information to Kozlov," he stated bluntly, watching Dmitri's face for any tell-tale signs of guilt.

The accusation seemed to hit Dmitri like a physical blow. His shock was evident, his brow furrowing as he processed the words. "That's impossible," he protested. "I've been loyal to you, to the cause. You know that, Max."

Eleanor stepped forward, presenting the coded messages and financial transactions they had uncovered. "Explain these, then. They were traced back to your systems."

Dmitri's eyes scanned the documents, his face paling as he read. "I ... I don't know. This isn't me, Max. Someone's setting me up."

The room was heavy with the weight of suspicion and the echo of betrayal. Max and Eleanor exchanged a glance, the silent communication between them speaking volumes. They had to decide whether Dmitri's words held any truth, or if he was merely playing them for fools.

Max's next words were measured, his decision clear. "We're going to dig deeper, Dmitri. If you're telling the truth, we'll find out. But until then, you're off the operation."

Dmitri nodded, resignation etched onto his features. "Do what you must. You'll see I'm not your enemy."

With that, Dmitri left, his departure leaving a void of uncertainty behind him. Max and Eleanor were left to ponder their next move, their trust in their allies shaken but not shattered.

Max and Eleanor delved further into the evidence, seeking the truth in a sea of lies. The enemy within had been confronted, but the veracity of Dmitri's allegiance remained a question mark that hung over their operation like a dark cloud.

*

After Dmitri's departure, Max and Eleanor returned to their screens, diving into a detailed investigation of the digital trails and financial records. They worked with the meticulousness of surgeons, dissecting the layers of encryption and hidden files that Dmitri had been accused of manipulating.

Eleanor's expertise was invaluable, her legal background allowing them to navigate the complex corporate structures that Kozlov had used as fronts for his illicit activities. "We're looking for anomalies, patterns that don't match the established behaviour," she instructed, her eyes not leaving the screen.

Max, meanwhile, kept an open channel to John, who was using his network to cross-verify the evidence they had against Dmitri. "Keep an eye out for any disinformation," Max said into the secure line. "If Dmitri is being framed, the real traitor will want to cover their tracks."

The investigation was tedious and time-consuming, but slowly, the web of deceit began to unravel. Max was the first to notice a series of transactions that didn't align with the others. "Here, look at this," he called to Eleanor. "These transfers originated from a different source."

Eleanor leaned over, her sharp eyes quickly parsing the data. "You're right. These aren't Dmitri's signatures. Someone's been using his credentials."

The revelation was a breakthrough, but it also meant that the true enemy was still at large, perhaps even closer than they had feared. They needed to act quickly, to flush out the mole before they could do more damage.

Max's decision was immediate. "We go on the offensive. Whoever this is, they're still out there, and now they know we're onto them."

Eleanor nodded in agreement, her mind already racing through potential strategies. "We could set a trap, leak false information, and see who bites," she suggested.

Max was already on the move, his military instincts kicking in. "Let's do it. We'll set the stage for our mole, make them think they've won. When they show themselves, we'll be ready."

The trap was set with precision, a piece of bait that no double agent could resist — the promise of a final piece of incriminating evidence that would supposedly seal Kozlov's fate. All they had to do was wait for the traitor to reveal themselves.

As the hours ticked by, the tension in the room was palpable. Max and Eleanor watched the digital breadcrumbs they had laid out, waiting for the tell-tale signs of their unseen adversary taking the bait.

Finally, a hit. An IP address, previously dormant, sprung to life, accessing the false information they had leaked. Max traced the connection, his hands steady despite the adrenaline coursing through his veins.

The digital trail led them to an unexpected name, a player they had never suspected, revealing the true extent of Kozlov's reach within their ranks.

The enemy within had been unmasked, and as the chapter drew to a close, Max and Eleanor prepared to face off against the betrayer in a confrontation that would determine the fate of their mission and their lives.

*

The dim glow of the computer screens in the makeshift command centre barely lit the determined faces of Max and Eleanor as they stared at the name now highlighted on the monitor. A wave of betrayal, deeper than they had ever anticipated, washed over them. The mole was not just a peripheral member of their team; it was someone who had fought alongside them, who had shared their victories and setbacks alike.

Eleanor's voice broke the silence, a mixture of anger and disbelief lacing her words. "George Blackwell? But he's been with us since the beginning. How could he?"

Max's mind raced, memories of past operations where George had been instrumental flashing before him. He had trusted George, had considered him a friend and a brother-in-arms. But the evidence was irrefutable; the transactions, the covert communications, all led back to him.

"We need to confront him. Now," Max said, his voice carrying the weight of command. He reached for his phone, but Eleanor stopped him with a hand on his wrist.

"Wait," she urged. "If we confront him directly, we might spook him. We don't know how deep this goes or who else might be involved."

Max considered her words, the tactical part of his brain kicking into gear. "You're right. We need to be smart about this. We need to draw him out."

The plan formed quickly between them. They would use the same tactics that had served them so well against Kozlov — subterfuge, disinformation, and the element of surprise. They set up a meeting with George, a ruse that would bring him out into the open.

Eleanor sent the message, her fingers steady despite the storm of emotions she felt. They baited the hook with talk of new evidence, of a breakthrough that would require all hands on deck. It was the kind of message George couldn't ignore.

A secluded location was chosen as the meeting place, an abandoned factory that had been one of their safe points early in the operation. The area was open, hard to approach without being seen, and even harder to escape from quickly.

Max and Eleanor arrived first, taking positions that would give them a clear view of the area. They were armed, more with the knowledge of George's betrayal than with the firepower they carried. This was a confrontation that would rely on wits as much as weapons.

George arrived, his steps hesitant, a sheen of sweat on his brow that wasn't entirely due to the summer heat. "Max, Eleanor, what's this about? What breakthrough?" he asked, his eyes flicking between them, looking for the evidence that was promised.

Eleanor stepped forward, her voice cold. "Cut the act, George. We know it's been you all along. The mole inside our operation."

The accusation hung in the air, and for a moment, there was a silence so deep it seemed to absorb all other sounds. Then George's facade cracked, his shoulders slumping as the fight went out of him. "I had no choice," he said, his voice barely a whisper. "They have my daughter."

The revelation hit Max and Eleanor with the force of a physical blow. The enemy they had been fighting had been one of their own, coerced into betrayal by a threat to his family.

Max's decision was immediate, his next steps clear.

"We're going to fix this, George. Together. But from now on, we do it our way. No more secrets."

Eleanor nodded, her gaze hardening with resolve. "We're going to bring Kozlov down, for all of us."

The trio stood in the fading light of the day, the truth laid bare between them. The next move would be as a united front, a blend of their collective resolve to end the tyranny that had held them all captive.

The action didn't cease with George's confession. It was merely the beginning of a new chapter in their fight, a chapter that would see them stand together against the darkness, with the knowledge that the enemy within could be as deadly as the one lurking outside.

*

Under the heavy silence of the abandoned factory, the trio quickly devised a new strategy. Max, Eleanor, and George, united by circumstance, began to weave a plan that would turn their dire situation into an advantage.

"Kozlov thinks he's got us cornered," Max said, his mind racing with possibilities. "We'll use that. George, they believe you're still their inside man. We feed them information, control what they know."

George nodded, a glint of determination returning to his eyes. "I'll tell them we're planning to lay low, that the gala fiasco has scared us off."

Eleanor interjected, "And while they're busy patting themselves on the back, we strike at the heart of the organisation." She pulled up a map on her tablet, pointing to a series of locations. "These are Kozlov's remaining strongholds in the city. We hit them all simultaneously."

Max approved the plan, already visualising the operation.

"We'll need to coordinate with John and the others. Precision is key; there's no room for error."

They worked into the waning hours of the afternoon, each detail meticulously planned, every contingency accounted for. The factory became a hive of silent activity, the air charged with the electric current of impending action.

As the plan took shape, the roles were clear. George would be their voice inside the enemy's camp, sowing disinformation. Max would lead the strikes, the tip of the spear in their assault. Eleanor would be the architect, her knowledge of the law and Kozlov's organisation guiding their hand.

The setting sun cast long shadows across the factory floor, the dying light a metaphor for the fading influence of Kozlov over the city. The trio stood together, an alliance of necessity and newfound trust, ready to reclaim the streets from the darkness that had held them for too long.

With the pieces in place, they dispersed, each to play their part in the grand scheme. Max and Eleanor shared a final look, one of unspoken understanding. They had come far, through trials and tribulations, and now they stood on the brink of retribution.

The city, unaware of the silent war waged in its heart, continued its eternal rhythm as dusk fell. But within that rhythm was a new beat, a pulse of defiance that grew stronger with each passing minute.

There would be no retreat into the night but with an advance towards a new dawn. Max, Eleanor, and George, each a catalyst for change, moved through the cityscape, their plan a whisper on the wind that promised a storm was coming for Marcus Kozlov.

*

As twilight descended over the city, Max, Eleanor, and George dispersed to set their intricate plan in motion. The false information George fed to Kozlov's inner circle was designed to lure them into a sense of complacency, to make them believe they held the upper hand.

Max and Eleanor, meanwhile, rendezvoused with John and other key allies they had gathered over their long campaign — each one a specialist in their field, each one vital to the operation's success. The targets were Kozlov's remaining strongholds: hidden warehouses, covert financial centres, and clandestine meeting spots that formed the sinew and bone of his criminal enterprise.

Eleanor took charge of the logistical side, coordinating the attacks with military precision. "At twenty-two hundred hours, we hit the first location. Every fifteen minutes, another falls," she instructed, her voice clear and authoritative. "By the time Kozlov realises what's happening, it'll be too late."

Max, with John and a handpicked team, would spearhead the assaults. Their approach was direct and unyielding — a series of sharp, surgical strikes intended to cripple Kozlov's infrastructure beyond repair.

The rest of their allies were spread out across the city, each unit with a specific role in the operation. They were the unseen warriors of the night, their presence only felt by those who would wake to find their world had changed.

In the hours leading up to the operation, the city pulsed with unseen energy. The participants moved like phantoms, their actions unnoticed by the civilian populace, but each movement was a note in the symphony of their strategy, building to a crescendo that would break the silence with its impact.

Eleanor remained at the communications hub, her

fingers dancing across multiple keyboards, relaying information and confirming that each team was in position. "All units, stand by," she radioed, her voice the thread that tied the disparate elements together.

Max, cloaked in the anonymity of the night, gave a final nod to John. "Let's finish this," he said, the edge in his voice matching the blade he was prepared to drive into the heart of Kozlov's empire.

The city seemed to hold its breath as the clock ticked closer to the hour. In the quiet before the storm, the vast machine of their vengeance hummed with readiness, the tension of anticipation palpable in the air.

And then, with the arrival of 2200 hours, the night erupted into a controlled chaos. The first stronghold was hit, the element of surprise complete, the execution flawless. As Eleanor had promised, every fifteen minutes, another part of Kozlov's empire crumbled.

In the command centre, Eleanor monitored the progress, marking each success with a silent cheer. With each report that came in, a piece of the darkness that had shrouded the city was lifted, revealing the light of a new dawn on the horizon.

The situation reached its zenith as the last stronghold fell, the culmination of months of planning, of sacrifice and determination. Max and his allies had set the stage for the final act — the confrontation with Marcus Kozlov himself.

The city would wake to a new order, the balance of power irrevocably shifted. The enemy within had been exposed, the lines redrawn, and as the first light of dawn approached, Max and Eleanor stood ready to face whatever came next.

Chapter 27: Tangled Loyalties

The Moral Labyrinth

The cold light of dawn had never seemed so stark to Max as it did now, revealing a city that was a battleground of shadows. In the aftermath of their calculated strikes against Kozlov's network, Max's mind was a whirlwind of past and present. Memories of comrades fallen and battles fought juxtaposed against the here and now — where his war was no longer against distant enemies, but against a corruption that had seeped into the very streets he walked.

In an old, derelict building that had once been a symbol of prosperity, Max convened with his closest allies. Eleanor was there, her sharp intellect a guiding light. John stood ready, his loyalty as unwavering as his aim. And then there was Liam, the friend from another life who now walked the tightrope between lawful duty and the deeper calling of justice.

"Liam, you're sure Bennett doesn't suspect?" Max asked, his gaze intent on the detective.

Liam nodded, the lines on his face speaking to the nights without sleep. "Bennett's focused on the fallout from the strikes. She sees it as a victory for the Met, a step closer to bringing Kozlov in."

"And she's right, in a way," Eleanor interjected. "But she doesn't know we're not done yet. That we can't be done until the whole network is dismantled."

The plan they had was risky, reliant not just on their cunning or strength of arms, but on the very loyalties that had brought them all together. Max needed to draw out the final loyalists to Kozlov — those who would act to protect their master or seek vengeance for his capture.

"John, I need you to leak our location," Max said, turning to the former operative. "Make them believe it's an accident, a slip-up in our operational security."

John's nod was curt, the understanding clear between soldiers. "They'll come," he said. "They'll come for you, for revenge."

"That's what we're counting on," Max replied, his eyes steely. "We'll be ready for them."

The day wore on as they prepared, each member of Max's team taking on their role with the precision of a well-oiled machine. Weapons were cleaned and loaded, positions fortified, and escape routes meticulously planned.

As dusk approached, the tension within the walls of the building was palpable — a living thing that thrummed in the air. They were ready, their trap set, their resolve unshakable.

And then, as the first shadows of evening began to stretch across the city, the enemy made their move. A convoy of black vehicles, sleek and ominous, approached their location. Max's hand clenched around his weapon; the moment of truth was upon them.

The vehicles stopped, and from them emerged figures clad in tactical gear. They moved with purpose, their intent clear — they were here to wipe out the thorn in Kozlov's side once and for all.

Max and John knew that the men they were observing were not trained soldiers, their movement a telltale sign of their inexperience despite the high-spec weapons and equipment that covered them head to toe. They moved as individuals and not as a team, experience that was instilled in Max and John through many years of special forces training and operations.

The would-be soldiers finally organised themselves to a point where they were ready to bring violence to Max and his team.

But Max and his team were not so easily bested. The fight was swift and brutal, the air filled with the sound of gunfire and shouted commands. When the dust settled, Max's team stood victorious, the would-be avengers of Kozlov's empire lying defeated at their feet.

It was a turning point, a clear message to any who still supported Kozlov that his reign was truly over. Max stood among his team, their breathing heavy, their bodies wired from the adrenaline of battle. They had won, but at a cost that would weigh heavily on them all.

Max and his team had faced their enemy and emerged victorious, but the war was not over. As they looked towards the horizon, where the last light of day was giving way to the darkness of night, they knew that the final showdown was still to come.

*

As the dust settled in the aftermath of the skirmish, Max surveyed the dim warehouse. The air was thick with the residue of gunpowder and the heavy breaths of his weary but resolute team. This had been more than a firefight; it was a declaration, a clear signal that the endgame was upon them.

Eleanor's voice cut through the aftermath, grounded yet urgent. "We need to move now. They know where we are. Any element of surprise we had is gone."

Max nodded, his mind already racing through their

next steps. "We'll split up," he instructed. "Meet at the secondary location in two hours. Use the back alleys, stay off the main roads."

John, checking his weapons, looked up. "What's the play, Max? They'll be coming for us with everything they've got now."

Max's eyes were hard as flint as he replied, "That's exactly what we're counting on. We want them to come."

Liam interjected, stepping forward, his allegiance to Max now more evident than ever. "I'll head back first, throw Bennett off the scent. Keep her focused on the clean-up here. It'll give you more time to enact the next phase."

Max clapped a hand on Liam's shoulder, a gesture of deep trust and gratitude. "Be careful," he said, knowing well the delicate line Liam walked.

The team dispersed, slipping away into the shadows of the encroaching night. Max and Eleanor remained for a moment longer, the weight of leadership heavy upon their shoulders.

Eleanor looked to Max, her voice steady. "You've always known this might be a one-way trip."

Max met her gaze, the understanding between them unspoken. "We finish this, Eleanor. For everyone who's fallen, for everyone who's still standing. We finish this."

They left the warehouse by separate exits, melting into the cityscape that had become an extension of the battlefield. Max moved with purpose, his thoughts on the friends and foes alike who had coloured the tapestry of his life. The past, with its clear demarcations of right and wrong, seemed a distant memory against the present's complexity.

He arrived at the secondary location, an abandoned

print shop that had once told stories of the world but now stood silent. There, he began to prepare for the final act, the one that would see Kozlov's downfall or their own.

The city breathed around him, a living entity unaware of the silent war waged in its heart. Max stood ready, his past and present colliding in the single goal that had consumed him. The night was far from over, and the darkest hours were yet to come.

Max and his team regroup, with the knowledge that their battle has only intensified. Their loyalties, both old and new, drive them forward, setting the stage for the final confrontation. As they navigate the treacherous terrain they have created, they are ready to face whatever comes next to bring their fight to a close.

*

Max hunched over the cluttered table strewn with maps and scattered reports, the low buzz of a lone fluorescent light above mingling with the silence of anticipation. The print shop, with its walls echoing the hush of forgotten stories, now harboured the architects of a new narrative — one that would unravel the corruption woven into the city's highest echelons.

Eleanor's presence was a beacon of focus as she laid out the evidence they had gathered. "The corruption isn't just deep, Max, it's institutional," she said, her finger tracing lines connecting high-ranking officials and Kozlov's illicit operations. "We have MPs who've been puppets on Kozlov's strings for years."

Max absorbed the spiderweb of influence that sprawled before them, the tendrils of Kozlov's reach extending far beyond the criminal underworld and into the pillars of society. "Once we bring this to light, there's no going back," he said, the gravity of their revelations weighing heavily upon him.

He thought of Liam, now a crucial link between the lawful world and their shadow crusade. His friend was out there, in the heart of the Met's machinery, casting stones that would send ripples through the still waters of the establishment. "Liam will manage from the inside. He'll ensure that the fallout reaches the right ears."

A nod from Eleanor sealed their resolve. "It's time the city saw the true face behind the mask of propriety. The MPs, the financiers, the so-called pillars of the community — they're all about to be exposed."

As the cloak of night wrapped tighter around the city, Max readied himself for the next phase. They would leak the evidence to the press, to the public, and to every agency that had turned a blind eye, wilfully or otherwise, to the rot within. It was a calculated risk, one that could ignite the spark of justice or see them engulfed in the blaze.

The quiet before the storm was shattered by the sudden chime of Max's secure phone. A message from an unknown number blinked on the screen, its contents a jolt to his system. "It's a meeting," Max murmured, "between Kozlov's remaining lieutenants and several key officials. Tonight."

Eleanor leaned in, her eyes narrowing. "If we can catch them all together, we can tear down the whole structure."

Max knew the window of opportunity was narrow, the margins thin. "We'll need everyone on this. It's now or never."

They moved quickly, rallying their scattered forces with messages coded in urgency. John responded first, his reply a simple acknowledgment: *On it.*

The stage was set, the players called to their marks, and the final scene awaited its cue. Max and Eleanor, their every move now a convergence of past battles and the promise of a new dawn, stepped out into the embrace of night, where the city's fate hung in the balance.

As they made their way toward the clandestine meeting, the weight of their mission was a tangible force. They were about to shine a light so bright it would sear through the veils of deception, exposing the corruption that had burrowed into the city's heart.

*

The city's underbelly was quiet after the chaos that had reigned just hours before. Max, Eleanor, and their team navigated through the labyrinth of alleys and side streets, converging on the location where Kozlov's remaining lieutenants and their corrupt political allies were to meet. This was the fulcrum upon which the future would tilt, and they were the lever.

John, his demeanour stoic and movements precise, was a shadow flitting from one cover to the next. He was the embodiment of the skills honed through years of covert operations — a wraith, and tonight, an avenger. His eyes were keen, missing nothing, his hands steady, ready to act.

Max led with silent confidence, his own experience matching John's step for step. They were two sides of the same coin, warriors forged in different fires but tempered by the same resolve.

As they approached the derelict warehouse chosen for the clandestine gathering, Max signalled a halt, his hand raised. He turned to Eleanor and whispered, "Stay back. John and I will handle the entry. We need you to cover our exit."

Eleanor nodded, her trust in Max's judgment absolute. She found her position, a vantage point with a clear view of the warehouse's entrances and exits.

Meanwhile, Liam was a ghost in the machine, feeding disinformation to DI Bennett and the Met to keep them off the trail. His actions were subtle — a nudge here, a slight delay there — enough to give Max the time needed without arousing suspicion. He felt the weight of his dual loyalties bearing down upon him, a crucible that tested his mettle at every turn.

Max and John, communicating with hand signals, breached the perimeter of the meeting site. Inside, the air was thick with whispers of conspiracy and the rustling of expensive fabric. The figures gathered in the gloom were a tableau of treachery, their silhouettes betraying the opulence that ill-gotten gains afforded.

With a swift motion, Max and John incapacitated the guards, silent as the grave. They slipped inside, two spectres among the living, their presence unknown to the conspirators whose fates were soon to be sealed.

The voices within grew clearer, the arrogance and assurance in their tones igniting a fire in Max's chest. These were the puppeteers, the architects of misery, who sold their souls and their city for silver and gold.

Max's eyes met John's, and with a nod, they sprang into action. The room erupted into chaos as the two operatives dismantled the meeting with surgical efficiency. Gunfire was a last resort; they relied instead on the element of surprise, on speed and precision.

In moments, it was over. The lieutenants and their politician allies were restrained, the evidence of their collusion captured on the recording devices Max and John had brought with them.

As Max surveyed the captives, his expression was stone. "Justice is coming for you," he promised them, his voice the harbinger of retribution.

The team exfiltrated as seamlessly as they had entered, melting back into the night with their prisoners. The operation had been a success, but it was merely the prelude to the final act.

As they regrouped, Max's mind was already on the steps ahead. The finale awaited, the last push to topple Kozlov's empire and cleanse the city of its festering wound.

The night was still young, and the real battle was just beginning.

*

The backstreets of London served as silent witnesses to the procession of figures that emerged from the darkness. Max, leading the group with the restrained figures of the corrupt elite in tow, moved towards an unmarked van discreetly positioned in the gloom. Eleanor, her gaze fixed and determined, followed close behind, ensuring no detail was overlooked.

The air was electric with tension as they loaded their captives into the vehicle. Each member of the political cabal, their finery now stained with the grit of their capture, wore expressions of fear and disbelief. The reality of their situation was dawning on them; the game was over, and they had lost.

John, ever vigilant, kept watch, his eyes scanning the surroundings for any signs of an ambush. The silence was almost deafening, the city holding its breath as the wheels of justice began to turn in earnest.

Max turned to Eleanor. "Get these recordings to the press and the authorities. The public needs to see the extent of the rot that's been hidden from them." His voice was a low growl, the sound of a man who had fought too long in the shadows and yearned for the light of truth.

Eleanor nodded, her hands already working to secure the digital evidence. "It's time the whole structure came crashing down," she affirmed, her resolve mirroring Max's.

As Eleanor and John set about disseminating the evidence and securing the prisoners, Max's focus shifted to the final piece of the puzzle — Marcus Kozlov. The last act of their long campaign was at hand, and it was time to face the kingpin himself.

Max felt a vibration in his pocket — a message from Liam. It was brief, but it was all he needed to know. *Kozlov's on the move. Heading to a safe house outside the city.*

With a grim nod to John, Max made his decision. "Stay with Eleanor. Make sure the evidence gets out. I have to finish this."

Without waiting for a response, Max slipped away, moving with the singular purpose of a hunter closing in on his quarry. The night had one more secret to yield, and he was the key to unlocking it.

The city, so often a tapestry of light and life, felt like a stage waiting for the final act to commence. Max moved through it, a silent figure against the backdrop of looming buildings and whispered betrayals.

He knew what had to be done. Kozlov's reign of manipulation and control would end tonight, not with a trial, but with the finality that only their kind of justice could bring.

Chapter 28: The Final Confrontation

The Siege of Silence

The air was tense when John finally caught up with Max as they approached the derelict industrial estate on the outskirts of London. The estate, once a hub of productivity, now stood as a hollow shell, its skeleton housing the vestiges of criminal enterprise. Its walls, etched with the patina of decay, told a story of neglect, while the iron gates, twisted and rusted, groaned a foreboding welcome.

The sky above was a mass of brooding clouds, the city's ever-present fog a shroud that cloaked their movements in secrecy. Puddles from an earlier rain shimmered like mirrors on the broken asphalt, reflecting the dim glow of the moon that fought to pierce the fog.

Max's eyes swept over the scene, taking in the scattered debris and overgrowth that spoke of years of abandonment. It was here, in this forsaken place, that Marcus Kozlov had holed up, a fallen king in his dilapidated court.

John, ever the silent sentinel, communicated with Max in the language of subtle hand signals they had both come to master. Their approach was a choreographed dance of stealth, born from a kinship forged in the fires of countless covert operations.

As they breached the perimeter, the quiet was oppressive, the silence punctuated only by the distant rumble of the city and the occasional drip of water from a leaking pipe. They moved through the shadows, each man a spectre in this realm of desolation.

The entrance to the main warehouse loomed before them,

a gaping maw that seemed to swallow light and sound. Max paused, signalling John to hold position. He surveyed the entrance with a practised eye, noting the absence of guards. It was too easy, a fact that gnawed at his seasoned instincts.

With a nod to John, Max drew his SIG with fitted suppressor, the weight of the firearm both a burden and a reassurance in his hand. They entered side by side, senses heightened, every muscle tensed for the violence they knew would come.

Inside, the vastness of the warehouse was oppressive, the darkness almost tangible. The scant light from outside revealed a cathedral of industry defiled by its current use: a marketplace for the illicit, a haven for the corrupt. Amidst the ruins of machinery and the remnants of illicit transactions, they found their path.

They had not taken more than a few steps when the first of Kozlov's men appeared, a ghostly figure materializing from the shadows. The guard was seasoned but not enough to detect Max and John's approach. The confrontation was swift and silent, a brief struggle before the guard slumped to the ground, unconscious.

Max's heart pounded against his ribs, the rush of adrenaline sharp in his veins. He knew this was just the first. Kozlov would not be unguarded, and as they delved deeper into the warehouse, the truth of this became apparent.

Figures emerged from the darkness, a testament to Kozlov's paranoia and power. The ensuing conflict was a maelstrom of violence and precision, Max and John a whirlwind of lethality. Each takedown was a step closer to Kozlov, each moment leading to the inevitable face-off.

As they fought, Max was acutely aware of the building's skeleton around them, the way the light played tricks on the eye, the echo of their movements creating a cacophony of impending doom. This was a place of endings, and tonight it would live up to that grim promise.

They reached the inner sanctum, the heart of Kozlov's operation, where the crime lord waited. Max could feel the presence of his nemesis like a change in the air, a drop in pressure before the storm broke.

And then, from the darkness, the voice of Marcus Kozlov taunted them, a sound filled with malice and derision. "Welcome, Max. I've been expecting you."

Max and John stood ready, their resolve unbreakable, their mission clear. The final confrontation was upon them, and just one outcome was certain: only one side would walk away.

*

The warehouse was a cavernous space, long stripped of its industrial purpose, now repurposed into a fortress of illicit dealings. The scant light that infiltrated this domain did little to dispel the gloom that clung to the rafters and the long, desolate stretches of concrete.

Kozlov's voice reverberated through the expanse, oddly disembodied, as if the building itself were speaking. "You can't change what's coming, Max. You've already lost," he jeered, his tone echoing the darkness around them.

Max advanced, his movements deliberate, the SIG Sauer an extension of his resolve. Beside him, John's presence was a steady force, his M4 carbine ready to respond to any threat. The two men were not just soldiers; they were the embodiment of retribution, moving deeper into the heart of Kozlov's last stand.

As they navigated the gauntlet, a series of shadows detached from the walls, materializing into the forms of armed men — Kozlov's loyalists, his last line of defence. Each one was a symbol of Kozlov's influence, men who had sold their souls for promises whispered in the dark.

The confrontation was sudden, a clash of wills and weaponry. Max and John were a synchronized unit, their every move a practised choreography of combat. Gunfire tore through the silence, flashes of muzzle light punctuating the darkness as they dispatched Kozlov's men with clinical precision.

In the lull that followed, Max's breaths were heavy, his senses razor-sharp. He could feel the nearness of Kozlov now, the malevolence that radiated from the man like a physical force.

They reached the makeshift throne room Kozlov had erected amongst the ruin, an ostentatious display of arrogance and perceived invulnerability. There, in the gloom, sat Kozlov, flanked by his remaining henchmen. The crime lord's face was a mask of disdain, but his eyes betrayed the knowledge of his imminent demise.

"You think you are the hero, Max? You are just a killer hiding behind respectability," Kozlov sneered.

Max's reply was calm, devoid of emotion. "I am what the city needs me to be. And right now, it needs you gone."

The final dance of death commenced, an explosive exchange of fire that rocked the foundations of the warehouse. John covered Max's approach, each of his shots finding their mark. Max moved forward, the gap closing between him and Kozlov with every heart-stopping second.

As the last of the guards fell, Max stood before Kozlov, the two men locked in a gaze that was as much a battle as the physical struggle that had preceded it. John kept watch, ensuring no further surprises would come from the shadows.

"You won't walk away from this, Max. Even if you kill me, you'll always be looking over your shoulder," Kozlov hissed, attempting to rise.

Max's response was a swift motion, disarming Kozlov and forcing him back down. "Your time on this earth is over, Kozlov. This city will breathe free again."

A shot rang out, not from Max's gun, but from the shadows. Kozlov's eyes widened in shock as a bullet found its way to his heart. He looked down at the growing red stain on his shirt, then up at Max, his expression one of disbelief.

Max turned to see the shooter stepping from the darkness — it was Liam, his features set in a mask of grim finality. "He was right, Max. You can't have shadows hanging over you. Not when there's a city to rebuild."

Kozlov slumped to the ground, his lifeblood seeping into the cracked concrete as the echoes of the gunshot faded into the night.

*

The echoes of the fatal shot melded with the distant rumble of the city, a stark counterpoint to the silence that fell over the warehouse. Kozlov's body lay still, his empire ending not with a roar but a muted thud. Max stood motionless, the reality of Liam's actions sinking in. This was a justice delivered not by his hand, but by a friend who had taken the burden upon himself.

John lowered his weapon, his veteran's instincts

recognizing the shift in the air. His eyes met Max's in a silent exchange, a mutual understanding of the costs of war. Liam's intervention had been the final twist, the last cut in a night fraught with decisive actions.

Max approached Liam, his footsteps heavy, his voice a low rasp. "You shouldn't have had to do that."

Liam shook his head, holstering his sidearm. "It was my choice, Max. It was necessary, for all of us." His gaze was steady and resolute, that of a man who had made peace with his decision.

The warehouse, once a hive of illicit activity, now felt like a tomb — the resting place of a man whose life had been a testament to power's corrupting allure. Max felt the weight of the night's events, the culmination of every choice and every sacrifice that had led them here.

John broke the silence. "We need to clear out before the Met arrives. Bennett won't be far behind."

They worked quickly to remove any traces of their presence, erasing themselves from the scene with practised ease. The evidence of Kozlov's dealings remained, enough to ensure the remnants of his network would not survive the night.

As they exited the warehouse, the first hints of dawn were beginning to touch the horizon, the darkness receding inch by inch. The city was waking, unaware of the battle that had raged in its shadows.

Max paused, looking back at the industrial structure that had been the stage for their final confrontation. Kozlov's demise was the end of an era, but it was also the beginning of something new — a city free from his grasp, a chance to rebuild from the ashes of a long and costly struggle.

Liam's voice was contemplative as they made their

way back. "What now, Max?"

Max considered the question, the morning light casting long shadows across his face. "Now we make sure this never happens again. We use what we've learned to protect the city, to be better guardians."

John nodded in agreement, his expression sombre. "And we remember those who aren't here to see this new day."

The trio moved through the waking streets, their battle now behind them. The city stretched out before them, a canvas awaiting a new story — one they would write with the lessons of the past etched deeply in their minds.

The final confrontation had resolved the conflict with Kozlov, but it had also closed a chapter in Max's personal journey. He had faced his inner demons and emerged with a clearer vision of the future — one where the line between darkness and light was not as stark as he had once believed.

As they disappeared into the burgeoning day, the city began to stir, its heartbeat a rhythm of life that continued unabated, its people unaware of the silent protectors who had ensured their morning would be a peaceful one.

*

The first light of dawn was a brushstroke of pale gold against the sombre tones of the cityscape as Max, John, and Liam retreated from the warehouse, the locus of their operation's violent crescendo. The industrial estate, with its sentinel-like structures now silent witnesses to the night's retribution, was left behind, fading into the morning mist like a spectre of the night.

They moved with purposeful haste, aware that the

window of anonymity was closing rapidly with the approaching daylight. Their route was a zigzag through lesser-known paths, the trio weaving through the city's veins with the expertise of those who command the shadows.

Max led them, his thoughts a tempest of reflection and foresight. The scent of rain was on the wind, a cleansing promise. The city, he knew, would wake to a seismic shift in its underworld; Kozlov's death would ripple through the criminal ranks, a silent upheaval that would topple thrones and redraw territories.

Liam's voice, a low murmur, broke the silence. "I'll have to report back soon, give my account to Bennett and the others."

Max nodded, his response a murmur of acknowledgment. "Your role was crucial, Liam. Without your intel, we might've walked into a massacre."

Liam's silhouette was taut against the waning darkness, a man caught between the world he served and the justice he had helped deliver. "I'll play my part to the end. The Met needs to see this through the lens of the law."

As they reached the edge of the industrial district, the city began to stir, the first sounds of morning life blending with the natural chorus of dawn. Max halted, turning to John. "You should head back. The agency will want a debrief, and your cover is still intact." Although John had never formally acknowledged his involvement with the agency, Max understood the complex nature of the man before him and wanted him to know they had no secrets.

John's face, etched with the night's exertions, was a mask of solemn surprise, then understanding. "You're sure you don't need backup?"

Max's smile was a thin line, an echo of camaraderie.

"I have a few more moves to make before this game is over."

They parted ways at the mouth of an alley, John disappearing into the burgeoning light, a shadow receding from the day. Liam clapped a hand on Max's shoulder, a wordless exchange of respect, before he too melded into the city's waking embrace.

Max stood alone for a moment, the silence around him a relief after the cacophony of violence that had filled the night. The resolution of the external conflict was complete and Kozlov's dark reign ended, but the internal struggle within Max continued to churn.

He thought of the path ahead, the work that remained. The political scandal that would unfold in the coming days would shake the foundations of the country's leadership. The main MP involved, the lynchpin of Kozlov's political influence, would soon face his own reckoning. Max had ensured the evidence was irrefutable, and though he would not be the hand that delivered justice, he had set it in motion.

Max's journey was far from over. As the city awoke, he moved through its streets, an unseen guardian whose war was waged in silence and sacrifice. His resolution was clear: to continue the fight, to protect the innocents from the shadows that would rise in Kozlov's absence.

The sun crested the horizon, its rays cutting through the urban expanse, and Max turned his face toward the warmth. The new day was a canvas, and he was the unseen artist, shaping the narrative of the city in ways that would never be known.

*

Max walked alone now, his path taking him towards the heart of the city where the first hints of morning activity were stirring to life. The streets were slowly populating with the early risers, the workers, and the dreamers of the metropolis, all of them oblivious to the night's darker happenings.

His mind replayed the events that had led to this dawn. Each move, each decision had been a step towards this point. The fall of Kozlov was a victory, but it was not the end of the war against the corruption that had seeped into the city's veins.

Max's thoughts turned to the main Member of Parliament involved in the scandal, Jonathan Hales. His connections to Kozlov had been a shield of influence and power, one that had allowed him to manipulate the strings of governance with impunity. But the evidence Max had secured was a sword that would cut through that shield, exposing the rot within.

As Max neared a discreet café that was just opening its doors to the promise of the morning rush, he knew what he had to do. Inside, in the quiet before the day began, he met with a contact from Rebecca — a journalist with the integrity and courage to bring the truth to light.

He handed over the evidence, encrypted files that contained the proof of Hales's involvement with Kozlov's operations. "Make sure this gets the coverage it deserves," Max instructed. "The people need to see the extent of the betrayal."

The journalist nodded, understanding the gravity of the task. "It will be front-page news by the afternoon," she promised, her eyes reflecting the fire of a story that could change everything.

Max left the café, his part in the exposé complete. The

dissemination of the evidence would dismantle the web of corruption that Hales and Kozlov had woven, a task that would now unfold in the public eye.

The sun had fully risen now, casting a golden hue over the city. Max made his way to a quiet park, a place where the greenery offered a reprieve from the urban sprawl. Here, he sat on a bench and allowed himself a moment of solitude.

He considered the long road ahead. The political scandal would rock the city, and the vacuum left by Kozlov's empire would birth a power struggle in the underworld. Max knew that new threats would emerge, and he would be there, a silent sentinel standing against the tide.

As he sat there, the sound of the city coming to life around him, he reflected on his own journey. The man who had started this war was not the same man who sat on this bench. He had been tempered by the fires of conflict, by the knowledge of the cost of such a fight.

He stood up, leaving the park behind, his figure one with the multitude of citizens starting their day. Max had faced his inner demons, reconciling the soldier he had once been with the protector he had become. The resolution of his personal battle was in accepting that the fight might never end, but it was one worth enduring.

As Max disappeared into the crowd, the city pulsed with life around him, a metropolis that would continue to thrive, its heart beating a little stronger thanks to the unseen battles fought in its name.

*

The city, awakening to the rhythms of an ordinary day, remained unaware of the seismic shift that had occurred in its underbelly. Max, blending into the stream of early morning life, moved with a casual stride. His mind, however, was anything but idle, already anticipating the next moves in this intricate game of shadows and light.

The news of MP Jonathan Hales's involvement with Kozlov's network was a fuse that, once lit, would ignite a firestorm of scandal and outcry. Max knew the fallout would be extensive, reaching the highest echelons of power. The city would reel, but it was a necessary upheaval to cleanse the deep-seated corruption.

As he walked, Max's thoughts drifted to the team that had stood unwaveringly at his side. John, a brother-in-arms whose loyalty was as unyielding as steel. Liam, a man torn between two worlds, had made the hardest choice of all, straddling the line between law and justice.

Max's path led him to a quiet building nestled in an older part of the city. Here, in a secluded office space rented under an alias, he had one last task to complete. The room was sparse, functional, a hub from which many of their operations had been coordinated.

Seated at the desk, Max initiated a secure video call. The screen flickered to life, revealing the stern yet relieved face of Colonel Hammond, the man who had been both mentor and commander to him in past years. "Max, I've heard the news. Kozlov?"

"Dead," Max confirmed, his voice devoid of triumph. "And his network along with him. London's got a fighting chance now."

Hammond nodded, the lines on his face deepening. "And the cost?"

"High. But necessary," Max replied. He knew Hammond understood the price of such wars, the toll they took on those who fought them.

There was a pause, a moment of unspoken communion between soldiers of different eras. "You did well, Max. I always knew you were the right man for this fight," Hammond finally said.

Max acknowledged the compliment with a nod. "It's not over yet. The aftermath is going to be ... complicated."

"Indeed," Hammond agreed. "But you've given the city its best chance. We'll handle it from here. Come back in, Max. You've earned a rest."

Max considered the offer, the allure of stepping away from the frontlines. But he knew his war was not yet over. "I appreciate it, Colonel. But there's still work to be done here. I'm not finished yet."

Hammond's gaze was penetrating, understanding. "Then stay safe, soldier. And know you're not alone in this."

The call ended, leaving Max in the quiet of the room, surrounded by the echoes of battles past and those yet to come. He stood, gazing out of the window at the city sprawled before him. The sun had risen higher now, its light chasing away the shadows he had navigated through the night.

Max Fairchild, the soldier, the guardian, had made his choice. He would continue to stand watch over those who needed it, a sentinel against the darkness, a shield against the chaos that threatened to engulf the world around them.

As he left the office, stepping back into the light of day, the city moved around him, its pulse a steady rhythm of life and hope. Max moved with it, a part of it yet apart, always watchful, always ready.

Chapter 29: Aftermath

Ripples of Change

The morning after the warehouse siege found London awash in a sea of murmurs that soon grew into waves of outcry and demands for accountability. News of MP Jonathan Hales's illicit dealings, now irrefutably brought to light, sent shockwaves through the political sphere, toppling careers and shaking the foundations of institutions.

Max, now a silent observer removed from the fray, watched from a distance as the city absorbed the impact. The local newsstands were plastered with headlines that screamed of scandal and betrayal, while television screens in shop windows broadcast heated debates between pundits and officials.

In the privacy of his modest flat, which bore the spartan trademarks of a man accustomed to life on the move, Max took a moment to reflect. The walls were bare, the shelves devoid of personal effects, save for a single framed photograph of a younger Max in military uniform, surrounded by a team that was no more.

He pondered the ripple effects of his actions, how the dismantling of Kozlov's empire and the exposure of Hales's corruption would reshape the city's landscape. There was a bittersweet taste to the victory; justice had been served, yet the cost lingered in the air, a spectre of sacrifices made.

Max's contemplation was interrupted by the chirp of his secure phone. It was a message from Eleanor, who had been coordinating with their allies and the authorities in the aftermath. *The evidence is holding up. Hales is in custody, and the trials will begin soon. We did it, Max.*

He typed a brief response, a simple acknowledgement, before turning his attention back to the silent room. Eleanor was right; they had accomplished what they set out to do. But as the man responsible for setting events into motion, Max felt the weight of what had transpired: the lives lost, the families altered, the soul of the city forever changed.

Outside, the city continued its hustle, the populace moving forward, adapting to the new narratives unfolding around them. The criminal elements that had once answered to Kozlov were now scattered, their unity fractured, their purpose muddled without the iron fist of their leader to guide them.

Max knew that new threats would rise from the ashes of the old. It was the nature of the beast, the endless cycle of power vacuums being filled. But for the first time in what felt like an eternity, there was hope that the ensuing battles would be fought on a more even field.

He stood and walked to the window, looking down at the streets below. The people walked with a sense of freedom, unaware of the man who watched over them, who had bled for them in the shadows. This was his city, and he would continue to protect it, to serve it, in whatever capacity he could.

As Max turned from the window, he considered the future. The next chapter of his life was yet to be written, but the stage was set. He had allies, a network of connections, and a newfound purpose. He would use the lessons of the past to build a better tomorrow, not just for himself but for the city that had become his charge.

This was not an end but a beginning, a transition from one phase to the next. Max Fairchild, the soldier, the guardian, the avenger, had found a new role in the aftermath of the storm he had weathered. He would be a beacon, a shield, a silent promise to those who called London home.

*

In the days that followed, London seemed to move with a new sense of purpose. The revelation of Hales's deceit and the fall of Kozlov's empire had acted as a catharsis for London, purging it of a hidden malignancy. But for Max, the fight had been personal, and the victory was tinged with the hues of introspection and loss.

He found himself at a small, secluded memorial garden tucked away from the bustle of the city streets. It was a place for contemplation, where the names of the fallen were etched into stone, a sombre reminder of the price of peace. Max's fingers traced the cold, chiselled letters of comrades who had laid down their lives in battles far from home.

Here in the quietude, the magnitude of what he had accomplished — and the cost at which it had come — settled upon him. He had set out to cleanse the city of its demons, to sever the head of the serpent. But as he had done so, he had been forced to confront his own shadows, to grapple with the soldier he had once been and the man he had become.

A gentle breeze stirred the leaves, whispering through the garden like a chorus of voices from the past. They spoke of honour and sacrifice, but also of the burden of survival, of living to bear witness when others could not.

Max's reverie was broken by the distant sound of children's laughter, a reminder that life persisted, resilient and ever-renewing. It was for them, for the future they represented, that he had fought so fiercely.

He left the garden with a sense of resolution. His actions had ripple effects that would extend far beyond the visible horizon. The trials that awaited Hales and his compatriots would be a spectacle, a media frenzy that would dominate the headlines for months to come. But beyond the spectacle lay the real work, the steady effort to rebuild trust and to fortify the city against the return of such darkness.

Max's next steps were clear. He would continue to work from the shadows, his vigilance a silent safeguard for the country he loved. The network he had built, the alliances he had forged — they would be his instruments in the ongoing quest for justice.

As he walked the streets, Max was just another face in the crowd, but his gaze held the depth of one who had seen too much and yet still held hope close to his heart. The city was healing, its scars a testament to its enduring spirit.

The sun dipped low, casting long shadows that stretched across the pavement like fingers reaching for the coming night. In the interplay of light and shadow, Max found a semblance of peace, a balance between the battles he had fought and the calm that now settled over him.

He had faced the darkness, not just in the world around him but within himself, and he had emerged not unscathed but not defeated. The journey had changed him, but it had also reaffirmed the core of who he was: a protector, a sentinel, a warrior for the light.

Chapter 30: New Horizons

An Uneasy Dawn

Max sat on a weathered bench in Hyde Park, the first blush of dawn casting a gentle glow on the dew-laden grass. The park was a tranquil haven within the labyrinth of the city that surrounded it. He watched the sunrise, its serene progress a daily rebirth, a signal of new beginnings and the relentless march of time.

The city was just beginning to stir, the hum of early commuters a distant whisper carried on the breeze. Max's thoughts were adrift on the events that had brought him here, to this point where the line between soldier and sentinel had blurred. The takedown of Kozlov and the revelation of Hales's corruption had left a void, a vacuum that would inevitably pull him back into the fray. He knew the game was never truly over; it merely evolved.

His contemplation was interrupted by the arrival of two men, both dressed in very similar, dull suits that did little to conceal their disciplined posture and the subtle alertness of trained operatives. They approached with a respectful nod, an acknowledgment of a warrior from fellow warriors.

"Max Fairchild?" asked the first, his voice betraying no emotion. His companion remained silent, eyes scanning the surroundings with calculated discretion.

Max assessed them with a measured gaze. "I've been called worse," he replied, his tone even but edged with caution.

The man offered a thin smile as he extended an envelope. "We represent interests aligned with national security. Your recent ... endeavours have caught some attention."

Accepting the envelope, Max felt the weight of its contents and the gravity of what it represented. Inside were documents, photos, and detailed accounts of his actions against Kozlov's network. It was clear; his war had not gone unnoticed.

"We can offer you protection, Mr Fairchild." The second man finally spoke, his accent placing him as unmistakably from the United States. "Protection from those who would seek retribution for your ... justice."

Max understood the offer's contours, an exchange of freedom for service. They were not requesting his cooperation; they were requisitioning it.

"And if I decline?" Max enquired, though he already knew the answer.

The first man's expression didn't waver. "Then you and Ms Eleanor Petrova will find yourselves in a precarious position. Both here and abroad."

The threat was veiled but clear. They could offer sanctuary from the consequences of his actions, but the price was his autonomy. His skills, honed through years of service and sacrifice, were now a commodity to be bartered.

Max looked out over the park, where the first joggers of the day were beginning their morning routines, a semblance of normality he yearned for. He thought of Eleanor, of the peace they both deserved but which had been so elusive.

"You have my attention," Max said, his voice a low baritone of resignation.

"Excellent," the American replied with a nod. "We'll be in touch with instructions. When the time comes, you'll know what to do."

The men turned and left as quietly as they had arrived, leaving Max alone with the weight of his new reality. The sun crested the horizon fully, its rays chasing away the remnants of night, illuminating the path ahead — a path fraught with shadows and uncertainty.

Max considered the documents before him, the unspoken contract between him and a world that operated in the spaces between. He had fought to rid his city of one devil only to find himself in the company of another. This was the cost of the war he had waged, the price of the peace he sought to secure.

As the park filled with the sounds of life, Max remained seated, the protector of the city contemplating his conscription into a greater battle. He had walked through fire to forge a new future, not just for himself, but for all those who called the city home. Now, on the cusp of this new horizon, he stood ready to face whatever storms might come.

*

The early risers of Hyde Park passed by Max, their lives untainted by the shadows that clung to his. He remained seated, the documents from the envelope spread out on the bench next to him. Each page was a silent testament to his actions, a record of a war waged in secret, and now a leash in the hands of those who operated from the world's unseen corners.

As the morning matured, a jogger slowed to a walk nearby, stretching under the guise of routine exercise, but Max's trained eyes saw through the charade. The jogger, an athletic man in his thirties with a military haircut barely concealed under a baseball cap, gave Max a cursory nod and made his approach.

"Nice morning for some fresh air," the jogger commented casually, a forced nonchalance to his tone.

Max folded the papers, sliding them back into the envelope. "Sometimes fresh air is just a prelude to a storm," he replied, his voice low and steady.

The jogger, now identified as Agent Coleman based on the brief dossier Max had skimmed, didn't miss a beat. "Storms can be cleansing," he said, taking a seat on the bench, maintaining a respectful distance.

Max considered the metaphor. "Or they can uproot everything in their path," he countered.

Coleman's gaze was direct, the façade of an accidental meeting slipping away. "The offer we've made, it's not just about keeping you and Eleanor out of the spotlight. It's about utilising your ... expertise for a greater purpose."

Max turned to look at the man, his demeanour unchanging. "A purpose decided by whom?" he asked, the question rhetorical. "I've seen how these greater purposes often play out. They tend to leave collateral in their wake."

Coleman nodded, acknowledging the truth in Max's words. "Collateral can be mitigated, with the right people on the ground."

Max's eyes narrowed. "And when the ground shifts?"

"We adapt," Coleman stated firmly. "Look, Fairchild, the world you've been fighting in — the underworld, the back alleys of power — it's a microcosm of a larger battlefield. The rules are the same; only the scale is different."

Max understood the implications. The CIA's offer was

a pact that would bind him to their agenda, his autonomy sacrificed on the altar of national security. Yet refusal would mean a return to the crosshairs, a target on his and Eleanor's backs.

The park around them was a tableau of peace, a stark contrast to the decision that hung in the air. Max had fought to preserve such peace for others, and now he was being asked to extend that fight to arenas far beyond the city limits.

He stood up, the envelope in hand. "If I do this, I do it on my terms. I won't be anyone's puppet."

Coleman rose as well, a slight smile creasing his face. "We wouldn't want it any other way. You're not valuable to us as a puppet, Max. We need you to be the force of nature you are."

Max pocketed the envelope, his mind already turning to the future, to the new world he was about to enter. "I'll need assurances," he stated. "Eleanor's safety is non-negotiable."

"You'll have them," Coleman assured him. "Welcome to the bigger game, Fairchild."

As Coleman walked away, blending back into the normality around them, Max felt the weight of the devil's bargain he had just struck. He had navigated treacherous waters before, but now he was diving into an ocean, the depths of which were unknown.

Max walked away from the bench, his stride purposeful, his resolve hardened. He was a man who had walked through darkness to protect the light, and now he was stepping into a new horizon, where the battles would be fiercer, the stakes higher, and his will tested like never before.

As Max left the expanse of Hyde Park behind, his thoughts were interrupted by the familiar vibration of a message arriving on his secure phone. The screen displayed a message from John, a simple set of coordinates and a time for a meeting. The unspoken message was clear: there were still pieces moving on the board, and John was one of them.

He made his way to an old cafe that clung to its place amidst the modern sprawl of the city, its walls steeped in the aroma of strong coffee and the patina of bygone days. It was here, away from prying eyes, that Max found John waiting, a chessboard set between them as a cover for their less innocent strategizing.

John greeted him with a nod, his eyes betraying the weariness of the long night. "Max," he began, his voice low and steady, "the play's not over yet."

Max took a seat, his back to the wall, his eyes never still. "It seems our definition of over is open to interpretation."

John moved a pawn on the board, a metaphor for the conversation they were about to have. "I've been where you are now, caught between duty and autonomy. The CIA ... they've had their eye on you for a while."

Max's expression didn't change, but a flicker of realisation passed through his eyes. "And you? How long have you been playing both sides of this game?"

"I've been an asset to them for a few years now," John admitted, moving another chess piece. "It's not always straightforward, but it allows me to make a difference on a global scale."

Max considered the revelation, the chessboard before

him a mirror to the complexities of the world he was stepping into. "And my family? Emily and Lily?" he asked, the question laced with the protective edge of a father and husband.

"They're safe," John assured him. "The CIA has resources. They can protect them, keep them out of the crosshairs. It's one of the reasons I accepted their offer in the first place."

The conversation shifted subtly, the subtext clear. John had been inducted into this world of shadows and strategic plays before him, and now Max was to join the ranks, albeit reluctantly. There was comfort in knowing he wasn't alone, that a familiar face was already navigating these treacherous waters.

As they continued their game of chess, a symbol of the larger game at play, Max's thoughts turned to Eleanor. He had to ensure her safety in all this, to keep her insulated from the fallout of his decisions. And he would. Whatever it took.

John's voice brought him back to the present. "You're going to face decisions, operations that won't be black and white. But remember why you're doing this, Max. Remember who you're doing it for."

Max nodded, his gaze firm. "I always do."

The two men parted ways with a handshake that was more than a mere farewell; it was an acknowledgement of the path they both walked. Max stepped out of the cafe, the chessboard left behind, the game unfinished and yet so telling.

He walked the streets with a new sense of purpose, aware of the invisible threads that now tied him to a larger fate. His horizon had expanded beyond the city, beyond the tangible streets and alleys he had protected.

He was part of a larger world now, one where the stakes were higher and the battles were fought in the deepest shadows.

As the day progressed, the city moved around him, a tapestry of life and stories unfolding in every corner. Max was a part of it, an integral thread woven into its fabric, a protector moving through the new day with a resolve forged in the fires of his past.

*

Max's day was spent in transit, moving through the city with a new awareness of the invisible lines that connected the clandestine world he had just joined to the everyday lives of the people around him. With each step, he reconciled the man he had been with the operative he was becoming.

As afternoon turned to dusk, Max found himself outside the Met headquarters next to Westminster. From across the street, he observed the controlled chaos typical of a police department in the throes of a major case. He knew that within those walls, DI Bennett was likely piecing together the remnants of Kozlov's empire, her investigation now armed with the evidence that Max and his team had provided.

Inside, Bennett stood before a wall of evidence, photographs, and strings creating a web of connections that told the story of corruption and crime. She was speaking to Liam, her trusted detective, who had played a more complex role than she could imagine.

"We've got them, Liam," Bennett said, her voice a mix of triumph and frustration. "Kozlov's network, Hales's political machine — they're unravelling before our eyes. But the vigilante ... the one who started this... We're no closer to pinning down who he is."

Liam, his expression unreadable, nodded. "Perhaps some ghosts aren't meant to be caught," he replied carefully. "Maybe it's enough that the job gets done."

Bennett sighed, rubbing her temples. "Justice isn't just about the outcome, Liam. It's about the process, the law. Vigilantism can't be our way forward."

Liam offered a sympathetic smile. "I know, and I agree. But sometimes the lines get blurred. The important thing is we've made the city safer. That's a win."

Max, watching from his vantage point, felt a pang of solidarity for Bennett. She was a guardian of the city in her own right, her methods bound by the structure of the law he had once served. Their goals were the same, even if their paths diverged.

Turning away from the building, Max made his way to a quiet, unassuming bar where he had arranged to meet Eleanor. She was waiting for him, her eyes searching his face for signs of the inner turmoil she knew all too well.

"They approached me today," Max said without preamble, sliding into the booth across from her. "The CIA. They've offered protection, resources ... for a price."

Eleanor reached across the table, her hand finding his. "And?"

"And I accepted," Max confessed, the weight of the decision heavy in his voice. "It was the only way to ensure your safety, to ensure we can have a life without looking over our shoulders."

Eleanor squeezed his hand, her resolve as clear as the steel in her eyes. "We're in this together, Max. Whatever comes, we'll face it together."

The bar around them was a microcosm of the city, a place where stories intersected and lives unknowingly brushed against each other. In this space, Max and Eleanor were just two more souls seeking respite in each other's company.

As the evening wore on, they talked of the future, of possibilities and the promise of a horizon that was theirs to define. Max spoke of his new role that would take him to the edges of international politics and global threats, a world where his actions could tip the scales in ways he had yet to fully comprehend.

They left the bar together, stepping out into the night that had become their shared domain. The city stretched out before them, its heartbeat steady and sure. Max and Eleanor were part of that rhythm now, agents of change in a world that was forever evolving.

Max and Eleanor walked hand in hand, their silhouettes merging into the city. Tomorrow would bring new challenges, but tonight they had each other, and that was enough.

The city of London had always been a tapestry woven from threads of resilience and hope, its pattern complex and ever-changing. In the aftermath of turmoil, it found a new rhythm, a pulse that beat stronger for having endured the trials set upon it.

Max Fairchild stood at a vantage point that overlooked the River Thames, the water reflecting the city lights as dusk settled like a benediction. He was alone, a solitary figure against the sprawling canvas of the metropolis that he had sworn to protect. The events that had unfolded seemed now like echoes of a distant past, yet they were indelibly etched into the man he had become.

A soldier by training, a protector by choice, Max had walked through the darkest alleys and faced down the demons that lurked in the city's heart. He had sought redemption not through the absolution of his actions but through the conviction that they were necessary. And in doing so, he had found a purpose that transcended the call of duty, one that was grounded in the silent oath he had taken to stand as a guardian.

He reflected on the journey that had led him here, on the allies and adversaries that had crossed his path. Eleanor, whose strength and companionship had become his anchor; Liam, whose shared history and unwavering loyalty had been a light in the shadows; John, whose complex path had intertwined with his own in ways he could never have anticipated.

Max thought of DI Sarah Bennett, her commitment to justice a mirror to his own, though they served it in different ways. Her dogged pursuit of the vigilante had been a thorn in his side, but it was a role he respected, a counterpoint to his own methods.

And then there were those he had lost, whose memories he carried with him like scars. They were the unseen wounds, the cost of the war he had waged. Their sacrifices were a reminder of the stakes, of the fragile line that separated order from chaos.

The epilogue of his story was not written in the annals of public record but in the quiet moments like this, where he allowed himself to feel the weight of what had passed. He knew that his war was not over; there would always be threats to the peace he cherished, battles to be fought in the name of the greater good.

But for now, there was a respite, a chance to breathe and to watch over the city as it healed and grew. Max's redemption was not a destination but a journey, one that he accepted with all its burdens and its blessings.

As night claimed the city, Max turned away from the river, his silhouette merging with the evening. He was a soldier, a saviour, and a man who had found his place in the grand design. The storylines of his future were still unwritten, but they held the promise of adventure, of continued service, and of a legacy that would be defined by the lives he touched and the peace he kept.

London slept, its protector watching over it, a silent sentinel ready for whatever the future held.

The End

About The Author

Andrew Janes (A C Janes) is a debut author whose passion for storytelling emerged during his travels for work in 2018. Inspired by the reflective solitude of his downtime, he began weaving intricate narratives that explore the complexities of human nature and the profound psychological impacts of life's challenges on individuals and those around them.

With a keen eye for detail and a deep appreciation for the multifaceted nature of human emotions, Andrew strives to create immersive stories that resonate with readers. His writing delves into the intricacies of his characters, offering layered perspectives and rich emotional depth. Through carefully crafted plots, he takes readers on journeys filled with tension, introspection, and moments of raw humanity, ensuring they are fully engaged with every turn of the page.

Andrew's debut novel, *Beneath a Silent Banner*, reflects his dedication to character-driven storytelling and his interest in exploring the moral and emotional complexities of his protagonists. It is a testament to his ability to balance action and reflection, capturing the grit and vulnerability of the human experience.

As a first-time author, Andrew brings a fresh perspective to the literary world, combining his love for detailed narratives with an understanding of the emotional landscapes that shape us. He is committed to crafting stories that linger in the minds of readers long after they've closed the book.

www.blossomspringpublishing.com